S0-AKF-209

SAILOR

BOOKS BY RICHARD JESSUP—

THE CINCINNATI KID

THE RECREATION HALL

SAILOR

SAILOR

a novel of the sea

by

Richard Jessup

Little, Brown and Company—Boston—Toronto

LIBRARY OF CONGRESS CATALOG CARD NO. 69-12639

FIRST EDITION

Published simultaneously in Canada
by Little, Brown & Company (Canada) Limited

PRINTED IN THE UNITED STATES OF AMERICA

for my wife—
Vera Berlin Jessup

The most fearless person I have ever known, and it is always summer.

One man is the image of all men.
—Unknown

May 1909

April 1919

When Meg opened the door of the small apartment the child was playing on the floor with a set of building blocks. He worked and reworked the blocks into complicated structures. He made roads and trains. He talked to himself as he played, winning a battle, losing one, rebuilding the game. His soft voice penetrated the barrier of her world to a world that he alone could see and touch.

She stood looking at the child, a tall, almost gaunt woman with a boxy chin and long nose; yet in spite of this there was an aura of pure womanliness about her. If the child heard he did not show that he had. He went on building his blocks into new games, talking to himself. Time flowed in and out of his child's mind like the air in his lungs, unnoticed, unhurried. For the child, she thought, the world was just as it seemed.

Meg studied Howard, still not moving; a child's mind of infinite patience and care, she thought. All there was to know was still before him. There was the world, and there was time, and there was himself. I wonder, she thought, her female, motherly instincts rising, if he is aware that I have been gone all day. Most likely it's all the same to him. She moved then and the boy looked up.

Howard threw his arms around her waist. He hugged her close. Mama! Mama! Aunt Meg's home! Mama!

— Here is your block, Howard, Aunt Meg said, and gave the boy a chalk-white wooden block with the alphabet letter Q on all sides. That is the letter Q, Howard. Can you say that?

— Cue, Howard said, looking at it. It's funny. It's got a tail. He looked up into her eyes.

— Now, can you say your alphabet all the way up to this new letter? Aunt Meg asked.

Howard nodded furiously and rattled the letters off fast, because he knew that Aunt Meg liked him to do it that way. He managed it all on one breath.

— Go play now, Howard, Aunt Meg said. Later, after supper, I'll show you some more words with your other blocks.

— I saw Beau, Meg said.

— Where? Dolly asked, her eyes alert.

Meg removed her sweater and hat and sat down in her rocker and started unbuttoning her shoes. Dolly moved around to face her sister.

— In the courthouse square, Meg said quietly.

— Are you sure?

Meg did not answer what she considered a foolish question. She looked up at her sister's face, which had been calm when she entered the door and was now getting pink. She eased her bony feet out of the shoes, removed her stockings and placed her feet on the cool floor. Dolly did not move. She stood before her sister, waiting. She's learned about waiting, Meg thought, looking at her.

— It was him all right, Meg said. Do you think I could make *that* mistake?

— No, you wouldn't make that mistake, Dolly said.

— He was drinking, Meg said.

— Drinking? Right out there in the open? So it's come to that.

— It was always like that, Meg replied. It hasn't just come. I was cornering through the square, coming from Broughton Street, and there he was.

— What was he doing? Dolly asked softly.

— I told you, he was drinking. Like he used to. Just sitting there, like he used to, back up in Tasco. Sitting, looking, maybe thinking.

— But, I mean, what else? Dolly asked.

— What else is there?

— Please, Meg, none of your perverse talk now.

— He was alone, Meg said, watching her, rocking slowly. There wasn't any woman with him, if that's what you're wanting to know.

Dolly looked away.

— You always were one to rip right to the heart of things, she said.

— What are you going to do?

— What do you mean? Dolly asked.

— You know very well what I mean. He might be here tomorrow night, maybe even tonight.

— No, Dolly said, hushed. No.

— Well, it won't be long. What are you going to do?

— Please, Meg, I've got to think.

—About what? Letting him come back here and sweet talk you again?

—Please—just hush!

—That's all right, too, I guess. But one way or the other, tonight's the night.

—What do you mean by that?

—I am *not,* Meg said with a sudden driving fury, going to watch him sweep in here and make an impression on H-o-w-a-r-d!

Dolly moved restlessly around the room, twisting her fingers and looking as if she might cry. Expressionless, Meg watched her face.

—Well, she asked finally.

—He's my husband, Dolly said. I can't just—I can't. I'd be afraid to.

—Afraid to say no to him when he comes back here and sleeps with you?

—That is a horrid lie! Meg, you lie!

—I'm not finished. Wait until you hear what else I have to say before you call me a liar. Now, when he comes here, he sleeps with you, and—

—*He does not!*

—He does! And without a Papa round the house, and not knowing what one is, what is your s-o-n H-o-w-a-r-d going to think when he remembers that there was a strange man who used to drop around once in a while and crawl into bed with his mother?

Dolly tried to ride it out with a look of contempt. Meg began to rock faster, her feet slapping at the cool floor. Dolly cleared her throat.

—I want you to know, she said. I just want you to know that he hasn't touched me since before H-o-w-a-r-d was born.

—Crap!

—Will you stop using that filthy language in this house!

—Crap! Crap! *CRAP!* Meg shouted. She continued to rock furiously. They were silent for a moment in the hot Savannah night. Howard murmured to his brave captain and gave orders as the army of soldiers stood on one side of the river and waited for the morning and battle. Above him, in the strange world where his Mama and Aunt Meg lived, the tide of words continued to wash around his head.

— When was the last time you heard from him? Meg demanded.

— I don't want to discuss it. Dolly's voice was icy.

— Well, I'll tell you. It was three years ago. He was in some town in North Carolina working tobacco. Full of promises of coming home and being a good father and how he was finished once and for all, finally and for good, wandering around.

Dolly whirled on Meg. You've been reading my mail, she said bitterly.

— Of course I've been reading your mail. What the hell do you think? I'm not to know what's going on? All you tell me are fairy tales. Of course I read it.

— You are a liar and a cheat and I despise and loathe your kind of person, Dolly said.

— That may be so, Meg said, rocking with furious concentration, but whatever happens here tonight or tomorrow night or whenever he shows up, there had better be one goddam thing ringing clear! That no good sap-sucking husband of yours can pull a sneaky screw anytime he wants to, but not in *this* house, not under the same roof as H-o-w-a-r-d.

— You're disgusting! *Disgusting!*

— Better than you, letting him come up here while I'm at work and frigging from morning til night, probably. Just remember what I said, Meg went on, rocking hard and fast. H-o-w-a-r-d is yours, true enough, but just you remember this: Beau Cadiz is not going to change. He's been running since he was thirteen years old. Don't ask me why. God in Heaven might not even know the answer to that one, so this chile sure don't.

She stopped rocking. He's weak inside, Dolly. He's good-looking, as pretty a man as you could want, and a good worker, too, *when* he works, and he talks like a field hand and a saint, but he is thirty-one years old and he hasn't paid for a mouthful of food your son has ever eaten. A man that can't warm to his own son, that can run off, wandering all over hell and gone, knowing that he's left a woman and baby to shift for themselves, acting as if he was always nineteen years old and the world still—well, a man like that is *not* going to change. He's weak. Like jelly. He's yellow-livered, spineless and a plague to humanity. I don't care how smart he is, or how charming he can be, or was, there is *no* excuse for the man who abandons his children. Even a mangy dog in the gutter will stick by its young until they can shift for themselves. That is your husband. Beau Cadiz. H-o-w-a-r-d apostrophe s father. You love him. I *know* you love him. And he probably loves you. But you and Beau don't count anymore. It's H-o-w-a-r-d. It's him and him alone.

Dolly listened, her eyes dry, her hands loose. You love him, Dolly said. You love Beau. You love my husband.

— No, Meg said. I did once. Long ago. Before you were married. But not since then. Not since you were married and he got back from Cuba. Not anymore. No, I don't love Beau. I'll tell you what I do feel, though. I feel sorry for him. Sorry as I can be, because in spite of all he's done, and hasn't done, I know he's sensitive enough to understand *what* he's done, sensitive enough to know that he is weak, and weak in a place where all of his other courage and strength don't quite make up for it. And that must hurt him—deep and long.

Meg began to rock again, more slowly, more thoughtfully.

— Back, before H-o-w-a-r-d was born, and you came to me, and Beau was out west with that cattle ranch, going to be a writer, you knew then what you're afraid to face now. But time has changed things. It should have changed you a little, at least a little. You can see that, Dolly. You've got to see it.

— How is it different? Dolly asked.

— Many reasons, Meg said.

Dolly sat down opposite her sister.

— Tell me. Please.

— When you came here and we settled down to wait for the boy, and Mother Cadiz died back up in Tasco, do you remember?

Dolly nodded.

— Beau came back from Montana. He sold the Cadiz home place for four thousand dollars. He didn't come home, did he? He just kept going. We didn't see him until after the boy was born, until he was a little boy in rompers.

— I know, I know, Dolly said.

— I walked with the boy when he had the croup, Meg said, same as you. I did for him, same as you did, Dolly. I would move out right now, though it would break my heart—and I would, you know I would—if I thought you could take care of Howard—

— Yes, Aunt Meg? Howard asked, looking up from his blocks.

— Nothing child. Go on playing, Meg said.

Howard dropped his head and went back to his fort.

Meg looked at Dolly for a moment, her face stern. She lit a cigarette and snorted the smoke down her long nose. She is thinking about it, Meg thought. She is giving it serious consideration for the first time in her life.

— But you can't take care of the boy alone. Worrying about Beau all these years, Dolly, has taken something out of you. You need me and the boy needs me, and there is nothing for you to do but face it.

— Face what?

— The truth that Beau is *not* going to change, and that you cannot depend on him for one second, or believe any of his promises. He hasn't done anything for you or the boy, and he isn't going to.

— But I loved him! Oh God, I adored the man!

That's water under the bridge. We can do for each other, Dolly, and for the boy.

— You are so good, Meg.

— Crap!

— I'll do whatever you say.

— Make up your own mind.

— But you're right.

— I know I'm right. You don't have to tell me I'm right.

— There doesn't seem to be anything else to say. Except how are we going to tell him?

— I'll tell him.

— No, I'm his wife, Dolly said. I've got to tell him.

— Then tell him, Meg said. And if he starts any funny business I'll blow a hole in his goddam head. She stopped rocking and went into her room, coming back with a silver-handled forty-four pistol. I had this some time now, she said, just in case.

— You look silly with that thing, Dolly said. Put it away.

— He's going to look a hell of a lot sillier if he starts any funny business.

—No, Dolly said, half to herself, he won't. I know my Beau. I know him.

There was no funny business when Beau came, as he did that night, sweeping in with a smile on his face, his old charm fading now as the light in his eyes was fading, but still overwhelming to Dolly. Dolly surprised Meg by the calm way she handled it, getting right down to it without preliminaries, not asking where he had been or any questions at all. Beau stood, rocking back on his heels, fingering change in his pocket, staring at the boy on the floor, who stared back at him uncertainly. He listened to Dolly but looked at Meg, and he thought of the way it had all begun, knowing that this was the end of it, but remembering a bright morning in May many years before.

Beau Cadiz was going home after five months in the timber country of southern Mississippi. Home was Tasco County, close to the Tennessee line in north Georgia. He rolled through the low country of Mississippi and Alabama, enjoying the early summer green landscape of lush pines that he had roamed as a runaway boy, passed into the flatbed pastures and swampy cypress groves that he had tramped through as a man. All the way from New Orleans, where he had been paid off and in turn had paid off his gang of Negroes after delivering the cut timber. On coast lines of the railroad there had been much that was new, but getting closer to home in a land that he had never forgotten during the many times he was away, it was unchanged. It was still a soft country, just as he remembered it.

In Mobile, and later in Dothan, he had tried to find something to drink, and it was not until he chanced missing the connection for Atlanta and went off in search of a bottle that he finally got one.

A broad-shouldered man with blue eyes, there was a look of wildness and selfishness about him. He had the heavy hands of a man who has used a round-handled ax. There was also a sexuality that he wore somewhat cynically because he had learned early in life that women came easily to him.

When Beau found a place to buy his bottle, he was not too far from Blakely, Georgia, after crossing the wide, muddy Chattahoochee. The still operator took his half-dollar and watched as the young man tilted the quart bottle up to his mouth.

— I swear, I know you, mister.

Beau lowered the bottle and looked at the operator. He said nothing. He glanced around. The place was barren, two shacks on the cleared ground. He drank again.

— I was with Whoop'n Holler Teddy down yonder to Cuby, the operator said. Got this laig stiffened up from it.

The young man lowered his bottle again and wiped his lips. He looked down at the squatting operator, his stiff leg straight out like the branch of a tree.

— Give me another quart, Beau said. That damn train riding makes me thirsty so.

— I swear I seen you before, the operator repeated.

— You never saw me before, Beau said. And you probably got that busted leg right here on this patch of dirt you call a place.

— Is that so! Well, lemme tell you something—

— You going to give me another quart or not?

The operator glared. He gave over another quart and Beau tossed him a second half-dollar.

— I got me a medal inside proves I was in Cuby! And that's probably where I seen you.

— And who did you fight with? General Wheeler?

— No, did you?

— I didn't fight, Beau said. Did you fight with General Lawton?

— No, did you?

— I didn't fight, Beau said. Did you fight with General J. F. Kent?

— Listen here, now, you can't tell me—the still operator began, his big homely face sagging into a grin. Why, hell, whyn't you tell a feller—! Why hell, I could of—

— Anybody ever tell you you look like a chicken-necked sonofabitch? Beau asked.

The operator took a step forward.

— Maybe I ain't seen you before, but I know your kind. That's what I recognized, your kind. One of the hardnosed 'uns that went rousting through the camps and was so drunk they couldn't fight.

— Come another step and I'll gut you right where you stand.

— What? Now, you go on with you. Come around here threatenin' a man. Watson! You stand there, mister, just wait a minute. *Watson! Goddammit!* Maw! You, Maw, git the gun!

Somewhere behind and to his left, Beau heard the train whistle blow.

— So long, chicken neck, Beau said, and laughed as he sauntered away toward the railroad station. Behind him the still operator continued to call for Watson and his gun.

When he was home, Beau Cadiz proved to be an outrageous flirt, full of stories of places he had been and things he had seen, and after a while all of the mothers warned their daughters to stay clear of him.

Dolly would not be warned. The more Dolly learned about Beau Cadiz, the more she wanted to know. She met him the first time by accident, introduced by a girl friend as they were entering church for a Wednesday night prayer meeting.

— How do you do, Miss Dolly, Beau Cadiz said, moving out of the shadows from behind the wagon. And it is such a fine night, mam. And your father is really a fine preacher.

— Why thank you, Mister Cay-diz, Dolly said.

— KHA-DEEZ, Miss Dolly, Beau said.

— Yes, it was a wonderful sermon, Dolly said.

— Indeed, mam, Beau said, smiling. He turned to Meg. Good evening, Miss Meg.

— Good evening, Mister Cay-diz, Meg said slowly, and deliberately.

— No! Dolly said quickly. It's KHA-DEEZ, and then she stopped. Meg smiled. Beau regarded her with dancing blue eyes.

— It is the name of a famous port in Spain. Cadiz, Spain, he said.

— Yes, of course, Dolly said. Of course. I know of Cadiz, Spain. But you are not Spanish, are you Mister Cadiz?

— Irish on my mother's side, and my father is one quarter Spanish and three quarters French.

— Gracious! Did you hear that, Meg?

— I was born in Savannah, Beau said solemnly.

— That must be thrilling, living there, I mean.

— Savannah is a very sophisticated city, Miss Dolly, Beau said. There are many nationalities there. By way of explaining the mixture in my family tree.

— Savannah is a very sinful city, I've heard, Dolly said.

— Yes, that is very true, Miss Dolly.

Dolly turned and looked quickly around for her mother and father, who were just then leaving the church.

— Well, it has been so nice talking to you, Mister Cadiz, Dolly said lightly. Hasn't it, Meg.

— So nice, Meg said lightly. But it won't be if Pa catches you.

— Meg!

— I've just come from church, Meg said, and it's a little soon for me to be crimping on the truth. You know Mister Cay-diz's reputation as well as I do. Meg climbed into the wagon.

Dolly looked up into Beau's face. He smiled encouragingly.

— It has been most agreeable talking to you, Miss Dolly. And to you, Miss Meg.

And then he vanished into the darkness, only a few steps ahead of her mother and father.

Almost before Dolly knew he was gone, the letters began to arrive, the first one from Texas, where Beau had gone to work on a cattle ranch. Once and sometimes twice a week the letters came and at first there was some mention of Meg, offering best wishes or greetings. After a while, this stopped. Dolly was assured in the letters that she was not alone. She loved, and she had the letters assuring her that she was loved in return, and though Beau always signed a full, formal signature, never really declaring himself, Dolly was sure. To Dolly they were love letters, and to Meg, who read them on the sly, they were messages from another world. They transported her into the heart of deliciously wicked places like New York, Chicago, and Buffalo. And when she would come down from the hayloft over the shed in back of the chicken yard where she went to read Dolly's letters in private, she would look at herself in the mirror and despair at her plain, hard looks, her big bones and flat chest. She cursed her body. She wept that Beau Cadiz would never see her, seeing only Dolly's prettiness instead.

I would be with him, she thought at such moments. I would be right there with him. If he wanted to go to China, I would grow my hair and plait it into a pigtail, and I would be right there with him. Dolly will never hold him; Dolly will never shape him to what she thinks is going to be her life.

No one knew. She held it in tight and watched her sister glow with happiness.

No letters came for six months. Dolly moved like a ghost through her day. There was a war on in Cuba and they were sure Beau had joined up. Sean Cadiz and his wife promised to let Meg know the instant they received any news. And during that time Meg had to dry Dolly's tears and comfort and reassure her, while there was nothing for her to do but climb to the hayloft and cry until her throat ached.

Then word came on a cold December night.

— He's alive and home, Meg said. And sick. Mrs. Cadiz says he keeps asking for you. Will you go?

Like so many thousands of others in Cuba, Beau had come down with yellowjack. He was shaky, fever-racked, often delirious.

— I'm going to him, Dolly said firmly.

— You're going to what! Bowdry Calvert shouted.

— Leave her alone, Pa, Meg said, moving quickly between her sister and her father. Go on, Dolly, get your things.

— What's going on in my own home! Bowdry demanded.

Dolly ran to her room and started packing. At the last moment she took Beau's letters, putting them into her bag.

— You're not going to that sinful, no-good tramp!

— Yes, Father, I am going to him.

— Is this the kind of life I've tried to teach you? To run like a whore after a man who will leave you at the drop of a hat? How long has this evil thing been going on behind my back? No! As the Lord is my witness, you will not go.

Bowdry Calvert reached for the whip over the fireplace.

— Bowdry, Bowdry, please, Mother Calvert said.

—Meg, move out of the way. You're in on this too, and you should get what she gets.

—No, Pa, Meg said, facing him. Neither of us is going to get whipped. Colbert!

Her brother materialized out of the darkness of another room.

—Yes, Meg? His voice was quiet and steady.

—Do you remember when Dolly was sixteen and I was seventeen when you came back from Atlanta the last time, Meg said to her brother, and you said you wouldn't let Pa whip us again?

—Yes, I remember.

—Well?

—Pa, Colbert said, put the whip down. He was older than both girls by ten years.

—This is *my* house! A house of the Lord!

Colbert walked over and stood in front of his father. If you draw back your arm, Pa, I'll knock you down. I don't want to, but Dolly and Meg are grown women now. You can't hit them anymore.

Meg took her cloak off the hook and put it over Dolly's shoulders, then pushed her sister out the door. She turned back and looked again at her father.

—I'm going to hitch Jeem to the wagon and take Dolly over to the Cadiz place. She stared hard at the old man. And then I'm coming back.

—Listen to her, O Lord, listen to her!

—I'll hitch Jeem, Colbert said, and walked out past her.

She knew when she took Dolly to the Cadiz place that Dolly would never come back. It was all over. The dreams she had dreamed were finished.

Meg remembered all this, standing in the background, watching and listening, ready to step in if necessary. But it was not necessary. Relief swept across Beau's face as Dolly told him calmly, repeating almost word for word what Meg had said earlier, that she did not want him back.

Beau left the two women and his son without a word, nodding his head quickly, smiling a little as he went out the door. Neither Dolly nor Meg moved for some time.

Later that night, Dolly went over each piece of her life. She was surprised how easy it was, once you got started, to find out how and where the mistakes had been made. Surprised, too, at how many of them there had been.

She could not sleep. She rose with Meg, who had to get out early for the machine setups at the cigar factory on Bay Street. Dolly checked Howard in his room and then returned to the kitchen and stood looking out the window, a cup of tea in her hands, warming her fingers. Dolly saw the way Meg looked at her and knew that for once Meg was searching for some sign of reassurance. She spoke to her sister in a quiet voice, not looking at her.

— It's all right, Meg. I'm all right. But I ought to tell you, I feel like something inside of me has died. I guess it's because I lived on hope for so long. That Beau would change . . . Her voice trailed off.

Meg stood at the door, dressed, ready to leave.

— So! There isn't any hope left anymore, Dolly said. I'm all right, though. I'm all right. Yes, it's over, and I'm all right. Somehow I always knew it would end, but not like this. I used to have nightmares and wake up soaked with perspiration. It was always the same dream of getting a telegram from some far-off, distant place with a name I would have to look up in the Atlas, telling me Beau was dead, and inquiring what I wanted done with the body. And now—he really is dead.

Meg watched her sister. She made a quick, abrupt movement, stepping back into the middle of the room.

— I'm not going to work, she said, taking off her coat. You're going in my place.

— But—

— Go on. Ask for Ethel.

— But, Meg, I don't feel like facing *anything* now.

— Ethel! Remember that. She'll show you what to do. You need to *do* something.

— I want to think.

— You've just been sitting around here. And what about back up in Tasco? Waiting. Look at you. You're moldy.

— But I *can't!*

— Go on, git!

— Meg, I can't face things yet.

— Go! I'd rather be at home with Howard anyway.

— But I've never worked before—at a place, Dolly said.

— Try it and see. You might get to like it. Meg helped Dolly into her sweater.

— Go on now, she said. When you cut a thing off, Dolly, it's off. Like opening a boil, back when we were kids, and Colbert would hold us down and Pa would take out his razor. It hurt, but the cut was quick and deep and then it was all over. We started to get better. You'll see. Now go, and remember, ask for *Ethel.*

— Ethel.

Meg closed the door and leaned her head against the panel. She waited until she heard Dolly's footsteps fade down the hall and descend the stairs. She breathed deeply. She looked vaguely around the room.

It was a beginning.

— Howard! she called, going to the boy's room. Get up! Aunt Meg is packing a lunch and we're going to take the Tybee train and spend the whole day at the beach!

Howard opened his eyes.

— Beach?

And as Howard examined the wonderful world of warm sand and stretching seas, he stood on his little boy's legs and experienced his first shock at the size of it all. He was stirred, mystified, and then afraid. He turned and ran fast and threw his arms around Meg's neck, hugging her tight.

He sat all day with his face turned toward the sea, toward the endlessly washing ocean with its salt smells, and he would remember it always, for years to come, as the moment from which he would reckon time, the beginning of his existence.

Beside the school gate, he waited for Uriah and then they headed for the river, two very intent little boys in summer clothes and bare feet. They went straight through the heart of Savannah, stopping only for traffic corners until they came to Bay Street. They plunged down a dark hole of a dozen flights of marble steps that were cut so steep they had to slow down, and then they were on cobblestones that paved the bluff.

Howard closed his eyes, holding off until the last possible moment, getting into position to see the whole sweep of it at one time.

— There she is! Uriah said dramatically. The mighty ol' river! And there's the new boat I told you about.

Howard opened his eyes. The red, cloudy river waters flowed past him to the sea. Further out, on the other side, were the twin islands, Aunt and Uncle, and beyond them, diffused in the summer landscapes and heat haze, lay the mysterious, beckoning, unexplored lands of South Carolina.

— Didn't I tell you there was a new boat in? Uriah insisted. I heard it last night when it blew three times coming past the City Hall.

Howard studied the vessel on the opposite shore. He scanned the wharves and the huge warehouses that had once been offices of factors in the time of cotton. No sign of the watchman. He nodded to Uriah, a command gesture, then slipped forward to the edge of the wharf and sat down, making himself small.

Now he looked at the ship.

Across the river, swinging on slack lines, the thickly plated, riveted, rusting freighter was taking on cargo; clouds of dust mushroomed out of the holds as thc bucket was swung back and forth, dipping into the fertilizer hill and then back again to the ship. Howard watched the monotonous, hypnotic cycle, missing none of the details.

They sat quietly and studied the river. A Negro ferryman, a passenger in the stern of his rowboat, pushed out from the opposite shore and moved into the current. It was a small and decrepit looking boat to Howard, and he questioned the use of it for crossing the river and admired the courage of the passenger. The river was a quarter of a mile wide at any point, and further down it was even wider. The ferryman stood in the middle of the boat, facing forward, always looking at his destination. The boat was at a forty-five-degree angle, fighting current. He worked the oars with a powerful thrust of his arms and shoulders, making a quick recovery and then dipping the oar blades again.

—Looks like they're headed upriver, Uriah said.

—He's bucking the tide, that's why it looks like that, Howard said.

The ferry was nearing midstream where the tide would be strongest. There were little ripples on the surface as crosswind fought current. Then out of a nearby slip a tugboat appeared and headed upriver.

The thick rolling wake of the tug spread out as the vessel bore down on the ferryman and his passenger. Uriah and Howard leaned forward and watched intently as the tug drew nearer and nearer the ferry. The ferryman continued to rock forward in his jerky yet fluid motion, sending the rowboat leaping ahead.

—Boy! He's going to get some ride on those waves, Uriah said.

Howard looked at the wake of the tug and then back at the little rowboat. Was it possible, he wondered, that they didn't see each other? The tug and rowboat closed on what looked to Howard like a sure collision course, and then at the last moment the tug slipped past, blocking the ancient ferry from their view.

Howard and Uriah stood, straining to see. The ferryboat reappeared, and the ferryman was still rocking forward, leaning into his oars. The wake of the tug spread out and it was clear that the rowboat would be sunk in the wash. Then Howard saw the rhythm of the ferryman's stroking come to a stop. He held one oar still, pulled hard on the other, and the bow of the little boat was turned to a right angle, facing the waves.

At the last possible moment the bow of the boat was picked up and the ferry rode over the waves easily. Then another, and a third, and the danger was over.

The ferryman spun the boat back on course and settled into his rhythm once more, batting against the current and moving ahead in short jerks.

—That was *close!* Uriah said.

—Yeah, Howard said. But he was not sure. The ferryman had done something to avoid the wash of the tug, and while it appeared to be close, he sensed that it had not. Skill and knowledge were involved. He suddenly wanted to know what the ferryman had done to avoid the waves.

At the landing they waited for the boat to work into the shore. The passenger paid a dime and hurried up the bluff behind the City Hall. And then Howard stepped forward and slipped down to the floating dock where the ferryman was tying off his boat. He looked hard at the old Negro who had begun rolling a cigarette.

It took Howard some time before he found the courage to speak, and he stepped up to the ferryman only after he had lit his smoke and leaned against the piling to rest. Howard looked up into his lined, weathered face.

— Boy, that sure was close out there, he said.

The ferryman's eyes moved down to the ten-year-old's face and then he looked away, searching the river, reading it. He pulled deeply on his cigarette and began to work at the hard clots that cramped his arm muscles.

Howard eased away and watched the ferryman from a distance. After the smoke was finished, the man took a deep breath, mumbled somthing to himself that sounded to Howard like "Heahahgo," and stepped back into his boat. He began to bat his way on a return across the river for another fare, deadheading a quarter of a mile to make a dime. Howard stood watching the man work against the tide, his thoughts uneasy.

Leaning against the railing, Howard watched the ferryman eat away the distance on the empty return run. He did not take his eyes away from the little boat during the whole trip.

He's a sailor, he thought. Even in that little rowboat, he's a sailor.

The day was going fast.

— I'll bet, Uriah suggested tentatively, that if we went down to the bakery we could get some stale doughnuts.

— I don't think I can, Howard said. I can't stay out after the streetlights go on, or my Aunt Meg will beat hell out of me. You go if you want to.

— No, Uriah said with a lonely, defenseless gesture. It ain't no fun going by yourself.

And then, as if in answer to an unasked question, the huge clusters of milk-white globes were turned on all over the city.

— I have to go now, Howard said. So long, Uriah. We had a lot of fun, didn't we?

— Yeah, we sure did. Man, we had a *good* time.

— Yeah. See you tomorrow in school.

— Yeah, so long, Howard.

— So long.

They parted, each going his separate way, tired, hungry, their full day over, their curiosities satisfied for the time being, eager, anxious to get home, to return to the familiar, not to think about what comes next, or care, or be anything but just themselves.

Howard hurried through the darkening city, a boy hurrying toward manhood.

Tonight, as on all nights, his Aunt Meg waiting for him in the four-room apartment, her tall body looming over him, overwhelming him with her hardness and her bony spirit and her bony body.

— Go wash, Howard, Aunt Meg said.

— Yes, mam, Howard said.

He squinted against the harsh naked lights that were unshaded because Aunt Meg would not have just any kind of lampshade and was always going to make them herself. Howard wondered if she ever would, though there was a box full of silk scraps in the closet to which she kept adding pieces.

Aunt Meg looked at him as Howard squinted his eyes against the harsh light.

— Why didn't you come directly home from school today? she demanded.

— Because, Howard said.

— Because why?

— 'cause, that's all.

— Your mother—

Howard turned on the water in the sink to drown out the voice. He did not want to talk. He wanted to think about what he had seen at the river. It was always difficult when a ship arrived. He *knew* he would stay out after school, and knew the price he had to pay when he did so, and many times in the past he had sworn to himself that he would not go with Uriah anymore. He was prepared to pay up. But he did not understand why this had to be so.

While in the bathroom he heard his mother come in, her voice cracking a little as it always did after a long day selling, a little breathless, tired too. It happened so many times just that way, with him in the bathroom washing for supper and his mother coming home, her hoarse tones that were somehow still soft and easy, that he stopped this night and thought about how things repeat themselves.

— Meg, dear, his mother would say as she put her things down, how is Howard?

And Aunt Meg would answer, short, to the point, almost rudely, speaking around the cigarette in her mouth.

— He's fine. How was your trip?

— Good and bad.

— Tell me the good and keep the bad for later, after we've eaten.

— Howard! Howard! Mother's home, dear.

It was always the same, Howard thought, hearing it again. He wiped his hands on the towel and came out, greeting his mother with a kiss and a hug, seeing his Aunt Meg looking him in the eye.

— Have you been a good boy, Howard? While Mother was away?

— Yes, mam, Howard replied, looking at Aunt Meg.

Aunt Meg turned away to the stove where the supper was ready and warming. The meal followed quickly, eaten in haste with good appetite and little talk. After supper he turned to his schoolbooks, settling into the big chair by the window and letting their talk slowly fade out.

— I heard he left town again, his mother said.

— Where to? Meg asked quickly, in her no-nonsense way. And where did you hear it?

— I saw Arabel Wakefield in Augusta. She saw him in Atlanta.

— Was she sure it was him?

— She said she was sure. Passed him in the railroad station, face to face, and didn't say a word. Of course, he might not have seen her. And *she* wasn't going to speak first.

— She wouldn't, Aunt Meg said. She's always mannered. One of those women who pretend they're so innocent. They give me a pain in the ass.

— Well, I like Arabel.

—I like her, too, Aunt Meg said, surprised. What's that got to do with it?

— Well, it sounded like—

—I say what I think, Aunt Meg said. Sounds don't mean a damn thing.

— It's time to go to bed, Howard, Aunt Meg said.

He went to his room and waited on the side of the bed for the visit. His mother would come, he knew, and talk to him and touch his face and then kiss him. When she came, he complained bitterly about his Aunt Meg.

— My darling, his mother would say when she came, your Aunt Meg doesn't mean to be harsh with you. But she worries about you. And I don't think she understands little boys. And you mustn't make Aunt Meg worry about you, because that worries Mother, and Mother is exhausted from her trips. It takes the life out of me, son, and I wish I could get a job right here in town so that I could come home every night.

— Yes, Mother, Howard said, his bitterness toward Aunt Meg dissolved by his mother's needs. She was always exhausted from her trips, and sometimes she would lie in bed with pillows to ease the strain of her back and the nervous ache in her whole body.

— Your schoolwork is very good, Howard, and Mother is very proud of you.

— Yes, Mother—Thank you, mam.

— Come, give Mother a kiss. And go in and kiss Aunt Meg. She loves you, Howard, and I don't know what I would have done if you hadn't been in the hands of my dear sister after your father died. God always provides, and he provided me with the most loving sister in the world.

— Well, he didn't provide me with a very loving aunt, Howard said.

— Son, son.

— I'm sorry, Mother. Howard looked at her closely after she had told him the outright lie about his father. He saw no difference in her face for telling him the lie.

— Go on, now, and tell her goodnight, his mother said.

He walked out of the bedroom and stopped at the door of the living room. Meg sat in her rocker, reading, her cigarettes and ashtray at her side, smoke shooting out of her nose.

— I'm sorry, Aunt Meg.

— All right, Howard.

— I'm really sorry.

— No, Aunt Meg said, and drew back. Don't kiss me, and don't tell me you're sorry unless you mean it. There's nothing I hate more than hypocrisy. And I *don't* think you're sorry.

He stood, waiting.

— Boys, heaven knows, have to wander around. They're like cats. It's in their nature, I suppose. But you should tell me when you're not coming home from school. You had me worried half to death. I was going out of my mind when you walked in the door. Another five minutes and I would have called the police and had them tear the town apart looking for you.

Howard had visions of a swarm of policemen attacking a building, tearing it down brick by brick, searching for him, with Aunt Meg standing to one side smoking cigarettes, blowing smoke out of her nose, directing them.

His mother entered the room and stood watching them.

— Meg . . . she said.

— No, Dolly, Meg said stubbornly, he's done this too many times.

— Meg, he's only a little boy.

— Don't apologize for him, Dolly. He knows. By God, he's as smart as a whip, and he knows when he's doing wrong.

— Please don't swear, Dolly said.

— When you're away on a trip, Howard knows I need his help around the house for a few things.

His mother sat down and waited. Aunt Meg stopped rocking and stared at him, her pale blue eyes studying his face.

— Where were you?

— Playing.

— Where?

— Just around. Here and there.

— Around here and there, where!

— Out in the park.

— You were not! I went to the park and looked.

Howard thought hard. He could find no way to twist his lie.

— Where were you?

He decided on a defense of total silence. It was a dangerous thing to do, because Aunt Meg could easily take this and use it against him, accusing him of being sullen. There was nothing Aunt Meg hated more (unless it was hypocrisy) than a Sullen Child. There was a long list of things that Aunt Meg hated more than anything else in the world. So he waited, as she interrogated him, for the word "sullen" to come out. If it did, he knew he was in serious trouble.

— I know where he was, Aunt Meg said, turning to look at his mother. I know. Oh, yes I know!

Howard looked into her eyes, wondering if she really knew.

— You were with Uriah, weren't you?

— Yes, mam. How the hell did she know? Howard wondered.

— Why didn't you tell me that, instead of telling me a lie?

He remained silent. It was getting to be extremely dangerous, but he was committed. To speak up now would be called *talking back*. And there was nothing in the world that Aunt Meg hated more than a Child that Talked Back.

— How many times have I told you to stay away from Uriah?

— Many times.

— Yet you go against my wishes?

— But, Aunt Meg, it's fun and all.

— Meg? his mother said again.

Howard tensed. It was the exact time for his mother to speak and make a plea for him. He watched Aunt Meg's face for the surrender signs.

Meg sighed, wearily putting out her cigarette and immediately taking another from the pack. She opened her book and started to rock again.

— Go to bed, Howard. I'm tired and I've got a sick headache worrying about you. Thank God you're home safe. Now go to bed.

— I'm sorry, Aunt Meg, Howard said, and leaned over to kiss her smooth cheek. He kissed his mother and then slipped into his room.

There was another world waiting for him now. He stood at the door, listening for signs of reassurance to come to him. His mother stood and walked into the kitchen. Aunt Meg's rocking continued in an unbroken rhythm. He released his breath and the tension flowed out of him. He moved to the closet and took a chair. Standing, he took down an old suitcase. He reached inside and pulled out a three-cell flashlight that he had brought into the house secretly and that had been saved for, and that for months seemed beyond his reach but had finally been accomplished with his part of five dollars he and Uriah had found. He slipped it under his pillow, undressed hurriedly and took a book from his table.

Once in bed, he waited an interminable time for Aunt Meg to come and tuck in his blanket. He knew she would not move until his mother came back from the kitchen with the tea things.

It seemed hours, but the rattle of dishes finally came and the rocking stopped.

— I'll just check on Howard, he heard his Aunt Meg say, as she said every night of his life. The door opened and a splash of light hit his face. He remained perfectly still, eyes closed. Then he felt her near the bed, pulling the covers, tucking them, her face over his and the strong smell of tobacco combined with the smooth scent of her Paris bath soap, and finally her gentle cheek and lips. The door closed. He waited for the rocking to begin. Their conversation in the next room rippled pleasantly. He heard his Aunt Meg laugh at something his mother had said. It was the happiest sound he ever heard. She did not laugh very often, but when she did, he always stopped whatever he was doing and listened to it.

He slipped under the blanket, snapped the flashlight on and turned to page one of his book and read: *I was born. Whether I shall turn out to be the hero of my own life or whether that station will be held by anybody else, these pages must show.*

He lived now near Liberty Square, where innocent games of chance were played and tomorrow was a time when you might win or lose something important with the children from Cong. B. B. Jacob Temple and from the Widows and Orphans Home; Liberty Square, a naked, grassless park with swings and slides and baseball diamonds.

Howard Cadiz as a child was handsome. He had dark, curly hair and a pale, almost sallow skin and soft eyes. Women and girls would look at him and wonder what lucky female would get him when he grew up. He was never very tall: in fact, he seemed to be a little below average height, and with his pale skin, looking even paler in contrast to his dark hair and soft eyes, he was often called beautiful. He was strong at eleven, and he liked to have women touch him, as they often did.

— Howard is going to be a doctor, his mother would say when friends came by for tea, nodding her head, Howard thought, like a gobbler trying to choke down a piece of grain. He would look at Aunt Meg, but Aunt Meg apparently thought he was going to be a doctor too, because she never contradicted.

— Yes, his mother would say, my little honey is going to be a doctor. I just know. He just loves books and things to read. Why, would you believe it, just recently I caught him reading at one o'clock in the morning. Yes! And do you know, that child was reading a *National Geographic* magazine! Think of that! Just a little old *National Geographic* magazine, that's all.

He hadn't been reading it. He had only been looking at the pictures. The text bored him. The words were too big, and when he bothered to look them up in the dictionary, he always found very good small words that could have been used just as well as the big ones he didn't know.

Out of that conversation, about his reading the *National Geographic* magazine, from one of the pretty ladies that had touched his face and looked into his eyes and acted as though she might at any moment hug him (which Howard would not have minded at all), he had been given a subscription to the magazine after having been sponsored by two gentlemen strangers he never knew.

For many years after that Howard hated the magazine. But his mother somehow never let go of the idea that he was interested in it, and never stopped telling the lie that he had been caught reading it at "five A.M." in the morning until his eyeballs were hanging "right out of their sockets"!

Anyone that would read until their eyeballs hung out—a gory idea, Howard thought, the pale white orbs dangling on his cheekbones held by muscle and bloody sinew—would have to be some kind of idiot.

— And you know what? his mother would continue, wagging a bony gray finger up and down over the teacup, that precious Lily Crosby gave him a life membership to the magazine. That was before she married Doctor Furth.

And throughout all the tea parties, which were always the same, Aunt Meg would rock back and forth in her chair, smoking one cigarette after another, saying nothing, which was her way.

— Down where, son? the man asked Howard. Which way to Broughton Street?

— You're on Bull Street now, sir, Howard said. If you just keep on going down that way, you'll hit it, sir.

— Looka here, Martha! Now here's a boy that knows his manners. Say that again, son.

— Say what, sir?

— There! By God, I wisht Donnen would learn something like that. Donnen! Come 'ere, goddammit. I want you to listen to this boy talk to a man the way a man should be talked to. Say that again, son. What you just said.

Howard was confused. I don't know what you're talking about, sir.

Donnen was taller than Howard, with yellow hair and pale flat gray eyes full of hate.

— Sissy britches, that's all he is, Donnen muttered.

— Well, don't hurt none to hear a man paid respect by a young'un. I guess Broughton Street is further up along here somewheres. Thank *you*, young sir. Yessiree!

— Yes, sir, Howard said, and backed off from the menacing look of Donnen, who lagged behind his mother and father and, when they were a few steps ahead of him, suddenly hit Howard in the nose so hard that blood flowed.

Howard was shocked and enraged by the sneak attack. He watched Donnen run to his mother and father and grab his father's hand, and then he turned back, sticking out his tongue. He made a threatening fist with his free hand.

— You got any money? a tight voice asked at Howard's side.

Howard turned swiftly, ready to fight.

— Hold on! I'm on your side. I saw what happened. My name's Shad. I'll beat his ass for a dime.

— Shad?

— Shad Courtney. What are you doing over here on Bull Street, boy? I know you live down on Liberty Square. I saw you and your mother and aunt move in.

— He hit me when I wasn't looking, Howard said.

— Sure he did. He got away with it, too, didn't he? You have to watch those country bastards. I ought to know. I'm one of them. Don't trust them. Don't trust me. My name's Shad Courtney, and now you know my name, and I've already warned you not to trust me, so come on, I'll take you home with me and we can wash that shirt.

Howard learned that Shad had come to Savannah from the red, chinky hill country. He was not part of the gray cobblestone heritage that was soft and flowing, as Howard was. Shad's was a wild, free spirit, a legacy from forefathers who had given the Rebel yell, the naked opposition during the Civil War. There was a go-to-hell recklessness about him that ignored the consequences. Shad had made up a song about himself:

Oh, Shad, Shad, ain't so bad
for a white man
Oh, Shad, Shad, ain't never sad
loaned me a dime, las' he had

Little girls sang this song when they skipped rope during recess, and it was as popular as Keep the Kettle Boiling and I Went to the Animals' Fair. But one day they were singing *Strawberry Shortcake, Cream of Tartar*, and the schoolyard was filled with the screams of girls as Howard and the others began teasing them, throwing stones and sand. Howard hadn't meant to hit her. He wasn't even aiming at her. He wasn't even studying her, as they used to say.

— Is this the boy? the policeman asked.

— Yes, the teacher said, her flinty eyes glaring at Howard, that is most certainly him.

— Come on, boy, what you need is a good tanning. You damn

near put that girl's eye out. Don't you know better than to throw rocks at girls? To throw rocks at all?

He knew after that.

— A licking is what you're going to get right after supper.

— Please, Mother.

— Don't talk.

— Mother, Howard pleaded.

— I said *don't talk!* I'm sick of hearing your *voice!*

— Yes, mam.

— Stealing money from your poor Aunt Meg's pocketbook.

— Mother—

— *I say-ud do-unt talk!* You're going to get it *because* you're getting mighty big for your britches around *here!* And you're going to get it right *now!*

— Why right now? Aunt Meg yelled. And you are not! Not in this house, you are *not* going to touch a hair on his head.

— You said he took money, his mother insisted. He's got to learn.

— Well, I'm wrong. And you are not going to whip him.

— Meg, I don't understand you at all. When I come back from a trip, you complain about him like it was a trial.

— Don't you hit that child, Aung Meg said, meaning it. But when Howard tried to thank Aunt Meg, tried to make up to her when she came to tuck him in, she turned on him with one word, and he would never forget how it cut and hurt to be called "thief."

The crowd surged against the Negro standing wearily at the curb while the policeman held the back of his belt. They came for him with the wagon and thrust him inside, and Howard moved around the edge of the crowd, not daring to ask what the Negro had done, but listening to what was said.

— Stole to the grocery store, a black man near Howard remarked.

— Ax his name, another Negro said. Go on, ax his name, so somebody can tell his woman and she'll know.

— You don't talk to the law just lak dat! Throw *me* in jail with him.

Howard moved to the white side of the crowd and went on listening.

— When the hell are we going to keep these niggers on their side of West Broad Street? A white man elbowed his way past Howard and into the center of the scene.

— I only wish I knew, another white man said. But I say they oughta lock 'em up in a big boat and send 'em back to Africa where they come from. Every damn one of them.

— Well, I agree with you there, said a third white man, but I got a colored cook, like a member of the family. I wouldn't want Stella to go.

— I know what you mean, I know, I know. Well, she's a good nigra. There's a lot of good nigras. Had me a mammy nurse, myself. I'd fight now, you heah, to keep her off any goddam boat to Africa.

— Yeah, I heah. But the rest oughta be sent straight to hell back.

— All the bad ones, straight to Africa.

— You'd think they'd like it better over there. Why, they'd only be where they belong and where they come from. But tell me, where do you want to send all the bad white trash? All the loud-mouths? Huh?

— Who the hell are you?

— My name is Shad Courtney and I'm a white nigra, and I'd please like to know where you're going to send *me*.

— You smart-aleck little bastard! I'll slap you down!

— All I'm doing is asking a fair question, mister, that's all, Shad said innocently.

— You sound like a goddam kikey Jew sonofabitch to me, you Jew bastard.

That was when Shad hit him. The man went down and stayed down. Shad laughed and looked around, ready for anyone else willing to take him on.

— You did so, Howard Cadiz! You did so call me a kike!

— I did not, Sammy!

— You're a liar!

— I didn't call you nothing!

— But you were with them, and *they* called me a kike!

— Well, Howard said stubbornly, I didn't. Sammy, don't cry.

— To hell with them all. Goddam sonsabitches!

— Sammy, they didn't mean nothing by it.

— You too, Howard Cadiz!

— But I thought we were friends?

— I don't wanta play with you no more. I'm different. You heard them say so. You heard 'em. Just leave me alone and don't talk anymore to me and don't come around to my house and trade books anymore, 'cause I don't want to!

— Sammy—wait!

— Goddam sonsabitches!

— Sammy, Sammy, all I want to do is talk to you! Listen to me.

That night, Shad and Howard and Uriah sat on the curbstone and read about it on the back page of the paper.

> Sammy Kortner, age twelve, was struck by a speeding truck and died instantly. Witnesses to the scene said they thought the youngster ran deliberately into the path of oncoming traffic. Others dispute this. The boy was thrown into the path of a dray and four Belgian drafts. Thomas Cattls, Negro of 1234–29 Doan Street, Yamacraw, drayman, is now being held on charges. A group of young Sammy Kortner's friends, Howard Cadiz, Shad Courtney, and Uriah Lightfoot, witnessed the tragedy, declaring the drayman could not have swerved the double team of draft bucks.
>
> There is tragedy tonight around Liberty Square amid the shadows of live oaks, as friends of little Sammy Kortner sit and watch the silent arrivals and departures of relatives of young Kortner paying their respects. Liberty Square, usually full of laughter and games on these hot

summer nights, is quiet this eventide. There will be no Buck, Buck, How Many Fingers Up, nor Hide and Seek, nor Capture the General's Flag.

Liberty Square is in a deep and abiding state of sorrow.

— Uriah, do you remember the time we went out to Indian Hills and jumped ditches and saw that snake, with Sammy and me and you and Shad?

— Yeah.

— And the other times we had. Like when we went down to the river, and that German boat was in, and the cook took us aboard and let us eat all we wanted in the messroom with the sailors? Man! That was a time, wasn't it?

— Yeah.

— Sammy. Jesus. Dead and all.

— They wouldn't let anybody come close, Uriah said, he was tore up so bad. They wouldn't even let Mrs. Kortner come close. They said one of them big Belgian bucks stepped right on his head.

— Sammy Kortner dead, Howard Cadiz said, and he said it over and over and still could not believe it, nor comprehend it, and for a long time after that he cried when he remembered how Sammy had broken off their friendship.

— That makes it last a long time, Thelma. Just like friends. None of that love business. Just friends. Like a sister.

— Oh, Howard, it's such a pretty ring.

— But if my mother or Aunt Meg should find out—

— *Howard Cadiz!* I didn't know you smoked!

— Sure, long time now. Of course, I don't smoke at home in front of my mother. I'll *never* smoke in front of her, or Aunt Meg. I have too much respect for them. Both of them are very religious. But they know about it.

— The streetlights are on, Howard. I have to go now. Thank you for the ring.

— I'll walk you.

— Oh, that's nice.

They walked around the square and down the dark side of the street near the church, and it was there that Howard worked up his nerve to try and kiss her. He spun her around like they did in the movies and kissed, missing her lips and kissing, instead, her nose.

— That's about as bad an abscess as I've ever seen. Howard lay on the bed, his ear exposed, the pressure building to a hot pain that shut out the whole world.

— I'll have to open it up, Dr. Furth said.

— Where? Oh, God. Meg, they're going to have to open it up. *Where?*

— Right here, behind the ear. Just a little hole so the pus can run out and relieve the pressure. If it bursts inside, into the brain, he can die, Mrs. Cadiz.

— Don't talk to me of death. Don't talk about my poor precious baby dying.

— Open it, Aunt Meg said. The sooner the better.

— I have to have the mother's consent, Miss Calvert.

— She's just given it to you, Aunt Meg said.

— Mrs. Cadiz, do you want me to take your son to the hospital and open it?

— I can't bear to think of it. I can't bear it—

— Open the thing up, Doctor Furth. Get him to a hospital, or whatever it is you have to do. Don't pay any attention to her.

Howard opened his eyes. Aunt Meg moved in and stood over him.

— Am I going to die, like Sammy Kortner, Aunt Meg?

— No. Emphatically and once and for all, no, Howard. You are not going to die. You are going to live a long time and torment my poor soul straight to hell.

— Yes, mam. I'm sorry, Aunt Meg.

— *Doctor!* Aunt Meg said sharply.

— Yes, Miss Calvert?

— If you don't open that abscess right now, or take him to the hospital, or do something, I will personally throw your ass down the backstairs and break both of your goddam arms. Now *move it!*

— See here! The frail, delicate, pink-faced Dr. Furth retreated.

— The boy, Doctor! *The boy!* Never mind me. Or her! Attend to the boy. Do you realize he is only twelve!

— Here we are, so near to the end of school and you pull a stunt like that!

Howard had never seen his mother so angry.

— And right on the school grounds! God in Heaven! What have I raised, a pagan? A degenerate?

— Shut up! Aunt Meg said, and faced her nephew. Howard looked at them, embarrassed, unsure, his pants dropped below his knees, exposed, the pubic hair a tickle of fuzz, but all the same a man of sturdy character.

— Who is Shad? Aunt Meg demanded.

— Boy I know in school. Hangs around the square. We play and all.

Meg puffed rapidly on a cigarette. She turned and looked at her sister, who was fanning herself, sitting in a chair and looking away. Meg turned back to Howard.

— Who asked the girl?

— He did.

— Did he lay her too?

— Yes, mam.

— Oh *God in Heaven!* his mother screamed.

— Oh shut *up,* Dolly, Aunt Meg said. Has anyone ever told you you were a narrow-minded hypocrite? He's a man. That's goddam plain enough. With some men it comes sooner than later. You oughta know that, you were the one married, not me.

— Yes, but I know all about your little escapades! Dolly shot back.

If she heard Dolly's last remark, Aunt Meg did not react to it. She put out her cigarette and lit another one and glared at Howard.

— Pull up your pants, Howard.

— Yes, mam.

— Don't go yet. I have a few more questions.

— Yes, mam.

— What do you know about this girl?

— Name's Jane.

— Has she done this before, with the other boys?

— Yes, mam.

— You're sure?

— Yes, mam. Shad said he fu—, I mean, you know, did it lotsa times with her.

— But this time, did Shad do it with her?

— Yes, mam.

— You both did it? Is that right?

— Yes, mam.

— The same girl?

— Yes, mam.

Aunt Meg flushed and sighed and shook her head.

— Did you, ah—I mean—use anything? Aunt Meg asked carefully.

Howard nodded.

— You didn't, ah— Aunt Meg's directness broke down. She turned her head and looked at her sister, who sat upright, listening but not looking at them.

— I used a rubber, Howard said.

— *Don't you use that filthy language in this house!* his mother shouted.

— Shut up, Meg said. Just shut up!

— Go! March! Quick step! Straight to the bathroom and strip down and sca-*uld* yourself clean. His mother stood and marched ahead of him. I wish to God in Heaven I could get some of that hot soapy water into your sou-*ul!*

— Yessum.

Howard went to the bathroom and stripped down. He got into the tub of water that was so hot he had to wait fifteen minutes before he could sit down. And when he was finished and in his robe, moving toward his room, Aunt Meg stopped him.

— Howard, you're a man now, so this will happen again—

— Aunt Meg, I swear to you, never again.

— Yes, it will happen again. And when it does, there's no need to tell your mother, or me, about it. But don't do it too often, Howard. It's for adults. And when you do, be careful of the girl.

— Aunt Meg, I swear, I'm going to be good. I'll never do it again.

— Yes, you will, Howard. Just remember what I said about the girl.

— I don't know where I got the name, Howard, old boy. My old man has called me that since I was as big as a gnat on a skeeter's ass, Shad said.

— Heh, heh, heh.

— You got a funny laugh, Howard, old boy, like the scrape of dried chicken dooty over a blackboard.

— Heh, heh, heh.

— See what I mean?

His real name was Charles and he lived in an alley street deep in the backyard catfish section of Savannah and was just discovering there were people who left things in parked automobiles on dark side streets. Howard was a sharp-eyed lookout while Shad searched the seats.

— But where the hell are we going to sell a pistol? Howard wanted to know. Both of us are too young to go to a pawnshop.

— Know just the right person to take this off our hands, Howard, old boy. But he's out of town right now. And Howard was impressed because it seemed to him that Shad knew somebody for everything, and understood everybody, spotting their weaknesses quick as a wink—everybody, of course, except his own father.

Mr. Courtney heard them when Shad tried to sneak the pistol into the house. Where the hell you been! And who the hell is this you hanging around with!

— That's my friend, Papa.

— Don't Papa me! It makes me sick to my stomach, sick that I borned you. And don't tell me that you found that pistol, or somebody gave it to you, or that you nice and easy-like borried it. You *stole* it!

— Then leave me the hell alone, if you know so much! Shad said with quick violence.

— I'll leave you alone! After I've busted your ass for you!

— Yeah, you and what man's army!

— Goddam smart-alecky bastard!

Courtney hit his son four times with his fists, and Shad lay on the floor of the kitchen, the drunken, leering, triumphant father hanging over him, fists balled into hard rocks.

— Take to the road, boy, Shad's father said to Howard. And don't come around here anymore. You want to go to jail, hang around with this bum some more. He's going straight to jail. Even if I have to see to it myself.

Howard looked at Shad, his nose and mouth bleeding, sprawled on the scaly kitchen floor. Then he was sick, right on the floor beside Shad.

When he was finished and had staggered back to lean against the wall, he felt a cold wet thing hit him in the face; Mr. Courtney was holding a smelly towel to his forehead. Howard took the towel and wiped his face.

— Thank you, sir, he managed. I'll clean that up in a minute.

— You got a Pa? Courtney demanded.

— No—sir.

— Then somebody ought to bust your tail for hanging around with the likes of him. Courtney contemplated his son.

— But—Howard began a mild protest.

— Don't speak, boy. Don't sass me. I could give you the same I give my own. How do I know you ain't the one that gits him to do these things?

— But—

— Don't *sass!* Nothing in the world I hate more than a boy that sasses. Courtney picked up the pistol from the floor and looked at it and then looked at Shad. With one sharp blow against the stove he broke the gun in half and hurled the pieces to the floor.

After a long moment Courtney, who stood staring down at Shad, spoke to Howard.

— But I know you and the others ain't like him. I know it ain't you. It's him. His maw done that to him. She wasn't no good. A whore if there ever was one. Picked her up one night in Augusta. I came over from Tennessee and picked her up for a piece and then kept hanging around for just one more and then just one more after that, and then before I knew it, there it was, a woman tied around my neck, and this 'un.

Courtney rose to the kitchen cabinet and took down a flat pint flask and took a long drink. He came back to the table and sat down, resting his hands on his belly at the belt buckle, lacing his fingers, and looked at Shad.

—Fair-haired she was, his maw, and not bad when it came to doing little things around the house. She could cook enough, and clean right well, but when it came to chillun, she was tired of it all. She was tired when she borned him. Seems like she never forgave him for making her carry around that big belly and him in it for nine months. She had a tarrible time with him.

—I'm sorry, Mr. Courtney.

—You're a nice boy. I can tell. Don't pay any attention to me. I know you're a nice boy. How come you hang around with a good-for-nothing like Shad?

—I like him.

—Why?

—I—well—he's fun and all.

—What kind of fun? Because he steals? Because he likes to fight? What kind of fun is there in a boy that will talk back to his paw?

Howard tried to avoid answering. He licked his lips and asked for a glass of water. He hoped Courtney would have forgotten when he came back. He stepped over Shad's still motionless body and wondered if he might not be dead or seriously injured. He ran the tap and let the water get cold and drank greedily.

—Come here, boy. Come here. I won't hurt you.

—Sir?

—Do you really like my son? Do the others like him? Tell me. Tell me about my son, he said, still staring down at Shad. Boy, do you hear me?

—Yes, sir.

—Tell me.

—I can't say exactly, sir.

—Try.

—He—he isn't afraid of anything. Not anything.

—That would come from me, Courtney said softly. Look how he stood up to me. That was courage but not right, because I'm his father, see? But it showed what he had. We'uns, us Courts, we had it. Right back, way back, us Courtneys all had it. Anything else, son?

— All the others in school like him.

— They do, huh. In school. Is he good in school?

— Real good. Better than anyone else.

Howard saw the hunger in the red, whiskey-glazed eyes; the red was not just from drink but from work, too. He knew Shad's father worked in a boiler foundry for the railroads. Some said he had scabbed a strike a few years back to get the job. Some said it would be a cold day in hell before Courtney would live without his guilt bothering him for the men who had been killed during the strike. Howard Cadiz saw the lined and seamy face and the red eyes and the dark, thin nose, the bitter lips. It seemed to him that he was seeing straight into the core of another human being for the first time.

Howard lost his fear and lied, to help cover up the hurt he saw in the face of Shad's father. He focused on a point on Courtney's forehead. He told himself Shad *could* have been good in school if he had tried. But he was not better than everyone else. Howard himself was better than everyone else. The work came easily for him, and most of the time he was bored with school. Shad was smart, but he wouldn't work.

— Yes, sir, I reckon Shad, if he would study and all, would be better than anyone else.

— That would come from his mother, Courtney said. She was smart. And she could of been something. She could divide four figures into four figures in her head faster than I could write them down, boy. She was smart and she could of been something. A whole lot more than just getting me for a husband. But she was lazy. And she liked things. And wanted things without working for them. Give that woman a pretty frock and a bottle of whiskey and a good man for a weekend and she was happy. Too happy. She lived with it.

He gazed down at his son. Like him, Courtney said. They're alike.

— I'm sorry, sir, Howard said. I just like Shad because—

— Why, boy? Tell me more.

— He believes in things.

— What things?

— We talk and all, not just about girls and going to the show, but about things. Real things. He told me about the war in Europe, how it got started and all, and about the German king, and he even said the President was weak and no good. He said we're sure to get in it this year.

— Said that about the President, did he? I wouldn't have thought he'd even know who the President was.

— Yes, sir, and he had to go down to the principal's office, and he was with Mr. Jones a long time for saying it.

— What else?

— Said the country was in a terrible rotten mess.

— That too?

— Yes, sir.

— What else?

— Said things were going to get a hell of a lot worse before they got better.

Courtney stared down at his son and nodded. He's got it. He's got it. Can't you see that, boy? My God, he's got everything a man needs, if he would only—

— Only what, sir? Howard asked.

— If I knew, goddammit, I'd tell him, that's what! I'd bang his head on the floor until he understood. I'd do that, if I only knew what to *say* to him.

— Oh, Howard said quietly.

The soldier, a red-faced, red-haired, red-necked mountain boy who had joined the Army to fight in the coming war, was sprawled in the dirt.

— You don't think you've killed him, do you, Shad? Howard asked.

— He might be dead, Shad said amiably.

— Did you have to hit him so hard?

— I didn't hit him hard, not hard at all, Howard. I hardly hit him at all.

But the soldier's jaw was at a crazy angle.

— Well, we might as well make the most of it, Shad said, and stooped over the soldier to search his pockets. As he did so he heard the man breathing.

— Naw, he ain't dead, Shad said. But he ain't going to eat easy for a long time. And he sure as hell ain't going to get a chance to do all that fighting he was so hot about.

War fever gripped Savannah, as it did the nation. It was bonds and encampments and horseplay and emotionalism and pride of Company and pride of Battalion and pride of Regiment and pride of Division and pride in the section of your State and pride in the whole State and pride in your part of the Country and pride in the whole Country and finally there was pride in Old Glory. Our flag, look at her, boys, look at her. Don't you feel the pride swelling your chests?

— Slacker is what he is! How come he ain't in uniform!

The man was walking down Broughton Street when the drunken soldiers spotted him. They began walking in back of him and making remarks and then they got closer and surrounded him and demanded to know why he wasn't in the Army like the rest of them, and didn't he feel any pride in his country and Old Glory? And when the man tried to explain that the Army had rejected him because of a heart condition, they didn't listen and began to push him around as a crowd gathered and egged them on.

And then the man dropped dead on Bull and Broughton outside of a ten-cent store. The soldiers and the crowd hurriedly dispersed. The police came and took the dead man away, and the soldiers tried to explain. The next day there was a piece in the paper about the incident, and how the soldiers had taken up a collection for the man's family.

— Look, Howard, Shad said, showing him the item in the paper. Everybody in town has heard about how them stupid soldiers killed that poor slob on Broughton Street and then took up a collection to help the poor bastard's family.

— Yeah, I know that.

— Watch this, and I'll show you the easiest thing since screwing Jane.

Shad walked up to a man hurrying down the street.

— Mister, something for the slacker's family?

— What slacker?

— They tormented him, the poor man, on Broughton Street. You musta read about it in the papers. They're taking up a collection all over town to help out his family and starving kids. Real little kids. *Babies*, even.

— Oh, well, here, all the change I have. The man hurried on.

— See what I mean, Howard? Sixty cents.

They worked it hard for three days all over Savannah and collected nearly seventy dollars. And then the idea was dead, and there was very little talk about slackers because everybody was ashamed, really ashamed, until the incident of the Negro slacker occurred.

— Nigger! Slacker! Nigger slacker!

The voice was hoarse. But by then Howard had lived around Liberty Square long enough to recognize the cry for blood when men got together in crowds as big as this one.

— They got him pinned down in Yamacraw!

— Oughta go in there and burn 'em out!

— Must be a coupla hundred slackers in there, just hiding in all them dark crummy alleys, sneaking looks at white women from underneath where the rats live. They're just hiding in there, I tell you!

— More'n that. Thousands maybe.

— Well, what are we going to do about it?

To one side, watching, listening, circling the outer edges of the crowd, Howard and Shad and Uriah moved from group to group.

— Don't you think we'd better go, Shad? Howard said. I saw a man with a gun.

— What? A gun? Where?

— There might be trouble. Let's go.

— Not me. Hell, take your tail home if you want to, I'm going to go with them, down into the 'craw and get me a nigger slacker.

Howard looked at the crowd. They ain't going to do nothing, he said with contempt, and loud enough for several men to hear him. They're just talking and popping off and having an excuse to stand around and cuss out in the open.

— If you don't want to go, that's all right with me, Shad said.

— Shad—

— Leave me alone, will you? Will you?

— I ain't going to let you do this, and he hit Shad as hard as he could, knocking him down and drawing blood. Shad was stunned.

Howard was as angry as he was frightened, but he waited with his fists up. Shad looked up at him from his sitting position and stared. Howard was ready for him, ready to take his beating. But Shad did not move. He just sat there and looked at Howard a long time.

— Come on, let's go to a show or something, Howard said finally, when he saw that Shad was not going to fight. Or let's go see Jane. Her mother and father should be gone to work by now.

There was danger of a riot until the police came. The police were not after a Negro slacker at all. It was routine. A Negro soldier had been over leave, and before he had left his encampment he had been seriously ill. The Army just wanted to know if he was all right and needed hospitalization.

— You see, a simple explanation, the policeman said. But when a thing like this starts, it can get out of hand. You see what I mean? he asked the young rookie at his side. A crowd gathers. People get excited. And all it takes is one little incident to blow it up, or a simple explanation to cool it off. You can't let it get too big, because you'll always find more coming to see what's going on.

The night the troop train left Union Station there were people as far back as Montgomery Street, a whole block deep, all of them tying to get into the station and say good-by to their boys moving to camp up the line somewhere. It was all very military and very wartime secret.

Mothers and wives and sweethearts and sisters and girl friends and aunts and uncles and brothers and grandmothers and great-great-grandfathers had come down to see their boy leave for the war that would settle the Kaiser's hash. A sea of faces and clothes and bonnets and hats, and all of them crying as they sent their boys, the flower of southern manhood, Over There.

— Isn't that Shad? Uriah said.

— Where? Howard asked eagerly, because he hadn't seen Shad in months.

— Over there, talking to that soldier.

— Shad! Shad!

— Oh, hello, Howard. Shad only glanced at Uriah.

— How've you been, Shad?

— Fine. Just fine.

— We, ah, me and Uriah are going to a show. Wanta come with us?

Shad's eyes were absolutely flat. Howard saw there had been a change. He didn't know just what it was, but it startled him. It was complete. There was little left in the eyes that he recognized.

— I gotta go, Howard. Things I gotta do. It was nice seeing you again, and all. But I gotta go.

The soldier stood impatiently for a moment and then shrugged, aloof. Uriah stood to one side, watching Shad and Howard.

— I went around to your house, but it was closed up, Howard said.

— I don't live there anymore, Shad said. Jane ran away from her old man and old lady—and I had a room, and well, we sorta living together now.

— Oh? Howard was a little shocked. I asked about your father, too. But Mrs. Hennesy, next door, said she hadn't seen him.

— I don't know where he is, Shad said in a curiously uninvolved voice.

— What are you doing now? Howard asked.

— Working. Listen, it was nice seeing you, and all, but I got to go with this soldier. We got business.

— Wait a minute, Shad.

— Howard, I *gotta* go.

The soldier stepped back into it now, his voice a growl of irritation.

— Come on, kid, you taking me to that whore of yours or not?

— Yeah, sure. Be right with you.

— Good-by, Shad, Howard said.

Shad didn't say good-by. He just turned away from Howard and walked away with the soldier, their heads together as they hurried down the street.

Uriah eased up beside Howard. He knew about the friendship between Shad and Howard. He did not try to invade what he knew could not be invaded. He just waited. Finally he spoke up.

— We still going to the show?
— Yeah, Howard said.

Howard wants to be a doctor, and I aim to see that he *is* a doctor, Aunt Meg said.

Howard stood to one side, knowing in advance the outcome once Aunt Meg had declared herself.

His mother played out every trick she knew. Her back hurt. It *ached*. And would Meg *please* have some consideration for her and not discuss it just then. Her back was all trembly with nerves bunched up together and pulled into a knot. *There just wasn't enough money*. Howard was a child. She moved around the room and touched things, a sure sign that Aunt Meg was hounding her into a corner, was about ready to move in for the finish. Aunt Meg smoked cigarettes endlessly while Howard's mother roamed the room, always retreating until Aunt Meg backed away, knowing victory would come to her but letting Dolly off the hook just enough to think it was a standoff.

— My! How time flies, his mother sighed, sewing on a dress. Only a little while ago it seemed everybody was marking time until the end of the war, and talking about when the war would be over, and here it is done and over with, thank God! Our boys are coming home.

Aunt Meg was ironing. They were sitting in the front room. The grate crackled with pine pitch wood. Howard was curled in a chair with an anatomy book loaned to him by Dr. Furth.

— What are your studies now, Howard? his mother asked. She never asked what he was reading. It was always his Studies.

— I'm *reading* about the spinal column. The backbone.

— Read it out loud, Howard, Aunt Meg said, giving him a wink when he looked up. Maybe your mother can locate that place in her back where all the nerves get bunched up in a knot.

Howard smiled as Aunt Meg lit a cigarette and set the iron to rest.

Howard sat up in the chair and made himself comfortable.

— "The fixed, or immovable, vertebrae form the sacrum, consisting of five fused sacral vertebrae and the coccyx, the lowest portion of the spinal column, usually composed of four small fused bones. Each vertebrae has a somewhat cylindrical bony portion, the body or the centrum, a number of spinous process and bony arch."

—My, that's interesting, his mother broke in. Isn't it, Meg dear. Isn't it wonderful that Howard is going to be a doctor, Meg dear?

Howard and Aunt Meg looked at each other. An expression of sly amusement passed between them.

Aunt Meg continued to iron and smoke, her head cocked to one side to avoid the upward drift. She looked at Howard thoughtfully.

—Ever see that Courtney boy again, after the night he broke the soldier's jaw?

—Meg!

—Hello, Howard. I been around. You know how it is. I tried to join the Army, but I had the clap. You remember Jane. Where are you going?

—School.

—Oh.

—Don't you go to school anymore, Shad?

—No. Shad looked away. I got me a job now. I was lucky to get it, as a matter of fact.

—Where?

—I work at a place outside the city limits. Near the Army depot. Why don't you come out sometime. I have lots of girls out there, you know. If you want a piece, come on out.

—Well, I might come, but I wouldn't come for that necessarily. When did you start smoking cigars, Shad?

—Long time now. Say, what kind of book is this? Shad reached for the biggest book in Howard's arms.

—Book on the human anatomy. I think I'm going to be a doctor.

—Yeah? Shad Courtney's face changed when he heard that. A doctor, huh?

—Well, I don't know for sure, Howard said, watching Shad open the book.

—Tibula, Shad read. What's that, Doc?

—No, tibia, Howard said. It's the shinbone.

—Oh, yeah? Well, I got to go, Howard, old boy. Say hello for me to your mother and Aunt Meg. We used to have some good times, didn't we, kid? Eh, Doc?

— Yeah, sure did.

— Yeah, Shad said, not looking at him. It was fun. S'long, Doc.

— So long, Shad.

— Howard, Dr. Furth said, I am disappointed with you. I expected to see a little more progress than last time, at least a good knowledge of anatomy and pronunciations. It has been almost a year, and you're taking Latin in school, aren't you?

— Yes, sir.

— Being a doctor is important, Howard, even if it is important only to you. And then you can make it important to others. Dedication is the word commonly used. It is a good word. It means a man wants something and does it, with one hundred per cent purity of purpose and ruthless honesty. Do you understand?

— Yes, sir. Doctor Furth?

— Yes, Howard.

— Why does a doctor go on fighting when he knows he can't win? In the end, I mean. Everybody dies.

Dr. Furth looked at Howard a long time and did not answer, but only stared at the boy opposite him, his thin gold-rimmed glasses pushed back on his forehead.

— We go on, Howard, to sustain life as we know it. We cannot sustain something we know nothing about.

— Life?

— No, we know a great deal about life. It is death that we know so little about. Nothing, in fact, at all, except that it is a condition of nature, a mandatory law that all things living must die.

— But, sir—

— Yes?

— Why do doctors go on fighting, in the face of the mandatory laws?

— That is the truly mysterious part of the life-death miracle, Howard. On the one hand, there is life, and on the other, there is death, one as natural as the other, each a miracle in its own way, not to be denied, and in between we have man living out his time. Why does he do it at all?

— I don't know, Doctor Furth, Howard said.

— I don't know either, Howard. I'm going to give you a little note to the head of the City Clinic and Dispensary. He's a good friend of mine, a fine man and a fine doctor. The O.P.—that's the out-patient clinic—I want you to go over there as often as you can and sit and listen and watch. Then come back and let me know how you feel about things.

— Yes, sir.

— Very well, Howard, is there anything else on your mind?

— No, sir.

— How is your Aunt Meg? Better tell her to drop around for a check-up. The last time she was in, she didn't look too well.

— I'll tell her, sir.

— Fine, Howard. Tell the nurse outside to start sending them in as you leave.

— Yes, sir.

The City Dispensary was open to the public from 2:00 P.M. until 5:00 P.M. Howard sat to one side and watched and listened, feeling important and proud of the white smock they had given him because he was a guest of Dr. Furth's.

— Name, please.

— Deedee Simmons.

— Mother's maiden name?

— Deedee McVey.

— Age?

— Thutty-two this last month.

— Address?

— Fo'teen Fahm Street, Savannah.

— That in Yamacraw?

— Yes, mam.

— What is your trouble?

— Well, ah—mam, in my privates.

— Just take this number. When they call it, go through the green door and tell the doctor.

— This number?

— Yes. Twelve.

— Twelve. When they announces this number, I goes through the green door to see the doctor?

— That's right.

— Thank you, mam. Twelve.

The woman walked to the bench and sat down. Howard sat to one side, listening and watching and observing the shape, size and depth of pain.

— Name please?

— Quincet, spelled with a Q. Irmah Quincet.

— Spell it, please.

— Can't spell it, but heah 'tis wrote down.

— What is your trouble?

— This heah. Right heah! Swoll up somethin' bad las' night; and I up-chucks all the time.

— You do what?

— I varmits, mam.

— Are you in pain now?

— I can hardly sit in this chair, lady.

— Never mind waiting. Through that door, please, and just say it 's an emergency. You have an acute appendix or I don't know one.

Irmah Quincet did have an acute appendix and died three hours later.

— Name, please. . . .

— Howard, do your Latin now. I've got ironing to do. Get your homework finished before mother comes home.

— Yes, Aunt Meg.

— And do five pages, five full pages of Latin.

— Yes, Aunt Meg. Visum, visum, visum, visum, visum, and it was remembered.

— Tradere, tradere, tradere, tradere, and it was learned.

— Capere, capere, capere, capere.

— Fides, fides, fides, fides, *there!*

An ancient rite, a whispering litany of learning, with head bent over the pages, the finger searching out the word, the eyes closed tight, fighting out the light and the hundred other things that the mind wanted to dwell on, and seeing the word in the infinite space of the mind, making the word stick to the brain like a stamp on an envelope. And then back for more of the same.

— Dictum, dictum, dictum, dictum . . .

— What started it? Shad Courtney replied, trying to explain to the policeman. It was something he said to her. The blond whore was yelling in the corner and then someone got her out of the tavern.

— Well, boy, you sure should have tried getting him to shut up some other way besides breaking his neck, the policeman said, taking out a pair of handcuffs and putting them on Shad's wrists.

Shad turned and looked at Howard. They had been talking near the end of the bar where Shad worked as a bouncer. It was the first time Howard had gone there. He stood rigid when it happened. He had never seen such strength in his life.

— But I didn't mean it, Shad protested. You don't know what he said to her.

— Tell it to the judge, boy.

— The jury, you mean, the other policeman said.

— But you don't understand, Shad insisted.

The man lay on the floor where Shad had thrown him as easily as a man would throw a bundle of rags. The blood from Shad's wound was still on the floor and on the dead man. The head was angled off from the shoulders awkwardly. The knife the man had used on Shad was still there too, a cut-down kitchen blade that had come out of thin air; and before Shad knew it, the man had it in Shad's shoulder. But still, Shad had broken his neck.

— Fourth cervical vertebra, Howard thought, looking at the dead man, maybe the third, the third or fourth.

— Well, it was self-defense, the owner said. The guy had a knife in the kid. Got it in Shad pretty good. They'll probably let him off . . . Sure, I'll do what I can for Shad, but I hired a bouncer, not a killer. Jesus! What strength. That poor bastard didn't have a chance once Shad got a hold of him, and him with a shoulder cut up like that. Jesus. It looks like a beef steak, and the knife just hanging in there, like Shad didn't even know it. Listen, you damn dumb-head cops! Get him to a hospital before he bleeds to death.

— You know him, boy? a man said to Howard. You were talking to him, don't try to deny it.

— Yeah, Howard said, I know him. He watched Shad being put into a police car.

— Was he always that strong?

— Yes, and he was never afraid, Howard added, feeling something go loose inside of him. He wanted to tell them that things had gone wrong for Shad. He wanted to tell them about Shad's mother and father.

But he didn't. He just went home after giving his name and address as a material witness.

When Shad was convicted for manslaughter, Howard passed further across the subtle line that had divided boyhood from manhood. He had a friend who had killed a man and who was on the chain gang doing time.

Now that the war was over, the boys returned. They arrived unceremoniously in small groups of three, four and five at Union Station on West Broad Street to few cheers of welcome. The people most interested in the returning soldiers seemed to be the taxi drivers, who knew the soldiers would have pay in their pockets and who wanted to get as much of it as they could, steering them to the whorehouses on Congress and Indian streets. The soldiers didn't much care; they had just fought a successful war and were glad just to be alive and back home. They were still young enough to start putting to work some of the plans they had made in the muddy trenches. This was no time to worry, not *now*, not on this beautiful spring day in 1919.

They said there might be as many as five thousand cases of influenza in Savannah alone. The epidemic that had started in the Army camps had hung on, and now it was spreading over the country. Dr. Furth had had to suspend his afternoon talks with Howard Cadiz. He had no time for his office. Like all doctors in Savannah he was out making house calls and working with the serious cases that were to end in the hospitals. People stayed home. Broughton Street was empty. Even on Saturday afternoons, there was only half the usual number of shoppers making the rounds of the stores. At some of the lunch counters the food handlers were wearing face masks. The schools were near closing. For months now Howard had never seen more than half of his classmates in school at one time. They had not yet closed the theaters and the churches, but attendance was low.

It had been an early thaw and a deceptively early spring. A bone-chilling December and January's icy winds and freezing rains up from the southeast gave way dramatically over one weekend to a blossoming of hot sunshine. Long dreary days and nights in closed rooms were forgotten. Windows flew up, bedding was aired, rooms freshened, sweaters and coats thrown aside. From ten in the morning until four in the afternoon the sun blazed high in the seventies and eighties, and while it was still cool in the shade, who cared, the sun had come back. Normal springtime colds, normal March and April runny noses, normal numbers of cases of the grippe began to appear. Everything was normal, except that spring had broken too early.

For two weeks in early February the weather was burning hot, and then, as suddenly as it had appeared, the sun vanished and lead-colored clouds returned. Conditions were perfect; influenza moved in. Savannah was seized by the throat that was already a little tight and sandpapery, by the nose that was rubbed raw from wiping the constant running, by the chest that felt like a ton of bricks pressing down and in; the eyes watered and could barely be held open, and no light could be tolerated. Victims lay in darkened rooms. Their muscles ached and their fevers rose, they sweated under the covers, they took tea with lemon, they drank brandy straight, they drank moonshine cut with several drops of kerosene, they ate aspirin and cough drops and chewed Aspergum and sucked on sassafras root and had their bodies rubbed down with hot camphor; they hung over steaming kettles into which a few drops of codeine had been added to deaden the pain of delicate membranes. They sneezed, coughed, sweated, watered, ached, and many of them, in time, sank into pneumonia and died.

There was no record of the number of cases of influenza in Yamacraw, but it was true that the Negroes died by the dozens.

When Dolly Cadiz came in from a trip on the road that night, her face was flushed and she complained of not feeling well. Aunt Meg looked at her eyes, felt her forehead and ordered her to bed.

Howard and Aunt Meg moved his mother's bed into the parlor, out of the unheated back bedroom, and Dolly lay there those first few days more upset at the idea of being sick than by the sickness itself. And it did not appear that she was very sick. Aunt Meg hoped it was a light case. Dolly's fever was not too high, and she showed no signs of developing congestion.

During those first few days there was a spirit of gaiety and fun in the house. They talked and joked and played cards, and Aunt Meg did most of the cooking right there, using the wood-burning, sheet-metal stove.

On the fourth day, Aunt Meg began to heat up the egg-shaped stove until it was red hot and she put extra blankets on Dolly. Howard found it so hot in the room he stripped down to a cotton shirt and Aunt Meg walked around in her slip, but still she kept the fire in the stove going and would not let Dolly move from beneath the blankets.

— I can't breathe! Dolly complained. What are you trying to do to me, Meg! My God—!

— You've been running the same low fever ever since you came home, and you haven't perspired one drop. It's time something broke.

— But I can't breathe! I feel like I'm going to pass out. It's so hot! Please, Meg!

— Good! Start sweating, Meg said.

— Animals sweat. People perspire, Dolly said.

— You'd be a hell of a lot better if you'd do a little of what the animals do. She threw another piece of fat pine wood into the stove and brushed her hands lightly. The heat in the room became more and more intense. Two large pots of water boiled on top of the stove to make the air moist, but the atmosphere was still hot and dry. Dolly tried to slip her arms out from beneath the covers, but Meg was right there to stuff them back. Meg was perspiring herself now; huge drops of water ran down her long neck and into her thin bosom. Her slip was plastered to her body. But she kept the level of heat up, and the moment she could get another piece of wood into the stove she would shove it in.

After three hours of almost unbearable heat, the first drops of moisture appeared on Dolly's upper lip. A few minutes later her forehead was bathed in perspiration.

— Meg, I'm about to die! Dolly moaned.

— No, you're not, Meg said. You're doing fine. A little bit more and you'll be so wet you'll think you're in a summer bathhouse. Howard!

— Yes, Aunt Meg?

— Put some more wood in the stove, son, your mother is about to lose some of that fat she carries around on her stomach!

— Meg!

— Heave it in, Howard. She laughed and wiped her face on her arm and lit a cigarette that was soggy after a few puffs.

An hour and a half later Dolly was drenched in her own perspiration, and Meg sent Howard out of the room while she began to massage her sister with the diluted camphor solution she had warmed near the stove. Dolly fell asleep under the strong soothing hands of her sister, and after the terrific heat and her exhaustion from the forced perspiration, she slept through the whole night, waking the next morning clear-eyed, with no fever, and hungry.

The crisis was over. Dolly seemed to grow stronger with each passing hour. Meg, seated as always with a book in her lap, her cigarettes at hand, read and talked with Dolly during the long hours that Howard was away at school, or was shopping for the day. Dolly could get no satisfaction from her sister's conversation. Meg's eyes would drop to the book and she would read a line, or a paragraph, or a page as Dolly talked of her trips selling Perma-Maid Hair Colorer and Root Restorer, or described the people she dealt with: idle, prattling on, summoning up incidents in their youth, of Beau, wondering where he was (he had not been seen in years and it was believed that he had joined the Army) combing her hair over and over. Once out of the disciplined way of her father's house, Dolly had never found it easy to bide her time the way other women did, sewing, knitting, darning or reading. She was a woman who had to move, had to be doing something with her hands and body at the same time. She could not sit long, and six days in bed, growing stronger every day, was becoming a burden to Dolly's restless energies. And Meg, who could sit for hours and read or sew, content with her own company, could not talk of meaningless things all day, every day. Her mind wandered to her books, or her work, even as she sat with her sister.

— I was thinking about Mama this morning, Meg, when she came down here to Savannah to live with us after Howard was born and after Papa died, remember?

— Ummm, yes.

— That night she was dying. I shall never forget it. It was all so terrible. It was terrible for you, too, dear, I know, because you were always the strong one. But I remember how you must have suffered after she died. I remember, you don't know it, but I knew what was going on inside that unyielding body of yours. I know you suffered after Mama died, and that you couldn't even cry, do you remember, Meg?

That year, when Dolly was pregnant and Beau was gone again, Dolly called for Meg. And Meg came, peeling off ten dollar bills from her life's savings for a decent place for them to live and some furniture bought at the Salvation Army and for doctor bills.

While Dolly waited out her time, Meg went out and got one job after another until she ended up at the cigar factory, where she liked the work and the pay was good. Then she joined the library, and in the evenings they would sit together, Dolly at the window, listening for a familiar footfall on the quiet sidewalk below, watching the corner by the streetlight, waiting, always waiting, and Meg would rock in her chair and read one or two books a night.

The boy was born in a hospital not many blocks away from where they lived. He had his father's black hair. They thought for a while about naming him Bowdry, or after his paternal grandfather, Sean, but the doctor who had delivered Dolly had been so good to both of them, they took the doctor's last name and called the boy Howard, with no middle name.

It was then that their mother came to live with them after their father died. But not for long. She did not like the city. She was a country woman and hungered for the hills and her own land and her own garden vegetables, but Colbert had married and it was not easy to sit and do nothing in another woman's house after a lifetime of work. Meg understood this and took her mother in.

She was there only a few months when she caught a cold, went to bed and never got over it. The night she died, Meg and Dolly sat, one on each side of the old woman's bed, and held her hands. Dolly was distraught. But Meg sat with a strange coldness, almost detachment.

— Ma, Meg said softly.

— Yes, Meg.

— What was the matter with Papa? Why was he so mean? Religion mean, the worst kind.

— Yes, it is the worst kind, her mother said weakly.

— Why, Ma? He died without ever seeing Dolly again. Not after that night. That takes a special kind of meanness.

— Your father hated to go to war, but he went and did fer the Confederacy, but he jined up late. People to Tasco wouldn't never let him forgit he jined late. He took to religion. Religion can take the place of somethin' a man is cautious of, er if he wants to cover up a weakness, if there's somethin' missin' in him and he don't want to face it. I never larned what the weakness was. He was past forty when Colbert was borned. He started to hate one morning, that I saw, and he used his religion to hate more. It was a sad thing to see.

— But me, *and* Dolly, we didn't have anything to do with the war, Meg said. Why did he hate us?

— Meg! Dolly spoke sharply from the other side of the bed.

Meg paid no attention to her. Dolly started to cry. Then she saw that Meg was crying too. She had never seen Meg cry before.

— But, Ma! We were his daughters!

— Meg, please—Dolly got up and left the room.

— Ma, answer me.

— Don't fuss me now, Meg, the old woman said. You always was the hard one, the cold one. You should have been the boy and Colbert the girl. I always figured that. Let me rest.

— Answer me!

— Let me rest, Meg. I'm tard. Good God A'mighty, all them dishes I washed, time wasted doing that, and fer what! I'm tard! Tard of livin'.

The old woman closed her eyes and then opened them and looked at Meg.

— And you know, I never even loved your Pa. He came to me with a piece of land, and I married him.

And then she died.

Meg stopped crying as if someone had touched a button. She stood and looked down at her mother.

— Why you goddam old fraud!

Meg turned and left the room, went into the kitchen and made a cup of tea, poured a half glass of whiskey into it and drank it. Then she sat down in her rocker and began to read while Dolly moaned and carried on in the next room where her mother lay dead.

— Do you remember, Meg? Dolly asked again.

— Yes, Meg said, bestirring herself, yes, I remember. I remember very well.

— You were so torn up on the inside, Dolly said.

— Was I? Meg asked, dropping her eyes to her book. I don't remember it that well.

At the end of the week, Dolly asked for her dispatch case and began writing business letters, asking for appointments, setting up a calendar of dates. She wrote for hours on end and sent Howard out with thick packets of letters to be mailed at the corner box.

Dolly had lost a great deal of weight. She was much thinner and she looked better for it, though she was still pale and worn. In the middle of the second week, after receiving favorable replies to several of her letters, Dolly got up. She worked all day on her dresses, taking them in and fitting them to her slimmer waistline, and she felt very well indeed that night when she went to bed.

The next morning, without saying anything to Meg or Howard, she rose before they did, gathered her papers together and left the house. Three hours later she was on a train for Waycross, Georgia, allowing herself just that one trip, intending to make a single sale and then return. She did return that night and collapsed the moment she stepped inside the door.

She was put right to bed and slept through to the next morning, when she awoke feverish and unable to recognize either Meg or Howard. It was three hours before Dr. Furth could come, haggard, overworked and underweight.

He listened to her chest, felt her pulse and took her temperature.

— This woman has got to go to the hospital right away. Even then, you had both better prepare yourselves.

— What is it? Meg demanded.

— You know what it is.

— Pneumonia?

— In both lungs.

— All right, I'll come with her, Meg said.

— Just a minute, Dr. Furth said. Let me look at you. How do *you* feel?

— Fine, Meg said shortly.

— Let me see your eyes. He took her pulse and her temperature and pinched her cheek under her eyes. He nodded, setting his jaw.

— Get in bed and stay there. Don't even go to the bathroom. Use a potty. And you, Howard, keep the fire going and the room warm.

— Have I got the flu? Meg asked.

— You got it so bad I don't know what's been keeping you on your feet. Now get in bed, and stay there.

— I don't feel sick, Meg said.

— Meg, dammit, I've got enough on my hands with every person I see coming down with the flu, and if not the flu, then it's pneumonia, to have to worry about your stubborn hardheadedness! Howard!

— Yes, sir?

Meg had not moved. Furth looked at the intractable set of her jaw.

— Meg, listen to me now, and don't be bullheaded about this. Don't get the idea that as soon as I leave, you're going to do what you want. Howard, stay here with your aunt. I'll see if I can't get someone to drop in on you and help you out, though God knows where I'll find them.

Meg had not moved.

Furth looked at her and shifted his bag. I'm not going to order the ambulance for Dolly, Meg, until you give me your word that you'll get in bed and stay there—and I mean *stay* in bed until I say you can get up.

Meg snapped her eyes up at him. Howard watched her strong face as it reflected the conflict inside. She nodded, shortly, one time.

— All right, she said. And then, as Howard and Dr. Furth watched, she seemed to shrink. Her shoulders sagged, her mouth slackened, her eyelids drooped and her eyes began to water. Finally she began to shake. Howard and Dr. Furth reached out for her.

— In the chair, Howard, Dr. Furth said. Get some hot tea, and get that stove going. I'll call the ambulance. They settled Meg into her rocker.

Howard stood between his mother and his aunt, looking from one to the other. When he looked up, Dr. Furth was gone.

— Mother? he spoke to Dolly softly. She did not answer. Her breath was coming in hard dry rattles.

— Aunt Meg? She sat slumped in her rocker, head in her palms, eyes closed.

— Aunt Meg?

— Yes, Howard?

— Is there anything else I can do?

— No, Howard, just let me sit quiet and rest. Do you know where the clean linen is kept?

— Yes, mam.

— When they take your mother, do as the doctor said. Strip the bed and put on clean sheets. Then we'll see.

— Yes, mam. He looked down at his mother. There was no change. She continued to whistle thinly through her teeth. It was the most frightening sound he had ever heard.

The gloom of the parlor deepened, and it was quiet except for two sounds: the pine wood popping in the stove, making a series of small explosions that rapped the sheet-metal sides with bell-like percussions, and the whistling of his mother's breath.

Howard stood perfectly still before the stove, staring at his mother and his aunt, and gradually the noise of the exploding pine pitch and the harsh breathing of his mother no longer registered on him and he was alone. He was removed from the darkening parlor and the labored breathing, and the pine pitch explosions and the rain outside that had developed suddenly out of the cold afternoon. And he cursed his father for a scab, a gutless dog who was not there.

Now that his mother had been taken to the hospital and his Aunt Meg was in bed asleep, he too tried to sleep, but could not. His eyes still burned with the tears he had shed when the ambulance men had taken his mother.

He did not move from the pallet he had made on the floor near the stove. Again and again during the night he crawled to the head of his makeshift bed, reached into the wood box and took a piece of wood, opened the hole in the top of the stove with great care so as not to wake Aunt Meg, banked the fire, and then crawled back again. He listened to the dripping rain outside and wondered if his mother might not already be dead. The night was endless. He thought back over his life, and all he could remember was the two women, one now in the hospital and the other sick in the room with him. How sick she might be, or become, he would not allow himself to think.

And he dreamed about his father.

— Beau, he said softly, aloud, Beau Cadiz. You sonofabitch . . .

He woke with a start. There was a noise. He listened, bolt upright on the pallet. Then the regular clop-clop of the milk wagon horse—moving, stopping, moving in the silent morning streets—came to him and he knew it must be around six o'clock, though it was not yet light outside.

He was cold. He turned and looked at Aunt Meg. She had not moved. She was on her side, her bony shoulders exposed.

Silently, tiptoeing, Howard stood and waited until he had balanced and would not stumble and make a noise. He eased to the side of the bed.

Aunt Meg's mouth was open. Her arms were flung carelessly down over the side of the bed where she had turned in her troubled sleep.

Howard lifted the covers, lifting one arm to return it inside the covers. Meg woke up. She jerked up to her elbows and stared.

— Howard! My baby! She flung her arms around Howard and pulled him to her bosom. Howard's feet shot out from under him and he landed hard on the floor.

— Aunt Meg, he said softly, his head tucked awkwardly under her chin, his own cheek buried in the strange, yielding flesh of her breasts. Aunt Meg, please—

— Howard, my baby! Oh, my sweet baby boy, Aunt Meg cried out as if in protest.

— Aunt Meg, please, Howard said again, and began to struggle to free himself. She held him more tightly than ever, her hand against the back of his neck and pressing his windpipe against her chin. He was having difficulty breathing.

— Aunt Meg, you're choking me—

— Yes, my baby. Yes, my darling. I know. I know. She tightened her grip and Howard found it even harder to breathe. He brought his hands around and found her wrists.

— No! You can't have him!

— Aunt Meg, Howard said quietly, realizing that she was not talking to him now and that she did not even hear him. Aunt Meg, let go of me.

When she didn't, he took her wrists and slowly, using all his strength, brought her hands down from around his neck. Free of her, he took a deep breath.

She hurled herself upright and glared at him, her eyes wide and hard.

— God damn you! she said, and tore free of his grip. Where is my baby! She threw herself out of the bed and stood, looking around wildly, her gaunt figure almost comic in the cotton nightgown. Howard! Dolly! Beau! Where *is* everybody!

She started around the end of the bed and ran to the door of Howard's room and wrenched it open. Behind her Howard felt the rush of cold air from the unheated room.

— Aunt Meg! Howard jumped to his feet, running to her. He grabbed her around the waist, from the back, and tried to pull her around.

She spun and glared at him again. Then she slapped him across the face with all her strength, knocking him sideways.

—Don't you ever touch me, you slimy sonofabitch, or I'll gut you.

She towered over him, a little hunched over, her arms spread at the elbows.

Howard felt the sting on his face and when he lifted his hand to touch it, found himself crying.

—Please, Aunt Meg, get back in bed. You're getting pneumonia like Mother, so—*please* get back in bed. The tears flowed down his cheeks and he could not control himself. Please, Aunt Meg, oh, please!

—You come up behind me! There was loathing in her voice. I know what you been thinking!

—Please Aunt Meg, get in bed.

She did not move. She stood, her body set as if to spring at him. Howard looked away. He moved slowly away from her, still crying. He returned to his pallet and lay down silently. He stared out at the dawn that was coming up through the icy rain, leaden and dirty.

—Please, oh God, please, Aunt Meg, get back in bed—

She did not move. Howard tensed. He turned and looked at her. She began to pace back and forth around the center table, her arms swinging wildly. When she spoke, her voice was like nothing he had ever heard before. There was something low and animal in it, mean and terrifying.

—No, I won't tell on you. I won't say a living word to anyone.

She swung around the table, stopped short and spun around, speaking to someone Howard could not see.

—Not for *you!* There's others to consider. You count for nothing now. What about Dolly and Colbert, and Ma? And me? But you never did consider anything—

She walked the room again. She stopped and looked down at Howard crouched on the pallet, looking up at her.

She looked straight into his eyes and spoke.

—That's it! That's it! Get down on your knees and pray. But it won't do you any good. You do that one more time, Pa, sneak up behind me and put your filthy hands on me again, or come into my room while I'm dressing and I'll kill you. I'll do it, Pa, and that will make me as bad as you are right now. Killing my own Pa. That would send me straight to hell, where *you're* going. Oh, yes. Oh, yes, Pa, you're going straight to that hell that you're so afraid of.

Her low, cruel voice sent terror to Howard's heart. Her slitted, glittering eyes were fastened on him. Then, as he watched, her eyes rolled back in her head, her shoulders drooped and she collapsed at the knees, folding up, knees, hips, arms, head and neck, banging her head hard as she hit the floor. She lay still.

Howard fought down the nausea rising in his throat. He wanted to scream, to run away from there. He stayed still and looked at her on the floor. After a while, when he was calm enough, he said, Aunt Meg?

She did not answer.

He did not speak again. His tears dried and his heart stopped racing. He crawled to her side and lifted her head to slip the pillow under her neck. He wiped the hair out of her face and straightened her legs. Then he stood, went to the bed and remade it carefully, putting the covers down at the foot, and then went back to her. He tried several times to lift her under the shoulders and knees, but the weight was too much. He thought about leaving her there on the pallet, but decided against this.

He stepped quickly to the center table and shoved it out of the way, grabbed the end of the bed and swung it across the floor to her side. He went to her again, propping her up against the side of the bed. He straddled her body, took a deep breath and slipped his arms under her armpits. He lifted slowly. He got her halfway up the side of the bed and lost his grip. She slipped back down.

He looked at her. Aunt Meg? he said in a despairing whisper. Please Aunt Meg, get in bed.

She did not move.

—Aunt Meg! Howard screamed. Get up!

She did not move.

Panic flooded him.

And then his panic subsided and in an instant he was over the line, deepened, strengthened.

A sob shook his body. Then it was finished. He swallowed and rubbed his face with both hands. He looked down at his unconscious aunt.

He saw his mistake then. It was a question of leverage. He moved surely now, knowing just what he had to do. He lifted her nightgown, slipped one hand between her legs, aware only for a second of the naked flesh and the hairy matrix, then slipped his free hand around and under her back, laced the fingers of both hands together, braced himself and heaved. Aunt Meg rose steadily from the floor and fell backwards onto the bed. Howard fell on top of her. He recovered himself, pulled her legs up onto the bed, moved to the head of the bed and pulled her under the armpits, sliding her body to the center. He straightened her nightgown and covered her. He then pushed the bed back to its original position on the other side of the stove.

There was nothing else for him to do now. He turned to the stove, put in several pieces of wood and filled the kettle for coffee water. He went to the bathroom and washed his face and hands in icy water, scrubbing hard. He brushed his teeth carefully, found a clean white shirt in his dresser and went back into the heated parlor to put it on. He checked Aunt Meg and found that she was breathing without difficulty and had not gotten herself uncovered again.

When the coffee was ready, he poured a cup and took one of Meg's cigarettes and walked to the window. He sipped the coffee and smoked and watched the rain fall into icy pools.

Someone would come, or no one would come. Dr. Furth would bring news of his mother's condition, or he would not. He could take care of Aunt Meg. There was nothing to be afraid of. He would wait.

When Howard arrived at the hospital he had expected it to be quiet, tomb-like, hushed. Instead he found it in an uproar. People sat in cars, on the steps, on the porches of nearby houses. There was a steady stream of people into and out of the huge, double semiwinding stair that curved up to a graceful, screened porch and entrance.

He was tired. His eyes burned from lack of sleep. The woman who was now with Aunt Meg had not arrived until two-thirty that afternoon. It was now three. Aunt Meg was still sleeping when he had left for the hospital.

Howard pushed through the crowd, climbed the stairs, opened the screen door and looked up at a tall policeman.

— Close that door! the policeman said, keeping his voice low.

— I'm sorry, Howard said, backing off. My mother's in here.

— What's the matter with her?

— The doctor said it was double pneumonia.

— Oh, well, that's different. Not this door. The garden gate is what you want. Around the back. That's the pneumonia entrance. This is the flu entrance.

The door was closed firmly in Howard's face. He looked at the people waiting on the steps, huddled in the icy rain. He worked his way around to the back entrance and, once inside, stood alone by an empty desk until a nurse came up, her hands filled with papers. She glanced at him coldly.

— Yes?

— I'd like to see my mother. Or find out if she's all right.

— Name?

— Howard Cadiz.

— Not your name, the nurse said impatiently. Your mother's.

— Mrs. Dolly Bowdry Cadiz, Howard said.

— You wait in there and I'll see. The nurse pointed to a room off to one side.

Howard entered the gloomy basement room that had been a store-room before the crisis and still showed signs of its original function. He looked out into the gardens where a huge oak tree spread its gigantic limbs like the wings of a black angel, and he looked at the frostbitten dead flowers of the azalea that had bloomed too early in the false February spring, and he looked at the soft green grass that was now soggy with rain, and he could not believe that he was there at all.

After a while he turned his head and looked at the others in the room, and slowly he stopped feeling awkward and nervous. The people were very much like those he had seen at the City Clinic, all except one pretty young girl. A few years older than Howard, she sat opposite him. There was something different about her. Her face was delicate and pale. Her hair was brushed until it shone, and her clothes were expensive looking. She sat turned slightly away from the others, her legs tucked sideways under the chair, and stared out the window into the gardens, just as Howard had done.

No one spoke, and the only noise in the room was the constant sniffling of a man next to the door and the occasional clucking sounds a mother made to an infant two chairs away from Howard. Outside the room were sounds of whispered conferences between doctors and nurses and the pad of their hushed, cushioned-sole shoes on the floor; sometimes there was a sob, but he could never tell if it was far or near, a man's or a woman's, patient or visitor. When he looked at the door he could sometimes see the scissorlike flash of white stockings, white shoes and a stiff, starched uniform. Less often would be the larger, hurried bulk of a man's legs in white trousers and white shoes.

The day wore on. One by one the others in the room were summoned from their chairs and released from the deadening hiatus. The daylight began to fade. Though it was middle March darkness came quickly, as it did in the winter, and he realized that he was alone with the pretty girl sitting across the room from him.

As the last light faded, he stared intently at her face, averted to the gardens as it had been all day. She had been sitting still for so many hours, showing no emotion, dropping her eyes when she happened to look up and catch him looking at her, that it was a shock to see that she was crying.

— We've been here a long time, he said to her, surprised that his voice was steady.

— Yes, she replied.

— How long have you been here?

— Since early this morning. Her voice was soft and easy, and he could not remember any girl he had ever met who had a voice like hers.

— Is it your mother? he asked.

— My father.

— Flu?

— It was, but it's pneumonia now.

— My mother has double pneumonia, he said.

— That's very bad.

They lapsed into silence and watched the cars rush past the gardens.

—Why were you crying a minute ago? he asked. I've been watching you all day, and you haven't moved or made a sound.

—I was thinking about my father, she said, and something he read to me. A poem. I've been watching you, too. When the others left, when we were alone together, I thought you would speak to me. And then I cried, remembering the poem.

—Oh, Howard said.

—Have you read much poetry?

—Not really, he said, feeling suddenly awkward. He straightened up in his chair and cleared his throat. What was the poem?

—Would you like to hear it?

—Yes.

—You won't laugh?

—No, I promise.

She was quiet for a few moments and then began to speak in a soft voice that was neither hurried nor slow. Each word touched him with the rustle of whispered secrets.

—"I died for beauty but was scarce adjusted in the tomb when one who died for truth was lain in an adjoining room. He questioned softly why I failed? for beauty, I replied, and I for truth—the two are one; we brethren are, he said. And so as kinsmen met at night we talked between the rooms until the moss had reached our lips—and covered up our names."

As the last words washed against him—and he thought he could *feel* them—like warm drops of July rain—Howard felt a shudder twist his body.

—Goddammit, he said with low, bitter anguish.

—I'm sorry, she said quickly. Her voice was a rush in the darkness. I should have realized. I mean—I shouldn't have told it to you.

—I wish you hadn't, Howard said, just managing to hold back the tears.

—It was written by Emily Dickinson, she said. She was silent a moment. Now you're crying. I'm sorry. I'm very sorry.

—You think I'm crying because of some old poem? Well, you're wrong. I'm not.

—You don't have to apologize for tears. There are two things my father always said. A man should never worry about his tears or his laughter. That's what a poem is supposed to do. Make you happy or sad.

— It isn't the poem, Howard insisted. And I'm not apologizing.

— I'm sorry, she said, withdrawing, and he could hear her move in the darkness.

They said nothing for a time and gradually his tears stopped. He blew his nose, stood up and walked back and forth in the dark. He looked out into the empty hall, then went back to the chair and sat down.

I should speak to her, he thought. She's just like me. Waiting for something to happen, or not to happen. I could ask her about school, what her name is. He waited, lost in the deep darkness of the waiting room, and watched the lights of the city beyond the gardens of the hospital.

— I'm sorry, he said at last.

She did not answer.

— I never had anything like this happen to me before.

— I'm frightened, too, she said.

— Yes, I guess you are, he said. You really like poetry?

— Yes, she said. But I'd rather not talk about it anymore.

— All right, he said. Would you like to talk about something else?

— No, if you don't mind, I'd just like to sit here.

The words of the poem, taken out of the context of the tomb, once he could get past the melancholy connection with his mother, made him wonder about the one who died for beauty and the one who died for truth. What did it mean to die for beauty? For truth? Which was his mother about to die for?

He flushed with sudden shame as he realized that he had already given up, thinking of his mother as surely dying. The poem did it, he thought. It made me see my mother in the tomb.

— I didn't mean it, he said half aloud.

— Didn't mean what? the girl asked.

— Nothing.

She sighed. He hoped she would say something so that he might answer and they could talk.

— How long will you stay here? she asked.

— I don't know. I'd better be getting home soon. My aunt is sick.

— Where is your father? she asked.

— Dead, he lied, as he had always lied.

— And my mother is dead. It's odd, isn't it, she said. You're here because your mother is sick with pneumonia, and I'm here because my father is sick. Your father is dead, and my mother is dead.

— Look, he said, don't worry about your father. He's going to be all right.

— Thank you, she said.

— No, honest, I really mean it. Everything's going to be all right. You wait and see.

— Thank you, she said again.

— Don't you *believe* that everything is going to be all right?

— I don't know what to believe. I'm just hoping.

— Well, that's what I mean, he said.

— Are you trying to cheer me up? she asked.

— I guess I am.

— That's very sweet of you.

— You've got to believe something. We just can't sit here and be miserable, thinking about the worst that could happen. Why, if we did that, we might as well not be here at all, hanging around. We could be out somewhere, going to a show, and just take it for granted that your father and my mother were already dead, and all, and just come by and ask the nurse what happened.

He could hear her moving in the darkness.

— See what I mean?

— Yes, I see what you mean, she said quietly.

— Now, you take me, he said earnestly. I'm here because I know my mother is going to be all right.

— I wish I had your confidence, she replied softly. I'm always afraid the worst will happen.

— Cadiz? a firm voice intruded. The light was turned on. Howard looked up, half-blinded by the sudden glare of the naked white bulb. The man was dressed in white and looked desperately tired. He glanced at the girl and then back at Howard. Which one is Cadiz?

— I am, Howard said, standing up.

— Are you two together? the doctor asked.

— No, Howard said. Is my mother all right?

— Are you alone? the doctor asked.

— Yes, I'm alone. Is my mother better?

The doctor glanced at the girl. He looked down at his feet.

— Where's your father? the doctor asked, looking at Howard again.

— Dead.

— Is there anyone else? Aunt? Uncle? Older brother or sister?

— I have an aunt, but she's—

— Why isn't she here? the doctor asked, cutting in harshly.

— She's home, sick with the flu, Howard said.

— Furth taking care of her?

— Yes, Howard said. How is my mother? Can I see her now?

The doctor looked at the girl again and then back at Howard.

— You're to stay here until I come back. Do you understand that? What is your name?

— Howard. Howard Cadiz.

— All right, Howard. You stay here until I come back. Understand?

— Yes, sir. But how is my mother?

— She's dead. She died without regaining consciousness.

Howard sat down abruptly.

The doctor looked again at the girl. Are you a friend of his?

The girl hesitated a moment, then nodded.

— Stay with him until I get back, the doctor said. He turned to the door, hesitated a moment, then turned the lights out again.

Howard sagged and began to cry. The girl came to him and sat in the next chair. She put her arm around his shoulder and pulled his head gently to her bosom and stroked his hair and rocked her body back and forth.

When the hospital doctor returned an hour and a half later with Dr. Furth, Howard was asleep, his head in her lap.

They buried Dolly two days later. The sky was the same color it had been the day she died, and it was as cold. There were only four people at the funeral: Dr. Furth, a minister whom Howard had never seen before, the girl from the waiting room, and Howard.

That afternoon they took Meg to the same hospital and Howard, for the first time in his life, was alone.

Dr. Furth had wanted to take Howard into his home after Dolly died, but Howard pointed out the difficulty of going to school, which would be on the other side of town. More importantly, he wanted to be free to go to the hospital. The doctor was so pressed that he did not, after seeing Howard was apparently able to care for himself, give it further thought.

The first few days were the hardest. Getting up in the morning and fixing his own breakfast, or when he came home late at night after leaving the hospital, Howard would often cry; the emptiness of the rooms pressed in on him. Then a dullness set in, and he went through the routine of his day with a curiously detached behavior. The nurses and the doctors and his teachers noticed that Howard Cadiz never laughed or smiled.

He became a part of the hospital pattern. They stopped thinking of him as a visitor. He was simply Howard. In the mornings, before school, they would look up and there he would be. After school he was there again, and he stayed until it was time to go home. The floor nurses and doctors and interns saw so much of him they ceased to see him at all. He was always there, or just leaving, or slipping into the halls, quietly, quickly, never asking questions, never bothering anyone; just there, waiting for news of his Aunt Meg in 307.

— She's doing fine, Howard, a nurse would say, or a doctor, when they passed him standing at the door.

Toward the end of the second week, the regularity of his hours, the long, long days, the strain and worry, the holding back of his emotions, began to tell on Howard. One night he fell asleep in the waiting room, sitting close to the door, long after everyone thought he had gone home, as he always did promptly at nine. The night nurse did not look into the waiting room when she came to turn out the light but simply reached around the door and snapped the button.

Howard did not awaken until two in the morning. He was not sure at first where he was, but then he recognized the voice of the night nurse talking to someone in the hallway. He went to the door of the waiting room, standing in the dark. The hall was dimly lit. The nurse stood at the desk with another nurse and two doctors.

— Well, the doctor said, she's had it.

— You'd better get three-oh-seven cleaned up. We'll be needing the room.

The nurse looked up. Shall I call him and tell him?

— Who? the doctor asked.

— Howard.

— No, don't disturb him. He'll be here in the morning. Time enough. Poor kid, he's had it rough.

— I guess you're right, the nurse said. And I just remembered, there isn't any way to reach him anyway. No phone.

— I'll call Doctor Furth in the morning.

Howard stood transfixed.

The little group around the desk broke up.

— Hurry up with three-oh-seven, the doctor said over his shoulder. I have one down in the children's ward I want to get in there as soon as possible.

A little light flashed on a board near the desk, and the remaining nurse glanced up at it, flipped the release and hurried down the hall to answer the night call.

Howard slipped out of the waiting room into the hall and went quickly down to 307. The room was dark. He moved inside and over to the bed. The weak, soft light from the street filtered in, and he could see the bed was empty, the bedding still rumpled. To one side were hoses and other pieces of medical equipment. Howard stood there, frozen, touching the side of the bed.

Then he turned, walked out of the room and down the stairs. He made his plans as he walked home. When he arrived, he turned on the lights and began to pack. He did not take all that he owned, just a change of clothes, a picture of his mother and another of Aunt Meg. He snapped the lock on his mother's traveling case.

There was twenty-seven dollars and some change left of the kitchen money, and he emptied the jar into his pocket. He did not look back at the room as he closed the door, leaving the lights burning. He walked straight down Abercorn Street to the river and was at the ferry landing by the time it began to gray over. He studied the three ships in the loading slips across the river. He knew their names. He never failed to note the arrival and departure of ships into and out of Savannah. *Mandarin, America Glow, Delphi Star.*

They were all three American ships, but it made no difference to him. When the Negro ferryman arrived and found Howard waiting for him, he hesitated a moment and then nodded when Howard offered him a half-dollar to take him across the river.

He looked back at the waking city of Savannah as the rowboat was sent skimming across the red water: he watched the streetlights go out as the dawn came up. He had seen the lights go on thousands of times, his signal to head for home. Now for the first time he saw them go out. He shivered, and turned his back on the city, and faced the first of the ships, the *Mandarin.*

— Goin' to sea, white boy? the ferryman asked.

— Yes, Howard said.

— Eveh gone befo'?

— No.

— Lookin' fo' a job, then?

— Yes, Howard said.

They stood together on the cold pier and both of them looked back across the river at Savannah.

— Yo' know what kind of job you lookin' fo'?

— Any job.

— Yo' ax the captain to take you on deck, the ferryman said. Ordinary seaman. Don't go into the engine room, pitchin' coal, or git in the galley messin' around food. Ax fo' a job on deck.

Howard thought about this a moment. Thank you, he said.

— Ah happens to know which of these heah boats needs men. I fix it up fo' yo'. Yo' got any money?

— Five dollars, Howard said, thinking quickly.

— Gimme.

— How do I know you'll get me the job?

— Yo' git the job, white boy, the Negro ferryman said quietly. Yo' ain't runnin' away from home, 'r nothing like dat?

— My mother died, and my aunt died. I haven't got anybody else.

— The flu?

— Yes.

— Ah sorry, the ferryman said. Sho' yo' wanta be a sailoring man, now?

— Yes, Howard said. Which boat is it?

— Come on, I take you to Cap'n White. He take you on.

— Which one is it? Howard asked.

— This 'un, heah, the *Mandarin*. She sailin' nine o'clock fo' the Far East.

They walked up the gangway, the ferryman leading the way, and across the deck. Howard had never been on a freighter while it was working cargo, and he had never in his life seen such a tangle of lines and ropes and gear. He was stunned by the size of the ship, and even more by the solidity of it. There was no difference between the footing on the deck and on the pierside.

He followed the ferryman into a passageway and glanced into open doors where men slept in bunks. He had never seen anything so filthy. Someone had been sick; there was vomit all over the deck. Through one door he saw a man with a large bloody wound on his cheek.

He was about to turn and run when the ferryman stopped and said, Heah yo' is. Gimme the money.

— Not until I get the job, Howard said.

— White boy, yo' git the job. This heah flu got every sailor on the eas' coast sick to the Marine hospital.

Howard hesitated. The ferryman sighed and knocked on the door.

— Who is it? a voice growled.

— Cap'n, suh, this heah the ferryman from the rivuh. I got yo' a man, suh.

— Oh! Just a minute! The voice perked up. Howard waited. His grip on the traveling case slipped in his sweaty hand. The door opened and a man not much taller than Howard, stark naked, stood before them, rubbing his eyes.

— Oh, yes—well. The captain focused and looked at the ferryman and then at Howard.

— Heah he is, suh.

The captain looked disappointed.

— Ever been to sea before, boy?

— No, Howard said.

The movement was so fast in the semidarkness that Howard did not know what had happened. He felt something explode on the side of his head, around his ear and his eyes, and he felt himself going backward and down. He shook himself and when he had regained his senses, he stared up at the ferryman and the naked captain. They looked back at him blankly.

— You say *sir* to the captain and all other officers, the captain said quietly, sleepily. Get up and come inside.

— Yes, sir, Howard croaked, and stood up. He stepped inside the room and stood still, quivering a little.

— Close the door, the captain said.

— Yes, sir. Howard closed the door in the face of the Negro ferryman.

The captain sat on the side of his bunk and sighed, scratched himself and shook his head. In the better light of the room, Howard could see the thick arms and muscled shoulders. The man looked young, very young, for Howard's conception of a captain. He was clean-shaven and had unusually white teeth.

— You running away from home?

— No, sir. My mother and aunt died of pneumonia. I didn't have anybody else.

— No father? Brothers? Sisters?

— No, sir.

— Can you prove what you've just said?

— I don't lie, sir, Howard said.

— All right, son, the captain said gently. I believe you, but I've got to have some kind of proof.

— My aunt only died a few hours ago, sir, Howard said. But I have a little piece I cut out of the paper about my mother.

— Let me see it, the captain said. What's your name?

— Howard Cadiz, sir. He produced the clipping. The captain read it carefully.

— How old are you?

— Fourteen, sir.

— What? I didn't hear you.

— Uh—eighteen, sir.

— Do you know what you're doing? Just because you lost your mother and your aunt—what I mean is, there are plenty of people who lose their entire family and they don't go to sea. There must be friends, acquaintances, here in Savannah, who would take care of you.

— I don't need to be taken care of, sir. I want to go to sea.

— All right, Cadiz, the captain said. I've been delayed in sailing because of this flu business. Half my crew came down and I need men. We sail at nine o'clock for China. I'll sign you on.

— Thank you, sir, Howard said, feeling a wave of relief.

— Messman, twelve-fifty a month, the captain said. That suit you?

— I'd rather be on deck, sir. Ordinary seaman.

— I *need* a messman, the captain said. He watched Howard closely.

— I'd rather be on deck, sir, Howard said.

— But I also need an ordinary. All right, ordinary seaman, the captain said. Fifteen a month. But before I sign you on, I want you to go below, look the ship over, talk to some of the crew and then make up your mind.

— I've made up my mind, sir.

— You'll do as I damn well tell you, Cadiz, the captain said casually. Now go below and think about it.

— Yes, sir.

— Very well, that's all, if you're still aboard when we sail, I'll sign you on. The captain stood up straight and pursed his lips. He shook his head. You can go.

— Yes, sir, thank you, sir, Howard said.

He stepped out of the room and closed the door after him, turned and looked up at the ferryman.

— Well, white boy? the ferryman asked. Yo' git the job?

— Yes, Howard said. Thank you. Here's your five dollars.

— Thank *you!* Yessuh! Thank *you!*

The ferryman and Howard walked back down to the main deck. In the silence they stood a moment, awkwardly, the ferryman folding and refolding the five dollar bill over his forefinger.

— Ummhuh! Time slippin' by. Ah gotta go, the ferryman said.

—Yeah, Howard said, suddenly not at all sure he was doing the right thing, aware that this was the moment of decision—to stay or return across the river—not wanting the ferryman to leave just yet, reluctant to break this last, small link with home.

And then before he knew it, the ferryman was going down the gangway and Howard was left alone on the deck. He looked around him. He walked over the ship, making his way forward, studying the gear on deck, wondering if he would ever come to understand the use of it all, looking inside the huge maw of the holds, where turpentine barrels were loaded, then aft to the stern, looking, thinking, and feeling very little. He only knew that there was nothing left for him in the world he was leaving, and perhaps there would be something for him in this new world, the only one now available to him.

He blanked the past weeks out of his life, pulling a skein of ice down over himself. And as he did, standing on the stern, looking across red, muddy Savannah River, watching the sun rise over the familiar skyline, he felt the terrible pain of being alone. He let it rise in wave after wave of emotion, not fighting it, letting it spend itself, and then he quieted, and it was over.

At nine o'clock the *Mandarin* sailed down the Savannah River under pilot while Howard Cadiz stowed lines, working under the curses and threats of a new menace in his life, the bosun.

May 1919

It was the first land he had seen since leaving Savannah. He was enchanted by the weepy shores of Panama, with its distantly rising hills, the tops of which were then shrouded in a fierce tropical rainstorm. The rain would not come down as far as the Cristobal shore to dispel the heat and the humidity that enclosed the white buildings and was trapped under corrugated iron roofs.

The heat was like the heat of Savannah in the middle of August, and he did not mind it at all. He hung over the railing and gazed hungrily at the shoreline, the romantic sight of his first foreign soil beckoning to him in the casual dress of a beautiful woman, waiting for him and him alone. They heaved anchor after riding all night in the bay, and with the pilot aboard they began their approach to the Canal and the Gatun Locks. He could hardly contain himself as they inched through the Canal, the ship handlers coming aboard and leaving nothing at all for the deck gang to do but stand by. When they had made the transit from the Atlantic to the Pacific, he was ready for anything—for miracles, perhaps.

The engine room wiper joined Howard at the railing. They both studied the shore in the failing light of the tropics. The wiper was, as usual, filthy from his work below as the handyman of the engine room. Howard was very happy to be an ordinary on deck. The work was as hard as in the engine room but much cleaner. And he saw, accurately, that even with an advance in rating to fireman or oiler, the work below would continue to be hot and dirty. Howard already knew that what he wanted was to become an able-bodied seaman. The A.B.'s aboard were the journeymen sailors. They handled lines, gear and small boats. They were competent to do everything aboard ship except navigate and perform the more sophisticated duties of the bridge. They were, in the truest sense, sailors.

— It's the best goddam port in the world, the wiper said. It's going to be a night to remember, Howard. Just let me have time to wash some of this filth off me, shave and dress, and we be off this wagon and ashore! A bony, pigeon-chested youngster from Kansas City, he was only a few years older than Howard but had already been going to sea several years. Go on now, get slicked up. These Panama women are hell on *muchachos* like you an' me.

— What's that?

— Boys, the wiper grinned. They like 'em young.

— Why?

— Hell, I don't know. Maybe it's because we don't get falling-down drunk and are really only interested in getting pussy. These are hot women, man! All that sunshine and all, they sleep all day to hide out from the heat, then they ready for *amour* the whole night. Go on now, get slicked up. Meetcha in the messroom.

Excited, Howard showered and dressed, wearing his only pair of dress trousers and a clean shirt he had ironed himself. He took an extra pack of cigarettes, his shore pass and three dollars he had borrowed from the A.B. on his watch and hurried to the messroom.

Except for the fireman on boiler watch below, and the engineer, and an A.B. on gangway watch with a standby third mate on the bridge, Howard thought everyone else had gone ashore, so he was surprised to see Aubrey, the messman, still cleaning up.

— More coffee? Howard asked.

— I don't know, Howard. See for y'self, Aubrey replied in his friendly Tennessee drawl. He was a tall, lanky man with a deliberate way about him. Dave, one of the A.B.'s on the twelve-to-four watch, was in his usual place at the corner of the table with his model clipper ship. Howard poured a cup of coffee, added a thick stream of cream and took it to his seat at the table. He lit a cigarette and settled happily, a little less trembly, but with more zest for the coming evening (it had been a long time since he had seen Jane) and waited for the wiper.

Aubrey folded the clean rag flat and continued to wipe the tables. Smoke curled around his seamy face from a cigarette hanging at the corner of his mouth. His damp, colorless hair hung straight and limp over half his face. He paused in his swabbing and gazed out the porthole.

— I never saw her again, he said to Dave. She wasn't there when I shipped back three years later. He finished wiping the table. But I'm here to tell you, she was the prettiest thing, the *softest* thing, I ever saw.

Dave puffed his pipe, eying the clipper model before him.

— Why didn't you marry her?

— Couldn't, Aubrey said. Captain wouldn't let me. I woulda had to jump ship, and I wasn't going to do a thing like that. But I thought about it. The captain said it wasn't right for a white man to marry up with a yellow woman.

— Oh? Dave looked up.

— He was from Boston, Aubrey said, sadness in his voice. For a few moments he busied himself placing the sugar bowl, salt and pepper shakers, mustard and pickles back in the center of the tables. He slouched to the pantry and, moving with a sailor's fluid step, threw the rag into the sink, pulled the drain plug, watched the water swirl away, washed the sink and wiped his hands. He poured two cups of coffee from the urn and walked back to the messroom. He sat opposite Dave, slipping one of the cups of coffee toward him. The four bells of six o'clock were caught and held musically in the late-day stillness. The ship was very still. There was only the sound of the sanitary pump. Outside, the red equatorial sun was sinking into the Pacific, and dusk was settling over the Canal Zone.

Howard thumbed through the pages of a three-month-old magazine, unaware of the two older men at the other end of the room. Dave and his clipper ship model had ceased to interest him, and Aubrey was so gray and anonymous that he had long ago become part of the bulkhead and the general drabness of the messroom. Howard had looked at the magazine a half-dozen times already and now he shoved it to one side, lifting his feet to the bench, puffing languidly on a cigarette, sipping his coffee, unconscious of time, unconscious, even, of waiting for the wiper. He was already beginning to settle into the endlessness of this new world. But he was not yet old enough or mature enough to understand what was happening to him. He watched and listened to the two men on the other side of the room. Dave sipped his coffee and poked a finger into the rigging of the model and grunted with dissatisfaction.

— I can't seem to make that spar hang heavy, he said.

— What's wrong with it? Looks all right to me, Aubrey said.

— It don't, Dave said with emphasis, hang heavy.

— How the hell can it hang heavy with it not being no bigger or heavier than a matchstick?

— That's my problem, Dave said. I've got to make it *look* heavy.

Ever see a model yet that didn't look like a collection of polished sticks and cotton all stuck together?

Aubrey didn't answer. He looked around the messroom and over at Howard. He started to say something, but Dave spoke up first.

— That yellow woman the only one you ever saw that you thought about marrying? he asked.

— I thought about others, but never any as hard as I thought about her.

— I shipped with Boston skippers, Dave said. They're hard men.

— Not on themselves, they ain't, Aubrey grunted. They'll suck ass and fuck fist with any man, so long as nobody knows about it. They're all front.

— What are they trying to prove?

— We called it vanity down to home, Aubrey said. They got the Bible vanity.

— That's the worst kind, Dave agreed. I had only one woman I thought I might make it with. In London. She was a seamstress. A fine woman. A widow. She'd been married to a Welsh coal miner, and when he died of lung fever caught in the mines, she went to London. Two children. A fine, fine woman, Aubrey.

—I imagine she was, the Tennessean said with the proper tone of respect in his voice.

They were silent again. Aubrey watched Dave appraise the clipper once again, then turned and spoke to Howard.

— Going ashore, Howard?

— Yes. Me and the wiper.

— Well, watch out for yourself, 'cause Panama is a mean town for sailors.

— I will, Howard said.

Aubrey turned back to Dave and the clipper. He tried to be as casual as he could, sipping his coffee, almost hiding behind the coffee cup.

— Wanta go ashore and stretch your legs, Dave? he asked.

Dave hesitated.

— I guess not. I feel like working tonight.

— But you didn't go ashore in Savannah because of the flu epidemic, and that makes it five weeks. Don't you wanta go ashore and have a glass of beer even? You been working on the clipper every night almost.

Dave said nothing, but poked into the rigging with his finger. Howard had heard about them from the wiper, and from Allison, the A.B. on his watch. Neither Dave nor Aubrey went ashore very often, but when they did, they went together. They shopped in the five-and-ten, they had a few beers or dinner in a good restaurant, and they walked over the city inspecting monuments and historical sites they had missed in earlier years, when they were more concerned with women and good times. Sometimes they would return to the ship for supper and save money, then go back ashore again for a play or a concert. Between them they spoke enough of eight major languages so that foreign-language plays and jokes were no problem. If they were in a country famous for wines or liquors they might buy several bottles and smuggle them aboard and enjoy a secret ounce or two over their cribbage board.

Howard was surprised when Dave looked up suddenly and spoke to him in a friendly way. Usually Dave spoke very little or only to Aubrey.

— There are plenty of models that look right nice, he said, examining the tiny spar that was giving him so much trouble. Beautiful things. But I've never seen one yet that had the feel of the water to her. Now, when you see a smart vessel alongside, though you don't see many sailing vessels these days—but it's true even of steamboats like the *Mandarin*—there's a particular way she sits in the water. Light or loaded, even if she's trimmed properly, the vessel itself sits in the water a certain way. Ships have personality, like people. Dave picked up the tiny spar and looked at it. That's real Carolina ash. Got it in Charleston.

Howard and Aubrey looked at the polished bit of wood.

— And that deck, Dave went on, is Burma teak. Got it in Rangoon years ago. Those masts are the slow-growing Alaskan spruce. Everything in this vessel here before me is made out of the *same* material as the mother ship, built by J. Peabody and Son, of Boston.

— How come, Dave? Aubrey asked.

— What do you mean, how come?

— I mean, dammit, Aubrey said, getting irritated and not knowing why, how come you saved those dinky pieces of wood from all over the world? After you paint her hull, who's going to know if she's made of slash pine or Burma teak?

—I'll know, Dave said.

—What's going to happen to her when she's finished, Dave? Howard asked.

—He won't tell you, Aubrey said, turning away. I asked him that same thing many times.

Dave only smiled.

—If I press him, he'd only puff on his pipe and say he hasn't decided yet.

The two old sailors looked at each other, steadily, and then Dave put down his pliers and deliberately began packing his pipe.

—Howard, he said, this model clipper ship is going to the Metropolitan Museum of Art in New York. The first genuine art contribution ever made by a living American sailor. It might even be the beginning of a Marine Room.

—How the hell do you know they'll want it? Aubrey demanded. From what I've heard they don't want nothing unless it's a thousand years old and worth a million dollars.

—Not exactly, not ex-actly! Dave said. They recognize anything that is an outstanding work of art in its field. Cost don't concern everything. But that don't matter. I'm going to give it to 'em, as a present.

—Now listen here, Dave, Aubrey said, that's a fine ship model. *Real* fine, but who are you trying to kid with that kind of talk?

—You said yourself, Dave replied, that you haven't ever seen a model with a real feel of a ship that's put to sea, right?

—And you ain't neither, Aubrey said.

—That's right, I ain't. And that's just why the hell I'm building this one.

—Shit, Aubrey said.

—I am going to build a model ship so that when people come to the museum they can feel a real ship. A farmer from Kansas, for instance, never seen water bigger'n a sump in his fields, will be able to *smell* the ocean when he looks at my model!

—And this is going to be the best, huh?

— The best! Dave said angrily. And you can go to hell!

Aubrey stood up. And you can take your clipper and stick it in your ass, masts and all.

— If that's the way you feel about it, don't talk to me anymore.

— It'll be a cold day in hell, you betcha! Aubrey stalked out of the messroom. He, by God, was going ashore.

Howard stood to one side, feeling uneasy and not knowing exactly why.

— It's a fine model, Dave, he said tentatively.

Dave nodded briefly.

— The best, he said. He fingered the mainsail. Feel that, Howard. Feel that. That's Egyptian cotton. Same material used in the mother ship.

— But, Dave, Howard asked, why *Egyptian* cotton?

Dave's face was still red and his huge hands, usually rocklike and steady, were shaking slightly.

— Because that year, the year the mother was built, Egyptian cotton, for some reason, was cheaper on the world markets than any other cotton. And that's why I used it, cause it was used in the original outfitting. Feel that, Howard.

Howard fclt thc bit of cloth and nodded.

The wiper came in then, dressed and ready.

— Les go, Howard!

— Doesn't that feel like something, Howard? Dave asked anxiously.

— Yeah, it sure does, Howard said.

— Come on, Howard, the wiper said. We ain't got much time. Only one night. Man! We got to find the right ones!

— Now that bosprit there, Howard, Dave went on, that was the hardest thing for me to get, because—

— You comin' or not? the wiper demanded.

— Yeah, I'm coming.

Dave looked at Howard. His shoulders sagged and he stared at the model. He spoke without looking up.

— You go on ashore, Howard. This is your first port.

— Yeah, I guess I'd better. So, well, I'll see you later, Dave.

All over Panama City that night, the men of the *Mandarin* pursued their separate pleasures. Some went directly to a café, picked up a woman and spent the whole night with her; others went from café to café, drinking endlessly and not bothering with women; still others went from woman to woman and did not bother with drinking. They were not the only seamen in the Panama Crossroads that night. Howard saw sailors from a half-dozen different countries. There were tight-mouthed British Empire sailors who always went ashore in twos and threes, never alone, who were the closest with their money except for the Germans, who were the closest of all. The French never went ashore together and always spent their money almost as freely as the Americans. There were thin-faced, awkward Norwegians with cowlike eyes and slow, gentle ways; Swedes and Danes, as big as Germans but better natured. There were Japanese, small, tightly built little men who sat and drank, their eyes merry and alert, who would giggle like girls and never leave the table except to go with a woman, and who would very quietly pass out, sliding to the floor; Italians, who, like the Spanish-speaking sailors, were hot-eyed and quick to anger and just as quick to make up and break into song; and Americans from other U.S. flagship vessels in Panama that night, who were liked by everyone, and who liked everyone except the Germans; and the Germans, loud, profane, flat-eyed, in even larger groups than the British, singing their drinking songs, pounding the tables and taking over every place they went, eager to fight if the odds were in their favor, except when they met an American sailor from the south, especially Texans, who were always ready with the knife. The Germans backed away from knives.

Panama was like any other crossroads. The scene would be duplicated in Port Said, or Suez, Southampton, Singapore, Malmo, Hong Kong, Shanghai, Calcutta, or Istanbul, where incredibly bad drink would be sold at top prices and the women were invariably drawn from the interior farms and villages, ignorant, illiterate, often diseased, selling their bodies, knowing only that one thing about life and suspecting little else.

— Now there, Howard, the wiper said, see that one? The blonde? She don't look no older than you or me. How about her?

— I don't know, Howard said.

— Or that redhead, the chubby one. She ain't wearing no pants.

— I don't know.

— Or that pretty thin one. Dark. She's a hot-looking thing. Try her?

— I don't know.

— Jesus! What do you want?

— I don't know.

— Maybe you don't want any of them?

— I don't know.

— Why'd you come ashore?

— I don't know, Howard said miserably.

— Well, I ain't waiting no longer. I'm going to take that big-assed one. I like weight to it when I jounce 'em. You going to pick one or not?

— Well, the blonde, I guess, Howard said, and they walked across the dance floor, pushing through the couples, and stopped at the table of women and several expressionless, dark-faced, weasly-looking men who wore sunglasses.

— How old you, keedo? the blonde asked Howard. You sure you know what to do?

The others at the table laughed.

— I'm old enough, Howard said.

— Hokay, we see, keedo. Theesaway and you show me what you got and what you do with it, eh? She winked at the rest of the table and they laughed again.

Howard followed her through a back door and down a hall, her thin raunchy hips pumping up and down as she walked ahead of him on her high-heeled shoes. They turned into a room.

— One dollar. Gimme now.

Howard handed over the money. She tucked it in her stocking and in the same move swept the cotton dress up over her head. Nude except for the stockings and a thin brassiere, she lay back on the bed and waited.

— Hokay, keedo.

It was quick. Very quick, and very professional. Less than ten minutes later, Howard was standing at the bar with Aubrey and Allison, feeling flushed, breathless, and greatly relieved.

He was not at all sure how it started, but there he was, facing the compactly built, pale-faced, yellow-haired sailor who circled before him with fists high—looking very much like he remembered Donnen—and with a smear of blood on his cheek where Howard had hit him for calling him the dirtiest, filthiest name he had ever heard.

Vaguely aware that it was getting daylight, he was not exactly sure where the night had gone, but there he was, feeling the urgency of getting rid of the pale-faced sailor before him, who insulted him constantly in a language Howard could not understand, making the group of men he was with laugh.

Howard said nothing. But he heard Aubrey and Allison and the chief mate and the bosun and the wiper, who stood in back of him, giving him instructions and encouragement. The bosun, who was nearly falling-down drunk, was telling Howard that if he didn't lick the yellow-haired little bastard he personally would kick Howard's ass bloody, and then they were fighting again. He felt something smash into his face and when he looked up he was on the ground and the pale face was above him. He wondered briefly how he had gotten there and then he tasted the salty, creamy fluid that was his own blood.

He kicked out, catching the body below the pale face with both feet and watched with satisfaction as it hurtled backward and down. He sprang up and pounced on the fallen body and began to smash the blond, pale face with his fists; he saw blood and he kept going, not swinging, but doing as Shad had taught him, driving his fists like pistons, in and out, in and out. Then someone was grabbing him.

—That's enough! a voice roared. Cadiz! That's enough! You don't want to kill him! Stop it!

He was dragged off by Aubrey, Allison, the chief mate and the wiper and carried away, kicking and yelling to get back to the blond whose face was no longer pale, but splotched with blood and who lay unconscious on the green grass of the beautiful park with flowering bushes and stately palm trees.

It was several blocks before they finally calmed him down, and then not until the chief mate had coldly and deliberately stood him up against the yellow stucco walls of a warehouse and slapped him with a full palm across the face.

Chastened, hosed out, shaky, hung over, weary after their orgy ashore, finished with the land and heading back to their ship, they escorted Howard Cadiz, who was bloody and aching, with a swollen nose and blackened eyes. Now he was a fully accepted member of the crew. He was one of them, a recognized part of their world, a ship known as the *Mandarin* that sailed that morning in May, 1919, out onto the milky white waters of the Pacific.

That night, standing his lookout watch on the fo'c'sle head, alone in the dark and rolling ocean, searching the stars, all else was erased, all things past were canceled; there were no debts to pay, no promises to keep, no responsibility except to himself.

He had made a beginning.

August 1925

December 1930

The S.S. *Royal Tannerman* was in ballast, and he stood on the foredeck, remembering the first time he had come through the Canal on the old *Mandarin,* and thought about the "hokay" blonde, and his fight with the pale-faced sailor.

He was twenty. He had grown nine inches and stood six feet one and he weighed a hundred and seventy-five. In the six years he had been going to sea, he had learned well. He had ridden the old *Mandarin* around the world and into the boneyard in New York, and when he walked down the gangway he was a good deck sailor. Captain White had gone out of his way to help him get another ship. When the captain of the *Royal Tannerman* learned he could get an experienced ordinary who could do the work of an A.B. at ordinary's wages, there was no problem about his signing on.

He had thought it would be different aboard another ship, but it was much the same as the *Mandarin.* Even the crew was the same. There were different names and different faces, and there was a slight variation in the way things were done, but ultimately everything was managed in the way he had learned aboard the *Mandarin.*

He did not yet have the ingrained sailor's perceptions, almost childlike in their simplicity, as did Dave and Aubrey, Allison and Swede on the *Mandarin.* But he was an experienced enough sailor to see the value of thinking no further than the end of the voyage and the payoff. He was, however, still worried about what to do with his life, but even this concern seemed to be dropping away. His school was the sea, his teachers were his shipmates, men who defeated the sea every time they finished a successful voyage. Howard was beginning to realize that the sea could mold a man who was curious and at the same time unafraid.

If the line was not secured, or the hatch dogged, or the valve left open, the sea would steal in and win. He was achieving skills to defeat the sea, learning lessons that would stand him in good stead on any ship on any ocean, and he would do these things as naturally as he slept or ate or drank. But he did not know this yet. Not yet.

He learned that every aspect of wind or water could affect his ship, and he was learning to read the portents and anticipate what might be coming.

He had given himself over wholly to the sea and ships. He held nothing back. In six years he had succumbed to the sailor's virtues and to the sailor's vices, and found that the two were inseparable. The simple honesty of life at sea could not be left aboard when the sailor went ashore in search of pleasure, emotions simply felt and directly expressed. He learned also about the reaction to him and his life by the more complex land society that considered his simplicity ignorance and his pleasures vices, and it was hard for him to understand that unless one has ever been a professional sailor, one cannot ever know the truth about them, or ever understand.

In the years he had been away he thought often about returning to Savannah, getting a job, or perhaps living with Dr. Furth, returning to school and going on to be a doctor. But as time passed, as time hung above him like a mist over a quiet sea, as seventy calendar months had been lived a leaf at a time, the sea and its life became his life and he was committed.

There was no tie to the land for him. No mother, father, wife, or loved one, no home, nothing at all that his sailoring had parted him from. He did not suffer, as many did, the near unbearable melancholy of long night watches, remembering the smell of her hair, the touch of her kiss, the beauty of her smile, the caress of a love word. He did not lie awake in his bunk for hours on end wondering who she was with, or what she was doing. There were no letters for him at the next port, to be opened with nervous fingers, read with quick scanning eyes, picking out those key sentences that would bring joy or alarm, then a slower, painstaking rereading. And he did not go off into drunken, week-long rages at some bit of bad news, nor did he send cablegrams or hunt out little shops in ports for just the right thing to bring home.

He watched and listened to those who suffered from the "sailor's sickness," and was glad it did not touch him. When he walked into the nighttime cities of the world nothing stood between him and his next breath or his next drink or his next woman or his next thought. He was just what he was, and no power outside of himself could change that.

In those seventy-odd months, Howard Cadiz chose neither strength, nor courage, nor indulgence, nor self-sacrifice; he chose instead to be unafraid. And as he sailed out onto the bosom of the romance seas of the South Pacific on that August day in 1925, the unrehearsed world he had chosen for himself spread before him, motionless and waiting.

The motion of the ship, though slight, was still enough to give Preeb a problem in setting himself, causing the huge sailor to hesitate in his heavy workout on the broad canvas-covered hatch. Standing to one side, Howard watched as Preeb steadied the barbell, slung with two one-hundred-pound cast-iron disks, with his feet to keep it from rolling. The ship balanced momentarily, and in that moment—it seemed incredible to Howard that a man as large as Preeb could move so fast—the huge muscular A.B. had set himself, stooped and snatched up the two hundred pounds. He pressed them above his head. With a sure rhythm he worked the two hundred pounds up and down over his head with the ease of a father playing with a child. Once the barbell was aloft, no motion of the ship seemed to disturb him.

— What do you think of that, Howard? Preeb asked, still holding the weight above his head. He looked at Howard with a sly grin.

— Don't you get enough exercise with the work the mate puts out on this wagon? Cadiz said.

Preeb grinned, hoisted the weight up and down several more times and then lowered it. There was not a sound as the two hundred pounds were returned to the hatch boards.

— By now it's like brushing my teeth, Preeb replied.

— What do you mean, by now? Howard asked, sitting on the corner of the hatch. How long have you been doing it?

— Almost as long as I can remember, Preeb said. I'm from Pittsburgh. He looked at Howard as if the information would have special significance.

He set about his next exercise. Back in Pittsburgh, Preeb said, when I was a boy, my papa took me to the steel mills one day. Dusty, he said to me—everyone called me Dusty when I was young—Dusty, my papa said, this is going to be your life, like it was my life. What is, Papa? I asked. That, right there, he said, pointing to the furnace. When we left the mills, my father took me down to the Polish

Social Club on Palmetto Street. I had been there a hundred times to weddings and parties. My sister had her wedding party there. I thought we were going for a visit, have a beer and hang around, but my Papa took me downstairs. I was pretty excited because downstairs was a part of the club I had never been in. No one was allowed downstairs except the men. We went through the dressing room where everybody greeted my Papa in Polish, which I could understand a little because my mother was Estonian and the language in my house was a real mixture. English, Polish, Estonian and a little Yiddish. But I understood enough to know that the men were aware that my Papa was introducing me around in a formal kind of way.

— I stripped, and Old Harry came in then. He was like an old seed bull that couldn't stud anymore but was still mean enough to be the boss of the lot. He never got married and he was bigger and stronger than any man I've ever seen in my life.

— Harry was hung over. He was always hung over, and with that six-day beard—he only shaved on Saturday nights, and on Wednesday he would just shave under the neck and chin to keep it from scratching—he walked in and went to his locker without saying anything to anybody. He started stripping down. Everybody sort of waited for Harry to look our way, but he didn't. He stripped down and I remember everybody got very quiet. I knew why in a moment. I had never seen a body like his. His *pectoralis majors* were flat, like the bottoms of a skillet. The trapezoids were smooth and rounded, and his neck, the thickest I have ever seen on a man, was a good lift up from the trunk. And it was a good clean separation between the sternums and the trapezoids. His whole body was like that. He had the flattest *obliquus externus abdominis* a man ever had; it swathed his body like a thick blanket. His legs were like tree trunks and his arms were like tree limbs. And the whole body was covered with a kind of salt and pepper grizzle of hair. He looked like Michelangelo's God in the Sistine Chapel. He was sixty-eight years old.

— Harry pulled on a jock strap, stood up and started doing knee bends. It was then that my Papa walked over and spoke to him, and I remember Harry looked up at my Papa, almost surprised, as if wondering how my Papa got there. Up until then he acted like he was all alone in the room. After a few minutes, Harry walked over and stood before me, glowering down at me with those red eyes that probably hadn't been closed all night, and his breath whistled through his nose and he stood there, looking at me. He walked around me several times. Then he stopped in front of me. He looked down at my pecker and then up at my face, his red eyes boring into me. You old enough to stop jerking off yet? His voice was like thunder. Are you man enough to leave it alone? I stammered something, and it seemed to satisfy him and he turned to my Papa. Start him slow, Harry said to my Papa. Not more than seventy-five the first year. Not more than a hundred and twenty the second year. Then, without a word, Harry turned and walked into the gym.

Preeb paused long enough to light his pipe and look down at the barbell and roll it back and forth with his foot. He puffed several times and looked up at Howard.

— You see, starting as young as I did, I was prepared for the ten-hour days in the mills. But it wasn't until much later, long after I had shipped out, that I began to think there was something else to it than just keeping fit for the work at the mills, and why old Harry and Papa and the others worked out in the basement of the gym. Working with the weights wasn't just to keep the body in shape for the mills.

Preeb paused and puffed some more and Howard, unmoving, listening, forgetting his coffee, cleared his throat.

— What was it then? he asked softly.

— We were the strongest men in the world. There are no men stronger than the men who work in the steel mills. And we were making *steel*. The hardest man-made substance in the world. And *we* made it. My Papa, Old Harry—me. And the others. We had to match our bodies to the thing we were making. We had to be ready for steel. There wasn't any room for anything else down there in the mills, except making steel. No wife, no kids, no religion—nothing. There was the man and his body and his knowledge, and there was the coke and the ore and the ingots, and it was like we were ripping something right out of the pits of hell and purifying it, refining it and making it purer and purer until there it was—steel. And we made it. That ore is in the ground for a billion years or more. It's part of the whole universe. And then Old Harry and Papa and me, we come along and take it and change it into something that never existed before. You see, God made it one thing, and we came along and changed it and made it another. It was, in a way, like we were gods too.

Howard Cadiz listened, sitting at the corner of the hatch, watching as Preeb chewed on the end of his pipe-stem. He thought he understood, and he knew he would have liked Old Harry.

Preeb balanced his buttocks on the carpenter's bench, stretched his legs and caught the bar with his toes. Bringing it toward him at a gentle roll, he began to set himself and, after a few more moves, found his seat. Then he picked the barbell up a few inches off the deck, hooking it with his instep. The ship rolled gently, but Preeb was set and it did not bother him. Twin knots of muscle stood out in his stomach. He began to sweat. It made his skin glisten in the warm sun of that part of the Pacific Ocean, on the kind of day that is very accurately described as balmy and which the natives of Bali call *Tuoomoru,* or peaceful.

Endlessly Howard tried to reproduce the neat stitches that Gino made in the canvas. It was a fine art and Gino reminded him that regardless of what there was in the way of propulsion for future ships, there would always be ships with sails, and a good man with a needle and palm could always find work in the sail loft. Howard let the sweat roll down his face and neck and waxed his twine and his fingers, tucking the heel of the needle into the lead bullet of the palm and made his stitch and tuck, and it was not very long before they were short, strong stitches, though not works of art, like Gino's. And when Gino saw that Howard was sewing well and he did not have to check all of the work, he taught Howard a little stitching song that they sang together:

Alone
In the mists
On a darkened sea
My sailor wanders
Restlessly
The girl he loved
He has left ashore

Be she maiden
Or missus
Or fo'c'sle whore!

Sail on, sail on
Through eternity
There is no love
For thee
On a faceless sea
Sail on, sail on
Nor reach safe shore
My sailor man
My sailoring sailor man.

They were working on lifeboat covers, and by the time they were finished with the last one Gino said that Howard was a very good man with a needle and palm but that he had a terrible singing voice. Gino also said that it was too bad Howard was not a Catholic because he had a sister back in Brooklyn whom he thought Howard would like.

They had been in Hawaii for a week, and Howard had lost his draw money in a crap game. On Friday, Neely asked him if he wanted to make some extra money over the weekend. Howard, who was sitting on a stage over the side, painting the skin of the ship with red lead, squinted up against the hot tropical sun.

— Doing what?

— I tell you about it after mess tonight, Neely said, his red hair and red face disappearing over the railing.

Howard shrugged and went back to his painting. Neely was always coming up with ideas for making money, or making women, or making money and women. Lettmer, the A.B. on Howard's watch, had warned him about Neely, saying that Neely would do anything (with men or women) for money.

— Get spruced up, Howard, Neely said, after they had eaten.

— I've only got one pair of good pants and a clean shirt, Howard said. I don't even have a tie.

— Well, shave close then, Neely said, and make sure the shirt is nice and clean and ironed good and there's a crease in your pants and your shoes are shined.

— Where the hell are we going to, church? And you haven't told me yet what it is we're going to have to do.

— Never mind that now, Neely said. Hurry up. We ain't got much time. I meetcha at the gangway in thirty minutes.

When Howard appeared at the gangway after a steaming shower and ten minutes of careful pressing of his pants, Neely eyed him critically.

— You need a necktie, Neely said. Come'n, I'll loan you one of mine.

— To hell with it, Howard said. If I can't go like this, I won't go. He lit a cigarette and looked at Neely, who was dressed in his ice-cream britches, black coat and soft green tie and white shirt. He did, Howard noted with envy, look real nice.

— Listen, Neely said, I been working on this thing ever since we been in Wahoo, learned from a guy I meet back in Frisco. You want a good time? And make some cash to boot?

— So?

— Then come on, dammit. If it wasn't so late, I'd get somebody else.

Howard looked around the ship. If he didn't go ashore, all there was to do was play cards or read or sleep, and he sifted thirty cents in his pocket. Not even enough to take a round trip bus ride over to Waikiki Beach.

— Okay, Howard said, I'm your boy.

— Well, come on! They walked hurriedly for a quarter of an hour into the cooling Honolulu evening. Neely kept turning aside Howard's questions with knowing smirks. They never left the waterfront. Neely stopped abruptly.

— There she is, Neely said.

Howard looked out over the quiet evening waters. A schooner-rigged yacht stood offshore, her anchor lights up and riding the swells easily.

— We going to board her? Howard asked.

— Come on, we get the launch over at the little dock there.

—Wait a minute, Howard said, grabbing Neely by the arm. What's this all about?

—You'll see. Now I promise you'll make five bucks for the weekend, and all you can eat and drink.

—Who the hell is going to give all that to me? And for what?

—You coming or ain't you? Neely exploded. I ain't going to miss my good weekend. I'm late already.

Neely started off toward the dock, and Howard could see a motor launch was just then taking on a half-dozen women. Neely walked twenty feet, stopped and turned back to face Howard.

—Last time. You coming or not?

—All right! All right, Jesus Christ! I'm coming!

—Now look sharp when you get aboard, Neely said under his breath as they approached the dock. Just do what I do and keep your mouth shut.

—Okay, okay. I wasn't born yesterday, Howard grumbled. I know what's going on now.

Neely went directly to the man handling the launch and spoke to him. They both turned and looked at Howard. They spoke together again, and then Neely motioned Howard to get into the launch.

He sat in the stern with Neely, who had begun to talk to one of the women. She asked a lot of questions about the schooner. Howard listened to Neely reply in a voice pitched somewhere between respect and patronized attention. It was nearly dark, but he could make out the faces of the women, none of them young, all of them looking like women he would pass on the street without seeing. He tried to listen to their talk, but he found it dull. Neely was yes-mamming his woman to death and had casually slipped his hand around her waist in the darkness. A few minutes later he was rubbing his thumb over her nipple. Howard turned his attention outward and studied the yacht, giving it grudging, professional approval. They sailed straight out into the Pacific, and it was nearly midnight before the captain, a man in his forties with a deep suntan and smooth good looks, moved about the vessel, checking it.

—All right, Neely, the captain said. You and the kid are on watch. Keep awake and don't get drunk. And keep the lights burning. If the weather sharpens, call me; otherwise, lower the sails and let her drift.

— Okay, captain, Neely said.

There were eight women aboard, as far as Howard could see, plus two other crew members and the captain. The women had all remained below, talking and drinking and eating sandwiches. A few had tried to come on deck, but the captain had asked them to please remain below, saying it was unsafe on deck at the moment. But with the motion of the ship now no more than a slow and easy drift, the captain went below, spoke pleasantly and charmingly to the women, offering them the freedom of the ship. He then took the youngest and the prettiest of the women, went to his cabin, locked the door and turned out the light.

— What do you do on watch on a sailing ship, Neely? Howard asked, looking at the strange rigging, yet aware of the women.

— Same thing as any other watch, Neely said. And don't drink, because I'm going to and somebody's got to watch those broads don't drown or get too far away from the ship as we drift, 'kay?

— Okay, Howard said. The women came up out of the cabin chattering and giggling. Several of them had changed into bathing suits. One simply stripped down and dove over the side naked. They chattered together in the cockpit and yelled and squeaked with mock concern for the lone nude swimmer. Several more dove over the side. Howard watched all this and waited for Neely to continue, but Neely was watching the women intently.

— What else, Howard asked.

Neely replied without turning his head, as if Howard wasn't there.

— You pick one, Neely said. Or two. Or make a party of three and start fucking. And you don't have to be gentle. They want it rough.

Howard felt the steel wire tighten in his stomach; he went deliberately to a woman with a laughing face, slipped his arm around her waist and cupped her bosom—an absolutely cold move, checking into a wide-open game of stud.

Poker, pinochle and cribbage were the games they played in the messrooms on the long, off-watch nights, and though he liked the games well enough and was good with cards, winning slightly more than he lost, it was not enough for him. He began to read. And once he had regained his patience with a book, he fell back into the habit that had been started by Aunt Meg and that now was the final small piece that fitted into the puzzle of being a sailor: what to do on the off-watch time when sleep would no longer come and restless energy would not dissipate itself. His reading was like reestablishing an important relationship that had somehow passed out of his life, quite unconsciously and through a press of events, and then there it was again, to be seized upon and enjoyed. He read every spare moment, sometimes in a rush, sometimes slowly, tasting the words and the ideas as though savoring a special dish, utterly absorbed. He read himself around the world, and when he had had his fill, he came away surfeited, almost dazed from living in so many other worlds.

They had been in Japan for five weeks, three of which had been alongside the fitting dock in Yokohama, where the boilers were being overhauled. It was a hot, sultry day that had seen Howard at the backbreaking job of cleaning out the deep tanks. Now he sat in the messroom, sipping coffee, so tired he could hardly lift his head; the room was filled with men as tired as himself. The air was thick with cigarette smoke and the acrid odor of sweat and unwashed bodies. He sat with dulled senses, eyes closed, listening to the pounding of his heart, the same kind of noise in his ears that the jack-hammer working somewhere in the yard was making.

He had several more hours' work in the slime of the deep tanks and then he would shave and shower, eat and go ashore. Once ashore he would stop at the first bar he could find and have a few drinks and then walk around and look at another part of the city as soon as the drinks had eased his tension and weariness. Later, he would make his way back to the waterfront, where the bars lined up facing each other across the narrow street, and he might or might not pick out a woman and spend a couple of hours with her and then have a few more drinks before returning to the ship at two or three in the morning. He would turn to at seven-thirty and fight his way, cup after cup of blistering hot coffee, to some sort of accommodation with his hangover, and if the weather was hot and humid, it would not be long before he would sweat himself back into a reasonable state of clearheadedness. Eventually, if he stayed in port long enough, he would lose fifteen or twenty pounds, and he would be so tired and weak when they finally sailed that it might be two or three weeks before he gained his weight back and was again restless with energy and ready for the next port, where he would repeat the pattern that had become fixed in six and a half years.

That May day of 1926 in Yokohama, in the sultry, putrid atmosphere of the messroom, he recognized it as a sterile pattern, but it was useless and meaningless to try and break it. For what, he asked himself, should he save his time and energies—all right, his very existence?

Only for himself, he thought. All there was, was there for him, and he believed in nothing but his pleasures.

Reeling from his hangover, he watched as Ravitch, the third engineer, paced back and forth in the deck sailors' companionway. Someone was taking a shower, and Cadiz, unable to stand without holding onto something, knew he had only a few minutes to get in under the shower before turning to for his watch. He forced his eyes open, looking into the companionway, hearing footsteps. He vaguely remembered somebody had said the kid wiper was in the shower.

Ravitch had stopped packing and was leaning on the door grinning down at Cadiz.

— What'd you drink, Cadiz? Some of that slop booze that steward mixed up out of dried fruit? You must be crazy.

Cadiz said nothing. Ravitch shrugged and stepped to the shower stall and yelled over the roar of the water.

— Come on, kid, or I'll boot your tail.

Cadiz heard the kid reply something. It sounded like the bleat of a trapped animal.

— Why don't you leave the kid alone, Ravitch? Cadiz said.

— Mind your own fucking business, Cadiz, Ravitch said. Besides, the kid likes it.

— Sure he does, Cadiz said. And so do you.

Ravitch shrugged and let it pass.

— Tell me something, will you? Cadiz asked, his eyes focusing.

Ravitch grunted, his face blank.

— What's the difference between an honest queer and a guy like you that likes ringtails?

— I told you, Cadiz, mind your own fucking business.

— An old sea jock like you, taking a kid and making a ringtail punk out of him.

Ravitch's eyes grew small and sullen. Cadiz felt the blood pounding in his head. The shower water stopped and the kid wiper stepped out. Cadiz looked at him and then spoke to both Ravitch and the kid wiper.

— The bosun on the old *Mandarin*, you remember him, a guy with a broken nose and scars over his eyes? Well, the bosun tried to show me the shaft alley one day, and I broke his nose with a fid and was about to finish him with a ketchup bottle when they dragged me off.

— Anybody try that with me, I'd kill 'em, Ravitch said.

Cadiz stood up, surprisingly steady, and looked directly at the kid wiper. You don't have to go with him if you don't want to.

— You trying to get him for yourself, Ravitch suddenly yelled.

— I was hoping you'd say that, Cadiz said, and hit him with a footstool, knocking him back into the companionway. Blood streamed down Ravitch's face. Somebody yelled for them to cut it out and take their fight on deck. One of the mates came down the ladder, started to say something, then turned and walked away.

— You sonofabitch! Ravitch felt his face and head and, seeing blood on his hand, started to groan.

Cadiz turned to the kid, who had not moved and who stood looking down at Ravitch. Cadiz handed him the footstool.

— Do a good job on him now, kid, and he'll never bother you again.

The kid looked up at Cadiz and then at Ravitch. He licked his lips.

— Unless, of course, you *want* to be his punk.

The kid wiper grabbed the stool and stepped in on Ravitch and hit him in the face. One of the stool legs caught an ear and ripped it. Ravitch screamed. He tried to scramble away and the kid went after him, bringing the stool down on his head and shoulders.

—Please, Marion! Please! Please—don't hit me anymore, Marion, please! Ravitch's voice became shrill and hysterical.

—You gonna leave me alone, you sonofabitch? the kid wiper yelled. You gonna?

—I promise, Marion, I promise, just don't hit me anymore.

—What the hell's going on here? a voice bellowed from the end of the companionway. Cadiz turned to see the chief mate hurrying forward. Cadiz jerked a thumb.

—Ravitch's ringtail just got his discharge, he said with a grin.

The mate sobered, taking the situation in.

—Oh, he said. All right, Ravitch, your worm turned. If you try to jock him again, I'll do a job on you myself. Drop the stool, kid, it's all over. The chief mate strode off to have his breakfast coffee.

Ravitch struggled to his feet and disappeared up the ladder to his cabin. The kid wiper turned to Cadiz, his hands shaking, his whole body trembling. He tried to grin.

—Thanks, Cadiz. I don't know how I let him get away with it. But he kept threatening me and I was scared of him, him being an officer and all.

—Sure you were, Cadiz said. Everybody knew that.

—You mean, everybody *knew?*

—You think you can keep a secret like that on a ship?

—But if everybody knew, how come no-damn-body did anything about it before? The boy was close to tears.

—Why should we? Cadiz shrugged. It was you that was getting greased. It was up to you to do something, *if* you wanted to get off the Chocolate Speedway.

—Oh Jesus! I coulda cold-cocked him the first day if somebody had only told me.

—School's out, kid, Cadiz said. This is life.

—Buy why did you help me just now?

—I didn't help *you,* Cadiz said. He insulted *me.*

The boy was bewildered.

—Insulted you? How?

—He thought—or suggested—that *I* wanted to fuck you.

—But—but—I—

Cadiz laughed.

—*And you knew!* The wiper lunged at Cadiz. Cadiz stepped to one side, pressing himself against the bulkhead, and as the boy lurched past him, he brought up his knee. The wiper flipped over backwards. Blood spurted on both bulkheads and all over Cadiz's shirt and trousers.

The wiper writhed in agony on the deck.

—Don't fuck around with anything you can't win, kid, Cadiz said coldly, and turned away to go have coffee before going on watch, wondering where he could get a few aspirin for his overwhelming hangover, which indeed had come from the slop booze the steward had made.

In London, Cadiz got into a fight in the Monument Hotel and wound up in the hospital with a knife wound in his shoulder that made him miss his ship. After three weeks in the hospital, he was allowed out on a Sunday stroller's pass. Hungry for sunshine that bleak fall day, he had gone to Hyde Park. He had walked and walked, looking for a sunny spot. When he found it, he saw her sitting and reading. He had hesitated, but then at the moment he was about to turn away, not wanting conversation, feeling dispirited and alone, she had looked up and smiled. The impersonal white phantoms who took care of him in the hospital were dispelled by her smile. Her eyes were warm and her face was smoothly pretty, and his suddenly awakened hunger prompted him to return the smile and introduce himself. She listened quietly, apparently interested, as he blurted out in the very first few minutes of their conversation that though he was not inclined to be religious, if he had to be something he would be a sun worshiper, explaining that he had seen and felt the sun all over the world and that there was no balm like that of a hot day. Within ten minutes, her eyes, her lips, the quickness of her breath had worked their magic and he had, improbably, fallen in love with her.

They had tea in a small little tearoom with lace tablecloths, and they talked the whole time against a background of Mozart played softly and methodically by an elderly woman in a purple dress. By the time he had taken her to her bus stop, they were trading confidences, and he kept repeating, "You know what I mean?" and she kept replying, "Oh, yes. Yes, I do!"

After he was discharged from the hospital, it had not been difficult to avoid being shipped out through the pool. There were plenty of American seamen on the beach in England, and all of them had to report to London as a clearing station before shipment to Bristol, Liverpool, Manchester, or wherever an American flagship had lost a member of the crew. At first he had lived at the Seaman's Pool Dorms, checking in every day and waiting for her to finish her work in a dress shop in the West End, when they would spend the evening together. When he learned that he could get a job, so long as it was not reported officially, and provided he kept in touch with the Seaman's Pool, he no longer checked in every day but found a job as a flour handler for the gigantic Lleeds, Ltd., Bakers, moving into a one-room flat on the edge of Whitechapel. He had not been in his flat a week before she proposed that he move into her house and pay the rent and board money to her mother, who would put it by, and with this additional saving, they would build their nest egg more quickly. He was reluctant to move, but she refused to come up to his room and visions of the security of a home, with her so handy and available, crept into his mind and he accepted. Cadiz found himself getting progressively horny. Yet she had skillfully maneuvered him each time they had kissed and he reached for her breast. He was beginning to wonder if she was ever going to sleep with him. Doubt, too, began to enter his thoughts. Was she a professional virgin, or a sly conniving bitch or was she truly shy and domestic? He did not know. His improbable love was beginning to thin out. Not much, but instead of building, it was going downhill.

On a Saturday night soon after he had moved in, they were alone in the house together. Mr. and Mrs. Hopkinson were out at the Three Boar Public House. Mr. Hopkinson played shove ha'penny and darts while he drank exactly seventeen pints of mild and bitter, and Mrs. Hopkinson sat in the corner and gossiped and drank exactly twelve pints of mild and bitter. Both of them timed their consumption so that when Bayse Dunham walked through the rooms calling time, they would not have to hurry their drinking, but could finish their last swallow with dignity before staggering out into the night and going home.

It happened after they had put young Angus to bed and were sitting alone in the dark in the front room on the sofa couch. Ulrica's head was against his chest. His arm was around her shoulders, and now and then he dropped the palm to her breast, knowing that she would tolerate *that* for just so long, and then would move it away, snuggling closer, making a cozy, soft sound in her throat, teasing him, aware, so very aware of what she was doing. He smelled her body and was conscious of his own rutting scent. And then he found himself standing up, pulling her from the sofa couch. One hand pinning her arms behind her, his free hand ripped her dress away, neck to knee, before she could speak or make a sound, and then he was pressing her back onto the couch.

She kicked, hard, and tried to bite him. He was blind to everything but his own need, and all her twisting and wrenching was futile. Finally, she ceased resisting, and as she smothered her moans and cries of pain with a piece of clothing she had stuffed into her mouth, he pursued his course to the end. Whereupon she screamed.

When sanity returned and he was, with awkwardness and guilt, incapable of saying anything except how sorry he was, she brushed and kissed his face and whispered her virginal, innocent love into his ears, as much passion pouring from her lips as had spilled from her loins, enveloping him, soothing him. And, dumbly, still involved in his guilt, he said that he would marry her anytime she wanted, repeating that he was sorry, so sorry that it had happened this way.

Almost immediately she began planning their life. The change in her was not even subtle, and in the days that followed he saw clearly that he had made a terrible mistake, that he was trapped.

Oh, Christ, he thought. It was going to be difficult. All he wanted was to get in and out of the house without anyone seeing him. He wouldn't hide, or even go out of his way to avoid being seen, but he wanted very much to escape a confrontation with Mrs. Hopkinson. Angus would probably be playing rugger on the heath across the street, he thought, but that couldn't be helped. Besides, he wouldn't have to explain anything to Angus.

He got off the bus and walked slowly to the corner. It was hot for

England at that time of the year, and he had a headache from too much tension, too many cigarettes and too little food. Glancing up as he passed the corner jewelry store, he saw his reflection in the plate glass. He cringed. The cheap cotton trousers were wrinkled, and the cheaper shoes pinched his feet.

It had started, really, to burn itself out the night he had raped her. At first there were little excuses and lies that he used to get out of the house and away from Mr. and Mrs. Hopkinson, Angus and Ulrica; and at first there had only been long walks through London, winding up usually at Westminster Bridge where he would listen to that great clock tearing away at time, and stare into the river listening to the tugs, puffers and distant steamboat whistles further down the Thames. Then slowly he began to drop in on old haunts where he knew sailors would hang out, not even aware that he searched the faces at the bar or the tables for a familiar face, nervously, like a cat scenting the air. He was nearly always disappointed, and when he did meet someone, he felt outside of their party. He was a "usta"—a sailor who usta-go-to-sea. It was an easy step from the long lonely walks, to the familiar bars, to hanging around the shipping pool. And all the time there was not one single question from Ulrica as to where he was going, or why. There was only one thing in her life, and therefore his, and that was counting shillings and quid. Weeks stretched into months and every night was the same. The Hopkinsons sat in the kitchen and gossiped while Angus did his homework, never stopping in their outrageous and slanderous remarks about their friends, neighbors and distant relations. It became like a dirge. And he was out of it. They even seemed surprised that he was sitting with them when he would make a comment on something that was said. Then, finally, a last cup of tea and everyone off to bed, with Ulrica giving him a quick kiss in the dark, allowing him just enough of a feel to get him hot, and then ducking into her room. Once he had confronted her with this and demanded his due. Ulrica had been so afraid she would be caught by her parents or Angus they had made love standing up in the kitchen with the lights on. That night in the kitchen had so unnerved him, and had been such a stunning assault on his dignity, and in consequence revealed Ulrica even more to him, that he started actively looking for a ship and a means of escape.

He stepped to the curbing and surveyed the quiet residential street carefully. The row houses were exactly like those he had seen in Brooklyn and in parts of Queens, only smaller, uglier. Worthrington Gardens was lower middle class, not shabby but plainly struggling. He studied the heath. It was clear of games and he felt relieved. Angus had either stayed to play with his school chums or was inside reading. He glanced at his watch. Quarter of four. Mrs. Hopkinson would be in the kitchen starting supper. She usually listened to the Gramophone as she worked, singing along with the Italian operas she loved so much. It might be, he thought, that the Gramophone would give him the covering noise he needed. He hurried toward the house. If only he could get his suitcase and leave without having to explain to anyone but Ulrica. He would call her later. After he got on the ship.

The Gramophone *was* playing very loudly and Mrs. Hopkinson was accompanying the tenor. The way was clear to his room upstairs. But he would have to be quick.

Once in his room, Cadiz pulled out the Florida alligator Gladstone and began packing. Everything he owned went into the bag except his topcoat, which he would carry over his arm. He packed quickly and expertly, as he had done hundreds of times before. Snapping the locks, he flipped the straps and buckled them tightly. He stepped back, breathing hard, and looked around. On the top of the chest of drawers was Ulrica's photograph. How could he have forgotten that? He undid the straps, unsnapped the locks and was reaching for the picture when he froze. The Gramophone had stopped. There was a moment of silence and then he heard Mrs. Hopkinson trilling once more as she cranked the machine. The tenor started up again, but Mrs. Hopkinson did not join in this time. As he stood, straining his ears, he could hear a *la-la-la!* here and there, but she was not yowling as she usually did. He could even hear her footsteps distinctly. He could not wait any longer. He stepped to the door, opened it with great care and started down the stairs. He held the suitcase tightly so that it would not bump the banister and eased downstairs one step at a time. He looked at the door, at the doorknob, wiping his free hand on his trousers to be sure his grip would not slip. He was down the last step and into the small vestibule, reaching for the knob.

— Angus! Is that you, love? Angus?

Cadiz set the suitcase near the wall in such a way that it would be hidden if she came in from the kitchen. He walked quickly through the sitting room and a small pantry to the kitchen door.

— No, it's me, Howard, he called. He pushed through the door and stepped halfway into the kitchen. It was hot and steamy. Two pots boiled on the stove. The table was piled high with wet clothes ready for the line. Then he remembered it was Tuesday and of course she would be doing the laundry. On the top of the pile was a pale blue slip belonging to Ulrica. He recognized it as the one she had worn when they had gone to visit her sister in Didsbury, near Manchester.

Angus had gone with them as chaperon. He had often thought about the trip, wondering if Mrs. Hopkinson had really been so naïve as to think that Angus's presence would make any difference. Angus had gone to sleep almost at once and Ulrica's sister was only too eager to escape the house for an evening and leave them alone to mind her three-year-old twin girls. Howard had been amazed at the deliberately cool way Ulrica had waited at the window to make sure her sister and brother-in-law had left. Then, smiling at Howard, she began to undress. This was her way—a deliberate move, giving in just enough to hold him. It was a cold night, he remembered, and there had been a coal fire in the grate and she had undressed before the fire, strangely casual about the whole thing, as if she had worked out every detail beforehand, turning this way and that before the warm firelight in the grate as she disrobed, letting the light and shadows play on her rounded thighs, hips and breasts. He had put off his own clothes and had taken her right there on the floor before the fire: hard, brutal, he tore into her with cruel abandon. She had not uttered one word, one noise, one sigh of pleasure or satisfaction. She was, in fact, staring at the fire. Sweating, Cadiz stood up and wiped his brow. He looked down at her.

— Why? he asked.

— You needed it, luv.

— You mean, he said stupidly, that you decided I needed a piece of ass and arranged this whole thing to give it to me?

— You seemed to enjoy it, she said.

— Yeah, sure I did. Nothing like a good fuck.

— Don't be crude, she said in the same flat tone. Don't ever use that word to me again. Sexual intercourse between men and women is something quite, really, quite different.

— 'kay, you have your sexual intercourse and I'll have my fuck, 'kay?

The rest of the evening she had worn the blue slip as they drowsed before the grate, sipping tea while she talked of the future. He took her twice more that night and each time it was the same. He was shattered. He knew then that regardless of his own personal sense of dignity, he would have to get the hell away from there—and her—any way he could.

The blue slip on the pile of wet wash in the steamy kitchen gave off an aroma of soap and water, but he imagined he could still smell her body and the faint odor of her perfume.

Mrs. Hopkinson was wiping her forehead. Her hair was tied up neatly, but a few wisps had worked out and the dark hairs were plastered to her temples. She was a pleasant, handsome woman, direct in her manner without being brisk, as so many English women he had met were to Americans. She was dressed in a house dress with huge floral design; the dress was wet around the waist from handling the wash. She smiled.

— I didn't expect you until after six, love.

— I had to come back for something I need down at the bakery. I have to hurry. He stepped back through the door.

— Try not to be late for supper, Howard.

— Yes, Mrs. Hopkinson.

— Oh, love?

He came back to the kitchen door.

— Yes?

— Now, there's a good chap, see if the grand and mighty Lleeds Bakery, Ltd., hasn't got a cake from yesterday that you could bring? She smiled. I've made the sauce, you see, and a cake would make it grand.

— All right, I'll try, Howard said.

— There's a good lad.

In the vestibule, he waited to see if she would follow, then he reached for the handle of the Gladstone. The door opened before he could touch the knob, and Angus stepped inside, slamming the door back and knocking the Gladstone out of his hand. The eleven-year-old backed off awkwardly.

— Oh, I say, Howard, frightfully sorry! Angus said, and then saw the bag. Going on a holiday, Howard?

— I'm in a hurry, Angus.

— But where are you going? The boy stepped to one side and Howard bolted to the sidewalk. Behind him he could hear Angus calling to his mother. He didn't look back, and the last thing he heard was the tenor reaching for his F above high C. To hell with them, he muttered to himself.

The bus ride, which took him right across London, was long and tiresome. He sat near the back on the long seat, and passed the time counting the endless streams of passengers who got on, paid their fares to the conductor and then filed in through silence and heat; the bus filled and emptied twice before he got off and changed for the Eastham connection that would take him to the docks.

In Eastham Cadiz got off the bus and angled to a huge gate where a stream of railcars were being shunted into a siding at the pierside, stopping only to check the slip and the pier number, then going on to the gate.

— *African Carrier*? Cadiz asked the guard, flashing his slip from the Seaman's Pool.

— You in the crew, Yank? the guard asked, looking at the slip, and Cadiz smiled at the Yorkshireman's dour, hardnosed manner of speaking. In seven months ashore in London, he had learned the difference in the accents.

— Just going aboard.

— Right you are then. There's your vessel. The *Carrier* is the last ship on the quay, aft of the pier. It's a long walk, mid. Carry on.

— Thanks, Cadiz said, picking up the Gladstone, moving slowly past the slide side of the pier, passing the mooring lines and the gangways of other ships working cargo. It was a very long walk, close to a half-mile, and he stopped halfway to get his wind and rest his hands and gaze speculatively at the S.S. *African Carrier*, with her staggered superstructure that ran, as if cut out by a jigsaw, fore and aft in a clean, uncluttered way. It was a Hog Islander, as familiar to him as the mole on his cheek. He walked on, wanting a smoke but not able to have one until he got aboard.

He climbed the gangway, balancing the heavy Gladstone on his knee, kicking it out with each step, gaining the deck finally and standing firmly amid the tangle of lines and filth of the ship deep in the business of discharging cargo. He looked up. At each hold there were huge gantry fly hoists picking out the cargo, lifting it up and away, looking for all the world like the legs of huge insects—especially so because of the long, skinny underpinning structure—digging into the carcass of some dead beast.

Someone bawled something indistinguishable to his ear. Then he heard the reply.

— G'wan, screw y'sef, ya bastid. It was unquestionably Texan. He was home.

Standing still, lighting a cigarette in the sanctuary of his home, feeling the good feeling of being on a ship again with the rattle of the galley finishing up supper, encouraged by the yells and laughter and noise of the ship's crew as they ate, soothed by the creaking of the gantry fly hoists, he left his bag on deck and walked into the messroom. No one took any notice of him. He drew a cup of coffee from the urn and sat there a long time, soaking up the rich aroma of this, his place, feeling warm and secure, with the guilt he had felt mounting for days and days gradually draining out of his system as though purged by some magic cathartic fed into his body with each whine and hiss and throw of the steam piston in the sanitation pump.

Later, standing on the fantail, signed, sealed and delivered and with no way of turning back—the ship was sailing that night—he decided that whatever else was to be considered, he could not just walk away from it, from her, without seeing her again. He knew that he would have to endure her bitterness—she was a very expert woman at scolding—but it was the price he would have to pay. He went back to the midship housing, showered, put on a clean shirt and walked down to the end of the pier, where he dialed her number. His hand shook a little. Angus answered the phone. His voice was sullen.

— Angus Hopkinson here.

—Hello, Angus? Let me speak to Ulrica, please.

—Ully! Ully! It's Howard, Mummy! It's Howard!

He could hear movement on the open line and then Ulrica's voice saying, "No, Mummy! No! Let me!" It was hot in the booth and he opened the door.

—Hello? Her voice was soft.

—Ulrica?

—Yes.

—I'd like to see you.

—All right.

—I mean tonight.

—Tonight's all right.

—How about—Charing Cross, near the largest bookstall. It's halfway for both of us.

—Why not come up here, Howard? she asked, still soft, but he could hear the uneasiness.

—I can't.

She sighed and there was a long pause. Then she came back on and her voice was a little firmer, as if she knew, her suspicions well grounded now.

—All right. What time?

—It can't be too late. Can you leave now?

—Yes. What time?

—Quarter past eight?

—All right.

—Good-by.

—Good-by, he said, and hung up.

He stepped into a bar across the street from the pier and had three quick ones with his new shipmates, then excused himself and headed for the underground. He stopped, cursed and hailed a cab at the corner. Sometimes things change very quickly, he thought. The cab would cost nearly fifteen shillings, including tip. It was only a few weeks ago that Ulrica had asked him to stop buying magazines to read on the underground and read a penny paper instead, to save money. "It amounts to a tenner a week, darling."

He exploded inside, pressing against the springs in the back seat of the cab. Christ! Two bucks, roughly. Two shillings pinched here; this cost eighteen and six—too much; Spanish oranges, twelve and six, too much; Bond Street shirts are too dear, take a little less expensive one.

In the dark back seat of the cab, Cadiz told himself that it wasn't the money, it was the attitude. That was the way you had to think if you wanted to live ashore.

Ulrica was standing near the first table of the largest of the late-closing bookstalls. Swarms of people moved in and out, examining the books, angling them so that the light would catch the page. It was his favorite place in all of London, and he had, on previous trips, spent hours wandering from stall to stall. She did not see him right away, and he watched her from across the street, telling himself that what he was doing was right, yet dreading the need to face her. She was wearing her working tweeds. He could not tell from that distance if she had been crying or not.

— Waiting long? he asked.

— Few minutes. It's a ship, isn't it, Howard?

— Yes.

— Did you sign on yet?

— Yes. This afternoon. We're sailing tonight.

— You've been drinking, she said.

— I had a few.

— Where are you going?

— I don't care. You want to walk?

— I don't mean now, she said briskly. I mean the ship. Where is the ship going?

— Gold Coast, Africa, then back to the States.

— Let's walk, shall we, love? she said, sarcasm curling around the word "love."

They walked not slow, not fast, and not close at all. They were silent. They walked almost aimlessly, turning this corner and then that, pausing at curbstones and then drifting across the street, not looking at windows but not avoiding them either. Not a word was spoken for a long while until they were near the Thames. A stern-wheeling tug moved upriver. The engine room door was open and a bare-chested man stepped out for a moment and was framed in the light behind him. The man then closed the door and the silhouette of the tug was there again, unbroken by the engine-room firelight. They both looked at it, their eyes drawn to it because the sudden shaft of light in the black river and the blacker tug was startling.

— Would you like to sit down? he asked.

She moved without a word or gesture to a bench and sat down, carefully, smoothing her skirt. She sat very still and looked out over the river to the opposite shore.

He offered her a cigarette. She shook her head ever so slightly and he lit one for himself. They sat a long time, perhaps a half hour, in the building, brooding, painful silence. He smoked and she stared at the water and the opposite shore. There was a great deal of traffic on the river.

— You're very selfish, she said finally.

He didn't answer.

— You either lied to me, or you lied to yourself. Either that or you are the most selfish man in the world.

— I never lied to anyone in my life, he said. I don't know if I'm lying to myself. I don't know about that, but I never lied to anyone about anything that was serious.

— If you'd just tell me why you're going? There was no plea in her voice. Do you know? Do you really know, and if you know, can you tell me why?

— I guess I'd tell you if I knew.

— Are you sure you're not deceiving yourself?

— How do you mean?

— I've noticed that in you.

— What?

— Sometimes you deceive yourself.

— The whole world gets by by fooling itself.

— Well, she said, if you choose to believe that. Personally, I don't.

An East Indiaman moved downriver then, loaded to the insurance marks, heading out. There was a herky-jerky feeling about the ship and he studied her, looking for what was wrong. Scotland, he decided. Built on the Clyde. The oddness lay in her conversion from coal to oil. The ship was not moving fast enough to send out a full bow wave; it seemed to move forward without any effort at all. They both watched it.

—When did you decide? she asked.

—This morning. I was in the Nicker-Tea-Stalls across the way from the bakery. Mr. Jacobi came in and told me to get to work unloading a lorry. I was drinking my tea. It wasn't seven-thirty yet. He wanted me to start right away. I said I would finish my tea. He said if I didn't start right away I was through. I walked out.

He saw her fist tighten in her lap.

—You didn't think of me, did you, when you walked out? Didn't it occur to you that by walking out it might end everything between us?

He was very slow in answering. He took the time to light another cigarette.

—I guess I didn't think about anything. I looked around the street, at the bakery, at the walls, and out on the Mews where the people were hurrying to jobs they hated but had to go to, scared, nervous little people with no way out—and there I had a way out.

—And you took it. Her voice was flat.

He didn't answer.

—Do you remember the time we went up to Didsbury to see my sister?

—Yes, he said dully, I remember.

—Her husband knows someone in the renting agent's office of that sector. He told my sister there were a lot of people who couldn't pay for their houses, or lost them for one reason or another, and that we could pick one up cheaply. It would have been easy for us to get one of those houses. For three hundred pounds we could have moved in, and with luck we could have gotten one with a little furniture.

—I didn't know that, Howard said. So that was why she fucked that night in Didsbury, he thought. A piece of ass to soften him up for the big hit; the house, the little bit of furniture.

She stood up. She held out her hand.

—Good-by, Howard.

He got up.

—Ully, wait.

—For what? I don't know what it is you want, but it certainly isn't me.

—I—

— Mummy and Dad are very upset. They liked you. It's going to be very difficult to make them understand.

He stood there and took it. He didn't like it, but he took it, stiff faced, glassy eyed, and let her have her innings. He spoke around the stiffness and his self-imposed sense of "taking it."

— I think I loved you, Ully.

— That's what it amounts to. You think you did. You're not even sure of that.

— I tried for half a year.

— Good-by, Howard. I think I loved you too.

He watched her walk to the bus stop. After a moment a bus came along and she boarded it. The bus roared off.

He stood there a long time, without moving. From somewhere down on the river he could hear the pitiful hooting of a small vessel. He looked for it but could not find it. The hooting continued. It sounded like a child whimpering, wandering around in the dark, looking for its mother. He started walking. He walked and watched the river, the busiest and dirtiest in the world, searching it, and came unexpectedly on a private-yacht landing. Laughter, a woman's laughter that sounded a little drunken, drifted up from a sixty-five-footer. A trim-jacketed figure raced silently forward on the teak decks and pulled in the bowline. Another smart sailor surged a spring line amidships while the vessel made sternway against the tide. The tiny tones of the engine-room telegraph came up to him from the silent water, and then a surge of power sent the water boiling white under the stern as the beautiful boat cut cleanly downriver. Big Ben struck ten times.

Cadiz watched the yacht until it disappeared, then he simply stared out over the waters of the dark Thames and listened to the soft slap-slap of the water.

He knew he had badly hurt another human being, yet all he had done was make a decision. He would have to live with it. Life, after all, was everything that had not happened yet, in a time that had not yet been lived. All he could do was wait.

— But I think, he said to himself as he made his way back to Eastham and his ship, I loved her. If there could only have been some other way.

But he knew there could never have been any way acceptable to him. He had not deceived himself. That was all that mattered.

The months that followed were unstructured, and his earlier sense of *gaining* began to slip away and he began to indulge. There was nothing he would not do or experiment with.

— What the fuck are you *doing*, Cadiz? the captain asked.

— Meditating, Cadiz replied. He sat cross legged on the hatch and stared into a round red ball in his imagination.

— That Calcutta cunt musta really got to you, huh? You going Hindu on me, huh, what'd she have, two pussies? Jesus! I really don't care what you do, you know what I mean, but Jesus, steward tells me you ain't eating anything but dried apricots an—I don't want you to get sick. We a long fucking way from a doctor and you looking kinda down. Now, come on, get your ass up and I'll give you some of my bonded stuff and get drunk with me and then it'll be all right, what do you say to that, huh?

His mystic beliefs did not last very long. The captain was right and he never did reach Nirvana. But he did get drunk.

The Burmese girl did not look more than twelve, but he was assured she was fifteen. She had skin the color of a Miami Beach cutie.

— Why are you so thin, Sailorman.

— I have been seeking truth, Little One.

— This is truth, she said and slapped his hand to her crotch.

They had to come to the house and physically subdue him with three big tough British-trained and -instructed Burmese cops to help get him back to the ship.

— But I don't want to go ashore with Cadiz! the voice said.

— But dammit, he's got the money!

— But Jesus, all he wants to do is sit in one joint and drink. And then when he gets drunk he wants to fight. And Jesus, it ain't worth it. I never seen anybody drink like him. He must have a liver like a lead ball. I stood his watch so fuckin' many times he oughta just give us the goddam money and let us go and have our fun and all.

But they did go ashore with Cadiz. And he did sit in one joint and every ten minutes he would take a two-ounce shot of gin, straight, and sit and stare at himself in the bar mirror, and then, as if a light had snapped on in his head, he turned and hit the first man he saw. He was absolutely insane. There was no way to reach him, except with a chair, or a bottle or, when the cops came, with a blackjack.

He drank until he could no longer do his work and became flabby gutted and every morning was so hung over that whiskey postules dripped from his face and nose and he reeked. Finally those who knew him and had in one way or another expressed concern about him, or even spoke to him in a friendly way, turned their back on him and when the ship sailed they didn't bother to search for him as they had done so many times before.

He did not know and he did not care how he got to the beach village on Bali. He had a woman who fed him and who made him palm beer and kept him warm at night. The five months he spent there was one prolonged, drunken vegetable existence. When his woman, who was pregnant with his child, and who loved him, finally realized that he would never be any different from what he was, she left him unconscious on a low-tide beach and then sat on the fringe of the jungle gardens and watched while the sea came in, hoping that he would drown. When she returned the next day, he was gone. She was happy. She returned to her village and a funeral service was held for him.

The port cities of the world washed around him like garbage rising with the tide out of some fouled channel. There were no beginnings and no endings. Time stretched limitlessly before him and all of it became one and he was in the middle of it. And then his very existence seemed like a millstone around his neck. The *burden* of living overwhelmed him. When he sought release, he discovered he had done it all. He had been there. There was no release. He felt washed out at the age of twenty-four.

— Are you one of them stupid bastards, a quarter-deck voice roared at him, that think life is something disgusting, to be thrown away?

— To hell with you, Cadiz replied. Leave me alone Mister Whitcomb.

— I been watching you.

— Up yours, and leave me alone, Cadiz said, glaring at the river. Go back to your bridge and play third mate.

— You know what life is worth? I mean, do you *really* know? Or maybe you one of them inbetweeners squat to pee. Huh?

— Get away from me or I'll bust your face, Cadiz said.

— I'm a little high from my drinking, son, the quarter-deck voice said to Cadiz, but I'm still man enough to wrap your ass around that telegraph pole yonder and put two half hitches in it to boot. Wanta fight? Or do you wanta bellyache about the misery of it all? Here, have a drink. No? Okay, you ganna jump in that river, go ahead, I'll hold your hat and watch. I'll be your audience. I'll be your last will and testimony that you couldn't cut it. But don't make me wait too long. I hate to wait.

They stood, Howard Cadiz and Elisha Whitcomb, on a railroad bridge that spanned a swamp reaching the loading pier in a west-coast Florida port. Their ship, the S.S. *Indenter*, a small, dirty, rusting freighter, was taking a cargo of phosphate. A yard engine was shunting gondola cars up to the bridge, huffing and puffing, and Whitcomb, a big man with a barrel chest and a hard gut, spat in its direction.

— Now, I can respect a man who wants to go quick, so if you don't wanta jump into the water where there are most certainly sharks, 'cause I seen 'em today, then you can lie down on the tracks and let that train run over you. But make up your goddam mind. Like I said. I hate to wait.

Cadiz turned and looked at him. The third mate stared back solemnly, his lips making a near-perfect O around a ten-inch Havana cigar.

— Is this the way you get your kicks, Mister Whitcomb? You some kind of degenerate? You going to throw your hocks if I jump?

— Have a drink, son, and don't be disrespectful.

— I had enough to drink already.

— Then let's go on ashore and get laid.

— I been laid already.

— Then let's fight.

— I fought enough for a lifetime already, Cadiz said.

— None of it worth the candle anymore, eh?

— I can't see any way out, Cadiz said.

— Well, if that's all there is, she won't give you a second chance, you know.

— I know.

— I ain't going to be disrespectful and ask you if it was a woman—a particular woman.

— You're not disrespectful. It's only partly a woman.

— And you ain't no queer all trussed up with double trouble, like a man with a hernia who can't even take a good crap. So what else is there?

— I don't know, Cadiz said.

— How old are you?

— Old enough.

— I mean how long you been a brine pecker?

— I been going to sea ten years.

— That qualifies you to know what you're doing.

— I figure, Cadiz said.

— Here comes the train, son. You going to take the train or the water?

— You sonofabitch!

They both stepped out onto the edge of the bridge and let the train pass within a foot of them. The hot breath of the steam boiler and the fire box rolled past them.

— Git off'n the bridge, ya crazy bastards! the fireman yelled back at them.

When the last gondola rolled past, Cadiz and Whitcomb stepped back to the middle of the bridge.

— Well, I ain't got much more time, son, Whitcomb said. You gonna jump?

— I haven't got the nerve.

— Very few good men have, son, Whitcomb said. Very few. I'm a stupid old sonofabitch. I got me a master's license, and I know you got a mate's license, 'cause I seen it when you signed on, and I guess we been to most of the places the other has been—maybe even screwed the same women—and you get this fit at some time or other in your life. I had it, most do, and then you get over it.

— I don't want to get over it, Cadiz said. I really want to say piss on it and let it drop off me, all of it.

— But you can't.

— No, Cadiz said, I can't. But I don't want to go on fighting either.

— Okay, I understand that, Whitcomb said, passing a bottle to Cadiz, who took three long swallows before passing it back to Whitcomb, but there ain't no other way. You live or you die. That's all there is.

— Yeah.

— Yeah. So! Lemme tell you something. You been putting your faith in the wrong things. I know you. I seen your type. You been going around the world humping and drinking and fighting and you walk around with your arms stretched out letting anybody that comes along have a little piece of you. And you left little pieces of your own true self all over the world. And being a sailor you musta left 'em with some pretty sorry people, and in some pretty sorry places. Now all of a sudden, there doesn't seem to be anything of yourself left for *you*.

Cadiz was listening.

— What the hell, son, you think you're original? You think you're the first man that ain't felt down over the loss of a big hunk of your life, and you ask yourself, for what? and you have to say, for nothing, and then you get into a fit and you think, ahh, piss on it!

They had another drink, passing the bottle between them.

— The only mistake you make, that we all make, is that at this bad moment in your life you can't see a place to put what's left of your real self. And there is always a place for a man to do that. Why, hell, you can pick out anything and say that's what I'm going to live for, and then go do it. The rest of it, the living with people, the being with people, the being anywhere at all on the face of the earth, why, hell, it doesn't matter a tinker's dam. It's your goal, son, your dream, the thing you do, and women and drinking and having good times and bad times, somehow that all comes along and you learn to take it in stride. Drinking ain't important. Screwing ain't important. And fighting, why that's the way the apes in the fo'c'sle live.

— So, what is important? Cadiz asked, taking another drink and giving it back to Whitcomb.

— I'll tell you what's important, son. It's being the very best in a thing. Like I'm the best goddam navigator in the world. I went seventeen days once without a sight around the Horn on a sailing ship when I was a lad just on the quarter deck and I dead reckoned her right around. That's what I mean. It's something inside of you that's—well—that's purely you. Lemme ask you something.

— Okay.

— Let's take a beautiful broad, best you can imagine, all right?

— Okay.

— Now the ship is in danger, and you're ashore with this broad, okay?

— Okay.

— You going to leave her to come back to your ship?

— Sure, Cadiz said simply.

— That's all there is, son. It's a thing that a man does and does well that makes him important in the scheme of things.

— I see that, Cadiz said.

— Then you got it.

And as they went ashore that night, getting drunk and getting laid and getting into a very good fight, he really felt he had it.

Ride the sonofabitch, Howard, that's what we'll do. Ride the sonofabitch to hell. A big blow, eh, Howard, and we'll take her through the bowels of the earth.

Elisha Whitcomb, his big sagging gut hanging before him, stood on the bridge, braced against the heaving deck. He turned to Howard, who was jammed up against the wheel.

— Now wouldn't it be a shame, Howard, if you never got a chance to sail on that brand-new chief mate's ticket you just sweated out back in New York, and have to bust hell in the ass as an A.B. But never mind, Howard, just think of me, thirty years on the bridge a master of my own vessels and the onliest thing I can get is a third mate's berth, and here I walk into a blow like this with a skipper that's so shim-shivering scared he's down below there, drinking away his pukey guts 'cause he can't face the weather and what it might do to him. Never could understand a man that was only interested in going to sea when it was calm and then ran from her when she started to growl. The sea's like one of them black-assed women in Portugee East Africa that snap back when you prong 'em. By God, look at that water! Howard, you know we might *die* right here in the middle of this fucking ocean? Well, as f'me, I always did favor the western seas over that bastardly eastern ocean. All day and all night with the fantail humping and jumping out of the water 'cause there isn't enough weather to give the vessel a roll and a heel to her and take away the bumps and grinds of the main engine, just like a damn old burly queen throwing her hocks at you from the runway and some greasy-haired drummer, probably her pimp, beating the bass drum and grinning from ear to ear. Howard, goddammit, look at the ocean. Seas as big as Cleopatra's barge, by God! Hold on to that wheel, Howard, we'll ride her through this blow and then when I write my log, I'll make that sonofabitch drunken-ass captain we got look so silly they'll beach him faster than a young bride grabs at her husband's pecker. Then they'll give me this crummy ship and I'll sign *you* on as my chief mate. Hold her up, sailor! Hold to the wind! Ahh, if only my Sara back home could see this she wouldn't give me such a bad time every time I tell her I'm going to ship out again. Howard, we're going to ride this gale so long as you can hold her to the wind, and I will *make* this vessel stay afloat!

Elisha Whitcomb, himself so drunk he could hardly stand even while holding on to the stanchion, threw the window open and roared into the wind.

— You will not get me, you motherfucker!

He slammed the window, in that brief moment getting soaking wet.

— What do you think of that, Howard! Say something to me, goddammit, let me know you with me. I might not be able to hold this vessel afloat all by myself. Say something, goddammit, quartermaster! Here, get your face wet and lemme hear you tell her off!

Whitcomb threw open the windows in the wheelhouse, and water and rain, driven by the high winds, slammed into Cadiz's face.

Whitcomb hung over him, his face only inches away from Cadiz's.

— Well? Whitcomb roared.

— I'll hold the wheel to the wind and once more you and I will stalk Caesar's ghost on the Plains of Philippi! Cadiz shouted.

— Goddam you! We'll bust this ocean in half! Why, you got fire in you, Howard. Real fire!

The ship snapped and rolled. Whitcomb was thrown to the deck. The door swung wildly to and fro as Cadiz fought the wheel. Whitcomb did not try to move. He remained where he was and grinned drunkenly at Cadiz.

Cadiz looked down at Whitcomb's huge, drum-tight gut and the pink flesh of his balding head, blood trickling down over his face from a cut on his forehead. Cadiz knew him to be by far the best sailor—drunk or sober—he had met in all his years at sea. He laughed.

— Say something to me, goddammit, Whitcomb roared.

— Why then, lead on! Howard yelled above the scream of the wind and the rain and spray. O, that man might know the end of this day's business ere it come! But it sufficeth that the day will end, and then the end be known. Come, ho! Away!

Whitcomb looked up at him admiringly.

— A Bible-quoting sailor! Whitcomb roared. No *wonder* you so mean!

— That's not the Bible, you stupid idiot. That's Shakespeare!

— It's all the same, Howard. All the same. No. Don't leave the wheel, just let me stay here. I'll only fall down again anyway. Whitcomb giggled. It's in your hands, Howard. Everybody else is down below, messing they britches, they so scared, or so drunk they don't care. And I am about to go to sleep, so it's all in your hands, Howard, and if you sink the sonofabitch, I couldn't care less.

Howard lashed the wheel and then dropped a few loops of line over Whitcomb's body to keep him from rolling around on the deck. He stood wheel watch for nine hours and it was not until the gale had blown out that he discovered Whitcomb had been telling the truth, that he was the only man on deck sober enough to handle the helm.

The owners of the S.S. *Indenter*, after they had read Whitcomb's entry in the rough log—a masterpiece of implication and subtle disloyalty to the present captain—met the ship in San Francisco to investigate. Had the captain really been drunk when the ship was in danger?

— A man who holds a deep-water ticket and sailed A.B. on your ship, Mister O'Hara, was on the wheel for nearly *ten hours.* And I remained on the bridge for more than twenty-four hours without going below. I saved your ship, Mister O'Hara, me and young Cadiz, who is one of the finest sailors I've ever seen. Well, I've got to be going.

— Going? Going where, man?

— Why, sir, Whitcomb said, standing straight, I wouldn't sail with this captain again for all the tea in China. Why, sir, he could of lost more than thirty souls out there! Not me, no siree! I'm through with him.

— But—

— There isn't but one way I'll sail your ship, Mister O'Hara, and that's as her master.

— Done! Nothing more to be said. Done, Captain Whitcomb. She's yours. The *Indenter* is yours! O'Hara, a small, spry little man, who with his brother owned sister ships and hoped one day to have a whole fleet of O'Hara ships on the seas, jumped up and grabbed Whitcomb's hand.

— Control yourself, sir, Whitcomb said sternly. There is one more trifling condition.

— The money?

— I'll want more money, of course, but we can discuss that later. I was thinking about rewarding that fine young man who held so steady with me on the bridge that dark and terrible night—

— Reward him? How?

— I want him to be my chief officer.

— But—

— Good-by, Mister O'Hara. Once more Whitcomb started to leave. And good luck, sir.

— All right, captain, all right. You can pick your own chief officer.

— Fine, Whitcomb boomed. Will you have a drink with me, sir, to seal the bargain?

— I didn't know you were a drinking man, captain, O'Hara said.

— Only on special occasions, Mister O'Hara. Generally I frown on the vice of sailoring men. Women and drink do not mix with good steamboating.

— Well, in that case, captain, just a breath.

— Naturally, sir, just enough to wet the bottom of the glass.

After Whitcomb had escorted Mister O'Hara ashore and solemnly shaken his hand, taking his orders to sail the next night with general cargo for Cuba, then sugar from Tunas de Zaza for Antwerp, he came back aboard and found Cadiz waiting for him in the crew mess.

— Howard!

— Did it work?

— It worked. She's ours. Yours and mine. Get your ass on the bridge and sign the log, then stand by for me. I'm going ashore.

— Wait a minute, Cadiz yelled after the retreating Whitcomb.

— Oh, yes, there *is* one more thing.

— There sure as hell is, Cadiz said nervously, standing hesitantly at the head of the gangway.

— Howard, this is your ship, you understand me?

— No, I don't.

— I mean, goddammit, I'm the captain and I sign the papers, but this is *your* ship, do you understand? I mean I'm not so much as going to lift a goddam finger as long as I'm aboard her. Mostly I'm going to be drunk. And when we're alongside, I'm going to be ashore, and drunk. And all the rest of it, Howard. I been looking for a sucker like you all my life.

— Sucker?

— You're a first-class sailor and you're young enough yet to care. So care for my ship and you can run her any goddam way you want. Just don't bother me. *Now* do you understand?

— I understand, Cadiz said. Whitcomb offered his hand, but Cadiz refused to shake it.

— One thing.

— Name it.

— I'll protect you and your ship. I'll cover for you and I'll do it all, but I'll do it *my* way.

— That's the deal.

They shook hands.

— Jesus, am I going to have me a good time. I got me a free ride to every place in the world and no responsibility. You can't ask for more than that, can you, Howard?

But Cadiz wasn't listening. He had reached out and touched the rusting, scaling bulwark like a man taking possession of his bride.

— Mister? It was a small voice at the bottom of the gangway. They both turned and looked down at the hard-faced kid with a mop of curly black hair, dark eyes and a warm wide grin on his Mexican face. You need a sailor on this ship?

— I ain't even going to tell you about your crew, Whitcomb said. I said she was all yours, and I meant *all yours*.

— Okay, Elly, Cadiz said easily. You got a deal.

Whitcomb trundled down the gangway and disappeared into the shed of the pier. Cadiz regarded the kid still grinning at him from the bottom of the gangway. He hooked a finger and the kid ran lightly up the gangway.

— How long you been going to sea?

— I never been to sea.

Cadiz slapped him on the side of the face and head, knocking him to the deck. The kid looked up at him with burning eyes, his hand inside his shirt, where Cadiz knew there would be a knife.

— You say *sir* to all officers aboard this ship, Cadiz said, watching the kid's eyes.

The kid's hand came out of his shirt and he stood up.

— Yes, *sir*, he said.

— What's your name?

— Juan Mazzoula, sir.

— You look Mexican.

— My father was Italian, sir.

— Where are your mother and father now?

— They are all home, sir, along with my brothers and sisters.

— How many of them?

—Altogether there are fifteen, sir. My mother and father were very young when they got married, sir.

—Why don't you go home?

—There is no room for me, sir.

—All right, Max, walk around the ship. Have yourself a cup of coffee, talk to the men if you can find one sober, and then make up your mind. I'll be around somewhere.

—I made up my mind already, sir.

—You'll do as I damn well tell you to do! Cadiz roared.

—Yes, sir, Max replied. *Yes, sir!*

Cadiz smiled as the boy walked off.

Six weeks now, and he was still trying to explain to the young Mexican. Below is not downstairs, Max. You say *below*.

—I call it downstairs.

—And the railing is *not* a fence.

—It's a fence to me. What's a fence anyway? To keep something out, or something in, right? So, it's there to keep us in, outa the water. It's a fence.

—But you *call* it a railing, goddammit!

—Look, Mister Cadiz, sir. All my life when I see smoke coming outa something, everybody around me calls it a chimney. I call it a chimney.

—It's the *stack!*

—Smoke comes out of it, it's a chimney.

—*Stack!*

—So, chimney stack.

—Let's start all over again, Max. The front of the boat is the bow.

—That's the sharp end, right?

—Not the sharp end, goddammit, the *bow!*

—But we're talking about the sharp end, ain't we?

—Yes, and the sharp end is called the *bow!*

—But if I say sharp end, you know what I'm talking about, don't you? Like if I say the back, why, you know I mean where the—

—The *stern,* Max. The back of the boat is the stern. Or fantail.

—The back of the boat, any way you call it, is still the back, because it ain't the front, and it ain't the sharp end, so it's the back, the part trailing behind. Where the fuss is at.

—What fuss?

—All that water mixing up, fussing.

—That's the *wake.*

—The trail of the ship. Yeah.

—*Wake,* you stupid sonofabitch!

—You don't have to get nasty, Mister Cadiz.

—Max, listen to me. If you're on the bow, on lookout, then—

—I'm at the sharp end, yes, sir, I'm with you.

—And you see a light on the starboard side. How would you report it?

—Well, I'd say I saw a light on the right.

—No, you'd say you saw a light so many points on the starboard bow, going away, or you could say you've picked up a light so many points off the starboard bow falling off, meaning that it was not crossing the sharp end. Ah, to hell with it!

Max grinned.

—Max, I want you to go downstairs to the kitchen and get me a cup of coffee. You had better come back upstairs on the left side facing the sharp end because the wind is blowing on the right side. From the back, coming in over our fuss.

—Okay, Mister Cadiz.

—*Yes, sir,* Mister Cadiz!

—Okay, yes, sir, Mister Cadiz.

—Max?

—Yeah?

—Why did you go to sea?

—See what?

—The monkey wrap his tail around the flagpole and kiss his asshole! Now git below!

—Ah, you're kidding me, Mister Cadiz. Sir.

—Hard over! Whitcomb yelled.

The stern of the vessel, maneuvering in the tight basin approaching the locks into Antwerp, was swinging dangerously close to one of their tugs. The double side-wheeler churned the water in a vain attempt to get out of the way. As Whitcomb sent the engines full ahead, the tug on the bow made stern way, trying to pull the bow around and get the stern away from the trapped tug.

— Captain Wheetcum! The Tog! the Tog! the pilot screamed. He made a grab for the telegraph and rang it full astern.

Whitcomb whirled from the outside bridge and knocked the pilot down with one blow. He rang the telegraph again. There had been so little time between the signals to the engine room that nothing had been done to alter the speed or direction of the engines.

— Elly, Cadiz yelled from the wing of the bridge, you're going to mash that tug sure as hell!

— And if I get way on her going astern, I won't be able to back off and I'll slam right into that goddam lock! Whitcomb pointed to the heavy steel locks that formed the major basin in Antwerp. The masts of fifty ships in various smaller basins were plainly visible. A goddam ocean of water comes spilling out of there and ships are hung up on the beach and Christ knows where we'd land up!

— But there are men aboard that tug! Cadiz yelled.

— Let 'em jump, Whitcomb snarled.

Hardly had Whitcomb finished—all the time moving and watching the quickening forward thrust of his ship—when there was a sound as if someone had fired a pistol. This was followed by a wrenching of metal and steel and splintering wood; all of it was shrouded in the screaming voices of men, on shore and on other small craft and on the *Indenter*. Cadiz raced below to the deck, fighting his way through his men to the railing.

The double side-wheeling tug was squashed flat against the stone wall surrounding the basin, but the men were safe and they now stood on the quay wall, shaking their fists at Whitcomb and cursing at him.

Whitcomb ordered Cadiz to return to the bridge. When Cadiz had climbed to the wheelhouse, he found Whitcomb sipping a cup of coffee and smiling easily at the pilot, whose mouth was bloody and swollen. Whitcomb offered the pilot coffee.

— Anybody hurt? Whitcomb asked Cadiz carelessly.

— No.

—Good. Didn't think there would be. Have yourself a cup of coffee.

—But—

—Howard, listen to me, Whitcomb said patiently. See this poor slob here who I had to coldcock? Well, he's responsible, not me. All I did was, in a moment of emergency, reassume command of my vessel, concerned only for the protection of my crew, my ship and my cargo. Now, if I *had* tried to save that tug, I would have been placing myself and my ticket and my ship, crew and cargo in great jeopardy. I didn't think I should do that. So now we stand having coffee, I'm waiting for the lock to open, whereupon we'll proceed inside. My ship is in good shape, and the only damage is a tug, an old tug, which is covered by insurance and will be replaced by a new one. Now, would you expect me to endanger myself, my ticket, my crew, my ship and my cargo because this stupid sonofabitch didn't know what he was doing? He loses his ticket. So what? Maybe it's better that he loses it. And he knows, too, look at him. He's not even sore about my knocking hell out of him, he's so worried. There's going to be an investigation, and he's so stupid with worry at the moment, I bet he doesn't know he lost one of his front teeth, and that I got my foot on it. Now, not only that, Howard, but we are going to come out of this clean. And we are going to get an extra week here in Antwerp, because these Belgians take a long time to investigate. As a matter of fact, we might even plan on a weekend in Paris.

Paris would always be Paris, but Whitcomb and Cadiz would never be the same. The weekend had stretched to a full week and they had sold everything they owned, their watches and all of their clothes except what they wore, and had continued their party with Jacquette and Zenia, until finally there was nothing left to sell and Jacquette and Zenia, sensing this, disappeared, leaving them near the Etoile where, pale and shaky, bearded and dirty, they waited for a family of American tourists and told them they were starving painters and got enough money to have three glasses each of red wine and a cab ride to the American Embassy, where they described how they had been beaten and robbed by thieves in Montmartre and needed train fare back to Antwerp and their ship, sailing the next day for Genoa.

— I hit the beach about a year ago, Phil Lehmer said, sipping wine, looking past Cadiz out over the Genoa Harbor and south to the Mediterranean. They sat in a café near the statue of Christopher Columbus.

— You been on the beach a whole year? How come so long?

— Genoa isn't such a bad place, Lehmer said, except that I have to live off my whore, which I don't particularly like. On the other hand, I'm lucky I got her.

— Come on, Lehmer, answer the question, Cadiz said. I'm chief mate on the *Indenter*. Got a great captain, Elly Whitcomb. Know him?

— I know Elly, Lehmer said, light breaking into his eyes for the first time since Cadiz had bumped into him on the street. So you and Elly Whitcomb are together, huh? And you chief mate. Sounds great, keed.

— I can't get you on the bridge, Cadiz said, but I'll sign you on as ordinary.

Lehmer didn't answer. He didn't seem to hear. He sipped his wine and gazed out over the harbor.

— Are you going to answer my question?

— What's the question?

— Why have you been on the beach—and of all places, Genoa—for a whole year?

— How come you're so interested, Howard?

— In the first place, Cadiz said, it isn't like you to be on the beach for so long. Second place, it isn't like you to live off a woman, especially as a pimp. Everybody gets hung up now and then and takes it where he can get it, but a year is a long time. Long enough to get you past entrance exams for the profession of pimping. Third place, you look like hell. You need a shave, your clothes are filthy and you probably haven't had a bath in six weeks, because I smell you and I'm sitting to windward.

— You still, Lehmer said, haven't said why you're interested.

— I'm interested, Cadiz said, because I sailed with you for eight months back on the *Tannerman* with Neely and Preeb and we never had any fights and we had some good times together. That's all.

—Sounds reasonable, Lehmer said. You springing for another bottle of this red?

—You want something stronger? Cadiz reached for his wallet.

—No, just the red. You'll be gone soon, and then I'll have to go back to red, and it's hard to do after drinking good stuff, so I'll just stick with it. He paused.

—It's a crazy story, he said.

—Is it true?

—It happened. Right here. You see, I'm waiting for a guy.

—Oh?

—Sounds silly, I guess.

—Not if there's a reason.

—You sure you want to hear it?

—If you tell me the whole thing and don't leave anything out.

Cadiz ordered another bottle of red. They lit cigarettes and Lehmer drank for a moment before speaking.

—My mother married young. Fifteen. She had to. She was pregnant with me, and my old man ran out on her. She got married again when she was seventeen or eighteen and had a girl with my stepfather. I didn't get along with him after I grew up. I was a snotty kid, so I quit school and ran off to sea. It's an old story. Lehmer looked at Cadiz and smiled, tipping his glass to Cadiz, who he knew had run away to sea himself.

—I liked my half sister, and after about eight or nine years, after I got my license and was on the bridge, I went back home. First time. The old man, my stepfather, had done pretty well in the stone monument business and they lived well enough. It was a pretty good reunion, and then I left and came back to sea, but not before I found out again how strong I felt about my half sister. I mean, we really cared for each other. She wasn't very pretty. Wore glasses and read a lot, and didn't have too many dates. It was sad because—well, she was a nice kid. Anyway, there was a freak accident and my mother and stepfather were killed in a trolley car smash-up one rainy day in Philly. The motorman had already used up all the sand in the box that sanded the rails and he was going too fast, couldn't make the curve. The car jumped the tracks, hit the side of a building and my folks, along with several others, were killed outright. The money of course was left to Jeannie. The monument business and cash came to about two hundred thousand. I didn't even know all this until I saw her, or we caught up with each other, a year and a half later. She sold everything and started traveling. I met her, the first time after it was over, in Paris. She hadn't changed much, except of course she had money now and lived okay and it was easy for her to have a guy around. Jeannie traveled all over Europe and I saw her again about a year later, in London, and she was pretty down. She let it all come out, about being unattractive, and when she did find a guy it was because of her money. I told her to forget about the money, come here to Italy, live easy, especially since the money really didn't mean too much to her. She still lived kinda slap-dash. For instance, she would live in a swanky hotel but wear clothes she bought off the rack. That kind of thing. She wanted me to live with her, go into business of some sort, but I was already a brine pecker by then and it was out of the question. Anyway, she took my advice, came here to Genoa, got a small room and lived like a student. She painted a little and she got to know a few people around here who thought she was a student, a poor one, and nothing else. Then she met Palmero. They fell in love. He was a stone cutter and they had that in common since she knew all about stone and that sort of thing, and she even converted to a Catholic so there wouldn't be anything standing in the way of their getting married. All of this didn't take very long. Less than six months. They set the date, and she still hadn't told him she had money. She was going to surprise him. On the day of the wedding, she took a suite in a hotel. They were going to be married in his church, then go to his house for the feast, then back to the hotel for their honeymoon. In the meantime she had moved into the hotel where he was supposed to come pick her up and take her to the church. She was dressed, she had a few friends by then, and it was all pretty good, a happy time for her. Well, came time for her future husband to show up, and he did, right on the dot, only he wasn't alone. His papa was with him, and three of his uncles and a priest. They came into the suite and laid it on the line. They knew all about the money. They knew to the penny, almost, how much she had. There would be no marriage unless she signed the contract. I said that Jeannie was not very pretty, but I never said she was stupid. She dug it right away. She'd been taken and she knew it. She begged Palmero to marry her and to hell with the family. She suggested they leave and go back to the States. He refused. Then they all started to work on her. You don't really appreciate what that means unless you've lived with Italians for a while. Palmero, the father, the uncles and the priest, all trying to force her to sign the contract—which would have put Palmero in control of every dime she had. All this was done in front of quite a few witnesses, because as soon as Jeannie found out what was up, she called a few of her friends inside. They yelled and screamed at her for nearly six hours. There she was, dressed in her wedding gown, everybody all dolled up to go to church, and then—no dice. Well, she finally got it through her head that Palmero was nothing but a pawn of his family and that he was doing the whole thing at their instruction, so she excused herself, walked to the window and jumped. Five floors.

Lehmer paused, drained his glass and looked at Cadiz.

—Nobody knows but you. I don't know why I told you. I'm glad it was you, though, instead of that pig I sleep with who supports me. Or some of the beachies I see drifting around here—bums, like me, but without any reason for being on the beach.

—And you're waiting for Palmero? Cadiz asked.

—Waiting for Palmero, Lehmer said. I've had to be very careful about this. Nobody knows who I am. Different last names, see. No connection. I hit the beach after I piled off an Export that ran over here from New York. I had cash and I just played it like a beachie who keeps hanging around after his money has run out. I shacked up with this broad I'm with and finally got the whole story in bits and pieces.

—Where is he now?

—Here, in Genoa. He's been working for the past six months in Milan on some kind of building. I had plenty of time.

—You going to kill him?

—I thought that was going to be the way for a long time, but then I found out he's going to get married.

—Oh?

—Yeah, a beautiful girl from San Remo. Everything's been set. Banns posted, contracts signed, the works. They've only been delaying it until he gets back from Milan with his money from the building job.

— What are you going to do?

Lehmer looked Cadiz dead in the eye.

— Guess.

— I can't, Cadiz said, backing away from what he judged to be a very accurate guess.

— I'm going to give him one night, the first night, with his beautiful bride from San Remo, so that the contracts can't be broken. After that one night—see, I've learned a few things in the year I've been a beachie—after that one night, if he tries to back out or leaves her, every one of her relatives will be after him. No, I'm going to fix him, but not until after that first night. He's going to live with her the rest of his life and he'll never be able to get it up again.

— Jesus, Cadiz said.

— And I'm going to tell him that it's for Jeannie. It'll be dark, he'll never know who it was. But he'll know why.

Lehmer took another sip of wine. He stood and held out his hand.

— Maybe we'll ship out again, somehow or somewhere along the line, after I'm finished here.

Cadiz shook hands with him.

— Here comes my pig, Lehmer said, nodding toward a thick-ankled woman with large hips and a sullen mouth. I'd introduce you, but I don't want any connection with me and any of my friends.

— Lehmer, are you really going to do it? Cadiz asked.

— Bet on it. He turned quickly and shambled off to meet the approaching woman.

— Falls of that sort always kill 'em, Howard, Whitcomb said. They looked down at the A.B. crumpled on the deck. They hit a steel deck and if they're lucky they land on their head so they don't have to suffer.

— He just didn't follow the rule, a voice said in back of them on the crowded deck. All work on the ship had stopped. In the distance there was a siren wailing, but it was no use. The man was plainly dead.

— What rule is that? another voice asked.

— When aloft, there's only one way to be. One hand working for the company, and one hand hanging on for me.

— I saw a sailor fall once, from the cross trees, and he saw that he was falling and pushed off, like he was diving, trying to get over the side into the water.

— What happened? Did he make it?

— Yeah, he made it over the side all right, but it was the pier side, and he hit the concrete floor, which made it another thirty feet down.

— I'll bet he was one surprised sonofabitch.

— Or disappointed.

— Yeah, real disappointed.

Tahiti was the mirage in all sailors' dreams. There was Paris, which was good but expensive, and a conflict between the very good booze and pretty good women; there was New York, which was very good for women and not so good for booze, and too expensive; London, Liverpool, Manchester, Glasgow, all inexpensive, but poor in women, booze *and* food; Hamburg, good for beer and fat women and fat sausages; Marseilles, not good for anything at all; Hong Kong, good for everything; all of Japan, very good for food and women, but poor on booze; Honolulu, not very good for anything because of the Army and Navy; and generally speaking, most of the ports east of Suez were considered pretty fair. But none of them, or any combination of them, came close to a layover in Papeete, and there was nearly always a layover because if there was anything needed to be done to the ship, it was saved for Papeete.

— Elly? Cadiz stood in the doorway of the captain's cabin. Whitcomb, his great bulk making the bed sag, a pair of steel-rimmed glasses hanging on the end of his red, bulbous nose, read a mystery magazine held propped with one hand on his huge chest, while his other arm dangled toward the deck to an ice bucket full of beer. He peered at Cadiz over the glasses.

— Yeah?

They had been at sea for seven days, bound east from Papeete for Rio de Janeiro around the Cape, with Australian wool taken from a

Sydney freighter which had lost its propeller. The *Indenter* rolled languidly in the Pacific swells.

—We have two problems, Cadiz said.

—Well? Whitcomb snapped his glasses off and heaved himself to the side of the bed. His feet dangled near the ice bucket. You got the clap from your Papeetebaby?

—No, I didn't get the clap from my Papeetebaby. That would please you, wouldn't it?

Whitcomb wrinkled his nose and opened a beer, handing it to Cadiz. He opened another for himself.

—It can't be too serious or you wouldn't be standing there gaping at me. A conscientious mate like you is a boon to a weathering old captain like myself. I don't know what I'd do without you, Howard. That's a fact.

—Up yours, Cadiz said amiably. You want 'em both at once or one at a time? You're going to pee green, I promise you.

Elisha Whitcomb swilled his beer.

—Roll 'em.

—You remember that Papeetebaby that Mylross was shacking up with?

—Yeah? Whitcomb said guardedly, not liking the tone of Howard's voice. I remember. Why?

—She's in the galley having a cup of coffee.

—*What!* Beer shot out of Whitcomb's nose. He coughed and gagged and Howard had to pound him on the back until he was breathing normally again.

—I'll break that sonofabitch's head for him! Whitcomb roared. Bringing a broad aboard and—a stowaway, by God!

—Here, put your shorts on, Cadiz said, kicking the underpants toward the naked captain. Remember, we have ladies aboard.

—I'll keelhaul the punk! Jesus Christ! And where are we going? *Brazil!* It takes four days just to enter port with a healthy crew and sound cargo and everything in order! They don't even *have* regulations for illegal entry into Brazil! They make 'em stay on board the ship. *That* means she'll have to ride—Whitcomb had pulled on his trousers and was stuffing a shirt into his waist when he stopped abruptly. *Ladies?*

Cadiz held up two fingers.

— I'll kill him. I'll kill him with my bare hands! I knew that goddam Mylross was some kind of—

Cadiz grabbed Whitcomb by the arm.

— Hold on, Elly, wait until you hear the whole story.

— *Two* broads! Who else is in on this?

— Elly, now shut up a minute and listen to me.

— Get a cable off to Papeete, tell 'em we got two of their Papeetebabies aboard and we're putting back. Then send a cable to O'Hara, tell 'em—Oh, Jesus! tell 'em—tell 'em we busted a boiler. Yeah, that's it. A busted boiler and we're putting back to Papeete, and *don't* send the cable to Papeete. We'll just sneak them ashore and nobody will ever be the wiser.

— Are you finished, captain?

— Did Mylross really sneak two broads aboard? Jesus! A skinny little guy like that! Well, you never know. I heard stories about skinny guys being billygoats. But, Jees, one Papeetebaby is usually enough for a good strong man, but *two!*

— Will you shut up! Cadiz said. They might hear you down below.

— Okay, okay, but get on with it.

— Mylross is in love.

— Oh, Christ.

— Deeply in love with his Papeetebaby, and since she was in love with him, naturally she accepted his invitation to stow away on your ship and go back to the States and build a happy and prosperous life in the farm-supply business in Petite Falls, Kansas—

— Petite Falls? Kansas?

— It's a natural spring four feet high, Cadiz explained, deadpan. Some of our illustrious forefathers watered their stock there as they drove west through the Indian country.

— Never mind the goddam history, get on with it. *Two!*

— So, Papeetebaby Mylross, using good logic, foresees that she will be lonely in Petite Falls, Kansas, and invites her sister to come along too. Just to have somebody to talk to during the long summer nights, when Mylross is out delivering a wagonload of grade-A horseshit to the local farmers.

— Sure, sure, I can understand *that!* Whyn't you say so in the first place. Sure, the little thing would be lonely. Very considerate of Mylross to think of it. That all?

— Not—quite, Elly, Howard Cadiz said.

— If you tell me they brought the mother or an aunt or their grandmother, Cadiz, so help me I'll throw Mylross over the side.

Cadiz smiled. Well, it's not *exactly* a grandmother, or aunt, or mother—

— Then what the fuck is it *exactly!* Whitcomb roared.

— Well, Papeetebaby Mylross's sister—

— Yeah?

— is going to have a baby. Cadiz looked at his watch. In about four hours. Labor pains have already started. As a matter of fact, that's how she was discovered.

— She is *not* going to have a *baby* on *my* ship!

— Will you come down below, Captain Whitcomb, and pay a call on the expectant mother? It's her first, and she's a little worried. And she's such a little thing—

— You sonofabitch! Whitcomb hurled the beer bottle at Cadiz, who ducked. The bottle splintered against the bulkhead in the companionway.

The steam whistle blew suddenly, making them both jump.

— What's that! Whitcomb jumped to the porthole.

— Noon, Cadiz said. We always blow the whistle at noon, captain. It was your order. Will you make your duty call now?

Huge shoulders sagging, his face red and unshaved, Whitcomb jammed his bridge hat onto his head and stepped out of the cabin.

— How long you say we got? Whitcomb asked as they went below.

— Four hours, Cadiz said.

The usual clutter and yammer around the galley and the messroom at noon were missing. Whitcomb took note of the silence and the emptiness, pretending not to see the heads peering around corners at him as he moved toward the fo'c'sle of Able Seaman Mylross.

After reading every scrap of information about childbirth that they had on the ship, they were more confused than ever.

The crew mess had been turned into an operating room, with Cadiz's mattress—which was wider and longer than the bunk mattresses of the crew—placed on the table and secured with line. There were stacks of clean sheets and towels nearby. The entire contents of the medicine chest had been brought in and made ready. While the chief engineer supervised the setting up of the operating room and the second mate sat with the expectant mother, timing the labor pains with a chronometer, Cadiz and Whitcomb had taken over the saloon. They used the menu blackboard for diagrams to illustrate what they understood from the material they had read.

— "The first stages of labor produce uterine contractions of about twenty to thirty minutes and last about a minute or less. Labor pains produce two effects: first, they compress the cavity enclosing the child, and second, since it is completely enclosed, and there is but one opening, the cervix—"

Whitcomb, seated at a table, a cigar clamped in his teeth, a bottle of gin at his elbow, looked up over his glasses at Cadiz. What the fuck's a cervix?

— Just a minute. Cadiz flipped the dictionary at his side. He thumbed through pages, stopped, looked up at Whitcomb and said cheerfully, the mouth of the womb.

— Ya sure?

— Read, dammit, we're losing time.

Whitcomb turned back to the medical book. He cleared his throat, paused, took a slug of gin from the bottle and continued reading.

— "Labor pains, when it is a first-born, last from twelve to fourteen hours. These labor pains, or contractions of the uterus, force the bag of waters and the child downward."

— That would be toward the cervix, Cadiz said.

— The mouth of the womb, right?

— Right.

Whitcomb had another shot of gin.

— "If the cervix is excessively scarred from previous births and/or operations, a delay may be anticipated in the dilation of the cervix—" Whitcomb tore off his glasses and glared at Cadiz. Why can't they say mouth of the womb, or opening of the womb, if that's what they mean!

— Because Latin is a language which cuts past language barriers. If you say cervix to a Polish doctor or a Chinese doctor or any kind of medical man, he knows right away what you mean. If you said mouth of the womb, he'd look at you and shake his head and offer you a Coca-Cola.

— Okay, okay.

— Keep reading, dammit, Cadiz said.

Whitcomb put his glasses back on, picked up the book and continued.

— "A premature escape of waters may effect a closing of the cervix around the head of the child, making a descent into the pelvis difficult and prolonged." What does *that* mean?

— The child has to move through the dilated cervix at the time the waters are released. It's water pressure and—well, it sort of greases his movement.

— Okay. Got it. "When the cervix is broken and the waters issue forth, it is an aid to have the mother bear down, in effect, help force the child into birth." He looked at Cadiz. Clear?

— Clear. She's got to strain.

— Right. She's got to strain. Whitcomb continued to read, following the lines with his finger. He tore his glasses off and squinted accusingly at Cadiz. She's got to take a breath between each labor pain, between each bearing down. It's important, the straining. It helps a hundred percent.

— Okay.

— Got that?

— Yeah!

— "Usually the head of the child will rotate slightly, so that the occiput"—what's that?

— The head, the back of the head.

— You know for sure?

— I know. Keep reading, Elly, f'Christ sake!

The door to the saloon opened and the second mate poked his head in. He was white-faced and nervous. He held a chronometer in his hand.

— We're down to seven minutes thirty-five seconds point five. I ran it out on the exponential curve. We're picking up speed vertically.

— Okay, okay, we ain't finished. Get back to her, Whitcomb snapped.

The second mate, a hurt look on his face, vanished.

Whitcomb read on.

— "The occiput will turn slightly to the left side of the mother (the right side of the operator) while the body, still within the sac, will be turned slightly to the right side of the mother."

Cadiz got up and began to draw a diagram, side view, of the position of the child on the menu board. Whitcomb read the passage again and Howard checked it. It seemed right. They read once again.

— Okay, I got it, Cadiz said.

— "The child then starts into the birth canal and moves toward the birth canal, with the head of the infant, the longest diameter of the infant into longest diameter of the pelvis—"

Again Whitcomb stopped. Cadiz drew another diagram on the menu board. They discussed the meaning and definition of the two described diameters and were almost satisfied they understood what was going on.

She screamed. Cadiz, Whitcomb and the mother, who lay supine on the table, were the only ones in the crew mess. They had opened the books to the pages studied, and after a long debate about giving the mother an anesthetic in the last stage, decided against it since they felt it was important for her to bear down.

Cadiz and Whitcomb, both dressed in clean white trousers and mess jackets from the steward's department, sweated and soothed the fifteen-year-old girl twisting in pain.

— Okay! Here come the waters! Cadiz said. Stand by to lend a hand!

— Jesus! Whitcomb said under his breath.

— Here comes his chin! Cadiz announced. What does it say about his chin? There was something about his goddam chin—

Whitcomb hastily scanned the pages.

— "If the birth is a face presentation, and the chin is the first to emerge through the vulvo-vaginal orifice, *it will be an easy birth!*" Whitcomb's voice rose triumphantly.

Cadiz held the head in his hand and rotated it slightly to the left, toward the inner side of the mother's right thigh. Slowly, first one shoulder, then the second, followed. At last Cadiz held the slippery child in his hands.

— All right, Elly, quick now, two half hitches on a short lead, close to his belly—

— It's a her! Not a him!

— Two half hitches, dammit!

The cord cut, Whitcomb supplied two knots slipped down close to the infant's stomach. No doctor could have done it better as the old sailor's fingers secured the line. Cadiz held the girl up by the heels and spanked her smartly. Once, twice. The baby coughed and cried lustily.

The party went on for twelve hours. The fires had been stoked and two white lights hoisted forward of the mast indicated to any passing vessel that there was no control to the ship. The *Indenter* drifted twelve hours in the open ocean as the entire crew, roaring drunk, paused to celebrate the birth of a girl, five pounds, five ounces (as nearly as they could figure on the galley meat scales) and so duly recorded in the ship's log, Captain Elisha Whitcomb and Chief Officer Howard Cadiz attending.

There was really nothing for Whitcomb to do but turn around and take Papeetebaby, Pateetebaby's sister and her daughter back to Tahiti. The girls were content to return; the trouble came from Mylross.

They had cleared the return of the stowaways and the newborn infant with the officials, leaving the question of French or United States citizenship for young Elisha Howard Soonbinkuk to be decided later. And then Mylross asked to be paid off in Papeete.

— But it ain't even your kid, Whitcomb said. It ain't even the kid of the woman you so dippy about.

— I don't care, captain, Mylross said. If you don't let me go, I'll jump over the side and swim for it.

— Mylross, Whitcomb said with genuine disgust in his voice, you are a goddam fool. How long do you think it will take you to get tired of your Papeetebaby? And saddled with your sister-in-law's kid? Ever think of that? Besides, I can't pay you off here. You'll have to jump ship, and if you do, then you get nothing.

— I'm going, captain, Mylross said stubbornly.

— The French aren't very partial to beachies cluttering up their islands without money, Whitcomb warned.

— And if I was sick, captain? Mylross said. Wouldn't you have to pay me off and put me in a hospital?

— Yes, Whitcomb said sourly, but you ain't sick.

— Okay, captain, Mylross said. Thank you, sir.

Twenty minutes later Cadiz entered Whitcomb's office and began going through the desk, pulling out papers. Whitcomb came out of the shower and stared.

— What the hell are you doing? Whitcomb asked.

— Got a man for the hospital, Cadiz said.

— Who? What happened?

— Mylross just broke his leg.

— He *what?*

— Nice and gory a compound fracture as I've ever seen. Stuck his leg in the fiddley door, then slammed it.

— That sonofabitch! Whitcomb said. That love-sick sonofabitch. Ain't it horrible what a man will do when he gets hung up on one particular piece of tail?

— It is, Cadiz agreed. But it's kind of beautiful too, in a way.

— Yeah, it *is* kinda beautiful, Whitcomb agreed. Then he saw that Cadiz was laughing at him. You bastard! I'll bet you told him what to do!

— No, I didn't, Cadiz said. But I won over two hundred bucks giving two to one that he *would* do something, with the understanding, of course, that Mylross and I would split fifty-fifty. The betting was pretty hot for a while. You missed out on a good thing, captain.

They deposited Mylross in the hospital and continued their voyage around the Horn. They unloaded their wool, took on Argentine hides for Japan and recovered their course across the Pacific. Then they began coastal runs from Tokyo to Manila to Shanghai to Saigon to Singapore back to Hong Kong and then another trackless run to Central America.

Reading manifest, Cadiz sat in his room, his mind only half involved with the customs house information, the sweat pouring from his body in steady streams. He swore that he would not take another shower. It would do no good, he knew. He had taken six showers since eight that morning. He threw the manifest to one side, not at all happy about the prospect of sitting in Puntarenas, Costa Rica, with hundred-degree heat and frequent rains for at least three weeks. He had been to Puntarenas once before. The port city was nearly fifty miles inside the Gulf of Nicoya, and landlocked on the Pacific side by the Nicoya Peninsula, which dog-legged out from the Central American coast and successfully blocked whatever good breezes there might be.

It was going to be hot and it was going to stay hot. There had already been one fight in the crew mess that morning. And, he thought, they had not even got alongside yet but were still riding on the hook, waiting for Customs and Immigration. During the day he could keep the crew under control by putting them to work over the side. The steady, chipping hammer noises broke the otherwise monotonous buzz and cry of the bumboats which circled well away from the ship; they would stay there until the yellow Q flag had come down and the Customs and Immigration officials had departed. It would be impossible, Cadiz knew, to keep the crew from sneaking rum aboard. After the fist fight in the crew mess, he had warned them that he would log anybody found with a bottle: twelve days' pay for one, plus restriction to the ship. It was a futile gesture. He knew from his own experience that they would figure out ways to get their grog.

Around him was the unnatural quiet of the ship riding at anchor after the seventy-seven-day crossing from Hong Kong. It carried a complete coffee railroad including a steam engine, tender, twenty-eight flatcars and carriages, sixty miles of single track and heavy-duty I-beams upon which hoists could be rigged for repairs in the shop. The railroad was close to thirty years old and had been part of a spur off the Hong Kong–Canton line which had fallen into the hands of speculators who sold it right off the ground to a combine in Puntarenas. The Costa Rican agents had wanted the Chinese laborers to salvage the spikes from the crossties, building huge bonfires and not realizing that when the fires cooled the spikes would crumble. It had been a hell of a job loading, and Whitcomb, who was floating around somewhere in a Chinese bumboat with a White Russian Princess (she said), had not showed up until the day they started loading the rails.

— How many pounds to the yard of rail? Elly had demanded of the shipper.

— Thirty miles exactly, captain, the Costa Rican agent, a withered, thin-skinned Chinese, replied.

— How many pounds to the yard of rail!

— Not more than seventy-five, captain.

— Howard?

— Right here, Elly.

— Don't load a goddam rail until you've sawed exactly one yard off the end of one and weighed it! Call me when you're finished.

— Where are you going?

— Back ashore, after I take a shower and shave. Call me.

It had taken two hours to get the cutting torch to work, and when the piece was cut, with the stevedores waiting and the Chinese agent screaming that they were destroying property, Cadiz called Whitcomb. Dressed in his best blues with new gold braid, Whitcomb had weighed the railing on his own bathroom scale.

— Eighty pounds! he said. That's the way you figure it, Howard. One thousand seven hundred and sixty yards to the mile, eighty pounds a yard, comes to—Whitcomb rolled his head back, closed his eyes and within seconds snapped them open—one hundred forty thousand and eight hundred pounds, divided by two thousand pounds to the ton, gives you—

— Not eighty pounds, you cheat, you cheat. Seventy-five, seventy-five. You take too big piece!

— Seventy and four tenths tons per mile, Howard. You load sixty miles of single rails and you put four thousand two hundred and twenty-four tons aboard, and not another goddam rail.

— But dammit, I never stowed rails before! Cadiz yelled as Whitcomb strolled off to a waiting rickshaw.

— You'll work it out, Whitcomb called back. I have great faith in you, Howard. You're a real conscientious sailor.

Whitcomb had not returned until an hour before sailing and had not even bothered to check the cargo. He was so hung he could hardly write his name on the insurance bill of lading.

Both Cadiz and Whitcomb happened to be taking a shower at the same time when the Costa Rican Customs and Immigration came aboard, starched and white and polite, only to be greeted by a buck-naked captain dressed in a cigar and a bridge hat. There was no sickness, there had been none, they had had a quiet crossing. The rough log was brought out for the Health Officer to check. There was no contraband aboard. The ship's manifest was handed over to the Customs man, who then turned and nodded to his crew of three inspectors, who went about their work, searching the crew's quarters like children looking for Easter eggs. Immigration was a checking of the crew list and inspection of passports of three of the aliens sailing. Finally, coffee, sandwiches and brandy were served on the captain's bridge. Whitcomb had succumbed to protocol and put on a pair of shorts.

At five that afternoon, when the land breeze might have come up for them, it began to rain, and it was then that the pilot and tug came out for them. The crew worked in the hot muggy drizzle for two hours as the ship was tied up.

Whitcomb, as usual, was the first ashore. Dressed in the white British shorts and Cubana jacket that he affected in the tropics, he looked trim and healthy.

— You oughta make more seventy-seven-day crossings, Elly. You lost about forty pounds, Cadiz told him as he saw him off.

— It'll never happen again, Whitcomb said, brushing back a fine red beard he had grown during the trip. It smelled strongly of shaving lotion and tobacco.

— How's that?

— That Russian Princess and me got so drunk that last couple of days I forgot to lay in my usual supply of booze. Why, did you know, Whitcomb said in aggrieved tones, that the last six weeks I was down to less than a pint a day?

— I didn't know, Cadiz said, but you should try it again.

Humming merrily to himself, Elisha Whitcomb descended the gangway, his pockets full of money, his confidence brimming, his appetite set to a fine edge. He lunged into a waiting cab and was whisked away. Cadiz turned to the beaming face of the new owner of the railroad below decks.

— Why is there a delay in unloading, Meester Mate?

— Mister Acosta, do you see any cranes on the docks?

— No, how could I, Mister Acosta smiled. There are none.

— Exactly so, Mister Acosta. And that means your railroad is going to be unloaded with the ship's cranes—the booms, here, there and there. Cadiz pointed to them. My crew will have to operate those cranes, Mister Acosta.

— But they are all going ashore! Mister Acosta said.

— Yes, and they will be back tomorrow, or the next day, and then your railroad will be unloaded.

— But that is stupid! Mister Acosta said. Cadiz looked balefully at him.

— I insist that work start immediately!

— You are not in a position to insist, Cadiz said.

— Where is your captain?

— He's probably, at this moment, entering the bar of your best hotel or restaurant, where he is going to get hopelessly drunk.

Mister Acosta was quite used to getting his way. I can very easily have your captain arrested, Meester Mate, and brought back to the ship. Also members of your crew.

— That would be unwise, Mister Acosta.

— I want work to start immediately!

— Mister Acosta, my crew has just spent seventy-seven days in passage from the far east. They are not peons, or serfs, or Indians whom you can abuse and order about. They're sailors. Seventy-seven days is a long time. Now, if I insisted they start to work today, they would be nasty, fights would break out, they would sneak bottles aboard and drink while they worked, endangering lives, your railroad, the ship and the unloading gear. This is an old ship. If something vital breaks, we will have to send back to the States for spare parts. That would take weeks. Perhaps months. But, if I let my crew go ashore for a day or two, let them get drunk and relax and discover that they are still part of the human race, why, when they return to the ship they'll be ready to do a full day's work and then go ashore at night. Doesn't it make sense to you?

— I am not concerned with the problems of your position, Meester Mate. I want my cargo delivered *now!* Or there will be serious, very serious, reactions to your men ashore.

— All right, you can have the captain arrested and brought back to the ship. You can also have the crew arrested. I grant that you may have such authority—

— I do, I assure you, Meester Mate.

— Granted. Cadiz smiled. No contest. Now, you get everybody back on the ship. How are you going to make them work?

— You will make them work, Mister Acosta said.

— No, Mister Acosta, I won't. I wouldn't even if I could.

— You refuse? Acosta asked tightly.

— I already told you what I was going to do.

— Then I shall have no recourse, Mister Acosta said.

— Just a minute, I'll go with you.

— With me?

— I might as well start the legal machinery going. You can drop me off at the American Consul.

Acosta hesitated. He made one last attempt.

— I am related to the American Consul, and—

Cadiz cut him off.

— I don't give a shit if he's your brother. When I walk into his office, chief officer from an American flagship vessel and ask him for protection and guarantees, he will see that I get them. Your threats of arrest, your power, nothing you can do or say or threaten will stop me from getting those protections and those guarantees.

Acosta nodded slightly. But I can see to it that your crew is restricted to the ship for the duration of your stay here.

— All right, you can do that, too. But if you do, every man will refuse to work.

— Wouldn't that be mutiny?

— Not if the captain orders them not to work.

— Would the captain be so stupid?

— That's the second time you've used that word. I wouldn't advise using it again. And to answer your question, why don't you ask him?

I've told you where to find him. Though I wouldn't advise it. Evidently you don't know what kind of authority you're dealing with. Don't you know about maritime law? A captain is the only power aboard his ship. The crew can be returned to the ship and you can post a guard at the gangway so no one can get off. But that won't get your railroad unloaded. The crew will sneak bottles of your rum aboard and get drunk, no work will be done for days, and your railroad will still be sitting in the holds.

— I will have our soldiers unload!

— The minute you do that, the insurance company will cancel your policy, and with inexperienced men working cargo, you might wind up with your railroad in the water. And the first soldier that comes aboard, armed, forcing access to this vessel, has committed piracy. He can be shot down or given a trial and hung, or sent to prison for a long term, all of which will still not get your railroad on the dock any sooner.

— You are talking a great deal, Meester Mate! I want action.

— Oh, I'm enjoying this. You see, I don't give a damn what you do. As a matter of fact, it might be interesting to see just how things would turn out. So do what you want, Mister Acosta. You can try force, or legal means. I couldn't care less.

— But you are supposed to care!

— No, just get the stuff here and unload it. It's here and I'm going to unload it. But not yet. It'll take us three weeks to unload. Now, suppose that we lose two or three days up front, that makes it eighteen days left, right? So, by the time we get to the other end of those eighteen days, my crew, my captain and myself will be so goddam sick and tired of you, your country, your women and your climate that in the last two days, a week's work will be done just to get away from here.

Cadiz pushed back from the railing and flicked the sweat out of his eyes. At that moment the chief engineer waddled down the deck and moved quickly to the gangway.

— That is the chief engineer, Mister Acosta. Hey, chief!

The chief engineer did not stop in his progress to the dock.

— When are you coming back? Cadiz yelled after him.

The chief engineer did not reply, but kept moving steadily toward a waiting cab.

— Come back in about two days, Mister Acosta. We should be ready to unload about then. Excuse me, but I've got to rinse off. And he left Mister Acosta standing alone on the deck near the gangway while he climbed to take another shower, swearing to himself that it would be the last he would ever take.

— Drag him to his fo'c'sle, Cadiz said to the sailor who had brought the bosun back to the ship. And make sure he doesn't get anything else to drink tonight. Let him sleep it off.

The sailor mumbled something, heaved the bosun up, and, hardly able to walk himself, half dragged, half carried the babbling, sodden man down the companionway.

Cadiz glanced at his watch. It was 3 A.M. and he had been checking the return of the crew for the last three hours. He did not expect there would be many more. Those that had not returned to the ship would have found themselves something to shack up with for the night and would not, in all probability, show until the second morning. They would be drunk, snarling, scrapping, half-crazed with the cheap Coffeegop and rum, which, when used in mixed drinks, and especially in this heat, was an alcoholic bomb. But luckily he had only had to deal with one serious fight since midnight. Skonk, an oiler, and a wiper, facing each other with knives, had been so drunk he had had no trouble sneaking up behind the wiper and knocking him out while explaining to Skonk that it was necessary to save the unconscious man's life.

— You'd have killed him, Skonk, Cadiz said to the truculent oiler. You're so much stronger than he is, I didn't want to see you go to the chair.

It pacified the man, but then Cadiz had to listen to a half hour's drunken bragging about the oiler's days in Indiana, where on Saturday nights farm boys would drink and fight and go looking for girls they never found and end up fighting with knives to relieve their frustrations. Cadiz believed most of it, except the part about knives. Many men carried them, but he knew from experience that there were very few who ever actually pressed an argument by using them.

A man, he had observed over the years, drew a knife as an impulsive gesture; it was meant mainly to intimidate. But if the other drew a knife, both would grow quiet. They would often turn pale and circle and circle, waiting for someone to intervene. Only in rare situations had he ever had two knife fighters refuse to drop their weapons when ordered to do so. As a rule the contestants were almost eager, afterwards, to continue their fight with fists, which, after all, could not *kill*.

Finally getting Skonk into his fo'c'sle, Cadiz closed the door, only to have it snatched open by the oiler who wanted to go ashore and get another drink. Tired, depressed, irritated by the long day and Mister Acosta and the heat and having to stay aboard while everyone else was ashore, Cadiz threw a short, jolting left that caught the oiler on the chin. The man went down and out. There wasn't even any blood.

He sat in the saloon sipping rancid coffee and trying to decide if he could sleep. His thoughts were quick and nervous, a sure sign that he was overtired. He knew then, suddenly feeling it overwhelm him, that he would sleep and sleep soundly. Relieved and even pleased with this prospect, he walked out onto the deck, making a last check on the lines, the skies, and then back into the midship housing.

He stopped, not quite sure what he was seeing. Then he realized that it *was* the wiper he had knocked out, staggering toward him, bleeding from several places in his chest. The man held his chest, as if trying to hold the blood inside, reaching out toward Cadiz with the free hand.

—Mis—Cadiz—the sonofabitch stuck me! He took a step and Cadiz lunged forward as the man collapsed head first in his arms.

The man sagged and Cadiz held him, looking down at the sweaty, oily head that reeked of brilliantine. He eased the heavy body to the deck and quickly examined the wounds. He felt the pulse. There was none. He listened for the heart, putting his ear next to the bloody mess. The heart was still. There was no breath. Cadiz ripped a cigarette free of tobacco and held the delicate paper over the wiper's nostrils. It did not move.

Cadiz wiped the blood from his cheekbone with his handkerchief, feeling his throat turn dry and cottony. He walked directly to the bridge deck and Whitcomb's cabin. He snapped on the lights, stepped to the safe, spun the dial, reached inside and closed his hand around the butt of a heavy .45 pistol. He checked the chamber, closed the safe, snapped out the lights and returned below. He went first to Skonk's fo'c'sle, eased the door open and looked down into the bunk. The light was on, but the bunk was empty. The entire fo'c'sle was deserted. There was a knife on the deck, and even in the dim light he could see the smear of blood on the blade and handle.

He stepped back out into the companionway, turned left, saw nothing, turned right and spotted the oiler thirty-five or forty feet away near the end of the companionway. The light from the galley, casting a shadow on the steel screening covering the open serving tables, created a tic-tac-toe pattern on the oiler's face. They stood facing each other at opposite ends of the companionway, which was not more than thirty inches wide.

— All right, Skonk, Cadiz said. He raised the gun as if on a pistol range, arm extended, hammer back, sighting down the barrel.

The man took a step forward. In the change of position, new light was cast on him from the galley. Cadiz saw the knife in Skonk's hand.

— Drop the knife, Skonk, Cadiz said.

The man took another step forward.

— Drop the knife, Skonk, Cadiz said again. He had the man sighted on the middle of his chest. If you move again, I'll kill you.

The oiler hesitated a moment, then lunged forward in a crouch, his arm extended, the knife held as far forward as he could get it.

Cadiz depressed the barrel of the gun several inches and fired. Skonk stopped as if he had run into a wall. His forward momentum and the force of the bullet acting against each other brought him upright. As Cadiz waited, ready to fire again, his arm still outstretched, Skonk stood straight, almost at attention, then fell forward. He was fifteen feet away, his arm outflung, his hand relaxed. The knife slid to a stop at Cadiz's feet.

The pistol shot reverberated in the narrow companionway against the steel bulkheads. Cadiz slowly lowered his arm and walked forward. No one came to investigate. The sanitation pump kicked over and whined, threw the piston and was silent.

—Hello, Shad, Cadiz said, looking down at Skonk. Now I'm a member of the club. I've killed my first one.

—First time in my life I ever been laid off, Whitcomb said, standing with Cadiz at the railing of the *Indenter*, moored alongside the Atlantic Coastline Railroad Docks in Savannah. The city, set against a deep red late-afternoon sun, was upriver. Howard Cadiz could see no change in the skyline. Their bags were packed, and boxes and suitcases were stacked in piles on the deck near the gangway.

—I wish they'd let us sail her on to Barcelona instead of bringing their own crew over here, Cadiz said. We deserved it after that miserable unloading job.

He glanced below. The unfamiliar ring of Spanish in his ears was caught and wafted up into the hot, humid air like a spiraling leaf. The formalities had just been concluded. The rest of the crew had been paid off and Cadiz and Whitcomb were the only ones left. The ship was now a Spanish flagship vessel, and he and Whitcomb were out of jobs. The Spanish captain, an elderly man of seventy with a silvery white beard and a sly way about him that was full of humor and some sadness, was now Master of the *Indenter* renamed the *Azuaga*.

—Economics, Whitcomb said. He took a gulp of beer and belched. Suppose we had sailed her to Barcelona, the company would have had to send us back here to the States at least tourist class. For a crew of thirty-five or forty, that would mean a lot of money. But this way, they only sent the captain, one man, tourist class and the rest of the crew, mates, engineers, came over steerage. Quite a saving. Besides, what kind of chance do you think you'd have getting another ship in Europe? The people over there are starving to death. You've seen 'em. Why, mates and skippers in those countries would slit your throat if you were to take a job away from them. They're not shipping anything out. They're shipping it in. That is, when they have credit to pay for it.

—You think this Depression's going to be any different here in the States?

—It doesn't bother *me* worth a damn, Howard. I been squirreling it away for years! I'll just go home to Sara and the two boys and that beautiful farm of mine in Lancaster, Pee A., and wait 'til the phone rings.

Cadiz grunted. You might have a long wait.

— Naw, not too long, Howard. Mark my words. Not too long. There's going to be another war in Europe before you can snap your fingers, then we'll be right back out there supplying them and feeding them. Won't be long.

— You really think there's going to be another war?

— Howard, wars and political change are caused by only one thing. Economics. And economics broken down to the poor bastards like you and me and the gun-toting soldier means food, clothes, a house and maybe a little something left over for a Saturday night bottle. Now, you've seen those people over there. Just about every country you've been to in the last few years is starving to death. Only this time, it's going to be a rootin' tootin' sonofabitch of a war, I *mean!* You can make some of the people kiss your ass some of the time, but you can't make all of them kiss your ass all of the time. This next war is going to be from below, not from above. Then we'll get ships. We'll get ships, Whitcomb said firmly, in a way that Cadiz had never heard him speak before. And we'll get them *before* the shooting starts, because there isn't a gun in Europe that's worth a damn and they've got to have guns first. So I figure we should start getting ships in about two years. I mean, get a ship *easy* in about two years. Not more.

— Those are my own sentiments, Captain Whitcomb, Captain Mundano said behind them. And I am sorry that I have taken your ship from you. His chief mate was with him, a tall thin man nearing fifty with dark circles under his eyes and long lines that cut deeply at the corners of his mouth.

— Don't be sorry, man! Whitcomb said with a smile. Hell, I can get a ship any time I want it, but it's about time I go home to my wife and family for a while. I have a farm, see. Bought it a long time ago and it's a good running place now.

— You are very fortunate man, Captain Whitcomb.

— There's our cab, Elly, Cadiz said.

They shook hands all around.

As Whitcomb and Cadiz rode up the waterfront, Whitcomb slapped Cadiz on the knee.

— We had us some good times, didn't we, Howard?

— Yeah.

— This is your hometown, ain't it?

— Yeah.

— Good to be home?

Cadiz didn't answer. They were climbing the cobblestoned, snake-like street around the gas tanks and the old foundry of faded red brick. Was it good to be home? He thought about this as they climbed on up the bay front to Bay Street, going west. He was not surprised that he had no personal feeling about the town. He had cut it out of himself years before. But there *was* the familiar, and he had learned that the familiar was a good substitute for the personal. When he saw the Bay Front Park with its lush green and multi-colored flowers, it was familiar to him, just as the gardens outside of Arles in France were familiar to him. And this gave him at least some comfort. The Cotton Factor's offices, extending across a deep chasm-like pit, level with the river, where bonded goods had once been stored, were now laced together with a series of delicately made steel walkways.

West now, to the City Hall. He listened as it struck the hour in that late afternoon, not quite hearing Whitcomb's farewell, not really hearing Whitcomb's offer to come live with him on his farm in Lancaster, Pennsylvania, hearing only the tolling of the City Hall clock as it delivered the hour.

Now it seemed to him, as he stood on the corner with his baggage on the sidewalk around him, staring into the deep green of the park next to the slab-sided bank building, that he had never gone away. The ships and the sea and the men, the countries, the rivers, the mountains were all of a piece, and the piece was cut off from some idle hour when he had dozed undisturbed before a *National Geographic* magazine, and at any moment now someone would say his name—

— Howard Cadiz! As I live and breathe!

— I'm sorry, I don't—

— Howard, it's *me*. Jane!

— I'm sorry—

— Jane! *You* and *me* and Shad Courtney—remember? She laughed delightedly.

My God, he thought, she can't even be thirty yet, and—

They talked for a few minutes and he learned that the Depression had hit Savannah hard. After she was gone it occurred to him he should have asked where he could get in touch with Shad.

He checked into a hotel, a cheap one. It would be a long time between ships.

April 1931

January 1933

He was three blocks from the store, but he could see it in his mind as he walked toward it with his rolling, unhurried sailor's gait. Alfred S. DeCunningham's store, with rooms above to let, was no different for him than any other place. It was a familiar part of the routine that had taken him over since leaving the *Indenter* six months ago. All he could do that day had been done. There were no ships and there were no jobs. Now he would lounge in front of the store and watch the rest of the day come, or go. A few cars would pass on West Broad Street. Perhaps a heavy dray and Belgian bucks would rumble their boiler loads over the junction tracks of the West Savannah Street Car. People would walk out into the hot night for a breath of air, swinging along the sidewalks with steps that would, later in the night, echo against the desolate, silent houses and store-fronts. Some of them would stop and test the fruit, a few would buy, but only a few.

There were two fruit stands jutting out into the sidewalk, laden with boxes and pyramids of apples, oranges, pears, grapes, backed up by rows of pineapples and smaller boxes of dates and prunes. Bunches of bananas hung from the ceiling on a rope. An aisle separated the two stands and led into the dark interior of the store. The produce Al sold was too good for the neighborhood that could boast only a working class and the Widows' and Orphans' Home. Seventy-five years of time and commerce had worked on the area and left it exhausted. If it had been caught twenty-five or thirty years before, it could have been saved, but it was too late now. Dead, used up, its slow prevailing way of post–Civil War life was something no one recognized anymore. No one had lived in the area very long. No one cared.

That afternoon Hessian wore a white apron and was sweeping the trash across the sidewalk toward the curb. A burst of laughter rose above the street noises and he looked up, squinting across the street, his thin body alert. He broke out into a white grin.

—Always did like girls in red dresses with a wiggle like dat! Hessian cried, watching the tall strutting figure, dark, lusty and impatient, moving along the opposite side of the street.

— That ain't a wiggle, the girl called back, her voice sultry, inviting. That's character.

Hessian eyed her closely and was satisfied she wasn't wearing anything underneath the red dress. His voice became correct and confident of the situation.

— You workin'? he asked cautiously.

The girl slowed and came toward him, her long legs scissoring indolently. Her voice was softer as she answered.

— Ah works to home. You don't look like you interested.

— Where's to home? Hessian asked. I'm interested.

The girl broke off the conversation with a burst of rich laughter and walked on, straightening up now, fully aware that Hessian was still watching her. Hessian *was* watching her, shaking his head in admiration. Then he went back to his sweeping.

Behind, Alfred S. DeCunningham walked out of the store and stood between the fruit stands. Al was a big man in his late forties with a big chest and stomach, and he wore, like Hessian, a white apron. He began to inspect the fruit, dusting, testing it, restacking the pyramids. The appearance of Al on the outside alerted Hessian and he finished his sweeping with a flourish, a stylish twist of the broom.

— How many times, Al said, his voice firm, but not mean, do I have to tell you not to try and get your women lined up while you're on duty? And besides, there's white women and children around.

— I hear you, Mister Al, Hessian said with a humility that was as easily worn and as easily shed as an expression on his dark face. I'm sorry, suh. But he was not sorry and Al understood this. It was an old game between them, a ritual. Al continued his careful handling of the fruit as Hessian returned the broom to its place.

— Mister Percey Kolb came by, suh, said to tell you he was gone. And he might be late for the game. Said to tell you that he might not come a-tall.

At a step on the sidewalk behind him, they both looked around.

— Hello, Mister Cadiz, Hessian said. Hot day, suh.

— A hot day, Hessian, Cadiz agreed.

— No need, I guess, Al said, to ask you how you made out. Your face tells me that already.

— No need, Cadiz said.

— There's some homebrew on the ice, Al said. It's a little high, but it's Bernice's stuff, so you won't get sick.

Cadiz nodded and entered the dark interior of the store and walked directly to the cool drink box. He took out a jug of light brown to gray liquid and poured a glass, and then he sat on one of the counter stools before the hot dog counter and sipped it. He rolled a Golden Grain cigarette, lit it and sighed, looking out at the street, listening to the conversation of Hessian and Al, their voices rising and falling like buzzing flies over the fruit.

— When was Kolb here? Al asked.

— 'Bout four o'clock. He was all slicked up like he had a big place to go. Smell like rose water on a high yeller to a funeral on Sunday, Hessian said. He spoke matter of factly in a voice full of deceptive humor.

— That cockster! Al snorted, shaking his head. He's in to me for nearly thirty dollars and he's going to spend it on that Thursby woman.

Hessian picked up a spotted apple, examined it, pressing his thumb into the rot, and then dropped it into a wastebasket. He turned and sighed contentedly.

— Yessuh, he said, looking around. Say, he's a big man with the ladies, huh, Mister Al?

— He thinks, Al grunted.

— Yes, suh! Hessian drawled, his voice sly. Ain't nobody got much of anything these days, yet it seems everybody getting a little piece now and then. Yet Mister Percey, seems like he's got to pay. Hessian held the back of a limp wrist to his nose and sniggled silently.

A distant rumbling made them both pause. Hessian stopped giggling and Al straightened from his restless, nervous picking over the fruit. They both watched the huge yellow streetcar roll to a stop over the junction tracks. The bi-fold doors of the West Savannah car flapped open as the brakes released a rush of compressed air. Passengers lined up and stepped down to the hot pavements and walked away. The electric motor slung underneath the car started running and building up more pressure in the compressed air tank.

The streetcar rumbled off, turning the corner and disappearing into the hollow of the Negro ghetto known as Yamacraw, leaving a group of transfer passengers standing across the street from Al's store. Al and Hessian came to life then. As if a hidden spring had been touched off, they began to chant the price and quality of the fruit, their arms and heads moving, gesturing to the pyramids of fruit, singing out the prices; they worked up a mechanical chatter that was almost a litany.

— Ah got DATES—Su-weet Horange! By-nanna! PINE-apple-and RED apple. Rightcheah! Rightcheah! Fifteen cents! Two for a quarter! Hessian's liquid voice floated out over the broad street.

Al stood at the opposite end of the store, his heavy chest and stomach protruding, and contented himself with repeating over and over the one word that, many years before had been three words—Right Over Here—and had by endless repetition become Rightcheah! Rightcheah! Rightcheah!

A few passengers came over and were waited on with a stylish snapping of paper bags by Hessian. It was over in five minutes and then, as the transfer car came along, the passengers were loaded aboard and the stir was over. The last customer, an old Negro man, walked away with a bag of apples, shuffling out of the protective shade of the awning into the hot sun.

As Al looked around and started to go back into the store, there was a sudden shout, a withering screeching voice, and a boy of ten ran across the front of the store, stopped and yelled back into the street.

— Hiney-hiney-Haro! He turned and darted across the sidewalk and was followed a moment later by three children, two boys and a girl, all barefoot, all poorly dressed.

Al bustled back out of the store.

— What was that!

— Just the chillun to the Widows' and Orphans' Home across the street, just playin', Mister Al, Hessian explained.

— Goddam brats. Why the hell don't them women keep 'em inside.

Hessian dropped his eyes and studied the far side of West Broad Street.

— Ah speck it's because they ain't got no place else to play, suh.

— Last week they upset the apples.

— Ah members, suh, Hessian said.

— Well, watch 'em, Al grumbled.

— Yessuh, Hessian said.

Al moved back into the store and grunted at Cadiz, who had not moved.

— Gotta go to the can. Be back in a minute, he said.

Cadiz nodded and continued to watch the street. Hessian, after a moment's pause, peered back into the store and then almost casually moved over to the last of the stands and bent over, cleaning and inspecting the fruit. At the far corner of the block, the small, round, blond head of the barefoot boy was thrust into view.

— Hessian!

Hessian made a motion with his hands for the boy to be quiet, and with one more quick glance inside for Al, dropped four apples to the ground and rolled them to the waiting, eager children. The children scrambled out into the open, grabbed the apples and ran off, disappearing around the corner with a wave of thanks. Hessian behaved as if nothing had happened.

— If Al saw you doing that, Cadiz said, he'd have you arrested.

Hessian jerked around, saw Cadiz standing there, watching, then he relaxed and grinned. He snuffled at his wrist and confidently fell into his sham routine.

— But they just chillun, hardly eveh get any fruit or candy or stuff. You wouldn't tell, Mistuh Cadiz. Would you, suh?

Cadiz was silent, watching him.

— Of all the folks come around to Mistuh Al's sto', you the las' one to do a thing like that to old Hessian.

— Don't Uncle Tom me, Cadiz said harshly.

Hessian straightened and looked Cadiz in the eye. A careful hood slipped down; the care that had to be taken all the time. Be careful. Be careful. Hessian waited.

— Suh?

Cadiz did not pursue it, knowing that Hessian was waiting for his next move. Perhaps, Cadiz thought, even wanting the issue pursued.

— Now we're in each other's debt, Cadiz said evenly.

— Suh? Hessian said softly, still dissembling.

— I have the responsibility of not telling on you, Cadiz said, which would make you lose your job. This, in spite of the fact that I might be dead set against stealing. And you're in my debt because I know something that could get your job lost for you. So, just like that, we're involved in a conspiracy against a man who has done no harm to either of us, who in fact, has been a good friend to both of us. Now, suppose you continue to steal his apples and fruit and give them away? If I don't tell on you the next time, I will be compounding the act. I will be in so deep that I can never tell Al, because he would then, naturally enough, demand to know why I had not told him the first time.

— You wouldn't tell, would you, Mister Cadiz? Hessian asked.

— Why shouldn't I? I didn't take you to raise.

Hessian was no closer to knowing if he was being baited or not. But he could not press it too far. There was an instinctive cutoff point when talking to a white man on a serious subject. He could not fight back. He had passed over the safety line. He returned to his only safe position and changed the subject.

— Mistuh Percey Kolb come by early.

— I heard you tell Al, Cadiz said. Hessian was perplexed; he could read nothing in Cadiz's face or his manner or his voice. He retreated even further.

— If he do come back from his jackassin' tonight, and Mistuh Percey Kolb *do* have money left, he prob'ly be so cut up from his woman, y'all git to him easy.

Hessian cleared his throat as Al came out of the door and looked around. He glanced at Cadiz to see if he could read his expression. He relaxed. He felt sure Cadiz was not going to say anything.

— He sho' look sassy in his ice cream britches and black and white shoes and gabardine coat. Yes, suh!

— That damn Thursby woman, Al grumbled. You look done in, he said to Cadiz.

— I don't think there's a job in the whole goddam town.

Hessian drifted away to the inside of the store, closing out the troubles of the unemployed white man.

Al moved a little closer to Cadiz and spoke confidentially.

— Well, there's still that opportunity I spoke to you about. It's still open. There's a bankroll to get, to start things moving, and you know how to handle a boat. And with Shad, why . . . Al let the sentence hang.

— And get my ass shot off by some thick-headed cop, or a Coast Guard sailor who's so scared that—

— I didn't think you was one to give risk too much consideration, Al said with a shrug.

— What else would I think about? The money? Just the money and not any of the possibilities that I might get killed, or maybe wind up in jail? If you want somebody like that, talk to Shad.

— For a man that's been outa work for six months, you're mighty goddam choosy. You ever think about how I'd like to get a little of the rent on that room upstairs?

— What do I owe you? Cadiz asked coldly. You worried about it?

— I ain't worried about a damn thing, Al said. It ain't as if there wasn't nothing to gain. You know how much is in it?

— You told me often enough, Cadiz said. I know. I dream about it every night. And in the morning, and during the day when I'm sitting in the offices waiting to see the port captain about a job and knowing I won't get one. I know.

— Ever think about what I'd be losing? Al asked.

— Your money.

— Well, you can sneer. And it ain't much. But it keeps me from bumming around and I pay my goddam rent on time.

— So now I'm a bum?

— What a hardhead! Christ! What a hardhead, Al said. I know what's the matter with you. Why don't you get yourself a woman? You look tight around the eyeballs.

— How about leaving my goddam sex life alone? Okay? I'm doing all right.

— Stubborn hardhead, pride walking around with a hole in the seat of its pants and nothing in its gut but a memory of the last time you had a steak. All right! I'm suggesting all of this to you, not because I'd like to see a little rent for my upstairs rooms from you and Shad but because I want to exploit you. I'm evil. Okay?

— Speak to Shad, he'll do it.

— I don't want to take Shad without you. You know that. And you know why.

— Rat shit.

— All right. So I got a full head of congestion, so what the hell, so has everybody else, ain't they? There *ain't* no decent way to make a living. So what the hell is there left to do? I ain't talking about like as if we were going down and rob the Citizens and Southern Bank and Trust in broad daylight. We taking a little booze away from some crooks, that's all.

Cadiz finished the last of his glass of homebrew and turned back inside the store and poured a second one. He offered it to Al, who refused.

— In the first place, Cadiz said, the crooks you're talking about have got the whole police department on their payroll. How long do you think we'd get away with it? The crooks turn to the cops they've been paying off for protection and say, Listen, some people just hijacked us for forty thousand dollars' worth of bonded Scotch. Then they say to the cops, You don't get any more pay-offs until we get our goods back. Then you know what would happen? Every cop in town would start hunting us down.

Al looked off into the distance. I didn't take the whole world to raise or have a conscience for.

— That's what everybody's saying. That's what's the matter.

— Now what the hell's that supposed to mean? Something big and important, I guess. Al heaved his gut. You guys that have gone to sea a little while, seen a few things, give me a pain in my ass. Why, I seen more and learned more about people and stuff—rightcheah—walking past my fruit stand then you seen in all those places you been, and I didn't go no further off than this block!

— That's what I like about you, Al. You're so broad-minded.

— Ahh! Up yours. Think I don't know what's eating you? Al said.

— Yeah? Cadiz asked, interested.

— Never mind, never mind, Al said. I know.

The thunder of the West Savannah Street Car was on them again, and Hessian came out of the store. As before, he and Al went into their act as Cadiz moved out of the sun and inside to sip his homebrew and listen to them hawk.

Al offered service twenty-four hours a day, not that there was any business, but because it was easier to stay open than to move all the fruit stands inside and close. Hessian did not mind; their arrangement was flexible, and Hessian did not have anything to do anyway.

Hessian's chant was now silent. The 3 A.M. streetcar rolled over the junction tracks and crashed into the silent night. The only light, after the lights of the streetcar had passed, was a milk-white globe over the door to the upstairs rooms. Near this, stretched out on a bench, Hessian slept, his arms folded beneath his head. It was this way that Cadiz found him as he walked out of the store counting small change. Hessian stirred at his step, came awake and then sat up. In the distance, halfway across town, the City Hall clock boomed three emphatic items.

— How you make out, Mister Cadiz? Have a good run of cards?

— I made a few, Cadiz said.

Cadiz looked tiredly down the street past the run-down Rummage Sale shop that shared Al's block with him, a small clapboard building badly in need of paint. A short alley at right angles to the street housed a cheap, second-hand furniture store. Across West Broad Street was a barber shop, white and clean, with its candy-striped pole, motionless now. On one corner stood a green painted bakery that sold bread and rolls and never made cake anymore because everyone was too poor to buy it. Next door was an ice cream parlor, then a fish market, a Chinese grocery store, a dirty, rutted alley that ran into Yamacraw, and beyond that a desolate looking, low, flat building that sold furniture. Cadiz had never seen anyone go into it. A harness shop, a white concrete paved street, and the faded red-to-brown Georgian-styled, three-storied, rat-infested, airless citadel of the waif and the bereaved—the Widows' and Orphans' Home. What a neighborhood, Cadiz thought.

Al came out of the store. He was sleepy and, like Cadiz, he looked around the silent streets, but he seemed to take comfort from the scene.

— I'm going to make fresh coffee, Mistuh Al, suh, for the paper boys and the dray drivers to the river, Hessian said. You like a cup a fresh coffee, Mistuh Cadiz? Only takes a few minutes.

— No, Cadiz said, I don't want coffee.

— Well, I'm going to hit the sack, Al said with a great stretch, and he patted his stomach; he followed Hessian into the store and on into the back rooms. He stopped for a moment to watch the last four poker players wind up a hand and then chased them out. It would be cool enough to sleep now.

Cadiz stood still, thinking. The steps of the poker players had faded; Hessian was finished with his making coffee; Al was asleep, Al's proposal, he thought, was not a bad one. But he wasn't ready to go that route yet.

Shad, he knew, would be willing to do anything. But Al was right: to allow Shad to go by himself was too much of a risk. Shad had gotten too wild. And now, of course, he was mean as well. It was not hard to understand how this had happened. Shad had told him a few things—not much, but enough. No, Al was right not to take on Shad without Cadiz.

He glanced up at the sky, looking for signs of a weather change, and then went toward the doorway leading to the room upstairs. She was standing in the shadows, watching him.

He looked at her closely and decided she wasn't drunk, though she had been drinking.

— Well! If it isn't the man of my dreams, Lainy Thursby said.

— Did you leave Percey Kolb in some gutter? Cadiz asked.

— You got a nasty mouth, Howard Cadiz. A dirty, low, nasty mind, and it pours out of your mouth like a sewer pipe. She stood looking at him, her head to one side. She was not really pretty, but she was oddly attractive. She wore a blue cotton dress and this helped, because she was one of the fairest blonds Cadiz had ever seen, fairer even than some of the Malmo Swedes.

— And you're out for a leisurely stroll at three o'clock in the morning. What does that make you?

Even in the dim light of the white globe, he could see her flush.

— I came down for some oranges, she said, tossing her blond hair. We're drinking cocktails. Orange Blossoms.

— I'll bet you are, Cadiz said. I'll just bet you're drinking cocktails. Bathtub gin and orange juice. Cocktails!

— Look who's hurting, she said, going over to the stand and

looking at the fruit. You don't hear me raising my voice. I'm happy.

— It didn't take long, did it? I mean, Kolb and his thirty bucks.

She swung around and faced him, her hands clenched.

— That's a dirty lie! My father and brother and Pete Danner is playing poker-cards, right this minute! She turned and looked inside, saw Hessian and called to him. Hessian! Come out here right now and give me a dozen of these sweet oranges!

Either Hessian did not hear or pretended not to. Lainy eyed Cadiz with amusement, flirting with her hips.

— My daddy's been talking about you.

Cadiz went to her and slipped his arm around her waist.

— Yeah? What's he been saying?

She twisted away from him, twirling around and tossing her blond hair.

— They *all* been saying how you always thinking crazy. And *I* remember you as the coldest, smartest one in school. Crazy smart.

— Yeah? What else do they say? Cadiz snaked his arm around her again.

— How you're full of hate. How both of you are full of hate—you and Shad. But they say there was a reason for Shad hating. He got all tore up on the chain gang. You haven't got that excuse.

— Yeah? And what else? Cadiz pinched one firm nipple through her dress.

— Stop that!

Cadiz pulled her close and tried to kiss her neck. She resisted, then gave in, lending her body to his. Then she stiffened and pulled free, once more twirling her blond hair and swinging her hips, watching his eyes on her body.

— Listen, Lainy, you want to come upstairs for a little while?

— Uh-uh! Daddy would give it to me!

— I'd like to give it to you, Cadiz said softly, and grabbed her wrist.

— There you go again! Talking dirty! He sighed and let her wrist drop.

— Hessian! Hessian! You wake up, hear! Hessian did not want to hear.

— I've got to get back, Howard. Listen to me. Listen, I don't want you to think I'm that kind of woman.

— I don't think you're that kind of woman, Lainy, Cadiz said, and pulled her toward the doorway.

— But you do! All of you do. I see the way you look at me. And the way you act. I don't see you acting like that with other girls. Like a piece of candy in the case, that's the way everybody looks at me. Like them kids across the street in the Widows' and Orphans' Home looking at a piece of candy they can't have without the price. As if all of you could just eat me up! If only I would let you.

— More than a piece of candy, Lainy, Cadiz said, pulling her into his arms and then into the doorway. He kissed her hard on the mouth, and again she put him through the agony of responding and then resisting.

— No, no—*no*, Howard. I want to get married.

— Sure, Lainy, sometime, maybe, but not right now. For now, let's go upstairs.

— Howard, please don't. Take your hand away—Howard, oh—

She tore free. What else am I good for! she said, spinning on him but standing at a safe distance. That's what you're thinking. What else is she good for but something to throw on a bed and do it to! Well, I'm good for something and it isn't only *that!* That isn't enough! You think I'm trash just because I can't talk without it sounding country and can't dress up and go eat in the Manhattan Restaurant uptown to Broughton Street. Well, there's more to me, Howard Cadiz! There's *got* to be more!

Cadiz leaned back against the doorframe wondering what in sweet Christ had gotten into him. He hadn't really wanted her—he *did*, but not enough to hurt her—and he was ashamed, seeing that he had gone too far too fast. He had been stupid.

— I know what Percey Kolb has been saying around here about me and all, but it isn't true. And you know something, the man that *does* get me for the first time is going to *know* it's not true. He is going to be one surprised man, I can tell you!

— Lainy—

— And you want to know something else? My daddy and brother are sitting up there right now, letting Percey Kolb think he's going to get something he isn't about to get, and he's going to lose his thirty dollars!

— Well, I'll be damned! Cadiz said with a grin.

— Yes! It's true. Now leave me alone, I have to go.

— I'll tell you this, too, though. And you can tell the others. I'm never going to do it until I can be sure I won't have to forget about it and won't hate the man's guts for doing it. Goddammit, Howard Cadiz, *listen* to me! I'm going to have something more!

Cadiz felt his stomach tighten. How hard would she fight and how long would she be able to resist?

— When the right man comes along, she said—and she seemed to Cadiz to have grown older, matured in just a few minutes—the only important thing is that *he* be hard up.

— Can you hold out? Cadiz said.

— Don't hold your breath, she said. I told you. There's got to be more.

— Good luck, Lainy, Cadiz said, meaning it.

The West Savannah Street Car rolled over the junction tracks. Lainy walked off with a swing of her smooth, rounded hips. Hessian floated up to his side.

— Going to bed, Mistuh Cadiz? Hessian asked.

— Yeah, Cadiz said.

— Looks like a hot day tomorrow, Hessian said, looking up at the sky. It's a good time for sleeping right now.

— Good night, Hessian, Cadiz said and went slowly up the stairs to his room.

Alone, he closed his ears to the street sounds and imagined he was on a ship. The perfect stillness of the room did not spoil this illusion for him. He stretched out on the small bed.

And then, because there was no will left in him to fight against it, he thought about Lainy, not about *her* but the taste of her lips and the soft giving flesh of her breasts and the tight flat surface of her thighs pressed hard against his urgent maleness.

Cadiz's eyes flew open. His heart pounded. His hands were sweaty. He wiped them on the sheet angrily and closed his eyes tight, willing himself to think about something else, to sleep.

He tried to think about where he would go the next day in search of a job; he tried to examine Al's proposal. Nothing worked. Like a thin sheet of ice under a hot sun, his conscious thoughts all melted before a burning vision of a small floating dock that was really a pathway in Shanghai. Passing the cribs that were small bumboats tied sternward to the floating dock-path, one walked along the endless rows and looked at the girls lying on beds of silken pillows, listened to their birdlike overtures and assessed them for age and heft, tried to determine the quality of bosoms, width of hips and thighs, looked carefully at the framed Police Cards and the Health Cards displayed on the outsides of the boats, being careful to check the dates. And then, finally, one made a choice and entered into the gently sensual, cocoon-like fantasy of the crib to be bathed in their silent, never hurried, restrained sexuality that made them so much better than even the very best of the professional prostitutes in the western world.

Cadiz cursed and sat up, rolled a cigarette and smoked it savagely.

He went downstairs to the street. He was surprised to see gray dawn stealing over the main section of town, not realizing he had been up in his room so long. He avoided Hessian, going down past the school, cutting across Liberty Square and straight toward the river.

At Congress and Montgomery he turned left and stopped at the first door, knocking hurriedly. He preferred another whorehouse, but this was the only one offering twenty-four-hour service.

— Why! It's Howard Cadiz! Hello, honey. We ain't seen you in a long time.

— Yeah, Cadiz said, moving inside. Too long. He moved quickly past the Negro maid and into the parlor. Several men and a half dozen women watched him as he stepped inside, coming as he had with a rush and now stopping dead still. He felt foolish. Then annoyed. He glared at them.

Without looking, he tapped a girl on the shoulder.

— You busy?

— Why no, Howard, honey. We surely have missed you. She hugged him playfully.

— You know, you lost a little weight. Yes, definitely, you used to be a lot heavier.

— I haven't been eating regularly, Cadiz said.

— That's the way it is these days, honey. Hardly anybody eats regular.

— Listen, Cadiz grated, are we going to go upstairs and fuck or stay down here and talk?

What had not worked for Lainy with Cadiz, worked with Shad. They fell in love. They went to the picture show every night. They went swimming at Daffin Park. They went to Tybee Beach on picnic afternoons. They were in love. They did all this on seventy cents a day, thirty-five cents a day, a dollar twenty-seven a day—whatever money they had between them was used to give them time together. Cadiz said nothing. He watched and listened and waited, and he played poker with Al's gang in back of the store and cadged his eating money and he shopped Savannah for a job, any kind of a job. It had not taken Lainy long. Not more than a month and a half and Shad was *hers*. But around Al's store nothing had changed.

A different sound from that of the streetcar rumbling over the junction tracks shattered the hot afternoon silence. Hessian was at the fruitstands, shifting, dusting, cleaning out the bruised fruit that was thrown bulk fashion into one of the bins. He picked up an apple and inspected it, then dropped it into the garbage basket at his feet. He paid no attention at all to the thunderous noise and glanced up only as the group of children passed in front of the store following a huge twenty-team dray with a foundry press aboard. Seven of the horses were white and the children stamped them happily, licking their thumbs and pressing the wet end into the palm of their free hand and then smacking it hard with a balled fist. The gigantic load was pulled on down the street and out of sight, and the traffic that was strung out in back of it began to flow around the bottleneck as the maneuvering of the dray over the junction tracks was finished.

Hessian continued picking over the fruit. Not until he was finished and inside the store did the children move, then they rushed six abreast toward the stands, like driver ants, their faces compressed and tense.

— First pick on the speck basket!

— Second!

— Third!

— You're behind me, Tiny! a voice shrieked in the hot afternoon.

— I am not! I said *first!*

— *I'm* first, a cold-eyed blond boy said. You wanna make something of it, you sonofabitch?

— Well then I'm *second!*

— You can stick second up your ass, the blond boy advised.

The others quickly lined up behind the leaders, stringing out across the sidewalk, moving in a steady line toward the garbage basket, thrusting their hands into the muck in search of an apple that was only partially bad, then running happily away. Those who were left behind, boys and girls, struggled over the remains. Like a nest of cats, heads, arms, feet, cries and shrieks, they fought over the garbage basket.

— My God! Percey Kolb said. What's going on?

Al came out then, shoving gently but firmly.

— Go on! Get out of here, you kids, you shouldn't be eating garbage. It'll make you sick. Go on, get out of here!

The children scrambled away. Those on the end of the line who had not gotten a chance at the basket were quick to demand a share of the spoils. They moved off quickly, noisily, without a backward glance.

Al moved out to the curb and looked up at the windows over his store.

— What's Mistuh Shad going to do? Hessian asked.

— I don't know what he's going to do, but I know what he *should* do. Al's voice was bitter with conviction. He'd better take that goddam job to feed himself and that little piece of ass he's got. Leave it to Shad to end up with sweet little Lainy.

— What job? Percey Kolb asked. As usual, he wore a clean shirt, his trousers were neatly pressed and his shoes were freshly shined. Shad's got a job?

— Over in South Carolina. Timbering.

— Oh, Percey Kolb said, backing away from the idea of any job that required manual labor.

— He sho' waited a long time fo' a job to be givin' it up now, Hessian said.

— You're damn right, Al said. Ordinary honest people can't get work, and for a man just off the chain gang to get a job and then even *think* about giving it up, well, I just don't know. He turned to Percey Kolb. Lainy says she's pregnant. Pregnant, my ass! And if she *is*, how the hell does Shad know if it's his?

Lainy and Shad moved carefully around each other in the tiny room. Shad was stripped to the waist. His body was tough and hard from his years on the chain gang, and it bore the marks of brutal beatings, a network of old scars and welts across his shoulders and down his back. He was packing a battered old suitcase.

— Seven weeks, there's no question about it.

— I believe you, Shad said.

— Do you believe me when I say it's yours, Shad?

Shad continued packing.

— You know it's yours! You know! That night, right here, in this bed, you—you—*know*. You're the only one! The first one!

— Lainy, listen, Shad said. It ain't as if I was leaving and wouldn't come back. I'll send you money.

— What do you know about timbering?

— What do you think I did for twelve years on the gang? It's about the only goddam thing I do know.

— No! Lainy wailed. If you leave, you won't ever come back. I know it.

— It's a job! Will you try and understand that? A *job!* I haven't had a job since I got off the gang.

— Please don't, Shad.

— Can't you get it through your head? It's a paying *job!*

— We're not married.

— I told you I haven't got time to get married, Shad muttered.

— If you go, Lainy repeated, you won't ever come back.

— I'll send for you, Lainy. You'll come live with me in Charleston, and if we can save enough money, we might get out of this part of the country altogether. Maybe New York. You'd like New York, wouldn't you, Lainy? We could see the Statue of Liberty and the big zoo and shows on Broadway once in a while. But I can't do any of that *unless I take this job!*

—You know what you can do with your Statue of Liberty and your Broadway shows! *I want to get married!*

—Do you know, Shad said, that this is the first job I've had since I was a *kid?* Living like an animal on the gang and then getting out and living like a bum, eating from hand to mouth, cheating my best friends at poker, cadging nickels and dimes and on a good day a quarter. Sponging for rent and not ever hoping to pay off. And now I've got a chance to work and earn a living. Can't you see what it means?

—Some things a woman knows, Shad, she said. Some things don't have to be said right out. If you go, I'll never see you again. I know it. I know it and you know it.

White faced, Shad picked up his suitcase. He went to the door and opened it.

—Shad!

He kept on going. Lainy lunged after him, clinging to him. She rode his back all the way down the stairs. Shad took no notice of her.

—Please, God! Don't let him go! Please make him stay with me! Shaad! I'll do anything you say. I *won't* let you go!

They were out on the sidewalk now, in full view of West Broad Street. Al, Cadiz, Hessian, Kolb and several of the orphan children stood mute, pretending not to look.

—Shad—SHAD! Lainy screamed and ran a few steps in front of him and threw herself to the sidewalk. Shad! Please! God, no!

He tried stepping over her, but she caught one of his legs and hugged it, pressing her head against his thigh.

—Hessian, stop him! Talk to him, Cadiz! Cadizzzz! Mist' Cunningham! Somebody DO something, Shad—SHAD!

A little crowd began to collect, coming from around the corner and across the street. The children stood in a rough semicircle and stared wide-eyed. No one moved.

—Lainy, Shad said, stopping and looking down at her. For Christ sake! Get up. Get up and let me go!

She moaned and clung even tighter to his leg. She had stopped crying now. The wild, shrill emotion was gone. She was cold and desperate, hanging on, teeth clenched.

— I won't. I won't, she said. You'll have to kill me. I won't let you leave me. I don't care about the job. I don't care about anything.

Shad tore free, jerking back, pulling his leg out of her grasp.

— *Leave me alone!*

She lunged and grabbed his leg again.

— You'll have to kill me!

Shad dropped the suitcase and raised his fist to strike her—then stopped. Again heaved and jerked free of her hold. He stared down at her, and then at the circle of faces around him. He clapped his hands to his temples and grabbed his hair and began to stomp the ground with his foot. He gave one anguished cry, throwing his head back and howling. He stomped the suitcase to pieces, scattering his few belongings around on the dirty sidewalk. Lainy did not move. She did not look at him. She remained where she was, on all fours, her head lowered.

Again Shad looked at the faces surrounding him. They looked silently back at him. Then, with great weariness, he started picking up his clothes and the pieces of the suitcase and turned and walked back to the stairway. Lainy moved slowly after him. They disappeared into their room.

— My! Percey Kolb said. That's what I call a real ball and chain. Did you see the way she hung on!

Shut your goddam fat face Al said. He turned on the assembled crowd. You people going to buy something, then buy it. If not, then move the hell on. I'm open for business.

Most of the onlookers drifted away but the children did not move.

— Go on! Get the hell out of here! Al's fury whiplashed them. Don't come around here anymore with your begging faces hanging out! Don't come over here any more unless you got money to spend! You hear? Hessian! Get out here, goddammit! How about hollering it up! What the hell you think I pay you for, anyway. Sell fruit—sell 'em something. Anything!

Still the children had not moved. Al spun on them again.

— Get *out* of here! He picked up a few apples and began to throw them at the children as hard as he could.

— Now! the blond-haired, cold-eyed boy said tensely. He caught the first apple on the fly with one hand and never broke stride as he ran on away from Al. The other children scampered after the fruit.

Out of range, the blond-haired boy waited for the others to join him. He munched his apple contentedly.

— See, I told you. When he gets *real* mad, he throws things.

The wail of the siren sliced through the hot, humid night. But the vehicle could not be seen yet and no one knew if it was an ambulance, a fire engine or a police car. Before they could see anything, the deep roar of a speeding, powerful car surged out of the north, a car moving from Bay Street straight down the middle of West Broad. Hessian stopped his sweeping and went to the curb. A moment later, he was joined by Cadiz, Al and Kolb, who all came hurrying out of the store. Danner came up too from around the corner. Neat, dapper, thin, Danner slipped up alongside them without a sound. They looked around and there he was. It was a talent of his.

Two piercing headlights bore down on them, and then the car flashed past. The pursuing siren grew louder, and seconds later the police car screamed down the middle path through the traffic.

— What the hell was that! Al said.

— Leggers probably, Kolb said.

— Jesus! Al exclaimed. Right down the middle of West Broad.

— He was loaded, Danner said with a short, brisk nod of his head. You could tell he was loaded. Yes, sir, loaded with something. I-just-happen-to notice that he was very low on his rear springs.

— That don't mean anything, Kolb said. They're making Caddys like that these days.

— Wasn't a Cadillac, Al said. It was a Buick.

— It was a Cadillac, Kolb said. And I'll just bet a dollar to a doughnut that it was that Sharkey bunch down to Tybee.

— Now how the hell could you see it was Sharkey's bunch? Al said with contempt. You know something, Kolb, you're full of crap and corruption. Hot air. First place, Sharkey don't operate out of Tybee anymore. Not since they changed over commands in the Coast Guard. Talk was he couldn't pay the price the new commander wanted. He's operating out of the county now.

Danner nodded. I-just-happen-to-know Al's right, he said. Sharkey and the whole bunch from Tybee quit two months ago. They been working out of the county ever since.

Kolb turned on Danner.

— Now how the hell would you know? You remind me of some of them hustlers down at the Blue Boy Poolroom that stand around all day and agree with the winners.

— Well, as you know, Kolb, Danner said, I-just-happen-to-of been a runner for the bunch.

— Sharkey? Al pressed.

— Noo, I-just-happen-to been a runner for another bunch, right here in town, Danner said.

— B.S. and R.S., Kolb said. The only thing you ever ran was your mouth.

— Yeah, well, you ask Cadiz. He knows. Tell 'em, Cadiz. It-just-so-happens that Cadiz bought bonded stuff and who was it delivered it to you? Tell him?

Cadiz grinned and nodded. He's right, Kolb. Several times he brought me a bottle. Which, by the way, you paid for when you thought you were checking a cinch to me, that wasn't a cinch.

— Fuck it, Kolb said casually.

Cadiz felt himself flush. He was not particularly proud of the fact that he outplayed his friends in the nickel and dime poker games. But it was the only way, the only honorable way he could get by. And he felt that he had just put a stain on it. It was one thing to take advantage of his friends, but it was another to voice it, openly. He felt ashamed and he wished he had not said it. When he glanced at Kolb again, he saw that the big man's character had taken hold. Kolb was ignoring the remark. Cadiz was relieved that no one had picked it up, but it did not lessen his pangs of regret. And suddenly he remembered Ulrica in London. Jesus! Had he hurt another human being, however slightly? But what did it matter? He had hurt so many in his life, what did it matter. But inside, he knew *it mattered.*

— Well, I still say it was a Caddy and it was Sharkey's bunch. Whether they're operating out of the county or not, Kolb said.

Danner, backed by Cadiz, began to elaborate.

— Not only that, mind you, not only that, But I-just-happen-to-know that he was mixed up with a tough New York crowd. I see them come into town. Once. They meant business. You could of taken a bath in old Sharkey's sweat.

— B.S. and R.S., is what I say, Kolb said, and spat eloquently into the gutter.

— I know. I remember, Danner said. They suspected Sharkey of taking stuff off the boat, cutting it, and then recapping and sealing it again, then shipping it north.

— New York, huh? Kolb said, impressed in spite of himself. That's what I'd like to get hooked up with, just once, just one big haul, grab me some of that New York money and then cut out cold. I mean cut out cold. Then I'd get me a woman that looks like Lainy Thursby before she got married to Shad.

Al looked hard at Kolb for a long moment.

— You'd better watch your mouth, Kolb, Cadiz said. If Shad ever heard you talk like that he'd beat you to death.

Cadiz turned on his heel and walked away.

— What's the matter with him! Kolb appealed to Danner. Everybody knows—

— Don't say it! I don't want to hear it. It-just-so-happens that I ain't talking about another man's wife. No siree!

— Why, you damn little rat-faced sonofabitch! Kolb said. I got a mind to read you off right here and now and slam the cover down tight.

There was a slight movement of Danner's hand and then the gleam of a knife blade shone in the streetlights.

— I don't want no trouble with you, Kolb, but it-just-so-happens that I'm in a cutting mood of mind if you want to start reading and slamming.

— I'd stick that in your ear, Danner, Kolb said with a lazy confidence, before you knew what the matter was. But he glanced around quickly to see if anyone was listening.

— Put that thing away, man, before you get hurt, Kolb said.

Kolb walked over to Hessian, who stood leaning against the lamppost, reading the comics in the evening paper.

— Hessian!

— Yes, suh, Mistuh Percey.

— Hessian, do you know what the whole trouble is?

— Naw, suh.

— There ain't enough free stuff in the world, that's what the trouble is.

— Ah reckons, Mistuh Percey.

The early-evening sky bore down gently on West Broad Street.

— Well, look here, Al! Danner called. Here comes Herod. Maybe he knows about that legger that just tore by.

Al and Kolb came back out of the store as Herod, the beat policeman, walked up to them. Herod had a big open face that was not unkind, with a belly that was as large as Al's, but all muscle. He walked slowly, taking his time, missing nothing. He was liked and respected along his beat. Kolb was the first to speak, cutting in before Danner could say anything.

— That a legger just went flying by here, Herod?

Herod spread his legs and balanced his big body on his flat feet. He nodded. New bunch, he said.

— New bunch, huh? Al asked. I guess they moved into the city after Sharkey was chased into the county.

Herod paused a moment and then decided that what Al had said must be common knowledge all over town. He nodded again.

— Bootleggers or moonshiners? Kolb asked.

— Shiners, I think, Herod said. Darkies from over in Carolina. They sure had that damned Buick turning over. The lieutenant lost them when they turned down into Yamacraw.

Al turned to Kolb and Danner triumphantly. I *told* you it was a Buick!

— Moonshiners, huh? Kolb said. Not very much money in something you have to sell two dollars a gallon. It's the legging where the money is. Bonded whiskey from outside the country. Snuck in. Real likker. Only kind I drink.

— But there's a point, Danner said. I-just-happen-to-know that a lot of people are drinking corn moonshine these days because they can't pay for high-price stuff. Now seventy-five cents a quart isn't bad money.

— But that's only a dollar a gallon profit, Kolb said with contempt.

— It's a profit, Danner said.

— Who's there that got money in this town these days? The rich ones. And you're not going to get any rich people drinking corn. They're going to drink bonded stuff right off the boat, and they've got the money to pay for it. It's legging where the money is, ain't that right, Cadiz.

Cadiz looked at Herod, whom he liked, and winked.

— Well, in the eyes of the law one is as bad as the other, Cadiz said in a judicious tone. It's breaking the law both ways. But if a man was going to break the law, wouldn't it seem to you that he would do it where there was a greater profit?

— You have a bootlegger's mind, Howard, Herod said. I'm going to have to watch you. The policeman jabbed Cadiz playfully in the ribs with his nightstick.

— Exactly! *Exactly!* Kolb said. Just what I said.

— You got a job yet, Kolb? Herod asked.

Kolb withdrew slightly, looked at his shoe-tops, and shook his head. A few prospects. Something coming up looks pretty good.

— Danner? Herod asked.

— Nothing, Danner said, nodding his head briskly. It-just-so-happens there ain't no jobs. I found it was almost the same as panhandling on Broughton Street.

— There's a difference, Herod said. A man shouldn't ever feel badly about begging for work.

— You been panhandling on Broughton Street? Kolb asked with open contempt in his voice.

— I been thinking about it, Danner said in a matter of fact voice.

— Where the hell is your pride? Kolb demanded.

— Right here in my stomach, you big mouth sonofabitch! Danner said, close to pulling his knife again. When my stomach's full, I got pride and when it ain't, and after the third day, I can do without pride!

— Call me a sonofabitch, will you, Kolb said.

— None of that. Kolb! Herod moved in easily.

— You hear what he called me? Kolb demanded.

— I heard, Herod said. I think you were out of line. You can't argue with a man whose belly is empty.

— Well, I manage, Kolb said, and I ain't begged yet. Have a little respect for a man who ain't begged yet.

Kolb glanced at Cadiz.

— You begged yet, Howard?

— It depends on your point of view, Cadiz said. I owe Al a lot of room rent and for an awful lot of milk and sweet rolls.

— It takes the bite out of a man either way, Kolb, Herod said.

— Well, I make enough playing poker to keep me going, Kolb said. Nothing wrong with that.

— No, nothing wrong with that, Herod said. As long as you don't cheat your friends.

Everyone looked at Kolb. He let it ride.

— How are the ships, Howard? Al asked. Anything doing on that tanker that came in yesterday?

Cadiz shook his head.

— Did you get aboard? Talk to the captain?

— Yes, I got aboard, Cadiz said. He looked at Kolb. And you know, it was about ten this morning when I went up to talk to him and he told me right away there wasn't any openings in the crew. But he said I could hang around and eat with the crew. So I did. I hung around from ten this morning until after supper. I ate three meals.

Al spoke up immediately. Smart! he said. Smart man, wouldn't you say, Herod?

Herod nodded.

Lainy appeared in the doorway to the upstairs rooms. The change in her was shocking. She wore a sloppy dress, her hair was uncombed, her face was puffy. She walked past the group of men without taking notice of them, her dirty slippers slapping against the sidewalk. She was having a difficult pregnancy.

— Hessian, she said tiredly, give me some more Co-Colas, and some of them peaches. And a Stanback headache powder, if you don't mind.

— Yes, mam, Mrs. Courtney. You don't have to wait. I'll bring it upstairs to you, mam. And then his voice was gently reproving. I told you, all you have to do is speak to me from the window and I would bring it up.

Shad was thinner and drawn down very fine. He walked with a tension that was just below the surface. He carried a jacket over his shoulder, and his shoes and the lower part of his trousers were muddy. He joined the group and rolled a cigarette.

— Hello, Herod, Shad said, smiling. How are your feet?

— Worser, Herod said. If that can be.

Danner and Kolb greeted him with a nod.

— How's the ditch digging, Shad? Kolb asked.

— I guess ditch digging, Shad said, lighting the cigarette, is ditch digging all over the world. Ain't but one way to do it. Shad glanced up at the window and then back at Cadiz. Everything okay?

— Fine, Cadiz said. They moved off a few paces together.

— I didn't hear her vomiting, not once all day, Cadiz said. But she came down for headache powders.

— Did she go out? Buy anything for—supper?

— Shaaad! Is that you? Why don't you come upstairs? Lainy leaned out of the window. I feel so miserable and you standing down there jawing and you've got to go out and buy some stuff for your supper. I didn't get any rest today. That damned old streetcar banging back and forth—Lainy pulled her head back inside, still talking.

Shad could see her standing just inside the window, her arms folded over her swollen belly.

— Well, I'm waiting, she said.

— I'll be right up, Shad said. I just want to talk to Howard a minute.

— Why can't you talk to him later?

— I said I'd be right up, Lainy. And I have to come right down again to buy something for supper, don't I?

— I want you upstairs right *now!*

Shad said to Cadiz, Don't go away. I want to talk to you.

— Where the hell would I go? He turned back to the others. The moths flapped around the street lamp and a game of Hide-and-Go-Seek was played out in the soft early evening. It was a beautiful time of day.

Al was feeling good. He stood in the aisle between the fruit stands and slipped the wrapper from a cigar; he was relaxed after a heavy meal. Hessian slipped out past Al. He was dressed in a flashy street suit, a man bent on committing sin that evening.

— Take care. Remember what the man said, Al warned.

— Says which?

— A man seeking evil will surely find it.

— Ain't after no evil, just a little bit of tail, real innocent, Hessian said.

— I've seen her, Cadiz said, coming out of the store entrance, and she isn't innocent.

— She the one going to do the sinning, Hessian said. I'm the pure and innocent party. Yes, suh!

— Don't argue with your boss, Al said. Or your boss's friends.

Hessian laughed and strutted away.

— See you in the morning, boss!

— Have you got enough money? Al called after him.

Hessian turned and walked backward.

— Don't need *no* money. No presents, no sweet talk, just this here what I've got!

Cadiz watched him dodge a horse and wagon and then slip into the dark and mysteriously beckoning hole of Yamacraw, a thin, strutting man, solemn, eager, drawn toward a lamp-lighted bedroom and moist warm kisses.

The Hide-and-Go-Seek game was nearly over. The wailing mothers from the Widows' and Orphans' Home broke through the last barrier of the children's long day, and finally the street was silent. Then someone cranked up a phonograph and music floated down. Cadiz and Al felt good in each other's company, sitting and smoking and talking.

Neither of them saw the man right away. He came from around the odd corner, shaky, a little drunk but more hung over than drunk, trying hard to hold up his head. His hands shook and his patience wore out because they would not be steady, and he jammed them into his pockets.

— Al? Marvin Thursby said, his voice so low that it was no more than a whiskey-hoarse whisper. Al, tell me. Is—is Shad to home?

Al winced. He glanced up and saw that the light was out in Shad's room.

— What are you doing here, Thursby?

The man scratched absently at a three-day beard. There was dried blood on his face; he had probably stumbled and fallen. He jerked his head toward the upstairs room. —Is—is—Shad home?

—Yeah, he's home, Al said. He worked all day and came home to no supper.

—That's bad. Man oughta—oughta have his supper ready—for him. I'll just have—to have a little talk with L-l-lainy about things like that.

—It would be better if you didn't talk to her at all, Thursby, Cadiz said.

—Yeah, Al said.

—She oughta be told, Thursby said. Since her mother d-d-died, well, bringing up two children . . .

—You didn't bring 'em up, Al snorted, you drug 'em up. Jesus! Why don't you leave 'em alone?

—I—I didn't mean to—

—He's got a lot on his hands right now, Thursby, Cadiz said.

—I didn't mean to bother 'em, Thursby said.

—Like hell you didn't! Al said. You know he's only making a little time now and then, hardly able to keep your daughter in Co-Colas and headache powders. He don't need you on his neck.

Thursby managed to straighten up and hold his mouth firm.

—Brother, Thursby said, m' brother's got something lined up. Good prospect. Railroad job.

—Yeah, what railroad? Al asked.

—Central of Georgia, it's—

—You're a goddam liar! Al said. I know that brother of yours got thirty days on the Brown for fighting and drinking, and the Central of Georgia ain't hired a man in so long they got last year's cobwebs on the applications.

—Now, it ain't right to—to—call a man a liar. You're younger'n me, Al—

—You ain't a man, you're a goddam drunken bum, and you ain't a day over fifty and neither am I!

—Al! Cadiz said. Easy. She might be asleep.

—How come you don't like me, Al? Thursby asked.

—What's to like?

Thursby gave up. He nodded his head, and started away. Al stepped to his side quickly and took him by the arm.

— Listen, Marvin, leave 'em alone tonight. She ain't been well and he worked like hell digging ditches—

— I just wanted to stop in a minute and maybe have a cup of coffee—

— There *ain't* any goddam coffee! Al said. Here's a quarter. Go get a bottle of shine and get drunk and leave 'em alone.

— I been trying to stop drinking, Thursby said.

— Well, don't try tonight. Al shoved a quarter into the man's hand. Go on, get drunk and leave 'em alone.

Thursby took the quarter but did not move. I just wanted to see her, Lainy, and ask about the baby, that's all. I been thinking about being a grandfather. I been trying to make it mean something to me so I could get a hold of myself. But I can't seem to make it mean anything. I can't even remember things about her when she was a little girl that used to make me feel good. It's like even the memory of good times is all gone. I used to work on the job when they were both little, brother and sister, and sometimes I'd break out and just start yelling a song or something or other. Just thinking about them. My pa fit in the war against Sherman's bummers just north of here, toward Augusta, before he took Savannah. That used to mean something to me, to be able to say that, Al. I was—I used to be a proud man. I had something to be proud of. I had a pa that fit against Sherman's bummers and I had a job and a wife and two fine children. Now I wouldn't give you a fiddler's damn for my pa fighting against Sherman's bummers. I don't know. It was like a judgment was set down against me. On us. All of us. What did it, Al? What did I do to deserve this way that's got to me and what I am now? I was a working man. A hard-working man with good memories and things to be proud of. And then it was all gone and I was left with my pride and whatever else there was, which I don't remember anymore. It all just slipped through my fingers.

Cadiz and Al looked away.

— Ever think about the future? Al asked. Ever think about how lucky you are you've got a *man* for a son-in-law? I was here the day he turned down a good job for Lainy. So he could be with her and the baby.

— I heard about that, Thursby said vaguely.

— And you got a grandbaby coming. Maybe a grandson. That's something.

— But when an old man's old—

— You ain't old. You just a crybaby drunk. Go on, get drunk and sleep in a gutter somewhere. And leave 'em alone. Don't come around here. I don't want you around my store. This ain't a hangout for bums. It's a place of business.

Al's last words were drowned out by the thunder of the West Savannah Street Car. Al opened his mouth to make his pitch to the passengers when Cadiz stopped him and pointed to the window.

Al nodded and looked around for Thursby, but he had slunk out of sight.

— Whew! Al said. I hate that bum. I don't care what happens to a man, Howard, he's got to keep scratching. You know what I mean?

Shad slipped out of the darkened doorway, walking lightly, as if he dared not make a sound.

— I finally got her to sleep. I hope she sleeps through until morning.

Cadiz looked at Shad closely.

— Did you eat yet? Cadiz asked sharply.

— Not hungry, Howard, old buddy.

— I'll ask you tomorrow when you're swinging that shovel.

— I'll get a bottle of milk and a pack of sweet rolls later, Shad said. He worked the palms of his hands together, looking at them, spitting into them and rubbing them again. He smiled.

— I never thought I'd have trouble with these hands again, not after what they went through.

— How much longer will the job last? Al asked.

— Month, I hope. If I can make a steady eighteen dollars a week for four or five weeks, I'll be in good shape. For a while, anyway.

Kolb drifted up, and Danner, and later, Herod. Though it was nearly nine o'clock, several dirty, pinch-faced children that had so far managed to escape their mother's summons raced past the store and raced past again, and when they saw Al wasn't looking, they snatched oranges.

— Come back here! Al yelled. Damn you! Come back here!

— Reminds me, Cadiz said.

— Of what? Al asked, heaving himself around with a sigh of impatience. Oh, yeah! You and Shad. You were a couple of pretty good little hookers as I remember it.

— Right here in this neighborhood, Shad said with a smile. Liberty Square.

— I remember, Herod said. I used to chase you.

— Yes, and we used to hide in the schoolyard, Cadiz said.

— You think, Herod said softly, that I didn't know that, Howard?

Cadiz looked at Kolb and Shad and then at Herod and they all grinned. He nodded.

— I also remember the time you gave me a licking for hitting that girl with a rock in the playground at recess, Cadiz said.

— So do I, so do I, Herod said. It was also the time that I met your Aunt Meg for the first time.

Cadiz looked up, surprised.

— You knew Aunt Meg?

— Evidently you went home and told her about our little conference in the school toilet with the belt—

— I did. I had to explain the welts on my ass some way.

— Well, several days later, I was walking my beat. It was about one in the morning and I saw a well-dressed woman walking toward me. I was a little curious and knew right away that she wasn't a whore out on the make, and the Widows' Home is locked up at eleven. Then I recognized her.

— You met my Aunt Meg on the street at one in the *morning?*

— I did, Herod said. She came up to me and introduced herself. She said that her name was Meg Bowdry and she was your aunt. She said that any time it was necessary for you to get a licking, to bring you home and she would give it to you, in front of me.

— That, Cadiz said, sounds like my Aunt Meg.

— And, Herod said, she also said that if I touched you without her consent again, she would take care of me and that I would never be the same afterwards.

— Did you believe her? Cadiz asked.

— I did, Herod said. I didn't like it, but I believed her.

— You were a wise man, Herod, Cadiz said.

The pay telephone rang inside the store and Al went to take it.

— Alfred S. DeCunningham's store, Al speaking. He listened, then nodded. Yeah. Just a minute. Shad! For you!

Shad hurried into the store, took the receiver, and listened. He said not a word. He hung up and returned to the group.

— I've been fired, he said. They've got somebody else. Cheaper. They got somebody for three dollars cheaper.

The cooling wind eased in and around them. All Cadiz could hear was the thunder of the West Savannah Street Car. He was off by himself, alone, and he thought he could hear something under the wind. What was it? It was more than the sound of the wind. In the distance, muted, a curlew cried. Lost in the hot night, it searched for the seashore.

The store had changed. The stands, once piled high with delicious, inviting fruit, were now bare except for one huge basket of shrunken apples and a smaller basket of runty oranges. The interior of the store was changed too. The vivid advertisements that had been regularly replaced when the happy-talking salesmen came around, were faded and torn. The whole place had an air of sobering, steely-eyed defeat.

The robust self-confidence that had never allowed any challenge to defeat Alfred S. DeCunningham, had been eaten away as if worked on by nerve gas: odorless, tasteless, colorless. People passed the store front but Hessian did not hawk the fruit or attempt to sell them the shrunken apples or runty oranges. He sat hunched over. A thick, tattered overcoat three sizes too big for him hung loose and floppy on his thin body. He protected his hands from the cold wind by keeping them under the bib of his apron. He stared at the sidewalk. Al moved back and forth across the front of his store and looked down at the fruit. Out of habit he stopped before the basket of apples and selected several of the smallest, the most wrinkled, and threw them into the garbage basket. He brushed his hands together. Suddenly he swore.

Hessian looked up. Al pulled the garbage basket out from beneath the stands and retrieved the apples he had just thrown out. Hessian watched him, saying nothing. Al tossed the apples back on the pile.

— Goddammit! Al said again. I could throw out the whole stock! Just take the whole basket and give it to the kids in the widders home.

— Yes, suh, Hessian said quietly.

— But somebody might buy 'em, Al said. He spun around, his big belly protruding before him. He yelled into the cold air, his bass voice booming out. The voice was as icily defiant as the wind was icily cold.

— Rightcheah! Rightcheah! He yelled at the top of his voice for a few moments and then, winded, his anger spent, he stopped as suddenly as he had started. He looked around. People hurried by in the cold, unheeding.

Cadiz stared out into West Broad Street as the thick, icy rain came down. The street darkened and the lights from a few passing cars went by slowly, mistily. The West Savannah Street Car lumbered up. A lone figure stood at the exit waiting to get off. Then, head ducked into the collar of a raincoat, the figure dashed off the car and into Al's store. Only then could Cadiz see that it was Percey Kolb.

— Hey, Cadiz! Come on! I got some news that will burn your ears.

Cadiz moved quickly, cutting the angle from his doorway to the entrance of the store, but he still got wet. Kolb stamped around on the floor, shaking water from his head and peeling off his raincoat. He warmed his hands at the stove.

— Where's Al?

— In back, I guess, Cadiz said. What's the big news?

— What a situation, man! Hey, Al! Come on out here, boy. Got news for you!

Al drifted out of the darkness of the rear of the store. I was back there washing my hands, and even through all this rain I could hear your big mouth.

Shad ran in then. What a rain! If we were up north, it would snow a foot and a half!

— How's Lainy, Shad? Al asked.

— She's okay, Shad said cautiously. I got a prescription to fill.

— Yeah? Al said. How much it cost?

— Will you listen to me, Kolb said. I just come all the way across town from the Blue Boy Poolroom to tell you. And in this damn rain.

— How's she feeling? Al asked, ignoring Kolb.

— All right. Kind of low. But I guess that's the way it is when they get this far along.

— You'll have to watch she doesn't get a chill in this rain, Cadiz said.

— She's in bed, Shad said.

— Godammit! Kolb yelled. They wiped out Sharkey this morning. Early. Right after midnight.

Al, Shad and Cadiz looked at him, reacting slowly, not quite taking in the significance of Kolb's news.

— You're kidding, Al said.

Kolb drew himself up.

— I mean to tell you I ain't kidding!

— When did it happen? Cadiz asked.

— They were coming in from Tybee, down the county road. The way I heard it, there were two cars and four trucks, and all of them loaded with bonded booze just off the boat.

— Hijacked! Al said. I knew it would happen someday. All the no-goods in Savannah know about him and his operations, it had to happen. He was hijacked! I'll be damned.

Kolb wrung his hands over the stove in a painful gesture.

— Will you wait a minute! I didn't say he was hijacked.

— Well, tell your story, dammit! Al said.

Kolb took a deep breath and spread his fingers over the stove. Well! They went out and met the boat, see? Got the load and brought it back to the beach at Simon's Place, loaded the trucks and were bringing it into town. They had the cooperation of the cops, because everybody knows Sharkey's been working outa the county for a long time—when whammo!

— Whammo my ass! Al snorted. What does *whammo* mean? Something out of the funny papers? Al looked at Shad and Cadiz with a shrug of hopeless despair.

— Get smart, go ahead.

— Go on, Kolb, Cadiz said.

Kolb addressed Shad and Cadiz, ignoring Al. They were stopped by a big pile of stuff in the middle of the road and all of a sudden— they started shooting.

— *Who* started shooting? Al demanded.

— The people that put the stuff in the middle of the road *and blocked it,* that's who! Kolb blew his cheeks out. Jee-*sus!*

— There wasn't anything about it in the paper tonight, Al said.

— No, and there isn't likely to be, either, Kolb said.

— Anyone hurt? Shad asked.

— Hurt! They were sprawled out of their cars with bullet holes in them big as quarters!

— Was Sharkey hurt? Cadiz asked.

— Not from what I hear, Kolb said. He was one of the few that got away.

— Ah, it sounds like a story to me, Al said. Just another story about Sharkey and bootleggers and bullshit. You remind me, Al said, of some of the kids running around here, Percey, always got something important to talk about, always got something hot to tell.

Kolb turned his back to the stove and stared moodily out into the street. He thought for a moment and then turned back to Al.

— You're talking, he said.

— Yes, I'm talking.

— You admit you buy a bottle once in a while?

— What's that got to do with it? Al demanded.

— Plenty! Who do you think gets the stuff into town? It don't fly in here packed on the backs of angels! Somebody's got to handle it. And you hear things hanging around the Blue Boy.

— Sure you do, Al said. A lot of other guys just like you, throwing the bull.

— But the stuff is coming in! Kolb insisted. And somebody's doing it. You admit that, don't you?

— Sure, but it ain't none of the people that you would know or would even have their names mentioned in poolrooms.

— People on Victory Drive, I suppose! Huh? Is that who's in back of it, Al? Maybe the Mayor, too, huh? And the rest of them down at

City Hall? I suppose they're all in on it, huh? Or maybe you think the preachers are in cahoots with the Catholic Brothers, huh? Maybe every respectable person in the whole city is in on it, and *nobody* that would hang around a poolroom, huh?

Al shrugged, suddenly losing interest in the childish argument. Yeah, yeah. Why not? Like you say, somebody's bringing it in.

— Some of the guys figured it with a pencil and paper, Kolb said. A hundred thousand dollars wouldn't be far wrong.

— Lot of money, Cadiz said.

— Sure as hell is, Kolb said. More money than God's got.

— I wonder if it's true. Cadiz looked thoughtful.

— Even if the story is half true, it's still a lot of money and a lot of guys shot, Kolb said.

The rain slackened a bit. Someone hurried up the aisle and burst into the store.

— Boy, I'm whipped, Danner said. My ass is *cut!* Let me in there, Kolb, I'm wet to the skin and froze to the bone. I'm so cold my pecker's shriveled up in my stomach and I don't know what I'm going to do when I have to go to the can.

— Working hard? Cadiz asked.

— Hard, Danner said, warming himself. Seventy-three pairs of shoes shined in one day. It ought to be some kind of a record.

Kolb cut in with his usual quickness, running his fingers over his thumb.

— At five cents a pair, comes to three sixty-five. Not bad.

— But I had to split with the man, Danner said.

— Then you still got one-eighty-two-and-a-half, Kolb said.

— And I have to buy my own shoe polish—

— Twenty cents. Thirty at the most. A buck and a half. Still not bad. For shining shoes. You're doing okay.

— What the hell do you know about it! Working! Hanging over shoes some farmer came into town with after walking through cow flop all morning! What the hell do you know about it? You don't know nothing about it!

— Don't worry, Danner, ain't nobody going to ask you for anything, Kolb said.

— They damn sure better not.

— All right, you two, I'm closing up for the night, Al said.

Before any of them could move, Lainy's voice wavered down to them, as much through the ceiling as through the open front.

— Shad! Shaad! Don't you forget to get that prescription filled!

— I'm getting it now, Shad called back.

— Did you get the money?

— I'll get it, Shad said, unsuccessfully trying to avoid the eyes of the others.

— Well, hurry, will you? My back is aching and I need—

They did not hear what she needed. The rain came down again furiously for thirty seconds and then tapered off. A moment later it had stopped and the shiny streets reflected the night lights. In the quiet they could hear the run-off in the gutters.

— Well, I got to go, Danner said.

— How about loaning me a quarter, Danner? Kolb asked, and winked at Al.

— I can't, Danner replied.

— Loan me a dime.

— I gotta go, Danner said. He slipped out of the door and was gone as quickly as he had come.

— Scared stiff I might mean it, Kolb said.

— Didn't you? Cadiz asked.

— Well, now that you mention it, Kolb said with a grin.

— I'm closing up, Al announced.

— Anybody going my way? Kolb asked, slipping into his raincoat.

— Where's that? Cadiz asked.

— Back to the Blue Boy, where the hell else? It's the only home I've got now that Al's thrown me out.

— Where do you sleep, Kolb? Al asked, suddenly interested.

— I don't sleep in the streets, Kolb said. So long! And he was out of the door and walking fast.

— I know where he sleeps, Al said with a smile, punching at the grate in the stove. He's had a room in one of those old houses on the east side for years. The old man who owns the place is crippled or something. Kolb gooses his wife once in a while.

— Is that true? Cadiz asked.

— Yeah, why?

— Funny he never mentioned it. You'd think a guy like Percey Kolb would wear a thing like that on his sleeve. A badge of honor.

— Yeah, you would, wouldn't you? Al said thoughtfully. I only heard it by accident. He never told me. She's a fairly respectable woman, as I understand it.

— I'm going down to Doc Hilton's about the prescription. Shad said.

A Negro woman appeared at the front of the store. She looked critically at the basket of apples. She looked around for someone to wait on her. Al bustled out of the store and down the aisle.

— Yes, mam! Al said with professional charm. They're small, but they're firm.

— They looks softy, the woman said.

— I have a good price on them today.

— Says how much?

— Take three dozen and I'll give them to you for sixty cents. You save fifteen cents.

— Can't eat three dozen apples.

— I happen to be closing the store now, so I'll give them to you for a half dollar! Fifty cents! Al reached under the counter and ripped out a brown paper bag. He flipped his wrist and exploded it with a sharp report and started putting apples in the bag. The Negro woman had not moved. She stood still and watched his huge hands run over the fruit.

— That there'n is specked, she said.

— All right, we'll just take that speck right out! Al said and began to search around in the bag for the offending apple.

The bag was full and still the woman had not moved. She looked up at Al, her eyes blank.

— I didn't expect to buy so many, mistuh.

— I'm giving you three dozen apples for fifty cents, Al said.

— I know, but—

— You won't get a better price anywhere.

— No, suh, I don't guess I will, but I don't need three dozen apples. I just wanted somethin' to eat on while I waits for my streetcar.

— Well, how many? Al said, reopening the bag.

— How much for one?

— One dozen?

— One apple, the woman said, her impassive face showing nothing. Al ripped the paper bag apart and dumped the apples back onto the pile, balled the paper bag into a tight, hard wad and hurled it away viciously. The woman had not moved.

— I don't sell apples one at a time, Al gritted, and slammed back into the store.

The woman slowly walked across the street to the passenger station at the curb.

Al stood at the stove, warming his hands. They trembled a little.

— You'd better leave now, Cadiz, I'm closing up. Al spoke curtly, without looking at him.

— You once made me an offer, Al, Cadiz said.

— Yeah? What kind of an offer?

— Hijacking a bootlegger, Cadiz said softly.

— That was a long time ago.

— I'm interested, Cadiz said.

— Al snapped his head around and looked at him.

— You think the world has stood still? You're interested. You're *interested!* If I didn't like you so much, I'd bust out laughing.

— I'm serious.

— You're serious. I'm serious. The whole goddam world is serious. But I'll tell you something. That proposition, even back then, was sketchy. And needed a bankroll.

— You said you had a bankroll, Cadiz said.

— That's right, I had. I *had* it then. Now's different.

— What would it take? How much?

— It takes a hell of a lot more than you or I have seen in the last nine months.

— Was Sharkey the bankroll man?

— Why do you want to know?

— Because I'm going to move, Cadiz said. It's time for a change.

— Change? For Christ's sake, tell me *from* what *to* what and I might change with you.

— I've come to the snapping place, Cadiz said.

— Snapping place? What the hell is that?

— Don't get cocky with me, Al. There's something in each of us. Call it a wire. Mine's been tightened and tightened and—

— Whatever you're thinking, Al said, put it out of your head. It won't work. It can't work. You don't know what the hell you're saying.

— It's broken, Cadiz said.

— Go to bed, Al said. And here, take this dollar for Lainy's prescription in case Doc Hilton won't give Shad any more credit.

— I have three dollars, Cadiz said. But I'll take yours anyway. See? That's the change I mean. I'll take your dollar. I'm going to move, Al. You can tell me what you know, or I'll dig it somewhere else.

— Tell you what?

— About Sharkey. What you know about bootlegging. Who're the people to see, and the rest of it.

— You're out of your mind. Leave it alone. A-*lone!*

— No, said Cadiz quietly. I opened it up. It won't close again. It happened all at once. Today. Tonight, maybe.

— You can't have snapped it in just one evening, Al said. I don't know what you're going to hold it together with, but you just can't let go. Something's bound to turn up.

— Don't snow me, Cadiz said. Just tell me where I can find Sharkey. I hear he's still operating, bigger than ever.

— I won't tell you, Al said. You don't wanta get mixed up in that stuff. Something's bound to turn up.

— Are you going to tell me where I can find Sharkey?

— No.

— Then I'll hunt him up myself, Cadiz said. So long. He started off.

— Cadiz, wait.

— Yeah?

Al sighed wearily.

— You don't want to go to Sharkey, Al said. He dug a nickel out of his pocket and went to the pay phone. You couldn't see him. I'll send you to someone else. He dropped the coin and dialed a number.

— Hello. This is Al DeCunningham. Yeah, yeah, a store on West Broad. I want to get a line on Glass. He is? Okay, thanks.

Al hung up and looked at Cadiz. He's home. His name is Isidore Glass. Al mentioned an address in midtown.

— Thanks, Al, Cadiz said. Thanks.

— You going to take Shad in on this with you, if you make something up with Glass?

— I probably will, Cadiz said. Why?

— I just wanted to know. Okay, you better get going. He's just finished playing poker with Chocolate and Boris and Solly at the Blue Boy rooms upstairs. You'll catch him at home. Good luck with him, Cadiz. And watch him, he's smart. Very smart.

— I'm smart, too.

— I hope you make a million dollars, Al said.

— And live to be a hundred?

— That too, you cockster.

— I'll let you know how I make out, Cadiz said.

Al warmed his hands and studied the hair on the backs of his thick fingers. He shook his head sadly.

— If you catch on with Glass, you won't have time for me anymore. And I wouldn't want it. Things wouldn't be the same. He'll like you. In some ways you're alike. I don't know what it is. Hardheads, I guess. No, things'll change now for you. Like you said, you snapped. And if you don't catch on with him, you'll probably go on up to New York or Baltimore looking for a ship.

— Why do you say that?

— This is your ace in the hole. I know you been thinking about it for months. Whether to go this route. Well, you're making a move, anyway. You're playing your ace. If you lose, there won't be anything to hold you in town anymore. You'll go looking for something else.

— You're smart, Cadiz said. But it's not quite like that.

— Something else holding you?

— Yes.

— It isn't Shad and Lainy, so what is it?

— I'll come back and tell you sometime.

— It ought to be interesting as hell, Al said.

Cadiz went out of the store, past the spongy apples, and into the crisp, late November night air. It was a long way across town, and he blotted everything out of his mind as he walked.

He found the house on a quiet residential street. He climbed the stairs and knocked anyway even though the house was dark. He waited. A light shone through the glass-paneled door. Someone moved inside. Then the door opened.

— Mr. Glass?

Glass was a handsome man with jet black hair parted in the middle. He had a sharp, large nose and a full mouth. He managed a Valentino quality without actually trying.

— I don't want to buy anything, buddy, Glass said.

— Al DeCunningham sent me.

— Al DeCunningham. Is he still running that fruit stand over on West Broad Street?

— Yes.

— What's your name?

— Howard Cadiz.

— Oh, yeah. Cadiz. The sailor. Come on in.

Cadiz followed him inside, closing the door and then walking into a room that was Georgian, a faded elegance from another era but still retaining a certain style with bookshelves and hooded lamps and thick, color-faded carpets.

— Al spoke to me about you. A long time ago. Something we had lined up. Glass sat down in an overstuffed chair.

— That's right, Mister Glass, Cadiz said, still standing.

— It looks like I'm only a little bit older than you are, so don't call me Mister Glass. I'm Izzy. Plain, straight Izzy. It's a badge I would like to shed at times. At other times I have been mad enough, or foolish enough, to die for it. Izzy. Besides, when someone calls me Mister Glass I always have the feeling I should make sure they're not talking to my Pop. Okay, Cadiz, what's the story?

— I would like to make a lot of money, Cadiz said slowly, letting it come out under control.

Glass reacted coldly.

— What did you say?

— You heard me, Izzy.

Glass studied Cadiz a moment and then settled back in his chair.

There was a long silence. The two men looked steadily at each other. Glass broke it off. He sat forward in his chair.

— Go on, Cadiz. You would like to make a lot of money. Obviously you think I can help you.

Cadiz noted the tone of voice; confident as all hell, he thought. Have you ever thought how it would feel to walk down the street and never have to touch money again? Cadiz said.

— I've thought about it, Glass said dryly. Sit down, Cadiz.

Cadiz hesitated. He felt a sudden compulsion to walk out of the house. But he stayed where he was because Glass's expression altered slightly and Cadiz thought to himself: He knows, or at least senses, that I'm about to walk out.

— Go on, man, for God's sake, Glass said easily. Pull the chair around so we can see each other. Al DeCunningham, as I now remember it, told me you were a steady boy. You look pinched to me. Is it because you've come here alone? Maybe cutting Al out of your big plan? Or are you hungry? What was it that finally propelled you to the doorstep of good old Izzy Glass?

— Want the truth?

— Why not?

— I'm so hungry I nearly fainted on the way over here.

— I've never been hungry in my life, so I can't sympathize with you.

— I didn't ask you to sympathize with me, Cadiz said. I told you the truth, answered your question. But I'm not always hungry.

— Oh?

— No, Cadiz said, only every other day. I eat one day and starve the next.

— Interesting. Must take a lot of discipline.

— It was hard the first couple of weeks, Cadiz said. But then it got to be a habit.

— Then you have some money? I mean, you could buy something to eat if you wanted to?

— I have three bucks, Cadiz said.

Glass got up and walked to an inner door leading to another room.

— All I've got in the house is an apple. It's the only thing I've got because I live alone and I never eat in. You want it?

— I'll take the apple, Cadiz said.

Glass grinned and disappeared into the next room, returning

almost immediately with a huge red apple. He flipped it onto Cadiz's lap. Cadiz took a big bite, chewing slowly, his eyes on Glass.

— Why did you ask if I'd thought of never having to touch money again? Glass asked.

— I've brooded about money a long time, Cadiz replied. It has become everything.

Glass nodded. He moved around to a table and took a cigar from a nearly full box. He lit the cigar. In the pause that followed, Cadiz knew they would talk business now.

— You got any idea about how we can make a lot of money? Glass asked, puffing the cigar. Suppose I just make you an offer to work for me? I'll pay you by the week and I'll give you a bonus for big jobs.

— Doing what? And how much of a bonus?

— I'll think about it. I'll give you a little cash in advance. Glass extracted five tens from his wallet and handed them to Cadiz. Don't come here again. And don't try to get in touch. You'll hear from me.

— I wouldn't want to wait too long, Cadiz said, folding the five tens and putting them in his pocket.

— It won't be long.

— One more thing.

— Yeah?

— I have a friend who'd also like to make a lot of money.

— Who?

— Shad Courtney.

— Sorry, Glass said. I can't afford to hire an ex-con.

— You'll be missing a good man.

— Then I'll miss. But if I hear of anything, I'll let you know. There are some moonshine boys operating out of South Carolina and Florida. I'll ask around. Is your man desperate?

— He's desperate, Cadiz said.

— I'll let you know. Where can I reach you?

— At Al's store, Cadiz said. Any time.

The store was closed. The stands were gone, the doors locked and the windows dark and dirty. The only familiar thing in the place was the long bench that Hessian slept on while Al played poker in the back rooms.

Al and Kolb sat on the bench before an oil drum and watched as Hessian fed the fire from a pile of rubbish at the curb. Holes had been punched in the sides of the drum to make a draft, and they glowed hotly in the night.

Time and defeat had taken its toll of all of them, but it was most obvious in Kolb. His snappy style of dress was gone. He wore an old sweater underneath his jacket, and his ice-cream britches were soiled and rumpled; he had been sleeping in them and they looked it. He spoke in monosyllables. He would start a story as before, full of enthusiasm, but he would lose interest midway and ramble to a stop.

Al had changed, too. He now wore an old army overcoat and his remarks were more cynical and biting than ever. Kolb and Al sat on the bench and stared into the fire, hunched over, for the most part silent.

Hessian dropped more rubble into the fire. Sparks flew up and Hessian shrank back.

— Don't burn it all, Hessian, goddammit, Al said. Save some for tomorrow.

— And then they started yelling, Kolb said, and the first thing I knew the cops were down there beating them over the head with nightsticks and clubs.

Al spit on the side of the oil drum and watched it sizzle.

— They had no business going on strike. I can see a man doing something crazy to get a job, but I don't understand his acting crazy when he's got one. People are starving to death all over town and they stage a fucking strike.

— Sign of the times, Kolb said.

— If I hear that goddam remark *one more time,* Al said, I'll piss green. A sign of the times! Jesus! What does *that* mean?

Kolb didn't answer. Finally he said, Ain't it about time for Lainy and Shad to have their kid?

— I don't know. I ain't seen either of them since they moved out, Al said.

— He still running with the shiners?

—No, he didn't stay long with them. Glass had a job and was hungry for more men, and Cadiz hired Shad.

—How'd it work out? Kolb asked. Did they score?

—How the hell do I know? You think I see them? I changed my social habits.

Kolb hesitated and sighed.

—Give me some tobacco, Hessian, Kolb said.

—Sorry, Mistuh Percey. I ain't got no tobacco.

—Al?

—I got enough left for maybe five or six butts, Al said. And I've got to stay up all night.

—Okay, Kolb said.

—Pick up a butt off the street, Al said.

—I'll stop smoking first.

—Well then, stop, dammit, Al said flatly.

Al got up suddenly, walked to the door of the store and looked inside. He wiped the glass on the door and banged very softly on the pane with his fist.

—I tried to explain to them that nobody else would rent the goddam place, and that if they'd let me keep it they'd at least have the chance of getting some rent and I'd be in their debt.

—What did they say? Kolb asked.

—I was a goddam fool, Al said, walking back to the bench. After Cadiz and Shad came back and paid me what they owed me, I only thought about putting good stock out front. It just didn't occur to me to put something down on the rent. I had to have stock, goddammit. What the hell's the use of having a store if you ain't got anything to sell?

Al sat down heavily and warmed his hands at the drum.

—You're right, Kolb said. Suppose you had paid the rent on the store, what would you do for stock? It seems to me you'd have been screwed either way. You have a store and no stock. Or you have stock and no store. What's the difference?

—I could have begged for more credit from *both* of them, and dribbled out the money. I coulda hung on. I was a fool.

—What made you think you could have worked it out with the renting office? Kolb asked.

— Never mind, Al said. Never mind.

Hessian said, Mistuh Al thought his name still stood for something downtown.

— A good name, Kolb said, isn't worth the breath it takes to say it.

— I learned that the hard way, Al said. If I ever get another chance, and I will, goddammit, right on this corner, I'll be the biggest bastard this town ever saw. You wait and see.

— I can't wait, Kolb said. I been thinking about moving. Out to California—or Florida.

— Ha! Al snorted. And get your ass in a sling working on some road gang?

— Maybe not, Kolb said. I might be lucky.

At least you *know* the cops around here, Al said. The only ones they're picking up off the street so far are the transients. They're not messing with the hometown boys yet. You're better off sitting on your ass right here.

— Maybe the election will change things, Kolb said.

— Sure, Al sneered. Two chickens in every pot. Did you know he's so rich he don't even take his salary as President?

— I know.

— Take a look and see if they're ready now, Hessian, Al said.

— Yessuh, Hessian said, and poked around in the ashes at the bottom of the drum, punching several large sweet potatoes. He straightened up. Not yet, Mistuh Al.

— Who'd you vote for, Hessian? Kolb asked.

Hessian looked quickly at Kolb to see if he was being baited. He sighed.

— I didn't vote.

— Me neither, Kolb said.

— Well, I did! Al said with an inner fury in his voice. And I wrote right across the face of the ballot. One word. Big as I could make it. S-H-I-T.

— Who's he? Democrat or Republican? Kolb asked. They both laughed.

Herod sauntered up, swinging his nightstick around in a cartwheel, his eyes fixed on the three figures before the oil drum fire.

— Hello, Al, Herod said quietly. He nodded to Kolb and Hessian. Al glanced up briefly and nodded.

— You heard of anything, Herod? Kolb asked.

— Not a thing, Percey, Herod said. The policeman looked at Hessian. How's your mother, Hessian? Still got a cold?

— Fine, suh, Hessian said. Just that bad cold is all. But she's getting over it. The welfare people gave us a chit for some wood. It helps. Every-little-bit helps, suh, Hessian said wearily, dragging the words out over a sigh.

— Tell her to keep warm, Herod said.

— Yessuh, I tell her, Hessian said. But she find it hard to do.

Herod made a gesture for Al to come with him. Al stood and walked to the curb a few feet from the drum.

— I got orders today, Al, Herod said. You can't sleep out here on the bench anymore.

— I see, Al said.

— It's the women in the Widows' Home—

— They didn't complain, did they? Al asked quickly.

— No, they didn't. But the Lieutenant—well, Kolb and Hessian and all the others. It isn't a store anymore, where people get together, like the old days. It's just a bunch of bums standing on a street corner around an oil drum fire.

Al nodded. All right, Herod, I'll keep them away.

— No, you don't understand, Herod said. This means you, too.

— But Herod, I've got to be here early in the morning—

— I'm just relaying orders, Herod said.

— But I've been on this corner nearly twenty years, Al said. I scrubbed that sidewalk so many time the city ought to give it to me as a present.

— Goddammit, Al! Herod said, *I'm* not telling you to move on— it's orders!

— Well, you know what you can do with your orders!

The relief on Herod's face was apparent. He had hated to tell a friend that orders had come down and that the friend would have to move on, but Al had taken him off the hook; he had snapped back at Herod's authority. It would be easy now. He was used to having to deal with people who resented his authority. He unlimbered his nightstick.

—Now, don't go getting loud, Al. I'm telling you: get off this corner tonight, or I'll have to run you in.

Al's face was tight, his voice bitter. Okay, Mister Herod. Okay. You've told me. You've delivered your message. Anything else?

—Don't get hot with me, Al.

—I'm not getting hot. I just don't give a shit.

—I'm telling you. Don't sleep on this corner. Don't even hang around here tonight or I'll call the wagon. Herod walked off quickly into the darkness. Al watched him go, then moved slowly back to the oil drum. He sat down heavily.

—It don't mean a thing that just about every night for fourteen years he's been sleeping in my back room while Hessian went and pulled his box for him, I have to be off this corner tonight.

—What can you do? Kolb asked.

—I can stay put, that's what I can do, Al said.

—Wouldn't be smart, Kolb said softly.

—I don't care if it's smart or not. If I wanted to be smart I'd have gone in with Izzy Glass and Shad and Cadiz. All I want is what's mine. I still got the license to sell on this street, and I've been on this corner—Al looked up at Hessian. His voice was irritable. How about them damn sweets, Hessian?

—Just about ready, Mistuh Al, Hessian said, and poked again in the hot ashes.

—They look done, Kolb said.

—They are done, Al said. When the skin gets tight and burnt like that, they're done.

—Here she comes! Hessian said. He flipped two sticks into the drum, worked them deftly and juggled a large, smoking sweet potato up and out. Al caught it, tossing it from hand to hand and then putting it down on the bench to cool. Hessian dug again and came up with a second potato, flipping it over to Kolb. Kolb threw it high in the air, his eye watching the potato like an infielder under a pop fly, wiping his hands on his trousers between heaves. He continued to do this until the potato was cool enough to handle. Hessian pulled out a third potato and let it fall to the ground to cool. Too hungry to wait, they split the peels open and bit into the hot, soft flesh.

— Little butter would go good, Kolb said.

— Or salt, just salt, Al said. Surprising how you miss the little things.

— I'm satisfied, Kolb said.

— You were always easily pleased, Kolb, Al said.

They each had three potatoes and laughed and joked and complained about how hot they were and when the meal was finished, Al offered his tobacco all around and they smoked contentedly and stared into the fire.

They did not see Danner in the darkness behind them. He stopped and spoke to someone in the shadows with him, a woman. She was nearly forty, thin, with too much rouge and lipstick. There was a nervous haggard manner about her when she spoke. Danner kept making short chopping motions with his hands as if trying physically to cut through her fears. He wheeled abruptly and left her in the shadows and walked toward the group around the oil drum.

— Hello, Al, Kolb, Danner said, his manner studiedly casual. He nodded to Hessian. Cold night.

— Heard you quit the shoe-shine profession, Al said.

— Didn't quit, they fired me, Danner said. Ask anybody.

— I heard you quit, Al said. And don't tell me to ask anybody. Why the hell should I ask? Who the hell cares? I heard you quit. You know who told me? The man that got you the job.

Danner's hands, though well down over the fire, trembled slightly. He did not move or make a sound. He eased his head around once, peering into the shadows.

— Any of you boys interested in a little pussy? Danner asked.

Al, Kolb and Hessian all looked at him in surprise. He did not meet their eyes.

— Well, I'll be goddammed! Kolb said.

— Go on, get away from here, Danner, Al said in disgust.

Danner whirled on them. His face was livid with anger and pain and shame.

— What the hell's wrong with you, Cunningham! he shouted.

— Keep your voice down and get the hell away from here, Al said again.

— Since when have you gotten so high and mighty! I see C-L-O-S-E-D on a sign over that door yonder!

Al started to get up, but Kolb put a restraining hand on his arm.

— I might be interested, Danner. How much? Kolb said.

— You got any money? Danner asked doubtfully.

— When a man's buying pussy, he has to be particular.

— Well, you don't have to worry about catching anything, if that's what you mean, Danner said.

— Anybody I know? Kolb asked.

— Aw, shut up, Kolb, Al said. Go on, get the hell away from here, Danner.

— Wait a minute, Al, Kolb said, winking at Hessian. I want to know what he's got to sell.

— You wouldn't be interested in her, Al said.

— Might be. Never can tell about a man's taste, eh, Danner? Let's take a look at her.

— Goddammit, Kolb, keep your big mouth shut! Don't you *know* about Danner—and her?

— Know what?

— You interested in getting laid or not, Kolb? I ain't got all night.

— Know what, Al? Kolb insisted.

Al closed his eyes and shook his head. It's his wife.

Kolb was stunned. You prick, he said to Danner.

— Well, it wasn't my idea, Danner said, his voice shrill. She was the one that suggested it—

— You dirty little turd, Kolb said.

— I ain't asking you to judge me, or her! Goddammit! You wanta get laid, pay your money! But don't any-*damn*-body stand around no oil drum eating sweet potatoes try and make me out to be a bastard.

Al got up quickly, his arms at his sides, and moved toward Danner.

— Leave. Just leave before I lose my temper. Al shoved him. Danner fell and the woman came running out of the shadows and helped him to his feet. They walked off into the darkness and disappeared around the corner.

— Jesus! His own wife! Kolb said.

— He's hungry, Al said.

— I'm hungry, too. But, Jesus, what a thing for a man to do!

Al sat down again, heavily. Yeah, what a thing for a man to do. You want to know something? When Herod came by here a little while ago, he looked at us the same way we just looked at Danner.

— Mistuh Al, Hessian said, I think it's about time for me to go down.

— It's early yet, Hessian. No need to go hanging around in the cold until they open. Wait a while longer.

Kolb stared at the draft hole and said in a tight, withdrawn voice, I'm leaving.

— Where you going? They won't let you in the poolroom anymore since you broke a cue over Solly's head. You were lucky he didn't have you arrested for assault.

— I mean leaving town, Kolb said.

— You're a damn fool, Kolb, Al said. You do that, you're worse than a damn fool. It doesn't make any difference where you are today. There ain't no jobs—nowhere.

— I got to move. I can't pull my weight around here anymore.

— You'll find yourself in a sling, Kolb. You leave town and you'll get into a mess, probably the same mess you're in right now, right here in town. Why leave?

Kolb began to pace back and forth swinging his arms restlessly.

— But if I set here and wait, I'll rot and stink my life away. They say there ain't going to be any quick recovery, and I believe them. Some say it will take twenty years to pull out. Twenty stinking years. I'll be an old man, Al, and my whole life would have been spent right here in this chickenshit town trying to keep hat and ass together because people know me and won't throw me in jail. Is that a way for a man to go through life?

— If that's the way you feel about it, Percey, Al said softly. But it won't be easy.

— I don't expect it to be easy. You make it sound like it was easy here. If I move around, I'll meet different people, hundreds of them, different people and different things. Somewhere along the line I'll make a contact. I been thinking about it a long time. I been out of work now for thirty-one months. Since then I been doing the same things and seeing the same people and just standing still.

— You're an optimist, Percey, Al said.

— No, I'm not. But I'm honest, in spite of what the man wrote. And I always saw the picture honest and was honest with myself. I know what I'm doing. I know a rummy down at the Blue Boy. Everybody looks down on him. He's always drunk, and when he isn't drunk, he's looking for some small change so he can buy some stuff and get drunk again. I talked with him one day, and I asked him why did he drink and stay drunk all the time. Maybe you know him. They call him Love.

— I know Love, Al answered.

— He said, look at it this way. How many problems have you got? I told him hundreds. Things like eating, sleeping, a job, my self-respect, money, pussy, a hundred things. He answered that he had only one. He had reduced everything to one single problem. How to get drunk and stay drunk. That's all he was concerned with.

— How does that fit in with you leaving town? Al asked.

— Where I'm going, the only problem will be me. Not my self-respect, or eating, or sleeping, or getting pussy, or a job. Just me. I won't have the problem of facing the world every morning. I'll be part of the world. *Really* a part of it.

— When would you be leaving? Al said.

Kolb did not reply. He looked off down West Broad Street.

— I'll take the next damn streetcar into West Savannah. There ain't any reason why not.

Al rolled a cigarette and lighted it. I never liked you, Percey. I always thought you were a big mouth. I'm sorry.

— I am a big mouth, but you just never had a chance to see me go. I'm a big man when I go, Al. I can charge with the best of them. Big man, big mouth, can go together. You just saw one side of me. I'm strong as a bull and can work twenty hours a day. You just never saw me go.

— I'm sorry, Al said.

— Are you really going to cut it, Mistuh Percey? Hessian asked.

— Might as well make it California, Kolb said, nodding his head.

— I heard a fella say, Hessian began slowly, that the state cops were meeting them at the line and asking 'em one question. You got five hundred dollars? If they don't, they wasn't allowed to come into the state.

— I heard that too, Al said.

— There ain't nothing in the Constitution says a man can't move from one state to another.

— You tell 'em that when they pull you off the boxcar you're going to be riding, Al said.

— I'm going. I'll regret it to my last day if I don't make this move, Kolb replied. What is there to wait for? A promise of something to come? I been romanced by promises and I didn't even get kissed.

The distant rumbling of the West Savannah Street Car could be heard. It had not yet made its turn from Broughton Street into West Broad, but it was coming.

— Leaving, by God! Kolb shouted. He stopped, stiffened, as if awed by the decision he had made. I'm not taking it lying down anymore. I got the whole world to move around in. Somewhere I'll find me something to hang onto. You stay. Both of you. Stick with the promises and you'll find them stuck up your creeks!

The streetcar rumbled around the corner, straightened and moved down on them, a single yellow eye up front beaming the way. The car crossed the junction tracks and braked.

— Last chance, Al, Kolb said. Come with me.

— Don't be a fool, Kolb. You'll sleep cold tonight and be hungry in the morning.

— Well, that may be, but I won't be sitting around waiting for it to happen. So long, Al. So long, Hessian. I'll send you a picture postcard from Hollywood!

Kolb turned and ran across the street, yelling for the car to wait. They both watched as he boarded and spoke to the motorman. Then the car pulled off, rounding the corner.

Al stood up. Crazy bastard. They'll chew him up and spit out the bones. He won't last ten minutes. He's like a kid.

— Still, he ain't sitting, Mistuh Al. He's moving.

Al sat back down, staring at the fire.

— How much do I owe you, Hessian?

— You don't owe me, Mistuh Al.

— You haven't been paid in how many weeks?

— It don't make no difference.

— I want to know, dammit, Al said.

— How are you gonna pay me, Mistuh Al? It's just a game, Mistuh Al, just a game. I come around here because I ain't got no place else to go. People know me on this corner, like they know you. That's why Mistuh Percey had to get up and run all the way to California, because he feels like he ain't got a corner to stand on.

Al nodded in almost violent agreement.

— A man needs a good friendly corner to stand on, Hessian. It takes the place of friends, home, and a lot of other things. There were lots of places I could of moved my store to, but I never did, not because I did better business here. I didn't. But this was like home. I spent so many months of the year outside, so many months inside. This is the first time I've been outside in the winter since France.

— You never talk about France and being a soldier, Mistuh Al, Hessian said.

— I did my talking with a gun. With my hands. And when it was over, it was over.

Hessian said, You want me to go down now? It's getting pretty late.

— Might as well, Al said, digging into his pocket. He pulled out several dollar bills. Now, Hessian, I don't want anything but prime fruit. I want New York State apples. And you open the box and examine them.

— Yessuh, Hessian said. Anything else?

— Nothing else, Al said, handing over the money. I'd go myself, but I owe so much they'd want to take this money and credit it to the bill and I'd be left with nothing.

— I don't mind going, Mistuh Al. You know that.

— But I mind asking you.

Hessian did not answer. He put the money away and took a last warming lick of the fire with his hands, buttoned up tight to the neck, and shuffled off.

A cold wind blew down on the oil drum and swept papers along the gutter; the wind whipped the corner of a nearby roof; the wind tore at the faded paper ads stuck to the side of the building; it bit into the night and made it seem endless as Al slept on the bench, stretched full out, his face to the drum.

Out of the cold morning darkness, a sputtering car broke the silence. A streetcar clanged. When Al opened his eyes he saw a figure standing beside the oil drum picking up rubbish and dropping it into the drum. Al raised his head, alarmed.

— Oh, it's you, Al said blinking. I didn't recognize you for a minute there, Shad. How's Lainy?

— Have you seen her, Al? Shad asked.

— No, I haven't. Why?

— She's gone.

— Gone where? What about the baby?

— It was born two weeks ago, Shad said, staring into the fire. While I was away. Up in Canada for a load for Glass. I came back and took her out of the hospital. We have an apartment over across town. Then I had to leave again. When I came back, she was gone. With the baby.

— You had a boy?

— Yes.

— Congratulations. How big?

— Big boy, Shad said quietly. Nine pounds seven ounces.

— That's fine, Al said, watching Shad's face. Now what about Lainy?

— No one's seen her. She took every dime of purchase money Glass had given me for another trip to Canada.

— Jesus!

— Have you seen her, Al? Izzy gave me until this morning to get the money.

— How much was it?

— Four thousand dollars, Shad said, hardly able to get it out. I can't even go to the police.

— Mother of God! Al said. Where's Cadiz?

— Out on the boat. He's gone to meet one of our loads coming in from Cuba.

— Can't he get you out of this?

— No. He's broke all the time. Spends it as fast as he gets it. Glass was very matter of fact about it. He said from his point of view I could of set it up with her to run off, could of arranged the whole thing. He doesn't say he believes it one way or the other. He just has a point of view. And I have until this morning.

— Was there some reason? Did you do something to her?

Shad shook his head. No reason I can think of. He looked up at the closed store. I only just heard about your having to close down. This is the first time I've had a chance to come around.

— What are you going to do? Al said.

— I'm supposed to meet Glass.

— Have you tried her father? And that creepy brother of hers? They're just slimy enough to have made her do it.

— Her brother's in jail for stealing a car and her father's drunk. As usual, Shad said.

— Then there isn't anything left for you to do, Al said.

— No, nothing.

— You wouldn't run?

— To where? And for what? Is there any place better than this?

Al threw a piece of rubbish into the oil drum and sent sparks flying into the air.

— No, I don't guess there is. Percey Kolb just pulled out for California. Danner's pimping for his wife.

— I know.

— Are you going to sit and wait for it? Al asked. For Glass to come and get you?

— I've done all the running I can.

Al nodded. He warmed his hands. Listen, Al said suddenly. Friend of mine would be glad to hide you out for a while, until Cadiz gets back.

— No, not Howard. Not again.

— Listen, that's stupid—

— No! You listen, Shad said. I'm finished. I want it over with.

— Don't *talk* like that.

— And it's not because a woman I was forced to marry and began to love ran out on me with money a man now threatens to kill me for. It's the boy.

— Your son?

— It's right that it ends up this way, Shad said. I never really had it. The difference. The something else that it takes to live in this lousy world. Maybe that's why we have a depression. To shake out the deadbeats who can't pull their weight. Me, Danner, Thursby, Kolb—

— And me? Al asked.

— Yeah, Al, even you, Shad said. But this way I won't have to play nursemaid to a son—even if Izzy Glass lets me off the hook.

— Nursemaid! Why you—you got it all wrong!

— No, not wrong at all. Going through life making out that I enjoy living the lies that I'd have to teach him. Telling him over and over that the world is something it isn't, afraid of the day when he finds out for himself and comes to hate me for lying to him.

— You're a pretty strong man to give up so easy, Shad.

— You can't rile me, Al. It's past the time for hot air and you know it.

— Yeah? Well, let me tell you something. I learned one thing when I had to close this store down. It ain't *never* too late! Not if you're selfish enough and greedy enough. It's got to be strictly hooray for me and fuck you. It's the only way. The way Izzy Glass operates. From the talk I heard around town he likes you a lot, but that ain't going to stop him from breaking your arms or maybe your head for his dough. And you'll survive, Shad. That's what I learned when they closed me down, and where I made my mistake. I tried to be a nice guy, letting you have the room for nothing, not pressing you about the rent, putting you on the cuff for everything, loaning you money when I shoulda been buying decent stock for the store. All that, when I should have been a prick, see? It wasn't just you. It was a lot of others too. A dime here, a quarter there—

— I've got to go, Al.

— You don't want to run? To take a chance and fight again some other time? I can't figure you. Personally, I think you're a goddam fool. And I wish to God I'd never wasted good money and time and friendship on you.

The thunder of the West Savannah Street Car rolled in on them and covered Izzy Glass's approach. Glass eased up alongside of the oil drum and warmed his hands. Neither Shad nor Al moved.

— Hello, Al, Glass said. Cold night. He looked around at the dark store. Too bad about your store.

— I'm doing all right, Al said.

— Sure you are, Glass said. Didn't say you weren't. He looked at Shad. Well?

— You know the answer, Izzy.

Glass shook his head, lit a cigar carefully and puffed it several times. If you could only make me believe that you didn't plan it . . .

— How could I do that?

— That's not my problem, Shad. Sorry. Do you believe me, Shad, when I say thank God it isn't my problem?

— Yes, I believe you.

Al moved suddenly and grabbed Glass from behind, pinning his arms in back of him. Glass made no attempt to resist.

— Run, Shad! Run, goddammit! Take his car—run!

Shad did not move. Three men appeared out of the shadows and surrounded all of them. There was no mistaking who they were. They just stood and looked.

When Al saw them he released Glass.

Glass shook his head in mild exasperation as he looked at Al. Do I interfere with your business?

— Never mind, Al said. Never mind.

Glass warmed his hands again, speaking to Shad. You're not going to come up with the money. I know I gave you until this morning, but you're not going to do anything but hang around here and talk to Al. Come on, let's get it over with.

Shad began pulling on his gloves. You going to kill me?

— What kind of a question is that? What I do is business. Glass jerked his head, and the three hoods moved out, taking Shad with them.

— Tell Hessian good-by for me, Al. So long.

— So long! *So long!* Is that all you've got to say for yourself? *So long!* Why you sad sonofabitch! You give up that easy, I hope they do kill you!

Glass raised his eyebrows. You're a tough old cock, Al. I never realized that before.

Al ignored him. He spoke to Shad, ignoring the three men who had paused a few yards away.

— Shad, say the word. Just say it and I'll—

Glass jerked his head again and one of the men approached Al, his hand in his pocket.

— Get away from me, Al said, the words coming out like the snarl of a trapped animal, or I'll break you in half. Al shoved the man to one side, sending him back against the plate glass of the store. Glass took a step backward as Al faced him.

— Listen to me, Glass! Who do you think you are, packing people off like they were cattle, playing God—

Glass jabbed a finger in Al's chest. He was about to speak when the hood he had shoved put a gun in his back.

Al sagged. Shad had not moved an inch.

— It doesn't have to be like this, Shad—

— So long, Al, Shad said.

Shad and the two men, joined by the third, moved off to the car parked in the shadows by the school. Glass remained, still warming his hands. The car started. Al looked at Shad, sitting in the back seat. The window was open. He knew Shad could hear him. He spoke loudly to Glass.

— What about Cadiz?

— What about him?

— Cadiz and Shad were kids together. I know Cadiz. You'll have to get him, too. He won't cave in like this one.

— Then I'll take care of Cadiz, too, Glass said.

— Did you hear that, Shad! Al screamed. Did you hear that, you spineless sonofabitch! You're going to let him get Howard too!

Glass shook his head. You really don't understand it, do you, Al? It's a crack-up of the whole system. Everything is coming down. It's a gamble just to stay alive. A grab-bag society. You reach in with your hand and you have no idea what you're going to come out with. Shad put his hand in. This is what came out. I put my hand in and I wind up having to do things like this. And there's no way to go back for another grab. One to a customer. That's the rule of the game. As long as I can remember, people have been wanting guarantees. You put in your hand and you pull out your prize. That's all, brother. Glass's voice hardened. You going to change it?

Glass dropped the cigar into the oil drum. Well?

Al looked him in the face. Shock was in his eyes. He shook his head and left Al sitting alone on the bench. He stared at the fire—he did not know how long—slipping sideways first to lean on his elbow and then gradually stretching out. He was unaware of Thursby, who watched him from the shadows.

Thursby moved forward cautiously, looking furtively around the empty streets, and then moved in quickly on Al and began to search his pockets. He found nothing. He settled himself near the fire, deliberately making a noise to awaken Al.

Without moving, Al said, I been awake all the time, Thursby, while you searched my pockets. I'd get up and break your arm, but you're not worth the effort.

Thursby backed away from the fire.

— If you run, I swear I'll catch you and mash your face in. Where's that goddam daughter of yours?

Thursby made as if to run. Al came up quickly, ready to move. Thursby froze.

— I don't know—I ain't seen her. You'd think she would of thought about her father when she stole that money—

— Why should she think about you? What the hell did you ever do for her? Do you know what they did to your son-in-law?

— I'm a sick man, Al, leave me alone.

— I oughta beat you half to death, Al said wearily. Somebody should. But then, why just you?

— What did I do? Thursby whined. I didn't do anything. All I ever did was try to be a good father—

— Go on, get away from me.

— Jesus Christ, Al, it's cold. I need a drink—

— Go on, get away from here. Al made a menacing gesture. Thursby backed away.

— You got no call to yell at people. You ain't no better'n a bum yourself. Look at you! Look! You need a shave, your clothes are filthy, you sleep in the streets. And another thing! I seen you let them take Shad! And—

— What! Al demanded. You saw them! And you didn't come out? You didn't try and help me stop them? Your own son-in-law!

— I told you I'm a sick man, Al—

Al choked back the fury. He stood. Get away, he said hoarsely. Get away—!

Thursby retreated to a safe distance.

— Al DeCunningham! Big shot! Big shit is more like it! That's all you are now! You're down on your face like the rest of us. You'll root hog or die, Mister Alfred S. DeCunningham.

Al made a run after him, but Thursby darted around the corner and disappeared. Al turned back to the fire and picked up the last of the rubbish and dropped it into the drum. The sparks flew up and he slapped at them, catching some in his hands. He rolled his last cigarette and stood with his back to the drum and watched the corner where he knew Hessian would appear. He had smoked the last of his tobacco and tossed the butt into the drum when Hessian walked around the corner carrying a box of apples on his shoulders. He put them down gently next to the oil drum.

Hessian hesitated. I can't help you today, Mistuh Al, he said solemnly. I saw a man down at the market and he offered me a few hours' work around his chicken stall. I gotta go right back.

— That's fine, Hessian, Al said.

Al began to open the box, expertly, with a small pen knife. He took out two apples, rubbed them, smelled them. He flipped one to Hessian.

Hessian took the apple and put it in his pocket. He mumbled something about his saving it for later. Al nodded.

Mistuh Al, Hessian said, there's something I've got to tell you.

Al looked up. Well?

— They found a body, a man's body—white man—in one of the lanes nearby the market just before I left—

Al straightened up.

— He was dead, Hessian said. It was Mistuh Shad. Hessian did not attempt to wipe away the tears. I thought I might be mistaken, it was so dark, so I went up close and took a good look. It was him. Mistuh Shad.

— Don't tell me. I don't want to know.

— Yessuh, I thought that—

— Never mind what you thought, Al said. Go on now, go on to your job.

— Yessuh, it's Mistuh Distenfeld. His chicken stall in the market.

— Get going, or you'll lose out, Al said.

— No, suh, Hessian said. Mistuh Distenfeld said if I did good today he might use me regular. I thought I'd tell you so you would know if I didn't come around no more.

— You help yourself, Hessian. It's every man for himself. That's the ticket.

— Yessuh, well, I better be getting on down. Good-by, Mistuh Al, suh.

— Good-by, Hessian, Al said, shaking hands with Hessian firmly. I'll pay what I owe you someday.

— Yessuh, said Hessian. He lingered a moment longer, then ducked his head and walked hurriedly away.

Herod, a lieutenant and a third policeman walked briskly up to the oil drum.

— Hello, Herod, Al said.

— Al, have you seen Shad?

— Yeah. Saw him here earlier this morning.

— He's dead.

— I know. Hessian just told me.

— Do you know anything about it?

— I know more about it than anybody else.

— Who did it?

— Glass. Or some of his men. They stood right here around the fire.

— Did Glass threaten him? the lieutenant asked.

— He did, Al said.

— Well! the lieutenant said, let's see what Izzy has to say about that!

— Old man Thursby heard it too, Al said. He was hiding in the shadows.

— All right, the lieutenant said, we'll pick him up too.

Al frowned. What do you mean, too?

— Go call the wagon, the lieutenant said, turning to the other policeman. Let's go, Al.

— Go where?

— Don't ask smart questions, Al, Herod said. The lieutenant said let's go, and that means let's go!

— What is this, Herod? What are you trying to pull?

— Do you have an address? Somewhere you live? the lieutenant asked.

— Right here. On this corner, Al said.

— You're a material witness, Al, Herod said. We've got to take you in. Besides, I warned you last night.

— But I'm in *business* here! Al shouted. This is how I earn my living!

— Business my ass, the lieutenant said. Selling apples like any other bum around town.

— Who the hell you calling a bum! I been on this corner for nearly twenty years!

— Even if it wasn't this, Al, you'd have to come as a material witness.

— But you can find me here any time, you know that! You must be kidding.

— No, we're not kidding, the lieutenant said. Are you going to come or are we going to have to take you?

— Are you arresting me?

— You have to go downtown, Al, Herod said. Either way.

— You can't arrest me, Al said. I'm a material witness. Okay. I'll show up when you want me. But you're not taking me in. I done nothing wrong—

— All right, bum, the lieutenant said, you asking for it!

He stepped in with his blackjack and started to swing. The apples were kicked over and rolled into the street. Herod looked away.

Al ignored the apples and stepped in to meet the lieutenant's blackjack. He took the force of the blow on his forearm, then grabbed the weapon, twisting it out of the lieutenant's hand. He threw it into the street and hurled the lieutenant to the ground. Al backed up.

— I'm telling you now, goddammit, I've been on this corner for nearly twenty years. I'm in *business*—I've got a *license!*

— Arrest him! the lieutenant shouted.

— No! You don't understand! Al backed up against the store. *I'm in business!*

Herod, the lieutenant and the third policeman all moved in on him. They swung their fists and nightsticks and kicked and stomped. Al fought back. He used his knees, elbows, fists, teeth, and all of his strength, ripping and tearing and wrenching; not one of the four was unmarked. But it was soon over. Al slumped to the ground unconscious. They continued to beat him until he was dead.

Across the street from a second-floor window in the Widows' and Orphans' Home the cold-eyed blond boy watched it all. When Herod and the lieutenant had taken Al away in the police car, the boy slipped out of the window and climbed down to the street. Working swiftly, he collected the spilled apples in the box and hid them in the school yard over the girls' toilet. The next day he sold them on the other side of town for one dollar and fifty cents; for the next week he and his mother and sister and older brother ate a hot supper.

May 17–18, 1933

The woman curled one arm around her blond head. She was big boned and her breasts, resting now, were spread over her chest. She moaned, rolled over in bed and opened her eyes. She did not know the man in bed with her. He was dark, much less Latin than Irish. He breathed deeply.

She stared through matted lashes at his smooth but bearded face and straight nose and thick black hair. Then suddenly she knew him. The night before came back to her. The words, the images, the laughter of the long, long night before, tumbling over themselves in a rush to her consciousness.

The man surprised her and opened his eyes.

— Good morning, she said. You're Howard Cadiz.

— Good morning. Yes. I am.

— When did I meet you?

— I don't know, he said. Then he added slowly, thinking about it, Does it matter?

— I'd like to think it does, she said.

— For what reason?

Neither of them had moved. They had just opened their eyes and there was the real world, the one that had been forgotten, blacked out. Cadiz looked at her.

— You're one of Sharkey's boys, she said. That bunch that hangs out at the Blue Boy Poolroom.

Cadiz said nothing.

She took a deep, cautious breath, as if she were not sure what would happen.

— We were all drunk together, she said.

— Yes, Cadiz said.

— And you had just come back from a big load brought into Brunswick.

— Yes. What's your name?

— Last night it was Sue.

— And this morning?

— What name do you like? She asked with a warm smile.

— That's nice, Cadiz said, letting me pick my own name. I've always liked the name Permilla.

— I knew a schoolteacher named Permilla, she said. I've been watching you Sharkey boys a long time. I used to sit up in my hotel room across the park and see all of you coming out of the Blue Boy and get into cars and leave. Sometimes, but not very often, I've seen you with guns. Shotguns and other kinds. Other times I've seen you drunk.

— Me? Drunk?

— No, Mister Cadiz, just the bunch of you.

— Don't call me Mister Cadiz. My name's Howard, as you know.

— All of you looked like crazy white-faced ghosts in your dark overcoats and getting into them cars.

— A white ghost, he said to himself. He turned over on his side. His hands sought her thigh. It was very nice of you to come with me, he said.

— Howard, you paid me enough to make the difference.

— What difference?

— Why you *must* have been drunk! Sharkey had his eye on me too. No, on the other hand, I guess you were so drunk you didn't care that it was the boss's girl you were taking. She laughed. But I wanted to come with you, honey.

— Yes?

— It was a hell of a party.

— You remember it all?

— Most of it.

— I don't usually get so drunk that I pass out, Cadiz said.

— You did last night.

— Yes.

— Are you glad I came with you?

— I don't remember a thing.

— That isn't much of a compliment, she said.

Under the sheet he caressed her stomach.

— Howard, she said, her voice tentative, honey, just gimme a minute. She slipped out of bed, naked, milk white, thinner than he would have thought, but still big boned, a short tangle of cropped blond hair in a bob of some sort and so uncombed it reminded him of the jungles on a trip up the Orinoco back in twenty-seven. Sue, now Permilla, he thought. And after this there would be another name. Time, Cadiz thought, did not stand still, not even for a name.

He heard water running. She was taking a quick shower. This pleased him.

He leaned forward on his elbow, found a cigarette, lit it and surveyed the room. Her clothes, spread out over the cheap furniture, were in good taste. He listened to the shower water and flopped back in bed.

He tried to dig into the night before. Not so much to find the beginning of Sue-Permilla as to locate the place where the night had ended for him. They had returned from Brunswick with three full trucks of Scotch. A big haul, and it had been easy. The sea had been as calm as plate glass and as dark. He had picked up the freighter within an hour. Sharkey had been pleased. That may have been the reason for the party and the girls, and his waking up with a woman in bed with him.

The shower water stopped. He did not open his eyes when she came back to the bed, still wet. He flicked the cigarette into an ashtray and turned to her. Her breasts glistened and quivered as she moved, half crawling onto the bed, looking at him, watching his eyes, his face, then lay flat, pressing her damp, cool body against his. Cadiz felt a sudden strangulation in his throat, and an unnatural pounding. His hands sought her breasts, her hips, thighs, feeling her lips close in over his own; she fell gently to his side, her arms locked around his neck, her long, hard body straining against his own.

Neither of them made a sound as they dropped gently, effortlessly, into warm, hungry copulation. He was the first to come out of the suspension. And then she looked at him, straight up into his face and flashed a quick, warm, open smile. She did not look like a whore. He wondered. And then, as she slipped back into the bathroom, he thought no more about it. He got out of bed and into a faded silk robe. The robe had been a parting gift to him by the last woman he had lived with. It had not lasted very long. A month. He thought fleetingly of her, and for a moment he could not remember her face, only her name. Mary Scott.

The gallery was full of brilliant sunlight, caught up in the top of the elm tree growing powerfully in the center of the cobblestone court below. Then a sloshing noise brought his attention fully away from the fading sexuality of a few moments before, and he stepped to the railing of the gallery and saw a man washing a bright yellow taxicab in the court below. It would be either Monday, Wednesday or Friday, Cadiz thought, because only on those days did the cab driver, a man named Clyde West, dare use the hose without permission of the constantly irritated, impatient landlady, Martha Kapp, a woman much endowed with hip and bosom, tightly corseted, constricted into what she thought she should look like.

— Well, honey?

The woman was in back of him, just inside the door, dressing. She dressed quickly, not in a rush or from a sense of making up time but simply because that seemed to be her way. Cadiz watched with amusement the neat way she did this. Her thinness was curtained off, her supple white nakedness shut away and hemmed in to provide her image of herself. The soft, rapidly dissipating musk of sex, so strong before, curled from her, cloaked in the scent of her perfume. She wore a flowered dress. It clung to her thighs as she walked toward him.

— Well, honey?

It was said without any particular inflection.

— Where will you go now? he asked.

She made an abrupt gesture, as if he had brought something to her attention that she didn't want to think about, and just as suddenly she dismissed it.

— Back to the hotel, she said. Maybe sleep.

They both stood at the railing and watched the driver below them wash his car with bar soap; a brush in one hand, the soapy suds sliding down the bright yellow sides, a trickle of water running freely out of the hose. The cab driver looked up at them and grinned.

— Saw you downtown last night. Blue Boy. Man!

Cadiz nodded.

— He brought us here, the woman at his side said. Is he a friend of yours?

I know him, Cadiz said. He's a friend.

— You've got a lot of friends, haven't you?

Cadiz shrugged.

— I mean, she went on, there are a lot of people in Savannah that like you a lot. If you know what I mean.

— I know what you mean, Cadiz said. But they don't really like me.

— Then what is it? People are talking about you. Look, didn't I know who you were?

— Who am I? he asked.

— Why, you're Howard Cadiz!

— Yes, but what else?

— Scout for the Sharkey bunch.

— Anything else?

— I don't know about it, honey, she said.

She waited a moment. Then in the same tentative manner and voice she had used when she wanted to take a shower, she asked, Should I know more?

— No, Cadiz said. Nothing else important to know.

— What do you mean, important?

— Nothing.

— Do you always behave like this, honey?

— Not always, Cadiz said. And please don't call me honey.

— But you sometimes act like this?

— Yes, sometimes.

— I have to go, she said.

He turned and took her in his arms, leaning back onto the railing and pulling her body close to him.

— How much did I give you? he asked.

— Thirty dollars.

— It wasn't enough.

—Ho-ward! It was, oh, it was, ever so much more than enough. She kissed him. She nuzzled up close to him. I don't have to go. I'm just going back to my room to sleep.

— Do you want to stay here?

He didn't know why he had said it. And he was instantly sorry that he had.

— You give me ideas, Howard, she said, and turned away from him, stepping back into the bedroom. A quick appraisal of the furniture and then she turned to him. Her voice was again uninflected.

— I don't know, she said.

— All right, Cadiz said, feeling relief.

— Is this a proposition? she asked. She was not going to let it go by so easily. She walked to the edge of the gallery and leaned over the railing. She examined the porches; a critical eye that missed none of the faded, blistering paint, the run-down old courtyard. At one time it had been elegant, a Belgian Cotton Factor's house, built seventy-five years before.

— You Sharkey bunch are crazy, she said. I don't know if I want to get mixed up with you or not.

Still, Cadiz thought, she is not completely rejecting the idea. He lit a cigarette, offering her one. She took it, inhaled deeply.

— You ever live with anyone before? I mean, are you married, or divorced, or something like that?

— No, Cadiz said.

They were strangers now, he thought, dickering for a chance at something better than either of them had at the moment.

— Perhaps, he said slowly, it would be just as well if we forget it. He did not look at her when he spoke. It was strange that he did not have a hangover, not even a headache. And it was unlike him to pass out. And no hangover! He smiled to himself—smugly, because he was in such good health—and thought how even Caesar complained after a night of drinking. A blessing, then, Cadiz thought. One of the balances: fresh from sleep after a hard night of drinking and wenching, and he needed no one. If he had someone whom he knew loved him, would he then indulge himself with a headache and complain and ask for pity? Possibly, he thought. But with no one, I guard against it.

— What kind of proposition did you have in mind? she asked.

Cadiz was silent. Hell, why not? he thought. It would be good to have someone waiting for him; to be with him. But he was doubtful that she would understand this. There were so many of them in Savannah who wanted to move in with their cheap dreams. He saw them often, hanging around the Sharkey crowd. They thought that their sex was all the pass they needed into a man's world.

Well, isn't this so? Wasn't this, really, all you wanted? Something to sleep with, to leave it all with, to hang onto at night? In the morning, with fresh, shower-dripping sex?

It wasn't, and it was. But how to explain this? It was so easy in this marvelous sunlighted morning to let the prodding of sex diminish, to shrug it away with impatience.

— Perhaps we should get to know each other a little better, Cadiz said. A suggestion, tentative, defensive, and then he became amused at himself. It was the same tone she had used on him.

— If you want to think about it, she said, fine. I guess I'd like to think about it awhile, too.

— Fine. He strolled away from the railing and back into the bedroom. She stopped at the door and looked around once more, carefully, committing it to memory so as to be able to call it up again and make her decision (really making it then and there?).

— It isn't much, she said critically. Cadiz decided she was sharp eyed but without malice. I mean, this is about all you could expect from a court like this.

— I've been living alone for some time, Cadiz said.

— Oh, I didn't mean for you to apologize, honey. I know how it is with men living by themselves.

— Do you?

— All they want is a clean bedroom, clean bed, a little light over the bed for reading and a private entrance. I've noticed that about men living alone. They like their privacy. It's different with women. They like to have people around they can talk to. As long as there isn't a man around, women get along.

— It's that way with men, too, I believe, Cadiz said. And then he smiled. Yes. You see, I'm very ordinary. His voice was soft.

— Don't be that way, she said, coming and standing close to him. He could feel her strong, deep hips through the thin robe.

— What hotel do you live in? You told me, but I've forgotten.

— Mariposa, she said.

— Yes, fine. I'll call you tonight.

— Honey, she said gently, you don't even know my name.

Cadiz felt the gentle reproach.

— I'm terrible about names, he said. He forced himself to look at her. Permilla. No, of course, Sue.

—Not Sue either, Mister Cadiz. Cadiz thought she was blushing, but it was only the way she lowered her eyes. She stood perfectly straight; high breasted, with those deep, mysterious hips that were not really deep but only seemed so. My name is Agnes, she said. Agnes Holden.

—All right, Agnes, I'll call you. He waved his hand (flicked away the flies with his African Fly Brush, dug into his silken robed toga and waved her away). The airy dismissal, not meant to be abrupt or mean, touched her. (She, now more than ever, looked like a slave girl out of antiquity. Agnes. Greek. A beautiful blond Greek slave who would oil and perfume him in his bath and succor him, feeding him her ripe breasts; then, at moments like this, while he took wine on the balcony overlooking the court gardens, would strum the lyre and sing songs of her homeland.)

—When will you call? she asked.

—Whenever you say, Agnes. After all, you should have time to think about it.

—Are you serious, Mister Cadiz?

—About what?

—My coming to live with you?

There it was. He could say no and right then and there he would be out of it. Did it matter that a Greek slave girl might get her feelings hurt? How long would the hurt last? Until the next man? Or would she be hurt at all?

Yes, it mattered. He slammed the door on his fantasy.

—Let's get to know each other, he said as gently as he could.

—Then you're backing out, she said. You're hedging. She turned to the door. I don't mind, Mister Cadiz.

He felt anger rip through him. Damn you! he thought. Damn you for seeing through me. He fought to keep it out of his voice.

—I'm not hedging, he said. I just suggested that we both think about it. We should get to know each other. A little better.

—Agnes Holden. Mariposa Hotel.

Cadiz nodded.

—Call me tonight?

—If I'm not busy.

—Do you expect to be busy?

— I don't know yet, Cadiz said, his patience growing thin. It had been a mistake to leave himself open this way.

— All right. You won't forget now? Agnes Holden. Mariposa Hotel.

— I won't forget, Cadiz said.

— Good-by. And thank you, Mister Cadiz. Call me.

Cadiz closed the door and leaned his suddenly aching head against the jamb, listening to the click of her high heels fade down two flights of stairs.

He paced back and forth in his room, not at all sure that he didn't really want her to come and live with him (and strum her lyre, Cadiz? He smiled at this). He also realized that he was angry because he had handled it badly and somehow lost control of the situation. He stepped out onto the gallery. Suddenly the woman passed out of his mind as if she had never existed and would have been entirely forgotten if not for Bernice, who shrilled at him just then.

— Good, cold homebrew, Bernice said, is the best thing in the world for a man hung over.

Cadiz leaned over the railing and looked around the old latticework that separated their porches. Bernice went into her kitchen, her fat behind wobbling under her shift.

— Is it green? Cadiz called.

— A little high, but not green. And ice cold. She had a harsh screech of a voice that penetrated through walls and sallied forth, drunkenly quite often, at all hours of the day and night. She was a huge woman, and dirty. She dipped snuff and it left a constant smear of brown on her lower lip and chin. She made the best homebrew Cadiz could find in Savannah, and he did not consider it important to judge her personal hygiene. Besides, he liked the old woman's coarse wit and her encyclopedic knowledge of all things immoral in Savannah. Her voice screeched at him again.

— I saw that dish you had in for the night. She waddled back with a pitcher of homebrew and slopped it on the table. Cadiz negotiated the railing and swung himself onto Bernice's porch.

— You're very nosy, Cadiz said, and drank a half glass of the ice-cold homebrew in one swallow.

— What else is an old woman like me got to do besides get drunk and be nosy?

Cadiz took another long pull. The homebrew was like a tonic. It was beginning to take hold. The headache was fading. He looked at her sharply.

— Did you put anything in this? he asked.

— Just a drop or two of codeine, she said, watching him. Ain't the headache going?

— Yes, he said. But I wish you hadn't.

— I picked up enough sore-headed gents in my time to know just how to handle them. It clears the head and settles the stomach. In a little while you'll be able to eat and it'll stay there.

— How do you know so much?

She shrugged. What was her name?

— I said you're very nosy, Cadiz said. And you are.

— Compared to some of the things I am—and have been in my day—nosy is practically a love word. What's her name?

— Agnes Holden.

Bernice poured herself a glass. She sipped it and frowned a moment.

— Made-up name, she said.

— I don't think so, Cadiz said.

— How the hell would you know? How the hell would any man know?

— As a matter of fact, Cadiz said, I picked her up at a church social. I know her mother, father, brother, sister—Cadiz paused—and husband.

Bernice laughed and sipped her brew. She never drank it in swallows, just sipped it all day long. Her jagged laugh was a match to the screech of her voice.

— You're a good man, Cadiz, and take it from me, there ain't many left.

Cadiz studied the elm in the courtyard, his eyes lazing over the court and the top-floor gallery that ran U-shaped around the lower galleries; a fourth side to the street was fenced off and gated with wrought-iron work; sandstone columns stood on either side of the gate, and the latch post was ringed with garlands of flowers.

— It was true love last night, Bernice, Cadiz said.

— I doubt it, Bernice said. You fail to appreciate me, Cadiz, and my working knowledge of men.

— What are your credentials?

— Three husbands, about twenty-five or thirty lovers—counting only those I was sober enough to recall the next day.

— You sound qualified, Cadiz acknowledged.

— You're not the loving kind, she said. You're what's known as a three P man. Personal, Particular and Private. It's hard to believe you were a sailor for so many years. Most of the sailors I've known were a hell of a lot dirtier than slightly soiled fallen angels.

— You're very wise, Bernice, Cadiz said mildly, and you know a great deal about Savannah. And I admit that you know a lot about life, but you don't know a damn thing about Agnes Holden. Or me.

— Well, you tell me about it, Cadiz.

— Tell you what?

— What's it like to be a three P man?

— Personal, Particular, Private?

— And lonely, Bernice said.

— I'm not lonely.

— You are! Bernice slammed the table. So tell me about it.

— Adding to your storehouse of knowledge? Cadiz asked.

— No, I know just about all there is to know about ordinary men, she said. And I'm curious about how a man like you lives with himself.

— Busybody people like you, Bernice, always bored me. They're nervous, irritable, never satisfied, like a two-dollar whore.

— But you still associate with me, Bernice replied.

— Never on purpose.

— That doesn't take the curse off it, Bernice replied. And I never was a working whore. I never slept with a man yet that I didn't want to. Not have to, or get paid to, but *want* to.

— I withdraw, Cadiz said.

— Thank you.

— You're welcome.

Both of them were silent and both of them watched Clyde West put away his hose and then brush the water from the puddles, spreading it so the sun would dry it quickly and all evidence of his illegal use of the hose would be gone.

— That's why I like you, Cadiz, she said. I never got the feeling you were looking down your nose at me. Somehow you see *me*. That was why I asked that question about your being lonely. I saw it. Maybe I shouldn't have asked. I took advantage of your liking me.

— Do you know why I like you?

— No. Christamighty, I don't know why you should, but I know you do and I know you wouldn't talk behind my back and I don't think you would let people talk about me in front of you.

— You're right. And if you don't know why, then leave it alone.

— I think I know why. You want another pitcher of homebrew?

— Yes.

— How's the head?

— Better.

Clyde West's wife came to the railing of the first-floor gallery, hugging her stomach with both arms, her shoulders slumping. She wore her hair done up in paper curlers. Her face was pallid in the hot bright sun. Cadiz knew she worked all night in a lunchroom. Some conversation passed between husband and wife and then the woman went back inside.

Bernice was still standing. Her pasty face was quivering.

— I know you took Lainy in, with the boy, and I also know you didn't take any money from her for it, Cadiz said.

— Cadiz—

— I don't want to know where they are. I don't care. It was—that part of his life—was his problem.

— And the rest of it?

— My problem. There is nothing unusual to learn or to know, Bernice, Cadiz said. I should have killed him. I wanted to kill him. It was for me to do, but Sharkey got to him first.

— Oh, Christ! Bernice moaned. Me and my big goddam mouth! I'm sorry, Cadiz, I'm truly sorry. So all that I've heard is true?

Cadiz said nothing.

— Did Glass know you were looking for him?

Cadiz did not reply.

— He must have. Goddammit! Me and my big mouth!

Cadiz looked at her, his face blank.

— What did you hear?

— Bits and pieces. From Hessian and old man Thursby and Danner's wife.

Cadiz's eyes sharpened. Then you know what happened that night?

— Yes. Most everybody does.

— What else did you hear?

— That Glass knew he would have to—that in the end it would be you or him. That was why he planned to go up against Sharkey when he wasn't ready, knowing that the chances were against him.

— Then you know all about it, Cadiz said. That's exactly what happened. But I should have killed him, not Sharkey. Sharkey didn't know Shad.

— People say there's a piece missing, Bernice said.

— What piece?

— Al. That you're still hanging around Savannah waiting for a chance to do something about Al.

— People say that?

— Yes.

— They're wrong, Cadiz said. I'm still in Savannah because there isn't any place else that I want to be.

— Back to sea?

— There are no ships, Cadiz said.

— Can I ask you one question?

— All right, Cadiz said.

— If you were set to do something for Shad, why not Al?

— You don't know?

— No.

— Don't people—don't *they*—have any suggestions?

— Some. They say you're scared.

— Do you believe that?

— No, she said. So why not do something for Al?

— Because Al did it all for himself. No one could ever do anything for a man like Al. Certainly not me. He would call me stupid to avenge him for what happened to him. He did what he did because he was a man who knew what he was. I only know one other man who was, is, so lucky.

— And Shad Courtney never knew who he was, is that it?

Cadiz did not answer. As she waited, hoping that he would reply and knowing without his answering that she was right, her phone rang. She trundled off to answer it and Cadiz could hear her talking. Someone was ordering homebrew. There was a disagreement over the return of her Ball fruit jars. This was settled. An order of homebrew to be delivered. The phone was hung up, and Cadiz knew she would not move from the phone before she screeched . . .

— Willllllburrrr! You Wilbur!

On the ground level, a door of the old carriage house hidden in the shade of the elm was opened and a ten-year-old Negro boy slid out—lithe, a brown reed rising out of the gloomy depths. The boy skipped up the steps in the hot, sweaty morning and into Bernice's kitchen. A moment later Wilbur returned to the gallery with Cadiz's second pitcher of homebrew, easing it onto the table with a shy grin, then backing off. Taking the pitcher with him, Cadiz returned to his own gallery. He walked to the shower, still carrying the pitcher, and turned the water on. He let it run for a while and drank.

When he finished his shower, shivering and gasping a little from the crashing cold water he always finished up with, he slipped on his robe without drying off, picked up the pitcher and went back onto the gallery. It was going to be a hot day. He was glad he had nothing to do. He would dress loosely and move slowly. Perhaps he would walk out Bull Street and feed pigeons around the fountain in the gardens. Then dinner. In the Manhattan. A steak. Then on around to the Blue Boy for some snooker, then home to bed. But if Chocolate had a game, he would play a little poker.

Bernice was nowhere to be seen. The cobblestones in the courtyard were dry. Only one small puddle of water remained. At that moment the front door banged two stories below and the strident voice of the landlady, Mrs. Kapp, filled the hot, fly-buzzing court.

— Cherrrrryyyybeeee!

Cadiz watched for the carriage-house door to open. Wilbur's mother hurried across the court. She looked quickly to see if there were any signs of Clyde West having washed his taxi, then she was inside and out of sight. Clyde West had won. It was good to see a man in a hurry win for a change.

Mrs. Kapp's harsh voice rose, and softly, under this, Cherrybee's passive, warm, sympathetic answers flowed. Mrs. Kapp's ill humor would last all day; Mrs. Kapp raging and Cherrybee warding it off. It would all be gone by early evening. Cherrybee was the only one who could handle the old lady. You are so lucky, Mrs. Kapp, Cadiz thought to himself, to have your Cherrybee.

He shaved and dressed quickly, but he was reluctant to leave the cool of his room. It had been a morning like so many he could remember aboard ship in tropic ports, sitting on the fantail drinking chemical beer. His agenda of pigeon feeding, steak dinner, snooker or poker was losing ground to the pleasant thought that he might spend the day right here.

It was unusually hot, even for Savannah in late May. He smoked languidly, enjoying the harshness of the tobacco in his throat, and sipped more of the homebrew. Mrs. Kapp's complaints from some remote hall were softened by the distance; and again he could make out the liquid warmth of Cherrybee's soothing reply.

He watched the light play on the elm leaves. A slight rush of sound from a breeze, the murmur of Cherrybee's soft, assured voice, the endless ringing of Bernice's telephone orders for homebrew . . . His own phone rang. He knew instinctively that it would be Agnes and was annoyed.

— Cadiz?

— Yes, he said to Boris.

— Get busy. We're going to need a run up to Barbee County, South Carolina.

— That's Jernegan's territory, isn't it?

— That's right, Boris said, and Cadiz heard the caution in his voice. That doesn't bother you, does it, Cadiz?

— It does, Cadiz said.

— Sharkey just got the cable. There's a load. A small one.

— They're always small ones, Cadiz said.

— Well, this one is very small. Almost tiny, Boris said with a chuckle. So you won't have to take the boat. Sharkey said it wouldn't be worth risking the boat for so small a load. Just one truck will do. And a scout, of course.

— For when?

— In the morning.

— If I left now, Cadiz said, not wanting to work with trucks, wanting to use the boat instead, I can meet them on the outside, fifty—maybe a hundred miles. It'll be safer and surer.

— No, that's out, Boris said with finality.

Each man listened to the other breathing over the open line. It was Boris who finally broke in, his tone now careful and mocking.

— Are you up to it, Cadiz? I saw you leave last night. With that woman. If you're all jocked out . . . Are you still drunk?

— No, Cadiz said. But I'll want more money for this one.

— Why, Cadiz, you're getting the fattest dollar we pay now.

— You said Barbee County, didn't you? Jernegan's country, didn't you?

— Sharkey won't like it, Boris said.

— Let him get Chocolate, Cadiz said.

— Well, hold on, Cadiz, how *much* more?

— Double, Cadiz said.

— Sharkey won't stand for it.

— Call me back after you've talked to him, Cadiz said. Or get Chocolate for the job.

— This is too tight for Chocolate, Cadiz, and you know it. Sharkey isn't going to appreciate your holding him up like this.

— Let Sharkey decide that, Boris. Don't you worry about it. Let someone else make your decisions for you.

— Someday you're going to get that cock stiffener just sucked right out of you, Cadiz.

— That may be, but it won't be a second-rate ass kisser like you that does it. I'll be here for another hour. He hung up.

Leaning on the railing of the gallery, he dismissed his plans for the day. It did no good to plan, he thought. It was only an opening for a disappointment later on.

The sun was moving rapidly across the top of the elm. Nothing had changed. There were no new sounds to distract him.

Bernice came out and began to record numbers in a small handbook, licking her pencil with each entry.

Savannah had passed its noon hour and was gasping in the one-hundred-and-three-degree temperature. Cadiz smiled to himself when the phone rang. He let it ring a dozen times, pouring himself another glass of homebrew before answering, thinking as he walked into the room that he would have a terrible headache if he didn't eat.

— It's all set, Boris said.

He started to say something else, but Cadiz cut him off.

— Then I'll go on over to the garage.

It was a faded brick building still splashed with the names of the bachelor brothers that had once operated out of it.

O.P. & S.T. GRAINGER
HAY—FEED—GRAINS
NEW HARNESS USED

The spacious interior, with shafts of sunlight spearing down from the second-story windows to the floor, still smelled of horse. The floor, though spotted with grease from Sharkey's trucks and cars, was still clean in the corners where for more than three quarters of a century bulk hay and feed had been stored in wooden bins. Cadiz found the building comforting to be in. Long ago he had played in the hay in the high lofts and had struggled knee deep in the dusty grain bins, coming out a dusky brown boy, and then the fun of slapping himself to see the dust fly. The huge doors, designed for another time when six- and eight-horse drays would pull into the building with their massive loads of hay or bags of grain, were perfectly suited to Sharkey's trucks.

Somewhere along the way, he thought, you were given something valuable and you lost it.

The mechanic came over to greet Cadiz, wiping his hands on a grease rag.

— Sharkey called and said you'd be going out.

— Sharkey, or Boris? Cadiz asked, walking along the line of trucks and high-powered Buicks.

— Sharkey himself, the mechanic said. Told me to give you anything you wanted. The mechanic watched Cadiz's careful inspection of the cars and trucks. Which one do you want? GMC or Ford?

— Ford, Cadiz said, thinking that he would need speed. And the same Buick I used last time. Is it all right?

— They're all all right, the mechanic said sharply. Every one of them is ready to roll.

— All right, then, Cadiz said, I'll call you on that.

— I'm ready to roll. You pick it and I'm ready. You going to arrange for your drivers?

— Yes, I'll get my own men. Is Teo around?

— Teo can't go. Drunk again.

— John Walt?

— For shotgun?

Cadiz nodded.

— No, but what about one of the Paulster boys?

— I didn't know they were in town, Cadiz said. Which one?

— Luke. Vergil got hisself shot up in a fight somewheres upstate.

Cadiz considered this. Luke Paulster was a man capable of holding his own, but he also had a hair-trigger temper. Still, Cadiz knew he needed a second man on shotgun going into Jernegan's country. All right, Cadiz said, see if you can get Luke for shotgun.

— What if I can't locate him?

— Then anybody but Fowler, Cadiz said impatiently, walking out.

He walked slowly over to Broughton Street, slowing his pace, seeking shade under the awnings slanting down before shop fronts. There were only a few people on the street. The lazy echoes of the morning were still with him, but under the heat of the afternoon and the tension of the coming scout they were starting to shred. It was like a dream, one rising and one falling, morning and afternoon. Parts of the same day, yet distinct and separate.

He plunged into one of the parks where giant oak trees spread like umbrellas and held the heat beneath and made the interiors shaded but still insufferable. People rested on the benches, sweating.

Cadiz crossed Broughton Street, glanced right and left at the twin lanes of shop fronts, waved at someone who called his name and then turned into a side street and one of the low-two-story office buildings that lined it. He climbed the brass-edged, creaking stair slowly, reading for the hundredth time the signs nailed to the front facing of the leading steps.

DR. ABRAMS—
DENTIST—
GAS—PAINLESS
10–1 2–5
APPOINTMENT ONLY

He walked the short, dark hall toward the far door. Somewhere in the building, behind one of the frosted glass doors, he heard two men talking. He heard the floor creak and an instant later a chair scraped and the door beside him was snatched open. The man's complexion was like gray putty. He peered at Cadiz over his glasses.

— Help you? he asked. Looking for Warren and Son?

— No, thank you. Cadiz pointed toward Boris's office. Blue Ridge Real Estate.

— Oh, well, there it is, the man said.

— Thank you, Cadiz said pleasantly.

The man stepped back, started to close the door, then brought it open again. You wouldn't be interested in a good policy—

— No, I'm sorry.

Inside Boris's office, Cadiz stood a moment beneath the ceiling fan. It must be over a hundred degrees in here, he thought.

Boris was on the phone when the secretary passed him through. It was a good morning for the phone company, Cadiz thought. Boris continued his conversation nearly five minutes. He sold real estate, insurance and dealt in mortgages. Occasionally he would represent a poverty-stricken Negro in court. He was a good lawyer. He would have to be, to be Sharkey's agent. Boris swung around in his chair and dropped the receiver onto the hook.

— Want to invest in a little real estate, Cadiz?

— Not unless it's on water. He turned and looked at Boris. I take it everything is all right. Sharkey called the garage personally.

Boris grinned. His mouth was like the peeled husk of an orange; his chin was massive. Boris tapped a pencil against his false teeth.

— He hates Jernegan's guts. He'd do anything to put one over on him. So you went over to the garage?

— Yes, and I don't want Fowler on shotgun.

— Parker just told me.

— Parker?

— The mechanic. And he said you'd get your own drivers.

Cadiz nodded.

— Hessian?

— Yes, Cadiz said heavily. Hessian.

— That darky again, Boris said. Couldn't you put one of the others in the car as driver and put Hessian on the truck?

— Have you ever seen Hessian drive a car?

— Nooo, but—

— Then you don't know what you're talking about, Cadiz said. I want Hessian. The scout on a run is either the boss or he isn't. That's what you're paying me for. I make the decisions. The time, direction, place, movement, everything. I don't want any argument on this, Boris. Hessian is the best driver in Savannah—in Georgia. In three states.

He stared at the other man, past the eyeglasses so fragile they looked as though they would shatter if you coughed too loud. A man with a gold tooth that winked at Cadiz like an evil yellow eye. Boris's cigar smoke curled around the edges of the room.

Boris pinched the bridge of his glasses. Are you going to pay him full wages?

— Of course, Cadiz said. Why not?

— A driver for the scout car gets more than truck drivers and guards. Boris wiped his face. Some of the boys might not like it. Especially Paulster. A nigger getting more than a white man. I don't know. Boris shrugged. Why start something, Cadiz?

Cadiz said nothing.

Boris leaned forward in the chair and looked at Cadiz carefully. Is that why you don't want Fowler? Did he make trouble about the last scout, with Hessian driving?

— You think Sharkey gives a damn who brings in the stuff? Cadiz asked quickly.

—Nooo, I wouldn't say that. But we've got a smooth running operation here, Cadiz—

—When I bring in a load, Cadiz interrupted, hearing the old quarter-deck iron in his voice and being a little surprised by it, you pay off and that's all there is to it. When I don't bring in a load, when I'm caught by some hick sheriff, then you can tell me how to scout.

Boris nodded thoughtfully, then shrugged.

—Who do you want on the trucks?

—Is there going to be more than one truck? You said it was a small load.

—Well, actually, there's going to be two trucks. That won't make any difference to you. He had a pencil poised over a yellow pad of neat figures.

—Clarence on tailgate guard, Cadiz said.

—Another nigger.

Cadiz ignored it. I'll get Bellybeans and Springer to drive the trucks.

—What about Paulster? Boris asked, looking up from the pad. You said you'd use him?

—I changed my mind.

—You oughta take Paulster, Boris said. He's a *good* man, Cadiz.

—And you'd like to give him the work, I know, Cadiz said. Then you hire him.

—Now, Cadiz, are you sure you want to take the chance of a nigger for your tailgate guard? I mean, you know how *niggers* are, they'll turn tail when the going gets rough—

—I wish, Cadiz said, you would tell that to Clarence.

Boris smiled.

—Yeah. I imagine he's a big buck with the strength of a team of field mules who'd break me in two like a matchstick.

—You know it, Cadiz said. And realized instantly that he should not have said it. He waited.

Boris continued to smile and nodded.

—Strange thing about niggers. I mean, the way you treat them. Only one way. Only *one* way, by God! And that's as if they weren't there *at all!* I mean, *shadows!*

—I haven't got time just now to argue the morals of a Psalm-quoting hootch runner, Boris.

Boris looked surprised.

—Why, Cadiz, I never been in church *spiritually* a moment in my life. And as far as my morals go, why, that's one of those ten-cent words that you can wipe your ass on. That's the trouble with a lot of you boys who leave town and then come back. You start with a *rush* after everything you see that doesn't cotton to your new way of thinking. But being new doesn't make it sound.

—You don't know a damn thing about me, Boris, let alone my thinking, Cadiz replied. And there isn't a new way of thinking at all, just the old way with worn horse traders like yourself, cornering a dime here and a quarter there, taking pot luck as it comes along. Cadiz shook his head wearily. I'm hot and I'm not sure I'm up to a scout. He tried to shrug away his irritation.

—Boy, you sound, you know, well, almost *pink*, with that kind of talk. Boris nodded his head, tapping his false teeth with the pencil.

—Ah, shut your fat lying face, Boris. Time, at the moment, is on your side. You have the Negroes to trade off against each other, and against the poor whites. So what? You want a medal? Before that it was the Indians against the settlers. And before that the gentiles against the Jews. And before that the heretics against the Christians. And beforc that the Christians against the Roman slaves. All the way back, Boris. The only thing you care about is your pocketbook and a little personal power. New ideas? Name one, Boris. It's just the old ideas handled in a new way. You're right, morality is something to wipe your ass on. I don't care about your being a liar and a hypocrite and a thief, prejudiced and stupid. As for Hessian and Clarence, they are adult males. They happen to be Negroes and that's their worry, not mine. What I say is that if they want it better, let them find a way of getting out from under lard-ass bastards like yourself. What does bother me is for you or anyone else to suggest that I must *also* be a liar and a hypocrite and a thief to protect *your* skin. And to you and anyone else trying to make me trade by your measure, I say screw you, Boris. You can horse trade and cadge dimes and quarters all you want but don't expect me to think of you as anything but a fat slobbing pig so stupid you don't even realize that I am supporting your right to exploit the Negroes or anyone else you can con or whip or beat down, just as I support the right of the Negroes to come up here and take your job away from you.

Boris had not changed his expression during Cadiz's speech, but he had stopped tapping his teeth with the pencil.

— Yessir, with a mouth like that, why, it could get you into a lot of trouble. A whole *lot* of trouble. Boris nodded.

— It's who has the power, Boris. Who has the edge. That's who takes the game. It's the same all over. I don't want to change it. I don't care if it changes or not. I don't rally 'round the flag at the top of the hill and I don't storm the hill to pull the flag down. I say, though, that male whores like you come a dime a dozen, have always come a dime a dozen and probably always will come a dime a dozen. The only thing I have against stupid whores like you, Boris, is that you never, you positively *never* do anything but open and close your fat mouth.

Boris slowly began to shake with laughter, then he threw his head back and hooted and slapped his leg. Cadiz shrugged, turned to the window and looked out over the park.

— Never, *never*, boy, let a man get your goat or you'll spill your guts. I know you now, Cadiz. Boris pulled a handkerchief and wiped his eyes. Yessir, I gotcha now!

— Yeah, Cadiz said. You liked what I said, huh?

— I don't agree, but I like the fire you put into it. Magnificent, Cadiz.

— It should be, Cadiz said with a thin smile, I stole it from Jefferson's second address to the Continental Congress while Washington was freezing his ass off in Valley Forge.

— You did?

— Didn't you recognize it? I paraphrased it, of course.

— You really did? Boris asked, his eyes shrewd.

— Sure, Cadiz lied. I'm surprised you didn't stop me in the middle of it. Lifted it practically word for word. Oh for Christ sake, let me show you my route and get the hell out of here. We'll argue some other time.

— You'll have to come have dinner with me sometime, Cadiz, Boris said, easing out of the chair and coming around the desk. I have a suspicion that under that hard head of yours there may be a tiny mind.

— Coming from you that should just about qualify me for selling second mortgages at fifty per cent interest, the way you do, eh, Boris? It takes a real sharp mind to steal from illiterates so scared about losing their farms they even come to you.

Boris chuckled and pulled a huge map from a desk and began to unfold it.

— You're not going to get me riled, Cadiz, Boris said. Told you. I make it a practice never to get riled.

— That means one of two things, Cadiz said. A man who never gets riled is either completely in control of himself or he's a sap-sucking coward.

The map was spread. Yes, sir, with a sharp tongue for arguing like yours, why, a man could go a long way, Boris said.

— And with a head like yours, Cadiz said, he could hire himself out to old ladies as a dildo.

— Cadiz, you're a ball breaker.

— Boris, you're a coward, Cadiz said. And you're riled. If you weren't so scared I'd walk out on this scout after Sharkey has set it up, you'd try somehow to give it to me. But you won't.

Cadiz saw him tighten. The rest, Cadiz knew, had bounced off the lawyer's thick hide and meant nothing. It had merely been a way of passing a few minutes. But now Cadiz had hurt him. When Boris spoke, his voice was cold and brief.

— Your route, he said. Show me. The man had come into focus in that last small exchange—dangerous, heavy-handed, willful and arrogant.

— Sure, Cadiz said, and leaned over the map.

The scale was a half mile, with a white background. Blue lines were state roads, red lines for federal roads, green lines for county roads, yellow lines for private roads and orange lines for rights-of-way and traditional cuts through fields and woods. As nearly as possible, every building, barn and outhouse was posted. The fields, and what was growing in them, and the direction of the rows was also clearly marked. Patient care and detail had twice saved Cadiz's scout and his run from the law when he'd found himself trapped between roadblocks. One time, checking his map, he had unloaded four trucks into a field of seven-foot sugar cane, left a man to guard the farmer and his wife and family, drove through the roadblocks and circled back later to pick up the stuff.

Cadiz put his finger on a green line on the map.

— Go up through here, South Carolina twenty-seven, to U.S. three-o-one, around Sumter, then back along Lake Marion, trace the Santee along Hilliard's field here and on into Georgetown.

— Coming back?

— The same way.

— How long will it take you?

— A week. Not more.

— If you want to take the load on down to Waycross, you can make an extra scout.

— Seven days with Jernegan is enough, Cadiz said. I want some money.

— Oh? How much?

— Half.

Boris hesitated, then pushed a button on the desk and the secretary entered.

— Give Mister Cadiz one thousand dollars out of the Brookclift Development account, Clara.

As the woman turned to her office, a distant noise settled over the city. It was a moment before Cadiz identified it; the slow, deep-chested throb of a steamship easing out of the river, making way to the Waving Girl Station, and then on out to sea.

— Sign here, please, Mister Cadiz, Clara said.

He signed the receipt for one thousand dollars in twenty dollar bills, thinking to himself that he had not been down to the steamship office in two weeks.

He walked back through the park and into the Liberty Bank Building. He waited for the open cage elevator to come down, took it to the eighth floor, got out and walked the length of a half-block-long hall, head down, studying the white tiles in the floor that had been washed down with Lysol and that smelled like some of the jails he had been in.

He walked through a frosted glass door and into a huge open office.

— Yes? The girl at the switchboard looked up, then recognized him. Oh, hello, Mister Cadiz. She smiled and then the smile faded into a slight rocking of her head. Mister Kibbee is busy at the moment, but I'll tell him you're here.

— Thank you, Cadiz said. Was that the *Schofield* that sailed a few minutes ago?

— Yes. Naval Stores for Sweden. She plunged a brass plug into a hole in the switchboard, pressed a key and spoke briefly.

— Yes, sir. She pulled the plug and turned to Cadiz. Mister Kibbee will see you—but—

— I know, Cadiz said with a smile. There are no ships.

— You know where to go?

— Thank you, I do. Cadiz pushed through the swinging gate and walked past several desks to a side partitioned room. He knocked once and entered the small office.

— Mister Kibbee?

— Come in, Howard. But God knows, I don't know what I can say to you. The *Schofield* just sailed. There was an ordinary's job open, but the captain had a cousin or a nephew—or maybe it was his son. I'm sorry, Howard. Sit down.

— I won't stay and bother you, Mister Kibbee, Cadiz said. I just thought I'd drop in and tell you I'd be out of town for ten days or so and you could get in touch with me through my landlady, Mrs. Kapp.

— I know, Howard, Kibbee said. He was a tall, spare man with gold-rimmed glasses and white hair brushed sideways. He stood. I'll call—but we don't have a thing coming in now for six more weeks. The *Redwood* is in Capetown and going over to Calcutta. The *Magellan* is coastwise—

— I know, Cadiz said, edging out of the office, I just thought I'd tell you.

— Glad you dropped by, Howard, and I want you to keep trying. I'm thinking about you all the time.

— Thank you, Cadiz said. I've been on the beach so long now, I'm wondering if I'll ever get another ship.

—Times are bad. Very bad. We're cutting down.

—I wouldn't have to go out on the bridge, Mister Kibbee. I'd go out on deck. You know that.

Kibbee sighed deeply.

—Well, there you are. A chief mate that I would love to have aboard one of our ships, coming in asking for a job on deck. And I can't hire him.

He was back on Bull Street again, feeling the heat, letting it cut at him as piercingly as it could. Then he walked to the river. He sat down on the edge of the rotting pier and watched the tugs and the ferrymen work the current. He was there for nearly two hours. Finally he got up and started walking again, stopping at a homebrew parlor where he sipped the high, very green beer until the sun went down.

The west Yamacraw hollow was washed in the pink glow of twilight, lending a subtle charm to an old, pearl-like section of the city. Cadiz walked the silent red brick sidewalks and watched Savannah as she tucked the ugly and the disfigured away for the night. Passing street-lighted games, he was aware of the faceless shadows sitting deep in the darkness. Mysterious men and women. Some leaned out of windows on pillows, the lights turned out in the rooms behind them; occasionally he saw the glowing red tip of a cigarette and heard the murmur of talk. But he could not catch the sense of what was said.

He plunged into the base section of the city, walking on the west side of the street, the wrong side—here Yamacraw, there the Montgomery section.

Yamacraw. The melody of that name conjured up for him Indians sitting crosslegged on such a night as this and worshiping before the firelight, their shadows thrown back by the medicine flame, or by full moonlight. A word was spoken in the hush. *Yam-a-craw*. Where the Negro lived in numbers totaling more than a third of the population of Savannah, lived in clapboard houses with cardboard walls insulating the rooms against the cold, and with pot-bellied stoves that burned coke and pine kindling. Hessian lived here.

He was on the wrong side of West Broad Street—longer than

Broughton, wider than Bull, older because it had known more pain, and pain was the yardstick of time on West Broad Street.

— Was that summer I got run down by the law.

— Before Chrismus, when I was shot back yonder.

— A summer, Ju-lye, when I was cut.

— Remember them two years I spen' to the chain gang?

He went down into the darkest hole of Yamacraw, though he knew white men who would not cross West Broad Street after dark. He dipped into the shadows of a side street and found the right house. It looked like all the other houses. He knocked softly, knowing that all the eyes on the street were watching him. He was the white man who sometimes came for Hessian on nights like this, and then Hessian disappeared. And after Hessian came back, there was money in that house.

— Who's there! the voice sprang at Cadiz through the door like a fist.

— Hessian?

Pause. Cadiz was about to call again when there was another voice: that of a child.

— Ain't nobody here called *dat!*

Cadiz could imagine what had happened. A quick decision inside the darkened house. Make the child answer, create confusion. They learned quickly in Yamacraw.

— Hessian! It's me. Cadiz!

A longer pause. Then from behind him, the voice of Hessian, who had slipped out of the back door, squirmed under the house to the stoop, observed the visitor from his hiding place and recognized him.

— I'm sorry, Mister Cadiz. If I know it was you, I'd have come right out.

— You're not always so cautious, Cadiz said.

— Law's been down here looking for a man that did something on the other side of town. Everybody a little jumpy tonight. Otherwise, Hessian said, standing up and brushing off his clothes, I would just open the door and see who it is.

— Want to make a run?

— This is Wednesday, Mister Cadiz, and I got a whole month of Wednesdays of doing nothing.

— Then you want to go?
— Yessuh.
— It's going to be a rough trip.
— How rough would that be?
— We're going up to Barbee County. To the Santee River country. Sheriff Jernegan's country. You know how he feels about colored people.
— That *is* a rough one, Hessian said.
— I told you.
— Yessuh, you told me.
Hessian gave a long, low whistle. Well, I guess I'll go if you need me, Mister Cadiz.
— You know I need you, Cadiz said.
— Yessuh, but there's plenty boys in Yamacraw that's good with a wheel.
— You're the best.
— Well, I reckon they might prove something if they had the chance.
— This will pay double, Hessian, Cadiz said. One hundred dollars.
— Man! Mister Cadiz, don't say things like that unless you mean it.
— Three days to a week. One hundred dollars.
— Lord!
— I'm paying you in advance. You can give it to your mother.
— That's not necessary, Mister Cadiz.
Cadiz handed over five of the twenty dollar bills.
— Thank you, Mister Cadiz, Hessian whispered. When do you want me? Mama sure going to have a fit about this money. I don't think she ever had a hundred dollars at one time in her whole life. I know I never did.
— Do you know where Clarence is?
— I know. He going too?
— If he's interested.
— He'll be interested.
— Can you take me to him?
— I'll get dressed, Mister Cadiz. He hesitated. I'd ask you inside, Mister Cadiz, but we never had a white man inside before. Mama, she might get upset.

— I understand, Cadiz replied. I'll wait here.

Only after everything appeared to be arranged between himself and Hessian did Cadiz notice an easy movement of the shadowy figures around him.

He had not counted on hearing the cry of Hessian's mother. He didn't want to hear it, but he didn't want to move away either.

The door scraped open and he looked up, expecting to see Hessian. Instead, in the yellow glow of a kerosene lamp, he saw the gray head of Hessian's mother. Her face was dry and in deep folds of age.

— My son done something bad, white man. And now he's going to to do it again. She came down to the bottom step. Ain't no white mistuh coming down heah to Yamacraw and handing over money and then taking my son without that boy doing something bad. Leave my son alone! Please, suh! He ain't but one boy and he's all I got. Take your money and go back across West Broad Street—

— Mama! Now, Mama. Don't go bothering this man. He's doing for me. He isn't a bad man. He's just about the best man I know, Mama. And then he took the old woman by the shoulders and walked her back into the house, closing the door, his mother's voice cut off with the click of the latch.

Hessian came out a few minutes later. They walked up to the edge of the block, creating eddies of dust in the dirt street, then turned toward the glow of the city.

— Mama's like most mothers, don't you guess, Mister Cadiz? They hunch over a man like they did when he was a baby. Hungering over him, and yet, I tell you, there's very few mamas who don't in the long run act just like mine. They want out of him, at the same time they hunching over him, for him to grow up strong and make his steps in the world.

They were on West Broad Street now, walking along the lighted sidewalks. They did not pay any attention to the silent eyes that followed them. It was a rare sight to see a Negro and a white man walk side by side on that side of West Broad.

Hessian knew exactly where to look for Clarence. They went straight down West Broad to Union Station and cut down the side of the gray, sooty pile of marble and into another cut that jogged down into Yamacraw again.

— This the bad section, Hessian murmured. The man comes down here got to be careful. Colored *or* white.

Cadiz had never been in this part of town before and he was curious.

— Doesn't Clarence hang out at the Half Moon Café anymore?

— Most of the time, but not tonight, Mister Cadiz.

— Why not?

— Just got out of Brown's Farm for thirty days. Fightin' and being drunk.

— Where would he be now?

— That big boob? Him? With no girl for thirty days? Mister Cadiz, that jocker is straight to Pearl's!

— What's Pearl's?

— That's the place, Mister Cadiz. He's there.

— Far from here?

— We practically there.

Still deeper into this section of Yamacraw, they stopped on a street much like the one on which Hessian lived. It was dark and silent.

— Looks deserted, closed up, Cadiz said.

— Suppose to, Mister Cadiz. Hessian stepped up to the porch and rapped hard three times. He paused. Then he rapped three more times, lightly, distinctly. The door opened and an old woman who looked like a carbon copy of Hessian's mother and was dressed in the same shapeless frock of cotton goods, stood framed in the light of a kerosene lamp.

— Looking for Clarence, Pearl.

Pearl stared at Cadiz, searching his face. When she spoke, she kept her eyes on Cadiz.

— Wha'cha want with that big good-for-nothing?

— Want him, Pearl, that's all.

— He ain't around. I wouldn't let him touch one of my girls.

— Now, Pearl, you looking at this man like you ain't never seen a white man standing on your front door step.

— Not lately.

— Looka here, Pearl, now, listen to me, hear? Go back inside and tell Clarence, but you tell him so nobody with a big mouth can hear you, you tell Clarence that Mister Cadiz is out here and he ain't about to wait long!

Cadiz looked on, letting Hessian carry on the delicate negotiations. Suddenly Pearl nodded, something in her satisfied, and melted back inside.

— Come on in and tell 'm yo'sef, she said.

Hessian and Cadiz went in.

— You sit. I wouldn't let you in a-tall 'cept for Hessian. Also I don't want nobody standing out front waiting for nobody.

Cadiz stood while Hessian, who seemed to know where to go, preceded Pearl through the side door. Left alone, Cadiz heard the music for the first time.

It was more than music. It was something alive, with a heart and soul of its own. It throbbed through the walls and he closed his eyes to listen. The door opened again and Hessian reappeared, a big grin on his face.

— That Pearl! She didn't tell me Clarence was funnin' with Mae. She just point to a door and say, he in there, and I go in—

Cadiz smiled.

— Come on. Least we can do is sit down and listen to the music while Clarence is bouncin'.

Through a long dark hall (from the outside, the house did not look that large) and into a huge room. Three men sat on straight-backed kitchen chairs: horn, piano and drums. There were four Negro girls sitting around and clapping their hands in time with the music. They did not bother to look at Cadiz. They did not sleep with white men.

— They sell a rotgut moonshine here, Mister Cadiz, Hessian said apologetically, otherwise I'd say have a little something.

Cadiz waved the offer away. He listened to the clean, suggestive dialogue of sound.

The noise that preceded Clarence as he came barreling into the room was enough to make everyone, including the musicians, turn and laugh.

— Might as well be playin' a *harp!* Clarence bellowed. What the hell do I care if her mammy lives to New York? What that make me? Or her? Talkin' the whole god-*damn* time! Lak the man say, all cats is pussies, but that Mae was tamed before she got to me! Pearl! You Pearl! You gone get yourself a bad reputation keepin' that high yeller, high *tone,* she *think,* to workin' when a man comes in for they lovin'!

Everybody rocked back and forth, laughed and clapped their hands together.

Only then did Clarence see Cadiz. The big man's face, not as dark as Hessian's but more sensitive in spite of his huge size, sobered. The eyes narrowed. He saw only the white skin, and he had been living under the lash of white-skinned men for thirty long days on the county work farm. He almost took a menacing step toward Cadiz, then he recognized him. He came forward as Hessian had come forward, easily, warmly, without reserve.

— Mister Cadiz, Clarence said, and almost put out his hand in greeting, then caught himself in time and collapsed heavily into one of the chairs. As he did so, he dropped a heavy hand on Hessian's shoulder.

— I suppose this nigga done told you that I spent thirty on the Brown, catchin' up on my homework. He beamed. You don't have to tell me why you're heah. If I see you at all, if I see you with this boy heah, I know that we going to roll. Where and when, Mister Cadiz?

Cadiz smiled. It was impossible not to feel good around Clarence.

— I'm sorry to interrupt, Cadiz said, with a nod toward the girls.

— Business before pleasure, suh. Always. A man got to look out for business before pleasure.

— I have a run, Cadiz said.

— Fine. Jes fine, Clarence said.

— Tough one. Not on the boat this time. Trucks.

Hessian interrupted. Big boy, we going to Jernegan's country.

— Mister Cadiz, Clarence said, closing his eyes and rolling his head from side to side, I swear, if you didn't give me them easy runs down to Brunswick and Jacksonville and Port Royal and all, I'd almost have to say I want to get back to my pleasures. But that Mae, she ain't no pleasure.

— Well? Cadiz asked, still smiling.

— But I am a man that is short of cash money and I need something quick. To Hessian he said, You think I got sent to Mister

Brown's for drinkin' and fightin', but that was just the way things worked out after the lawyer got to the right man.

— Says which? Hessian demanded.

— I had me a moonshine drop, Clarence explained, over to south side of Yamacraw, and all of four hunnert dolluhs worth of rotgut corn selling it like cotton candy to them po' sawmill niggas. But they came fo' me.

— Who?

— *Who!* Sheet! Yo' foot don't fit no limb. How come you goin' round hooting like an owl? Who! The mammy-rammy *law!* That's who! His voice was gruff but not bitter. It was Washinton law I stood against. That was, if I argued back. So I didn't argue, and The Man took over the drop and sold the corn to the sawmill niggas until the stock was gone, and we split the money, and then I paid a five hunnert dolluh fine for drinkin' and fightin' and got thirty on the Brown. I'm clean broke. Had to borry something to come here to Pearl's and make up for lost time.

The music started up again and two of the girls began dancing. One of them took a paper streamer from a fluttering fan and tied it around her neck.

— Tailgate guard, Cadiz said. The run is for Sharkey. It pays double because we're going into Jernegan's country. Seventy-five dollars for the trip. Three days to a week.

— That's a lot of money, Mister Cadiz, and I can sho' use it. But you don't have to pay me double.

— Why not? I'm being paid double.

— Easy money, man, Hessian said slyly, sitting back there, a shotgun acrost your lap, while I'm up front leadin' scoutin' with Mister Cadiz.

Clarence ignored Hessian. He knew what going into Jernegan's country meant. He looked Cadiz in the eye.

— Ready, Mister Cadiz. Any time you say.

Cadiz stood. He pulled sixty dollars from his packet of twenties and handed the bills over to Clarence.

— What's this, Mister Cadiz? You the one man in the whole world I really trust. You don't have to give me nothing ahead of time.

— I don't need you right away. Stick with Hessian, Cadiz said. Be at the garage at five in the morning, sober and ready to roll.

Clarence folded and refolded the three twenties.

— That enough for your pleasures? Cadiz asked.

Clarence grinned and goosed Hessian.

— Mister Cadiz, I'm a good man, but at a dollar a roll, that means sixty rolls. Now, this nigga ain't saying it can't be done. But if you want somebody strong enough to pull the trigger of that shotgun—! He broke off in laughter. Le's have some real music, Dingus! And where at is that Mae? You Mae! Don't put on your panties, baby, Clarence is still heah! You Pearl! Some of that terrible corn you sellin'!

The music started, the girls fell all over Clarence and Pearl brought a quart jar of moonshine and glasses.

Clarence winked at Cadiz and laughed.

Hessian hung back as Cadiz walked to the door.

— You need me, Mister Cadiz? His eyes lingered on one of the girls.

— No, I don't need you. But one of you has to stay sober enough to check the trucks.

— I'll check 'em, Mister Cadiz. I won't have a drink. Not one. And I watch the big 'un.

— Check the trucks and the Buick yourself. Be sure they have gas and oil, and that Clarence has roofing nails and his mixture of oil and gas in the last truck.

— Yessuh, I know. And I can call for you, if you want, save you a trip over to the garage.

— All right, Cadiz said. You know where I live?

— You still over to Miz Bernice's Court?

Cadiz nodded.

— I come fo' you at five with everything, after I check it out. And I'll take care of Clarence and make sure he's ready.

— All right, Cadiz said, turning away.

— Mister Cadiz, I hope that Mama, you know, what she said and all back at the house, didn't make any difference, you know.

— Not at all, Hessian.

— Thank you, suh. I sure appreciate you taking me like this.

Hessian dropped his eyes. Some of the others, the truck drivers on the last few runs, they said something about me having the bes' paying job on the run, and since they taking risks like everybody else—

— Let me worry about that, Cadiz said.

— Please, Mister Cadiz, don't say anything to them. Like I've been complaining, or anything like that. I just wanted you to know how I appreciate—

— All right, Hessian, Cadiz said, his voice businesslike. But tell me this. Do you and Clarence understand?

— Understand what?

— That the only reason I hire you and him is that you are both the best men I can get for the jobs you do?

— Yessuh, we talked some. We figured something like that. It would have to be, we decided.

— Why should it have to be?

— Why, suh, that's the way you are.

— Then forget it, Cadiz said shortly, and started out once more.

— Never forget, Mister Cadiz, Hessian said. Never.

After leaving Hessian and Clarence he felt suddenly tired. The weariness began to settle in his legs. He knew this was because he had not gotten enough sleep after the party the night before. He trudged the dirty streets and over the broken sidewalk to Union Station and onto the taxi stand, taking the first cab he saw.

— Uptown, he said to the driver, not looking at him. He was irritated with his fatigue. A throbbing headache reminded him that he had not eaten all day. He would have returned to the Court and taken a shower, paying Bernice to fix him something to eat, but he disliked the thought of being alone.

The driver, he now noticed, was his neighbor, Clyde West.

— Oh, it's you, Cadiz said.

— How you t'night, Mister Cadiz? Clyde asked politely.

Cadiz merely grunted and settled back. They rode in silence, passing the huge, sooty, red-brick façade of the Central of Georgia Railroad Station. Cadiz lit a cigarette.

— Anyplace special you want to go?

— What time is it? Is the lunch counter at the Blue Boy still open? Cadiz asked.

— Yeah, until ten o'clock.

— Blue Boy, then, Cadiz said.

A little further on Cadiz noticed that West was driving fast and recklessly. He gunned the cab around other cars and cut back in sharply, and he drove with one elbow on the open window of the door.

— Are you trying to impress me? Cadiz asked.

West was silent.

— Well?

— Tell you the truth, Mistuh Cadiz, it seems to me that you would be giving a white man a job before you would a nigra.

— What are you willing to gamble for a hundred dollars? Cadiz asked.

— A hell of a lot, 'cause that's a hell of a lot of money. West said.

— Hessian would get twenty years, Cadiz continued, any time he was caught by a county sheriff resisting arrest.

West said nothing.

— A Negro carrying a gun. Think about it, Cadiz said.

— Well, West replied, I can drive a car good as any man.

— You don't know what you're talking about, Cadiz said.

— I just wish you'd give me a chance sometime, Mister Cadiz. West dropped his tone to a confidential level. You see, I've been keeping my eye out for a situation where I could—

— Own your own cab?

— In Savannah? West laughed.

— Open a dry cleaning store?

— Sir?

— Run a delivery service?

— Ahhh, you're making out you don't understand me, Mister Cadiz. I just wish you'd remember me sometime on one of your runs, Mister Cadiz.

At the Blue Boy, Cadiz walked straight to the lunch counter and ordered shrimp soup and dumped an entire dish of Oysterettes into the bowl and began to spoon it mechanically into his mouth. His eyes focused on a point behind the counter where Jesus Bible, a wrinkled Negro man, washed dishes. Bibleman, as Jesus Bible was called, had a strange whiteness on the backs of his hands that were also mottled with liver spots; the rest of his hands were a rich dark brown. He washed endless dishes dumped at his side by the quicker, faster talking, mother-witted younger Negroes who worked at the Blue Boy's lunch counter. Bibleman did not speak or ever look up, just sang the same everlasting hymn over and over. He had been a rigger on a Savannah River dray, the largest in town, with six double teams of Belgian drafts, when he had been kicked in the head by one of the horses and had never been the same since. He was as much a part of the Blue Boy as the pool tables.

— Jesus is the rock in a weary land, a weary land, a weary land. Oh, Jesus is a rock in a weary land . . . Bibleman hummed the rest of the song through to the end, then he started all over again.

The Blue Boy was the sort of place, the sort of atmosphere that Cadiz had known most of his life, all over the world. In the foc's'les and in the messrooms of ships. A world of men. No women entered here. Here were the saloons of the old west, the pubs of England, the private clubs of the rich, the fraternity in a small-town jail or Salvation Army. A coarse, uninhibited world where a man could miss a shot with a five dollar bet riding and purge himself of irritation with any curse he wanted.

Kelly, the sadistic, no-neck bouncer with a mind like a child, sat hunched near the door and presided over Blue Boy's.

Down from Kelly's sentinel post at the door was a row of lunch tables with white marble tops. Hovering over them like masked figures in a tragi-comic play, Negro waiters in white coats buttoned up to their necks sweated and hustled to serve dinners.

In the wide, smoke-hazed main room, a dozen pool tables, green, brushed, sparkling under the brilliance of overhead lights, were in constant use. The whole place seethed with a bass rumble of talk and laughter. Occasionally a trenchant curse seared the air as a man missed his bet, and here and there the thumping of a pool cue butt on the floor applauded a good shot.

At the end of the counter where Bibleman washed his dishes, a jog in the room cut back and there was a huge baseball board where men stood and studied the starting batteries for tomorrow and made their bets.

All over the room, in the platform chairs set back in tiers, were the bums and the onlookers, the poolroom loudmouths who kibbitzed and cadged dimes and meals and read papers and gossiped and were there all day and all night. Some of them were vagrant salesmen of pocket combs, neckties, mechanical pencils and cheap fountain pens, or they sold newspapers or touted a horse or were ready with information about a homosexual who could be rolled, or they pimped or they sold packages of Sheiks or Trojans, or they rippled the pages of small pulp-paper books with famous cartoon characters performing degenerate sexual acts.

Once in a while Kelly would throw one of them out the back door into the alley, and everyone in Blue Boy's would stop and watch in admiration. Kelly had been a wrestler and he handled his job with professional zeal and finesse. Somebody had once stood up to him and beaten him nearly to death with a chair. After that Kelly armed himself with a sawed-off pool cue slung from his wrist like a policeman's billy.

The crowd would thin out at about ten or eleven and the serious big-money pool games would get under way. Later still, the big poker games would break up in the neighborhood hotels and the players would come in for hot corned beef sandwiches and homebrew. And so it would go, on and on into the night, until Solly would signal Kelly to close the door and make one last check with Chocolate, who ran the rooms upstairs where stud and draw were the only games played.

Cadiz felt warmed by the feel of the place. He eased off his stool and stretched, feeling the muscles in his back flex.

— Hello, Cadiz, Solly said.

Cadiz liked the squat little man who owned the Blue Boy. Cadiz had thought many times how much he resembled Al DeCunningham.

— How's tricks? Solly asked, his darting eyes sweeping over his private world, his ear tuned for a curse that was a little too shrill or bitter, a voice a little too loud and angry. Solly could isolate potential trouble and send Kelly over if necessary, or go settle it himself. Solly was referee in all disputes and he played no favorites. If you didn't agree with his decision, you were banned from the premises. You played by his rules. His customers knew he was fair; even the losers liked Solly and after they had cooled down, if they came back and apologized nicely and promised never to disturb the peace again, they were absolved and returned in a state of grace. If a player's behavior got him banished a second time, it was forever.

—Know how I can get in touch with Bellybeans and Springer? Cadiz asked.

—A run?

Cadiz nodded.

—Both of them are over in the corner at the five cent table shooting rotation, Solly said. I'm glad you're going to use them. They're living in my poolroom. They could use the money.

His eyes never stopped roving over the crowded room.

—Henry, he said to one of the waiters, when you get finished clearing table there, go back to the five cent table and tell Mister Bellybeans and Mister Springer that Mister Cadiz is here and wants to talk to them.

—Yessuh, Mister Solly.

—I hear you're going up to Jernegan's country, Solly said conversationally.

—I don't know why, Cadiz said, but I hoped it could be kept a secret.

—Boris, Solly said.

—That surprises me.

—Why? Don't you know who you work for? You're a goddam fool, Cadiz. Boris was in here laying two to one you wouldn't make it back.

—Don't con me, Cadiz said.

—How long we know each other? Since you was a kid and used to come in here with Shad Courtney before he got sent up, right? And used to shoot rotation on the five cent tables, right? Well, I liked you when you was a kid and I liked Shad and that makes you an old friend, and I don't con friends.

Cadiz smoked his cigarette, his eyes narrowed, thinking hard. In the poolroom a very stylish little Italian who had all the signs of being a hustler was working carefully around the center table before a large gallery of onlookers. The action in the Blue Boy that night was on the center table.

— What makes you do a damn fool thing like scouting for Sharkey? Solly asked.

— Know where else I can make the same money?

— That hasn't anything to do with it and you know it, Solly said. And then both of them watched the careful play of the Italian for a while. He was very good, but Cadiz knew the man he was playing against. The hustler was going to get sucked in. He was having it all his way now, but not for much longer.

Solly hopped off the stool to mix into the crowd at the center table. He watched for a few minutes, then walked back to Cadiz and spoke to him in a low voice.

— Take it easy up there in Jernegan's country and for Christ sake don't shoot him, Solly said.

Cadiz laughed. I'll take it easy and I won't shoot him.

Solly shook his head and went off again. Bellybeans and Springer came up then. Both were thin, raunchy men in their late forties. Both were married and they were enough alike to have been brothers. Cadiz quickly outlined the work. They readily agreed and accepted an advance on their pay, each getting two of the twenty dollar bills, forty against a total of sixty which would be double pay for the scout. Each promised to show up at the garage the next morning at five, ready to go.

All the arrangements made, there was nothing to do now but wait. He walked over to the five cent table, ignoring the action at the center table where Rufus, the local champion, was still enticing the Italian boy into his trap. He shot rotation, practicing his English and control until he was bored with it, then drifted over to the center table and watched as Rufus began to come alive. The gallery was silent while Rufus led the Italian into the final big-money game, and then slaughtered him.

Solly closed up after that and Cadiz stood outside with his back to the locked doors and listened to the soft rustle of leaves in the park across the street and sniffed the air of memories washing around him like a whirlpool of half-forgotten scents, too old to have retained their potency but still alive enough to prick his senses.

Through the branches, across the park, he could see the lights of the Mariposa Hotel. There was a woman in there he could sleep with. If only he could remember her name.

After some difficulty with the night clerk he learned that her name was Agnes Holden (oh, yes) and she was in room three-twenty-three. He climbed the worn steps, smelling the hundred-year muskiness that was part of the grainy wood, distilled from a thousand drunks, a thousand hushed confidences, a thousand business deals, a thousand stolen moments. He found her room. The door was slightly ajar. He pushed on in.

— The clerk, she said from the bed, called and said you were on your way up.

— I hope I'm not disturbing you, he said, but I had to see you.

— Why? You need a woman?

Cadiz shrugged and nodded.

— At least you're honest, she said.

— You told me to call, remember?

— But not at one in the morning. Or is it two?

— It's two. And I can leave.

— Why leave? You're here now. You want a piece of ass, I'll give it to you.

Cadiz felt himself tighten up inside.

— I'll leave.

— I couldn't go back to sleep now anyway.

He watched her as she threw back the sheet and slipped off the far side of the bed, pausing a moment as she felt for her slippers, then standing. Her transparent nightgown hid nothing from him. He remained at the door, holding the knob in his hand, leaning against it. He knew now, after seeing her, that he would not leave. He wanted her. He felt himself turn over inside, as if he were a locked steel vault whose tumblers had been poised, waiting for the right twist of the dial, the proper setting, to spill open.

— Have you got anything to drink? he asked.

— Homebrew. In the ice chest. In the bathroom. It's cold, but I don't guarantee it isn't green.

— As long as it's cold, he said.

— I'll get it for you, she said.

She walked slightly bent over, with a curious protective hunching of her shoulders, and he watched her almost thin body shaded by the light behind her. It made him think of a shadow screen theater he had been to in Japan. A man and a woman entered, throwing their shadows on the opaque screen, and then, disrobing with great ceremony, had proceeded to rut.

As she leaned over the ice chest her breasts swung forward. She straightened, turning to him with two bottles of the homebrew and saw him looking at her. She snapped out the light switch with the bottle. Cadiz went to the window and looked down on the dark tops of the trees that seemed close enough to touch.

They drank and he leaned forward, looking out of the window, holding the moist bottle to his forehead.

— How do you feel? he asked, not looking at her.

There was a slight hesitation, but he caught it. She sat on the side of the bed, a little hunched over, gazing sightlessly at the figured rug on the floor.

— I feel all right.

— Not annoyed that I came?

— What do you want me to say, Cadiz?

— Why don't you call me Howard?

— Cadiz is more like you. I'll call you Howard if you want me to.

— No, it doesn't matter, he said. He turned back to the window. After a long pause he heard her clear her throat. I'm sorry about what I said a while ago. I'm not ordinarily so vulgar.

— I know, he said. That's all right.

— It's funny you should come.

— Why?

— I've been thinking about you all day.

—You have? Why?

— This morning you didn't want to see me again. You backed down the moment after you suggested that I move in with you. No, not back down. You withdrew. After I showed that I might be interested, you just seemed to disappear. I felt I was talking to myself. Actually, I felt ashamed. For a while today I hated you for making me feel ashamed.

— I didn't mean to do that, he said.

— I know, I know. I realized that after I thought about it. She sighed, took a cigarette from the night table, lit it, exhaled quickly. Why are you here?

— Because I wanted to see you.

— Not to sleep with me?

— That was what I thought I wanted. I wouldn't admit to myself, or maybe I didn't know, but I think I just wanted to be with you.

Her face was calm.

— I'm tired of being alone, he said. When I reach out, I want to be able to touch something.

— Are you working your way around to saying you like me?

Yes, he thought, she cares. He heard it clearly and distinctly. She was with him. The mystery of man and woman coming together and held there, even for a moment, by some invisible tie. He would not deny it. He knew it could happen. He looked at Agnes, testing her, comparing her to Ulrica. Was it more strange that it should happen now with Agnes at two in the morning in a second-rate Savannah hotel than with Ulrica in Hyde Park?

— Well? she asked.

— Well, what?

— Are you trying to say you like me?

Ulrica had said the same thing.

— I think so, Cadiz said. I think that's what I'm saying.

— But you're not sure. Is that it?

— I'm pretty sure.

— Don't, she said suddenly. Don't move in on me like this, Cadiz. I'm not even sure about this morning. It was all pretty hazy—

— You're sure, he said.

— No, I'm not. And I've thought about it. I told you. I thought about it today and waited for you to call. And I'm thinking about it now, this minute, while we're talking.

— I wonder if I sounded as frightened this morning as you do now?

— I guess I do, she said. This morning, well, it was cut and dried. I was nervous about that too, to tell you the truth. I've only known three other men in my life, and you wanted someone to sleep with and I wanted to get out of this hotel and out of that goddammed department store.

—Yes, he said, that was the way it was this morning. That was what I wanted, and I guess that was what you wanted. But now?

—Now you want to make love to me, she said bitterly, and she shivered.

Cadiz closed his eyes. And you want to make love to me, he thought.

—Yes, that is what I want. To make love to you, Cadiz said.

—Or just give it to me? she asked, her bitterness cutting at him.

—I want to make love to you and I also want to give it to you.

—Did you know, she said, watching him slip out of his clothes, that you made love to me this morning?

—Did I?

—Yes.

—Then you're not surprised, are you, that I'm here now?

She held up her arms and he skinned the nightgown over her head. Still standing, he pressed her backwards, then buried his face in her breasts.

—After Harry left me, when he thought I was pregnant, she said, I swore that I—that it wouldn't be like this again.

He kissed her breasts, taking the nipple in his lips. She stirred.

—Harry was the only one, really, like you. As long as it lasted, he made love to me.

He reached for her mouth, bringing her face close to his. She moved in the bed, slipping under him, clinging to him. A quick, hungry thrust of her hips and she had taken him. Their passion was long. There seemed to be no end of their hunger for each other.

He lay awake long afterward as Agnes slept in his arms, curled against him.

He awoke with a start and looked instantly at his watch. Four-thirty. His arm was numb. As gently as he could, he eased her head onto the pillow. Then he crept out of bed and dressed. She did not stir. He dressed quickly and in five minutes was smoking a cigarette, standing at the bathroom door drinking from one of the bottles of green homebrew and looking at her blond head on the pillow.

—Agnes, wake up, he said softly, going to her side.

She moaned and opened her eyes.

— What is it? You're dressed—

— I've got to go, he said, taking her hand, squatting beside the bed.

— Go where?

— A job, he said. Now listen to me. Here are the keys to my place. Go over there any time you want and tell Mrs. Kapp that you and I just got married. You have to tell her that or she won't let you in.

— When will you be back?

— Not long. A week, maybe a little more. Take this money. He gave her five of the twenty-dollar bills.

She sat up in bed, holding the money and the keys, the sheet in her lap, her breasts exposed.

— Cadiz, she said, please don't go.

— I've got to go. When I come back, we'll talk about the future.

She put the money and the keys on the bed beside her. Then with a quick, desperate gesture, she reached for him, taking his head in her arms. She began to cry.

— Don't go, Cadiz. I—

— I need the money. Besides, I've given my word.

— What does that mean to someone like Sharkey—

— Agnes, he said gently. I've got to go. Now. He stood up. She came out of the bed after him, following him to the door.

— Cadiz, can't you stay? Please. I want you to stay.

— A week, ten days, no more, Cadiz said, framing her face in his hands and kissing her on the lips.

— Cadiz, I love you—

— And I love you.

He kissed her once more, then angled out of the door. As he rounded the corner of the stair, he looked back. She stood in the open doorway. He waved. She did not wave back. He glanced at his watch on the way through the lobby, checking it against the clock behind the desk. It was four-forty-five. He had fifteen minutes.

At five o'clock the caravan moved through the somber streets of a hot Savannah morning. Five men in all, experienced bootleggers. As planned, they headed north to the beaches of a deserted little village on the South Carolina coast near Georgetown.

Cadiz sat low in the front seat of the scout. Hessian, his lean, sure hands on the wheel of the car, hummed to himself. At the intersection of West Broad and Bay Streets, they caught a red light and Hessian worked the gearpost. Automatically both men checked the two trucks in back of them. The light changed and the car eased into gear, rolled to the brick-and-concrete post that supported the traffic light, glided around it and moved powerfully but not fast down Bay Street Extension through the ragged fringes of Yamacraw and up onto the viaduct that spanned the railroad freight yards. Cadiz again checked the trucks. One after the other they made the turn around the traffic light in back of him.

On the viaduct now, Cadiz looked down at the snorting yard engines. They reminded him of children playing in a sandbox. Except that the pierheads near the river and the dark maw of the giant doors would have frightened most children.

They rode on in silence and were soon in South Carolina, with the darkness of night peeling off into morning. Cadiz could see the ragged outlines of the pines and the grotesque shapes of the swamp cypress and the lacey effect of the random oak being strangled by Spanish moss; and against this, the dim reflection of the graying sky in slaking pools of water that would eventually move toward the sea. They were beginning to pass cars now, a few of them on their way to Savannah, others moving with them; and some, big logging wagons heading into South Carolina, moving with rattle-trap speed toward some dense growth of slash pine and loblolly.

He set himself to putting Savannah and Agnes Holden out of his mind. There was nothing now but make a successful run and return to Savannah. He felt he could do it, and he thought about the man in his path—Sheriff Jernegan.

He knew little about the man beyond the gossip at the Blue Boy. But he knew Sharkey was impressed by Jernegan. It was, Cadiz thought, enough for him to be impressed himself.

Jernegan, like so many county sheriffs in the south, was a law unto himself. But apparently he was different from other county sheriffs. In the time he had been bootlegging, Cadiz had come to recognize a certain pattern in the behavior of law officials. Generally speaking, as long as the sheriffs and their deputies received their cut, they didn't much care who bent the law. Cadiz knew of four counties in Georgia that were surviving the Depression by bootlegging or moonshining. This was not the case with Jernegan. He could not be bought off, and he would not allow any illegal trafficking in alcohol in his county. Cadiz wondered about such a man—whether it was integrity or a puritanical morality. The best guess—with which Cadiz tended to agree—was that Jernegan was a self-righteous, Bible-belt illiterate, a self-appointed moral judge for his county.

Cadiz knew Jernegan's territory well. It was the cleanest, prettiest, best-kept spot in the southern part of the country. The farms were trim, the houses neat and painted, and the county seat was a gem of orderliness set amongst the sand pits of South Carolina. Having seen the county, Cadiz had not found it hard to believe stories about how Jernegan would drive up to a home and demand that the owner clean up his front yard, or white-wash a fence, or tidy up a ragged field lying fallow, bristling with stalks from the year before.

— Rolling into Yamasee, Mister Cadiz, Hessian said.

— First stop and pay off, Cadiz said.

— Tucker's Café?

— Tucker's Café.

Hessian swung the car off the main highway and rolled down a side street heavy with traffic, many cars parked at an angle. There were no sidewalks. The edge of the road merged into gravel. In some distant siding, a shunting train huffed and puffed its way in the grass-and-sand country of South Carolina's glades to a cotton loading station. They pulled off the side of the road and parked. The drivers, Belly-beans and Springer, stayed behind their wheels. Clarence got out and stood sentry, hands in his pockets, leaning against the tailgate of the last truck, the double-barreled shotgun within easy reach just inside.

After checking the trucks Cadiz checked his own gun on the seat beside him in the scout car. He handed it to Hessian, who then got out, signaled to Clarence, who nodded and waved back that all was clear. Then he opened the warped screen door of Tucker's Café.

A row of enameled stools stood at attention before a grooved, pine-plank counter top; sticky swirls of flypaper hung from the ceiling. Cadiz proceeded to pay off the first representative of the law in the person of Deputy Emerson Fisk, at the going rate of ten dollars per vehicle for empty bootleg rolling stock. The right-of-way was secured.

They were rolling again, the caravan moving straight up 17, heading north, free of the first toll-stop of their trip. The purring of the big Buick—it could do a hundred and twenty-five miles an hour before slinging the tires from its rims—sounded good to him. As he listened to its steady, vibrant power, he grew icy calm.

He remained that way until late in the afternoon. As the red sun sank, they turned a long, narrow curve, swinging straight into the blinding sunset. Hessian hit the brake and Cadiz threw up his arm to shield his eyes. In the next instant, as the Buick slowed, Cadiz saw the roadblock. It was more than a roadblock; it was a trap. Three double teams of mules stood to one side, used by Jernegan to drag the huge tree across the road. Half a dozen men with guns, the same number of cars off the road and one steel, cage-backed truck waiting in the slanting sunlight.

Hessian hit the accelerator and spun the wheel. Cadiz heard the tires scream. Then another scream as the trucks behind them stepped on the gas. The Buick slowed, careening sideways, and would have skidded but for Hessian's fantastic whipping of the big wooden-steering wheel. Without waiting, Hessian slammed to a stop, reversed, shipped the wheel again. It was then that Cadiz heard the first shots. Then several more. Hessian had the car halfway around now and was off the road. The car tilted dangerously to one side as it hung over the edge of the ditch, but Hessian got it out and moving in the opposite direction.

They jerked to a stop before the open truck door where Bellybeans stood on the running board. He tried to use the open door as a shield and dove for a transfer to the Buick. Cadiz pulled him inside, but knew as he did so that he was already dead. There was a hole as big as a fist in his chest. Hessian jammed to a stop for Clarence and Springer. Clarence was standing in back of the last truck, coolly and rhythmically firing and loading. Springer made the transfer to the back, stepping on Bellybean's face as he jumped in. He turned immediately to fire out of the back window. The back of the Buick was being riddled with bullets. The smell of powder, burnt tires and seared brake linings, the yells of the men, the whine of gears and bullets created a world suddenly gone mad.

Clarence dove for the car. He was immediately hit in the head and pitched forward half in and half out of the rear door. Springer turned to kick him out. Hessian plunged the car forward. The fire power coming from the men behind the tree trunk was overwhelming. Cadiz had emptied his pistol and was reloading as the car ground forward and Hessian, hunched over the wheel, stamped his foot to the floor. Springer fired through the rear window and then slumped to one side, clutching his neck. Blood gushed and he tried to stem it with his hands. He started to move to the door handle. The car was in second gear by then and the clatter of bullets hitting the car slackened off abruptly as they got out of range of the shotguns. Springer fell forward on the door handle, spun it open and dove out. Cadiz did not look. He lowered his head in back of the front seat until he could see to fire at the rapidly receding roadblock.

He saw a figure, a man in suntans with a large reflecting metal star on his chest, leap to the top of the huge log and take aim with a rifle. There was no mistaking it; this was Jernegan himself. Cadiz emptied his gun at the figure but knew as he fired that his target was out of range.

The car spun crazily to the side of the road as Hessian fought the wheel. Cadiz knew a tire had been hit. There was nothing to do now but run for it. Cadiz pointed to the curve that had shielded the roadblock, and Hessian nodded his understanding. He could not control the car with one tire gone, and Cadiz helped him, grabbing one of the steel spokes and pulling hard. Around the curve and out of sight of the roadblock, they fled from the car and scrambled into the tall sand-weeds, keeping as low as they could.

Behind them the firing ceased. They ran blindly through the weeds, stumbling into ditches, falling into holes, moving west and into the sun, knowing that their pursuers would have the sun to fight as they themselves had fought it coming into the blind curve.

They ran until they heard the dogs and then they stopped, gasping for air. Then they plunged forward, taking a detour into the first ditch, away from the sun and more to the south, pitching into sinkholes, going down over their heads, coming up gasping, pausing, listening for the dogs.

It sounded like someone had slapped naked flesh with an open palm. Cadiz looked back. He saw that Hessian was dead.

He would never get back to her now. If he got out of it alive, he knew there would be no turning back, that he could only go on.

He ran all night without stopping for rest, and the next day, when the sun came up, he was free of them. He found a sand cave and after lighting a cattail torch and checking for snakes, he lived there for four days without food or water. When he slept he did not dream; when he was awake, he did not think. He was without fear or anger or remorse or anything that a man is supposed to feel at such a time. He knew only that he was there and that sooner or later he would be driven out by hunger and thirst, but until that breaking moment came, he did not really exist.

A June Weekend 1939

Out of the darkness Howard Cadiz could hear the plaintive voice of a singer and the plucking of a guitar, both light and expressive. As the voice rose and the words became clear, Cadiz moved aft along the deck toward the gangway. He did not intrude on the youth—hawkfaced, twenty-one or -two—hunched over the guitar; instead Cadiz walked around the midship housing to the slip side, observing and checking. He made a complete circle and came back to the singer. He stopped again, listening to the final chords. Turning his head slightly, he could see through the porthole into the messroom. A half-dozen men sat around a long table listening to the song. The messman, his long dark hair hanging in his face, leaned on his swab. A sailor stood at the coffee urn, cup in hand, listening. Cadiz recognized four men he had sailed with years before on other ships seated at one end of the table. The bosun, Perry, Harrison and Spanish had stopped in the middle of a hand of poker to listen.

Sail on, sail on, through eternity
There be no love for thee on a faceless sea,
Sail on, sail on, nor reach safe shore,
My sailor man, my sailor man.

In the middle of the refrain a thousand voices of the river and harbor chorused softly under the song and strings. A growl from a Diesel engine bucking current under a heavy load drowned out the music. When Cadiz looked up, the guitar player was chording, still involved with the lament he had just finished and feeling his way through the mood.

Cadiz moved down the deck and leaned on the railing. Nice song, he said. You played it well.

Startled, the young man jumped and spun around.

—Jesus Christ! You snuck up on me, man! I coulda fell over the side and been drowned.

—Sorry, Cadiz said amiably.

—That's okay. The youth eyed Cadiz critically. You must be the new chief mate.

—Yup.

The youth unslung the guitar and stood. He spoke with an open, aggressive pride.

— Well, I'm the goddam ordinary seaman on the four-to-eight watch, so I'm welcoming you aboard the *Sea Lover.*

— Thanks, Cadiz replied ironically, for nothing.

— You welcome, the youth said. He reslung the guitar and chorded it several times. Right now I'm coffee boy for that poker game going on in there. I figure to make enough cash to have a ball game with extra innings when this wagon gets down to Capetown, which is where we are going to palm off these reconditioned taxicabs we're loaded with. He chorded the guitar again. Reconditioned my ass. I been watching 'em come aboard. I examined about a dozen of them and there ain't a one that ain't got sawdust in the rear end.

— You a cargo inspector? Cadiz asked with a smile.

— No, I ain't, the youth said. I'm just a nosy sonofabitch, that's all.

— That's a pretty dangerous thing to be, Cadiz said.

— It's a way of life. The boy looked up and forward to the West Side Highway that spun like a ribbon along the western shore of Manhattan. I see something that tickles me, I got to laugh.

— Is it always funny? Cadiz asked.

— No, not always. Sometimes I get into a piss-pot of trouble on account of them tickles.

— But you don't stop?

— No, I don't stop. A man's tickle is his tickle.

The boy bent his head over the guitar suddenly and began to play with a driving fury, singing as he played:

My mama was a porcupine!
My papa was a wooly bear!
I got quills where pecker hair should grow
And a whanger from here to there!
Watch it girls—Hey! Hey! Watch it now!
Watch it girls—Hey! Hey! Watch it now!

He finished with a flourish. Cadiz grinned and nodded his appreciation.

— You're talented, Cadiz said.

— It's a natural gift, the boy said modestly.

A deep voice from the messroom growled out at them. Cadiz recognized the bosun and involuntarily flinched.

— Hey! Tender! the bosun yelled. How about some service!

— Is that your name? Tender? Cadiz asked.

— Leon Tenderling, but Tender is a term of affection for them that loves me.

Cadiz grinned.

— I get a cut of five per cent outa every fifth pot they play for serving them sandwiches and coffee and whiskey and anything else their little hearts desire, except ass. I don't pimp for no man. A screech of brakes and a blast of an automobile horn from the elevated drive interrupted them. Both looked off toward the lights of Manhattan. I figure a good man like me outa action during the crossing oughta be able to take on about four or five of them big ass Afri-kaan women with no strain.

— You look trim, Cadiz said, looking him over.

— I am! Tender said. And mean. Can't you tell at a glance?

— 'scuse me, Cadiz said.

— That's okay, Tender said elaborately. He chorded some more. You look like an all-right brine pecker to me.

— Thanks, Cadiz said. I didn't know it showed.

— Any way I look at you, Mister Mate, Tender said, stepping back and appraising Cadiz, I see only one thing.

— What's that?

— Man of action.

— You see that, do you?

— We all men of action, Tender said. Din't you know that, Mister Mate? That's why I'm trying to build up a stake with this poker game. I figure European women appreciate a real honest to God man of action better'n these dames in New York. So, I just ain't letting 'em get to me this last weekend ashore.

— You got a point there, Cadiz said.

— You can't argue with it, Tender said. Besides, money goes further outside the States. And besides that, I won't have none until we get to Africa where we going to make money on these pieces of trash called reconditioned taxicabs some sad sonofabitch got suckered into buying.

— Couldn't you get a draw from the Old Man? Cadiz asked.

— Naw, Tender said with resignation. He's been drunk for five days already. He's up there now in the sack with some broad. I seen her. Tender made a face. Jeese! I wish I hadn't.

Cadiz chuckled, and once more the bosun's voice broke in on them. Hey, *Tender! Coffee!*

— That bosun, Tender said wearily, casting his eyes to heaven. I wonder sometimes if he wants food with his cards or cards with his food.

— Last weekend ashore, Cadiz said, you'd think they'd all be shacking up.

— They did all the fucking and messing around they can, Tender said. They ain't as young as me. Besides, they're the big winners of the early payoff games, and this is the All-Star weekend game.

— Tender! Goddammit! Get your ass in here! I want a cuppa coffee and I want it *now!*

— Coming, coming, Tender called airily. He gave Cadiz a helpless shrug and entered the hatchway.

Cadiz listened to the swish of the cars on the highway, closing out as nearly as he could the scarring past. Shad and Al and Hessian . . . and Agnes Holden . . .

It had been nearly six years now and he did not think of her so often anymore, yet in the middle of a conversation there she would be again. When he did think about her, however, it was as if he were an observer seeing himself as he would watch a stranger.

The cards were dealt. The messman, finished with his cleaning chores, smoked a cigarette and watched the play.

— I got it all figured out, he said. A hunnert for her, and forty-five for the weekend's whiskey. She's waitin' for me. I awready got it lined up.

— Well, I seen her, Tender said, and if I was you, I'd go see one of them cowboy pitchers in Times Square instead.

— Yeah? the messman said sarcastically.

— Yeah.

—You saying that because you broke and I got her and you ain't, the messman said.

—And I ain't going to get the clap neither, Tender said.

—I suppose you wash your feet with your socks on?

—I wouldn't even look at her.

—Up yours, Tender.

—Let alone talk to her!

—Your mother's box, the messman said.

—Let alone *pay* her! Tender snorted with contempt and turned his back on the messman. Awright, Boats, I'm here, now what'cha want?

The bosun looked hard at Tender. He needed a shave. An old scar from a knife fight showed livid in his face.

—I want you here to serve me when I want you, that's what!

—Well, I'm here now, Tender said. Name your poison.

The room fell silent as Spanish, thick-chested, almost fat, but hard and weighty, dealt the hand. The cards were gathered up and the players concentrated on their hands.

—Gimme a cuppa coffee, the bosun said, reading his cards.

Somebody opened for five dollars. Everyone stayed. Tender went to the coffee urn.

—Fifth pot coming up! Build it up, big men. I want plenty of money when I ease up alongside one of them big-assed Dutch broads in Capetown. I don't want nothing restricting me.

—He gets a cut out of every fifth pot for doing nothing, the bosun complained. Doing something he woulda done for no pay in the old days. And then be lucky he didn't get his ass whipped by the losers for bringing 'em bad luck. That's the way it was in the old days. Tender plopped the cup on the table, slopping it.

—Well, you're up the creek, Boats, because this ain't the old days now, this is the new days.

The bosun stood up and backed away angrily from the scalding coffee. He glared at Tender.

—Goddam you! the bosun yelled. Look what you done. I oughta—

—Still bitching, huh, Boats? Cadiz's voice, low and firm, stopped the bosun.

The bosun took on a different tone and his body tightened as he recognized Cadiz.

— Well, well, the bucko mate himself finally comes back. How long has it been now—seven-eight years? Back to hold Captain Whitcomb's drunken hand.

— And you're still running off at the mouth, Cadiz said. He turned his attention to the other players, a quiet authority in his voice. Tender, having watched him put the bosun down, paid careful attention.

— Playing the whole weekend, huh? Well, try not to cut each other's hearts out, 'kay? Cadiz said.

— This is a friendly game, Mister Mate, Spanish said.

— There won't be any trouble, Perry added.

Cadiz looked at the bosun and smiled. I don't mind trouble, he said. I just don't like to see blood on the *Lover*'s decks—or investigations by the Coast Guard *and* the Company. If there's any knife fighting, take it onto the dock. Not on my ship.

— I told you, Mister Mate, Spanish said in mild protest, this is a friendly game.

— You must be winning, Cadiz said. But watch out for the losers.

— Seems like the man knows you, Boats, Spanish said.

— Screw you, Spanish.

— Will I get kissed good-by, Boats? Tell me, will I get kissed good-by? Spanish pursed his lips. Everyone laughed. The tension eased and the bosun resumed his seat at the table. Cadiz motioned Tender to the porthole.

— Make a fresh pot of coffee, Cadiz said. I'm going to wake up the old man.

— Sure thing, Tender said breezily, regarding Cadiz with new respect. Anything else?

— No, Cadiz said.

— Queens bet ten, Perry said.

— Ten and ten more, the bosun said.

— Call, Spanish grunted.

Cadiz watched the hand played out as the bets were made. It was quick, alert, professional poker.

— Three jacks, the bosun said, and started to pull the pot.

—Not enough, Boats, Spanish said amiably. Full house. Tens over fours.

The bosun slapped his cards down angrily as Spanish raked in the pot. Tender moved in quickly and held out his hand. Spanish cut several bills and some silver from the pot and handed it over to Tender.

—Six dollars and sixty cents, kiddo, Spanish said.

Tender took the money and waved it in his clenched hand. Six dollars and sixty cents! Man! I'm living! That oughta be enough for a good feel in Capetown, huh, Spanish?

—You'll give 'em a bruise, kiddo. A real bruise.

—See? Tender said to Cadiz. He knows me awready. I'm gettin' a reputation awready. When you ride the Spanish Main and see some old wart-faced hag crippled up, why, you going to know I passed by and gave her the prong!

—What's to eat, Tender? Perry asked.

—I looked inna refrigerator awready. We gotta da nice balon', Tender said, and we gotta da nicea yeller cheese, nicea sardines, and if you wanta anything else, gimme money and I'll go ashore and get delicatessen stuff.

Spanish looked around the table. Perry, Bosun and Harrison agreed. They all contributed and Spanish handed the money to Tender.

—Let's see, get some kosher pickles, ham, corn beef, a half dozen thick steaks for later, some rye bread, couple cases of beer and a couple bottles of bourbon and rye.

—Jesus Christ! Tender protested. There ain't but four of you!

Cadiz moved away from the porthole, smiling to himself. He entered the housing and climbed the ladder to the captain's deck. Behind him he heard the poker game progressing into the dangerous game of bet and buck the odds; heard, too, the brash voice of Tender as he prepared a fresh pot of coffee.

—Little Mary Jones, Tender sang to himself, had a ring around her asshole colored blue!

—Kings bet, the bosun said. How about it, Spanish?

—Well, Boats, Spanish said, I'll just give it a breath, a light touch. Kings bet a brand new twenty-dollar bill to open . . .

On the slip side of the pier, Cadiz stood for a moment in the darkness, smoking and listening to the harbor sounds and the sounds of the city. He flicked his cigarette away and turned to the office door of the captain. He did not knock.

Inside, he wrinkled his nose against the odor. A long couch spanned one whole side of the bulkhead. A desk chair was overturned. The glass on the eight-bell clock was cracked, and when he looked closely, he was surprised to note that the clock was still running. He picked up the chair and an old dress blue jacket with four gold stripes on the sleeve. He brushed the stripes absently, feeling the roughened surface of the tarnished metallic cloth, then laid the jacket neatly to one side.

On the desk were several opened whiskey bottles. He picked up one of them, smelled it, looked sideways at the bedroom door and put the bottle down. He stood still in the middle of the office, lit another cigarette and inhaled deeply, closing his eyes, trying to close out Agnes's face. Then, shivering slightly, he opened his eyes, searching for something to concentrate on. His glance fell on a stack of unopened mail and he reached for it hungrily, leaning on the desk and sorting it quickly. Several of the letters made him pause. He examined them, turning again to look at the bedroom door. He tossed the letters to one side with a flash of disgust, picked up the nearest bottle and drank. He slammed the bottle down, staring at the letters. He moved to the bedroom door and banged it open. It was dark in the bedroom and he waited for his eyes to grow accustomed to the gloom. Gradually he began to make out the form of a man and a woman side by side in the double-sized bunk-bed. The woman was only half covered by the sheet. Whitcomb's mouth was open. He breathed heavily. The woman opened her eyes and then closed them again.

— Wake up, Elly, Cadiz said sharply. Come on, goddammit, hit the deck!

There was a sharp intake of breath and Whitcomb groaned. He opened his eyes and fought to focus. With great difficulty, he pulled himself out of bed and tottered to the bathroom door on the opposite wall, trailing the sheet behind him. The woman, nude, turned her back on Cadiz and curled up into a ball. Cadiz grunted, went back into the office and slumped in the chair facing the bedroom. He listened passively as Whitcomb, in the shower, whined under the shock of the ice-cold water. It did not last long. The water was turned off and Whitcomb reappeared, sopping wet. Cadiz watched him through the open door as he rummaged vaguely for his robe and hat.

Whitcomb paused beside the bed and threw the sheet over the woman and then leaned over and kissed her back.

— Jesus Christ! *Lay off me!* the woman snarled.

— Get some sleep, baby, go ahead and sleep in. Nobody's going to bother you, Whitcomb said, and staggered into the office, closing the door after him. He looked at Cadiz and stared, seeing him for the first time.

— Hello, Elly, Cadiz said.

— Howard Cadiz! Whitcomb said, surprised and pleased. Well, I'll be goddammed!

Whitcomb had aged so much that Cadiz was shocked. His hair was gray and his face was mottled, the telltale badge of the chronic drunk.

— Well, well, Cadiz. The bucko mate himself, Whitcomb said. He sagged to the couch and held his head, groaning. What the fuck are you doing here?

— I'm your new chief mate, Cadiz said.

— You are, huh, Whitcomb said with difficulty, breathing hard. Well, well. Whitcomb lifted his head and stared at Cadiz again, as if lost in thought. Then he hauled himself off the couch and staggered to the desk. He sloshed whiskey into a water glass and drank it off, shuddering. Cadiz watched as Whitcomb sagged to the couch again.

— One of your sailors said you'd been on this jag for five days, Cadiz remarked, smoking languidly, hooking one leg over the chair arm.

— So?

— Five days, Cadiz said. Even for you, that's a long time.

— Well, whatever else has happened to you, Whitcomb said, his head buried in his hands, you damn well ain't changed much. You just as snotty as you always was.

— It stinks in here, Cadiz said.

— It sure as hell don't smell sweet, Whitcomb agreed, head still down. I never thought I'd see you again. Where you been?

— I hadda coupla good trips, Cadiz said.

— They're all good trips.

— Each one better than the one before, Cadiz said.

— I been around the Horn, Far East. Hong Kong is better than ever. The crew wasn't worth a damn for a week after sailing. Never seen a crew hosed out like them.

— That good, huh? Cadiz said.

— Cadiz, you'll never believe it, I had me a—

— Don't bother, Cadiz said. I've heard it before.

Whitcomb looked up sharply, then waved it away.

— Up yours, he said tiredly. You sure ain't changed.

Cadiz saw that the whiskey was taking hold.

— How's Sara? Cadiz asked.

— Okay.

Cadiz reached over and picked up the letters he had examined.

— You going to make your annual visit to see her?

— You been calling your shots ashore, or just having a ball game? Whitcomb said, trying to change the subject.

— It was a long depression, Elly. Then I saw O'Hara and he finally put me on standby. I've been waiting for you and *The Lover*.

— Yeah? Well, that was nice of you. Waiting for me, huh?

— Have you really been drunk for five days?

— Six.

— You going to see Sara?

— That's none of your goddam business, Whitcomb said. And what the hell's the idea of reading my mail?

— Same old Elly, Cadiz sighed. Let's see. We're going to sail Sunday midnight, and the train to Philly for that nine o'clock connection to Lancaster leaves Penn Station at seven. Cadiz slapped Whitcomb on the knee.

— What the hell are you—

— Coupla good nights at home and then back to sea, huh, sailor?

— trying to do?

— Same old Elly. I wonder how long Sara's going to stand for it?

— How long you been ashore? Whitcomb asked, his voice turning crafty.

— Long time, Cadiz replied.

— Why would a sailor stay ashore—for a long time?

— Maybe I was in jail, Cadiz said.

— Naw, you ain't no jailbird. And I heard about you on the Mo-Mac's *Pole Star* running north, how they didn't want you to leave. And you ain't no rummy. What else is there?

— I coulda had the clap, Cadiz said. The last port I hit was in the Red Sea. You know, all those little fellaheen broads. But the Marine Hospital doesn't keep you very long to clean up a dose. And besides that, I don't have that hospital look about me. You can see that. Cadiz paused and grinned. Even though you are drunk.

— No, but you look a little pinched. Like you ain't had none lately.

— Your eyeballs are twisted, Cadiz said.

— It ain't my eyeballs that's twisted, Whitcomb snorted, and glanced toward thc bedroom door. He jerked his head. She ain't what I like. Too big for one thing. I like'm small. More along the lines of that little Canadian Canuck up in Nova Scotia. Remember her?

— I remember, Cadiz said.

— And you had her sister, Whitcomb said with a chuckle that he immediately regretted, clutching his head. Tell me, Howard, tell me why'd you go ashore? I heard you got your open ticket and Mo-Mac was just dyin' to have you take one of their ships.

— There's a reason, Cadiz said.

— A woman!

Cadiz did not react, except that his deadpan detachment was momentarily broken, like a switchblade knife flashing open.

Whitcomb missed nothing. You! *You!* Of all people! Jesus, that's a hot one! You, the bucko mate, spitting St. Elmo's Fire, *you* hunkering around ashore mooning over some lost love! Whitcomb roared with laughter. Now I'll tell you something. I knew it! I just knew it! Of course I din' know how long you was ashore with her—

— It was, Cadiz said tightly, only twenty-four hours.

— but I saw Captain Hogan out to Hong Kong a few years ago and he told me. So, you snotty sonofabitch, I ain't so surprised as you would want me to think, that you come to *The Lover.* I remember laughing all the time I was snug up with some of that young Chinese stuff that you was suffering over a woman. An'—an'—Whitcomb gasped for breath, an' now you tell me you only had twenty-four hours with her! Why, Cadiz, you're a fucking romantic! You can't snow an old bull like me. Nosiree! But I thought about you, Howard, all the time I was cornering the market in Chinee tail, I thought about you and I *laughed.*

—You prick, Cadiz said mildly.

—I said to myself then, I said, he'll be back. And here you are!

Cadiz jerked his head toward the bedroom.

—Get rid of her. You're going down to Lancaster tonight.

—You're a pretty shitty bastard this morning.

—It's not morning, Cadiz said. It's five-thirty P.M. on a Friday.

—Just as snotty as the last time I saw you.

—These letters are from Sara, aren't they? Cadiz held them up. And you didn't even bother to open them. Here's one over ten weeks old.

—Gimme a drink, Whitcomb said. You sure got a nerve coming back here after seven-eight years and just like that, throwing your weight around. Screw you.

—You want me to sail your ship for you, Elly? Cadiz asked. If so, you're going down to Lancaster tonight.

—I'll go Sunday, Whitcomb said.

—We're sailing Sunday.

—Leave me alone, Howard, Whitcomb said wearily. Gimme a drink.

Cadiz poured a very small drink in the bottom of the glass. He handed it over.

—You'd better lay off this stuff.

—Well, if I'm going to Lancaster tonight, Whitcomb said reasonably you don't want me to have the shakes, do you!

—Personally, I don't give a damn, Cadiz said. Why didn't you open the letters?

—Because—because. Aw hell! What makes you so interested in my personal life?

—There isn't anything personal about you, Elly.

— Izzat so! Well, just answer me, how come you so interested in whether I go to Lancaster tonight or not?

— Your last trip you stayed drunk in Baltimore for three weeks and didn't go see her! Cadiz turned and jabbed the buzzer near the desk, signaling the pantry near the crew mess for Tender to bring coffee. Never mind how I know. I *know*. You'd better have some coffee.

— I'd better have a drink, is what I'd better, Whitcomb said.

Cadiz hesitated and then poured another small drink and handed it over to Whitcomb.

— You're a lush, Captain Whitcomb, Cadiz said. And if you didn't have chief mates like me to run your ship for you, you'd have been dumped by the annual company insurance surveys a long time ago.

— That's mighty interesting, but you know something—

Before Whitcomb could finish there was a loud crash from the bedroom. Both men jumped.

— Take it easy in there, goddammit! Whitcomb roared. He shook his head.

A knock on the door announced Tender's arrival. He came in with a tray and four cups, a pot of coffee, cream can and bowl of sugar.

— I brought my own cup, Cap'n, Tender said breezily, in case you ast me to stay. He put the tray on the desk and looked around. Where's the broad, Cap'n? You seen her, Mister Mate? She's got a pair of tits on her bigger'n grapefruit.

— Get him outa here, Whitcomb gritted.

Tender poured three cups of coffee.

— She's a real high-class-looking whore, Mister Mate. Nothin' but the best for the Cap'n—

— *Git below!* Whitcomb roared. Tender spilled the coffee as he set it down hastily and escaped.

— We lost a lot of the crew, Whitcomb said. You check the crewlist yet?

— We only need a couple of A.B.'s, otherwise you've surrounded yourself with the usual bunch of bums.

The bedroom door opened. The woman, about forty-five, big-breasted, blond, hung over, wearing only a sheet, entered. She did not look at either of the men. She moved unsteadily to the desk.

With one hand she held the sheet up over her bosom, and with the other she picked up one of the bottles. Cadiz and Whitcomb watched her as she took a deep pull. Finished, she shook her head hard and turned, still carrying the bottle. She reentered the bedroom and closed the door.

— Jesus! Whitcomb said.

— Were you desperate or just drunk? Cadiz asked.

— I musta been drunk, Whitcomb said. I ain't never been *that* desperate.

— I've seen you that desperate, Cadiz said.

Whitcomb sipped the coffee and regarded Cadiz balefully over the cup.

— You changed, you know that, Cadiz? You more snotty than you used to be seven-eight years ago. No, that ain't right. You was always snotty. Now I think you're getting mean. I seen plenty in my time. Sailors get to living high, you know what I mean, booze and broads and money and then something happens and they get mean. They go sour. I seen it in mates and bosuns and skippers. They just go bad. Plain rotten.

— You got a headful of congestion, Cadiz said.

— Yeah? Whitcomb blew on his coffee. Well, what happened to you down on the Gold Coast with that big A.B.?

Cadiz swung around.

— Sure, I seen Ike Trigger. And I saw Captain Johansen, too. I heard you beat the A.B. s'bad you scrambled his brains, is it true?

— Just stay the hell off the foredeck, Elly, Cadiz said, tense. You just sit up here and look at your smutty French movies and stay drunk, and I'll run the *Sea Lover* for you.

Whitcomb was watching his face. Yeah, some of them turn plain rotten.

— And some of them turn into drunks.

Whitcomb spit the coffee out onto the deck and threw the cup against the bulkhead.

— Stop treating me as if I was some South Street bum! So all right! So-all-goddammed-right! I like a little vino! But *I'm* the master of the *Lover*, and I don't have to take on any chief mate I don't want to. I could go to the Company—

— You're getting drunk again, *Captain* Whitcomb. If I were you, I'd stay away from the Company.

— I've had enough of this, Whitcomb said and lunged for his coat.

— I gotta go, Cadiz said, rising.

— There's the power, Mister Bucko Mate! There! Read 'em and weep! Whitcomb brandished the gold braid in Cadiz's face.

— You know what you can do with your four gold stripes, Elly?

— Ahh! Go on below, Whitcomb said, tossing the coat to one side. There was a time when I'd throw your tail off the bridge for sass.

Cadiz started for the door.

— What did you mean—what you said about the Company? Whitcomb asked.

— The seven o'clock train to Philly, Elly. I'd make it, if I were you. It might be your last chance.

— Now what the fuck is *that* supposed to mean?

— You're a sick man.

Whitcomb recoiled and stiffened, then let his great gut sag heavily.

— I'm okay, he said quietly. O'Hara, the—ah—Company, do they know about it?

— I don't know, Elly, Cadiz said gently.

Whitcomb's eyes lit up. So the Company *don't* know about it! he said craftily.

— Elly, listen a minute.

— How'd *you* find out?

— Listen, Elly, Cadiz said, why don't you quit—

— I know! That loudmouth chief mate I kicked off the *Lover*, that's who! The sonofabitch! You talked to him!

— Elly, goddammit, listen to me. You've got Sara and the farm and the boys—

— I shoulda brained that sonofabitch with a fid. And he *was* a lousy sailor!

— You owe that much to yourself, Elly. You've got it coming to you.

— Sure! You saw him at the office, or in a bar, and he told you. Sure. That's it! All about Baltimore las' trip, too, prob'ly.

— Why don't you go back to Sara?

— There's a reason—reasons, of a kind.

— What kind of reasons?

— Reasons, Whitcomb said. Leave me alone! All the ships in the ocean and in this Company's fleet, and how fucking lucky can I be to get *you* back! Jesus!

— All right! Cadiz snapped. It's not my funeral. You want to have me weigh you down with shackles and drop you over the side, I'll see that you get prayed over.

— Up yours, Whitcomb said. I got two more good trips before I tie up for good. Yes, sir! About two more good ones. I'd sure like to get back to Hong Kong and get some more of that young Chinese tail. And now that you're back with me, I don't have to worry about the *Lover*. Yes, sir! Two more *good* ones!

— What happens if you get an attack when you're crossing thirty-five west? Cadiz asked.

— Why, Whitcomb said, I got me some stuff. I just take a swallow. It's really pretty amazing medicine.

— Elly, Cadiz said, the last mate said you had two heart attacks the last trip.

— What a big-mouth bastard he is. Truly a big-mouth sonofabitch, and a *lousy* sailor.

— How long can you keep fooling yourself?

— You know something, Cadiz? I'm going to put in a request to the company for another mate! I'm master of the *Lover*. I don't have to take this, I don't have to sail with you again. I don't have to take that kind of bilge.

— Go ahead, Elly. Put in your request. I told you O'Hara put me on standby to wait for you.

— What happened to you ashore since I last saw you, Howard? It's been a long time. Beginning of the Depression. She give you a hard time ashore? Sure, that's it. You got hooked up with some broad and she gave you a hard time. I coulda told you you wouldn't make it. I seen it happen too many times. You have to do it the way I did it. Get married young, real young, and then start laying it in. Not very much, just a little at a time. Now I got me a beautiful farm, fifty head of dairy cattle, wife, sons—fine sons—and a grandchild. Whitcomb rocked back on his heels and spread his hands.

— Yeah, you got it made, Cadiz said.

— Goddam right I have, Whitcomb said, pulling his robe around him. I seen it, I tell you. Sailors go ashore working in a office, or clerking in a dime store, going home every night and staring at the same four walls, living in a two-room apartment with a kitchen the size of an Eyetalian postage stamp and a Murphy bed and eating hamburgers while they listen to Gangbusters on the radio . . . Balls! a hundred times I seen it. All kinds. Weak-minded idiots and tough guys like you, trying to walk away from it. I may be a rummy, Mister Cadiz, but I know this—you gotta get the roots started and then *forget about 'em!* You can't have it both ways. Then you sail off and have your good times while she's home pregnant waiting for you. Sure! I'm drunk and I might get drunker, but it ain't none of your business.

— You'd better make that trip down to see Sara, Cadiz said. Don't stop off at the Savarin Bar in Penn Station and come back and *say* you went down to see her, either.

Whitcomb picked up one of the bottles and Cadiz grabbed his wrist.

— I told you, Elly, Cadiz said grimly, that you're going down to Lancaster tonight. Either you go or I'll walk off *The Lover* and tell the Company about your heart. You had your wake-up shot—no more!

— Leggo my arm, Whitcomb muttered.

Cadiz released him, then quickly collected all the bottles in the room and heaved them out of the porthole. Whitcomb stood by helplessly.

— Now look what you've done! Goddam you! One of these days somebody's going to let you have it in back of the head.

— Don't you ever try it, old man, or I'll kill you.

The cool, almost detached tone of voice had an effect on Whitcomb. He relaxed. He drew the robe tighter around his stomach.

— I'm sorry, Howard, he said. I didn't mean it about your broad. I guess I'm still pretty crocked.

— You sure as hell are, Cadiz replied.

— There you go again! Lay off, will you! Why don't you go ashore and get laid or something. Get your thoughts on something else. Get another woman.

Cadiz picked up the letters and held them out to Whitcomb.

— You'd better take these with you. Read 'em on the train and catch up on all the news. Sara'll know if you didn't.

Whitcomb took the letters, glanced at them a moment and then turned away. He sighed. He opened a closet and took out an old briefcase, opened it and dropped the letters inside.

— I been thinking serious, Howard. Maybe it was time I piled off and for good. I mean—

Cadiz left the room abruptly and stood in the dark companionway outside, flat against the bulkhead, his eyes closed. Whitcomb continued talking, not aware that Cadiz had gone.

— . . . give you *The Lover* and go on down to Sara and the boys, but—Howard, I just can't make that decision. I—Howard? Howard? He slumped to the couch.

— You got a drink, Elly? the woman called from within the office.

— No, I ain't got no drink.

— I need a drink, Elly. Bad—real bad.

— Well I ain't got no fuckin' drink! Whitcomb shouted furiously. Drink water. Drink coffee!

— How come you let that man throw out the whiskey, Elly? I thought *you* was the captain?

— Aw, shut up, you stupid goddam dumb broad.

— Elly, that ain't no way to talk to a lady—

— Lady, my ass!

— Lissen, you mad on him, the woman whined, don't take it out on me.

— I ain't mad, baby, Whitcomb said.

— Elly, we had a good time din't we?

— What?

— Elly—I NEED A DRINK!

— *Well, we ain't got no drink!* So shut up! You have to go ashore. I gotta dress. I'd better make that train to Philly or he'll get snotty and ack like a prima donna and walk off. And I need him.

Tender walked out of the hatchway and onto the gangway, which was flooded with light from three cargo cluster lamps. But to Cadiz, as he prowled the decks, it did not seem light enough. The darkness of the huge empty pier shed absorbed the light as a sponge soaks up water. He walked forward and stood on the bow and watched the cars pass on the West Side Drive, then turned and walked aft, avoiding Tender and the gangway, keeping to the dark slip side, and stood on the stern. He looked out over the dark Hudson and at the Jersey shore, alive with neon. He saw a cabin liner moving upriver under tug. He studied the approach the pilot was making, judging the currents, making the decisions to himself, grunting satisfaction when within seconds he saw the proper move made—large lighted house on top the glistening waters, an incredible bulk moving about in the dark like a blinded giant, being guided by the strange little gnome of a tug attached with a line. No one made room for the vessel in the river. The heavy nighttime traffic continued. Barges under power and barges in tow, lighters and small craft and ferry boats skirted and hooted and bellowed against the big, overpowering vessel, a hundred different squawks and demands and appeals for the right-of-way, yet the huge ship came on. Cadiz did not move until he saw that she was coming into the next slip over and that he would be sharing the pier shed with her; and it was then, too, that he heard the voices and saw the lights in the shed as the stevedores, company officials, customs, immigration and pier police moved deep into the shed and stopped before a door marked with a huge number 5. The door was opened and Cadiz watched as the waiting officials on the pier stepped through to the pierside and stood on the stringer, all of them watching the tug maneuver the bulky, awkward hull into her slip. He studied her lines with professional curiosity and decided that she would be hell in a quartering sea. Then he walked aft and met Tender, standing on the deck. The ordinary was eating a sandwich and drinking a beer as he too watched the cabin liner angle into the slip. The vessel was close enough now for them to hear the jangle of the telegraph and the shouts of the men on deck.

—Looks like we gonna have company, Tender said.

—Looks that way, Cadiz replied.

—About twenty thousand tons?

—About.

—Limey?

—I can't make it out but it could be. It's a cabin liner. Five hundred passengers in the cabins and another twelve hundred in steerage.

—How the hell do they get that many down below? Jesus! They must be sleeping all over each other.

—They do, Cadiz said. That's the type of ship that was developed to bring immigrants over. Especially from Northern Europe. Ireland and Italy—

—You're right and you're wrong, Whitcomb said, speaking from above on the boat deck. He trotted lightly down the ladder, not at all like a man who had been badly hung over only a short time ago. Whitcomb joined them on the deck, dressed in a fresh dark navy blue uniform with four bright new gold stripes on the sleeve. His bridge hat and gray kid gloves held in one hand, his briefcase in the other, he was a different man—shaven, pink faced, smelling strongly of a masculine cologne. He wore a white shirt and black tie, the very picture of a deep-water captain. Cadiz was stunned at the transformation. He sensed a difference in other ways, too, and concluded that Whitcomb had probably had a reserve bottle secreted away in his room. The captain was strong, direct and confident. He's got his nerve back, Cadiz thought. For a while, anyway. Below them, in the pier shed, activity increased.

—You're right that she's one of the great human cargo carriers that hauled the big waves of Irishers and Eye-talians and class A-1 Northern Europeans back there in the old immigration days, Whitcomb said, squinting at the ship. But you're wrong that she's a Limey. She's a Kraut. Can't you see that red and black flag? And the Swastika?

Cadiz squinted at the vessel. It was closer now but he still could not make out her flag or colors.

—Can you see the flag, Tender? Cadiz asked.

—No, but then my eyes ain't so good.

—My eyes are excellent, Cadiz said, and I can't see it.

Whitcomb chuckled.

—One thing I still got is my eyesight. Yes, sir, cat's eyes. I got 'em.

—Captain Whitcomb, you are trying to pull the sheep shit over this poor ordinary's eyes.

— Whassat!

Tender became alert and took an involuntary step backward.

— You were up on your deck in the dark, watching her with the glass, weren't you? Cadiz accused.

— There's only one thing worse than catching a man in a lie, Howard, Whitcomb said soberly. And that's catching a man in a white lie, jamming him up over an insignificant detail.

— There's only one thing worse than lying, Cadiz retorted, and that's lying over something of absolutely no importance.

The three of them were silent for several minutes, watching the liner inch her way into the slip. The tug was sending up a boiling wake; offal from the bottom spun to the surface and filled the air with a sickening bilge smell. The dialogue between the pilot on the bridge and the tug captain was an articulate language of shrill policeman's whistles and deep, short replies from the liner's steam horn.

— Where do they get the people to go steerage these days? Tender asked, a careful politeness in his voice, making it obvious to Whitcomb and Cadiz that he was aware of the sharp exchange between the two men.

— They don't get many, Whitcomb said. They come over light, and pick up passengers over here for the summer in Europe. College kids and students and poor slobs make up the bulk of the lists. They haul them over most of the summer and then turn around and haul them back home again.

— I can't imagine anybody wanting to pay to ride on a boat, Tender said, half to himself.

Cadiz and Whitcomb looked at each other and both of them laughed.

— Spoken like a true brine pecker, Tender, Whitcomb said.

— A professional, Cadiz added.

Tender looked from one to the other, unsure. He frowned.

— Yeah? How's that? What's a professional?

— A professional, Cadiz said, is a man who gets paid for doing what he likes and does best, while others pay for the same privilege.

— Oh, Tender said. Then that's me, Mister Mate. I feel like I oughta get a pass when I ride the ferry.

— You've said it all, Whitcomb replied.

They fell silent again, watching the tug and the liner, appreciating the pilot's problem of getting the huge vessel into the slip, where there was a restriction on maneuvering room for the tug, while at the same time the current attacked the stern, still sticking out into the river.

— He's going to lose her, Whitcomb said. He'd better get a line on the dock damn fast.

The stern of the vessel was being carried away by the power of the current. The whistles became shrill and the answers deeper and shorter. The tug suddenly cast off the bow line and turned in the slip. It rushed aft alongside the liner and put its buffered nose up against the liner's quarter. Cadiz saw the heaving line go in.

— He's going to have a tough time bucking that current, Whitcomb said. Isn't that just like a krauthead, trying to get a twenny thousand tonner into a slip with a tide running with just one goddam tug when he oughta have three? Cheap bastards. Always trying to finesse.

The tug worked hard against the swinging vessel, and then it was over and the liner was three quarters inside the slip. Now the effect of the current, thirty seconds before a dangerous threat, was no longer a factor.

— Good man on that tug, Cadiz said.

— Damn good, Whitcomb agreed. We got the best tug captains in the world right here in New York.

— A Thames man isn't bad, Cadiz said. Especially a downriver Thames man.

— They're pretty good, Whitcomb said.

— Or a Mersey tug. Or a Clydeside man.

— Or a St. Johns, or a Malmo, or any of a dozen places, Whitcomb said. But you separate the men from the boys when you've got a ship in ballast, high out of the water, all light, with a high wind and going through Hell's Gate. Gimme a Moran tug and a New York harbor skipper any time.

The officials on the dock were joined by a few friends and relatives of the passengers on the liner.

—Not many down to greet the homecomers, Cadiz said. For a ship that size.

—They're probably all you going to see, too, Whitcomb said. I'll bet there ain't more than a hundred passengers aboard.

—Can they afford to run so light? Cadiz asked.

—It ain't what can be afforded, it's the way things are. You been there, you know how it is. Ships are running outa Germany light and in ballast these days and then going back full list and full cargo. Everything going in, nothing coming out.

—You'd think, Cadiz said, that the way things are over there, they'd be crammed to the overhead with people getting the hell out.

—Goddammit! the bosun's voice boomed from the messroom. And me with aces back to back!

—Three tens will beat 'em every time, Boats, Spanish said.

—But you went and checked a cinch to me!

—Sure I did, Spanish replied. And you went and bit like a three-time loser. And I'll do it again if I get the chance.

—But that ain't fair poker, the bosun whined. Checking a cinch and raising.

—No, it ain't fair, but it wins. It's called sandbagging, Boats. Now you know.

—That bosun is a lousy sailor, Whitcomb said to Cadiz. I wonder that I haven't kicked his ass off my ship long ago.

Before Cadiz could comment, Spanish stepped out of the hatchway and joined the group. He was chortling and shaking his head. He took a drink from a quart bottle he carried and leaned on the railing, still grinning.

—That bosun—

—You're drinking good stuff this trip, Spanish, Whitcomb said.

—Why not, Spanish shrugged. Bosun's paying for it. He stood up, then caught himself. 'Scuse me, Cap'n, have a drink, sir?

Whitcomb glanced defiantly at Cadiz and then nodded.

—Just a breath, he said, and took the bottle. Out of politeness, he did not wipe the top. He drank deeply several times. He looked at Spanish. I don't want no trouble on *The Lover* this weekend, Spanish. Whitcomb returned the bottle.

— No trouble, Cap'n, Spanish said.

Whitcomb slapped the railing.

— Well, I may be back and I may not. It depends on my luck and the kind of perfume she's wearing.

— That's the way I like to hear a man talk, Tender said. You got to smell for a woman to make time with her.

— A smell is mighty important, Spanish said.

— Mighty important, Tender said.

— The perfume, if it's right, Spanish said, can make all the difference.

Yes, sir! Whitcomb said expansively. The artificial lure replacing the old muskiness that our modern hygiene deems offensive. The female in heat—

— If the smell—if that *certain* smell is right, Spanish said, and kissed his fingertips. I *like* the smell of a woman, he added reverently.

— It don't have to be high class either, Tender said.

— Not at all, Spanish said, offering the bottle to Whitcomb again.

— Yeah, man, Tender said. It can be ten-cent-store stuff—

— Or even the smell of soap, Whitcomb said, wiping his mouth.

— Like them movie stars, Spanish said.

— Movie stars, my ass, Tender snorted. Just woman. Period.

— I agree, Tender, Whitcomb said. Just woman. Period.

— Fresh from the shower, Spanish said. Her hair a little damp.

Whitcomb had kept the bottle and took another swallow.

— With a light breeze coming through the curtains, Whitcomb said.

— And everybody else, working, Tender contributed. That's important. Everybody else working and you just laying there, waiting, with the taste of breakfast coffee in your mouth.

— Waiting for her. Just laying there while the world moves around you, Whitcomb said.

Whitcomb took another drink, and Tender summed up the mood with a long, horny sigh. And then, as if in echo to Tender's sigh, breaking into the mood, adding to it, the cabin liner blew one long sustaining blast. Whitcomb came alert and slapped the railing again.

— Well, she ain't much, my *Sea Lover*, but she's all I've got. At the moment.

The bosun broke into the circle then, complaining as he approached the hatchway, not expecting to see Cadiz and Whitcomb there.

— You playin' cards, or ain'tcha? And how about some goddam service, Tender? When I play poker, I like to sit and *play!*

Spanish and Tender looked at each other, shrugged and followed the bosun inside. He offered Cadiz the bottle.

— One for the road, Cadiz?

— No. And you'd better take it easy, Cadiz said.

— Go ashore, will you, f'chrissakes! Find her! Either knock her teeth out or—take her to bed. But don't stand around moaning and groaning. Life's too short.

— Go on, or you'll miss your train, captain. Keep the philosophy for kids like Tender.

— You know my Sara, Whitcomb said.

— I know her.

— She's a good woman, you know that, Cadiz?

— I know that, Elly.

— Funny, you get an idea of what kind of woman would please you, and then you make your choice, Whitcomb said. He paused. And that's it.

— And that's it, Cadiz said quietly to himself.

— Most women satisfy, Cadiz. You ever think about that?

— I'm thinking. But I can't get it to add up, Cadiz said.

— Hell! I've got grown children. Grandchild even. Boy five, Whitcomb said.

— You better go, Elly.

— Why are you so goddam *insistent* on me going to Lancaster? Whitcomb demanded. Will you tell me that?

— Because, Cadiz said slowly, I sailed with you before, remember? And I don't want you crying on my neck the whole goddam trip about how guilty you feel.

— Guilty for what?

— For not going down to see Sara! That was why you lost the last mate.

— That big mouth again, Whitcomb said scornfully.

— No, not only that. I sailed with you before. I know. And it doesn't take much imagination to see that being a dedicated drunk now, it'll be worse than ever. Now *go!*

— So that's it. Now it comes out, does it? Well, I'm *cer*-tainly glad that we've cleared the air. Yes, sir. Very fucking well, Mister Cadiz. Very eff well.

— Go on, Elly.

Whitcomb lifted the bottle to his mouth and drank again. He put the bottle down firmly on the gangway apron railing.

— You know something? he said. In those years we spent together back in the old days, I spent more time with you than I did with my wife, and I been married thirty-five years. That's the trouble. We didn't share anything.

— I've heard it all before, Elly.

— But when you're back—after a crossing, after been gone five, six, seven, eight months maybe—so much would have happened to the farm and the kids and Sara, too, I wouldn't know anything about it. Then she'd try to tell me. How it was and all. Howard, honest to God, I couldn't get into the spirit of how it was when a cow had a calf in a snowstorm one night, when I'd remember that on that *particular* night I was shacked up with three Swedish broads and a case of booze. That actually happened once, you know. It actually happened.

Cadiz saw the figure break away from the crowd surging around the gangway of the liner and walk quickly, militarily erect, trim in his whites, to the gangway of the *Lover*. The man stepped onto the gangway and climbed swiftly. Cadiz moved instantly to the head of the gangway to meet him.

— Herr Captain? the officer said in precise English. He was as tall as Cadiz, about the same age, ruddy faced with deep brown, almost black, eyebrows. He inclined his head a fraction.

— Chief officer, Cadiz said, still barring his way. Can I help you?

— I have compliments from Captain Hunzel of the *Thuringen*. He smiled. Ve are to be neighbors for several days.

— Who are you? Cadiz asked, not able to decipher the insignia on the uniform.

— I am deck officer Martin Thale. Once more he inclined his head slightly. He did not actually click his heels together, but that was the effect. And you, sir?

— Howard Cadiz.

The German's eyes moved over Cadiz quickly, coldly, and then he smiled again.

— Spanish?

— Georgia Cracker, Cadiz said.

— Pardon?

Cadiz did not bother to answer. He nodded in Whitcomb's direction.

— Mister Thale, Captain Elisha Whitcomb, master of the *Sea Lover.*

— Herr Captain! This time Thale did click his heels as he snapped a bow with his head.

— Mister Thale, Whitcomb said. Come aboard, sir.

— Thank you, Captain Vitcomb. Thale smiled again and stepped down from the gangway platform. Herr Captain, Captain Hunzel of the *Thuringen* sends compliments, sir, and vishes you to honor him for a drink in his cabin.

Before Whitcomb could reply, Cadiz spoke up. Captain Whitcomb is on urgent business, Mister Thale, and sends his regrets to Captain Hunzel. Perhaps another time.

Martin Thale gave Cadiz a cold stare and then said to Whitcomb, Ahh, Captain Vitcomb. Captain Hunzel will be disappointed, but he vill understand.

— We appreciate the gesture, Cadiz said, and you may inform Captain Hunzel that, acting for Captain Whitcomb, I shall pay a courtesy call myself.

Thale opened his mouth and Cadiz quickly cut him off.

— On my opposite number, of course, Cadiz said with a smile.

— Opposite number? Vot does this mean?

— Your chief officer, Cadiz said, hardly able to keep from laughing out loud.

— Ahh, so. Of course! Thale smiled thinly and turned to Whitcomb. He snapped another bow and clicked his heels again. Captain Vitcomb, sir!

— Mister Thale, Whitcomb replied formally.

Thale did not speak to Cadiz as he turned, only inclined his head a bare quarter of an inch and hurried down the gangway. Cadiz and Whitcomb watched him until he was lost in the crowd.

— I thought he was going to have a fuckin' heart attack when you said you was going in my place, Whitcomb said. But what did you cut me off for? I'd have liked seeing one of their new skippers.

— New ones? Cadiz asked.

— Those who are politically correct, Whitcomb said heavily.

— Oh, Cadiz said. Well, I'll find out for you.

— Poor bastards, Whitcomb sighed. They aren't bad people individually, but watch out when they run in packs.

— To hell with 'em, Cadiz said.

— Keep 'em off the *Lover*, Howard, Whitcomb said, picking up his briefcase.

— You got a half hour to make that train, Elly.

— And when the crew starts coming back over the weekend, keep our sailors off *their* boat. I don't want no fights.

— Go on, Elly.

— You ain't mad or anything, are you Howard?

— No, Elly, I ain't mad or anything. Just go see Sara.

— You're right, of course, Whitcomb said. But then you snotty enough to know you're right. He started down the gangway. Suddenly he froze, looking over the side. He pointed. My God, Howard, look at the size of that rat!

Tender came out of the hatchway just then and rushed to the railing.

— Christamighty! Tender said. That thing is bigger'n any cat that ever walked!

— I don't see it, Cadiz said.

Whitcomb retreated back up the gangway, walking backwards, and pointed into the murky depths between the skin of the ship and the pier stringers on the lower piling.

— There, right by the fluke of that big piling, Whitcomb said.

Cadiz saw it then and was revulsed. At his side, Whitcomb picked up the whiskey bottle and started to heave it. Then he hesitated and brought it down.

— Get a shackle, Tender. A big one. Maybe we can drop it on its head.

Tender moved off quickly and Spanish came out then, ambling over to the railing to see what was going on. He spotted the rat and his predatory instincts were immediately aroused.

— Why not get the gun, Cap'n? Spanish asked. That rat would shake off a shackle. Even if you hit him.

— Get up on the boatdeck, Spanish, Whitcomb said, speaking with authority, and turn on the spotlight. Hurry!

Spanish ran to the ladder as Tender raced back with a shackle, giving it to Whitcomb.

— He's moving! Tender said breathlessly. No, no, he's stopped—

— Spanish! The light, dammit! Whitcomb yelled.

The light sprung on and the spot trailed down the gangway in the darkness until the beam steadied on the rat. It sat on its hind legs, black, wet and slimy; its long snakelike tail was stretched out flat on the stringer for balance.

— All right, you've got him, Cadiz said. Not too far over, Spanish. That's it, now, hold it! Go ahead, Elly.

Whitcomb moved along the railing of the ship, leaning far out over the side with the heavy shackle in both hands, positioning it over the rat below him.

— Careful—careful—Cadiz cautioned both Spanish and Whitcomb.

The light moved.

— Spanish! Hold that light steady! Whitcomb said hoarsely.

— What the hell's going on here! the bosun demanded, erupting onto the deck.

— Shut up, Whitcomb said coldly.

— What is it, Mister Mate? the bosun asked.

— It's a big rat, ya jerk, Tender said quietly to one side. What the hell you think it is? Sally Rand buck nekked doing a dance?

The light moved inches at a time as the rat, with jerky movements, slipped along the stringer, constantly changing his position. Whitcomb and Cadiz moved along the railing, Whitcomb still trying to position the shackle, Cadiz offering suggestions at his side.

— Let me see! The bosun rushed forward and stumbled on the

whiskey bottle, sending it scuttling along the steel deck. It hit a stanchion and splintered.

— Goddam you, bosun! Whitcomb said angrily.

— He's running! Cadiz yelled, pointing.

— Spanish! Keep that light going! Whitcomb shouted.

— There he goes!

The last words were muffled as the whole crowd, led by Whitcomb and Cadiz, surged forward. Spanish remained at his post with the light, searching the stringers below him. In the distance he could hear the voices of the hunters.

— He's coming up the goddam lines! Whitcomb roared. Don't let him on the ship!

— Throw it, bosun! Cadiz yelled. Goddam you, throw it!

— Knock him in the water!

— He's coming your way, Spanish!

— Watch it! Tender shouted. He's loose on deck!

— Goddam you, bosun, Whitcomb bellowed. Your brains in your ass?

Tender crept along the deck near the gangway and glanced up at Spanish.

— That's the Cap'n for you, always gettin' his anatomy mixed up. You see him, Spanish?

— Naw, I think he went up the port side, Spanish replied.

Tender crept off, an eighteen-inch fid in his hand, his knees bent in the classical stalking tradition.

The *Sea Lover* was suddenly silent. Not a sound was heard for thirty seconds and then suddenly the hunt burst screaming onto the gangway deck, led by Whitcomb and Cadiz, followed by Perry, Tender, Harrison and the bosun, all rushing forward after the scurrying, terrified rodent. Spanish worked the follow spot.

Again there was a silence, and after a few moments Whitcomb and Cadiz appeared, tiptoeing aft. Cadiz carried a shackle in each hand and Whitcomb now wielded a broom handle. As they approached the lighted gangway area, searching the shadows along the railing, Perry and Harrison appeared in back of them.

— Here he comes! Harrison shouted.

Whitcomb, Cadiz, Harrison and Perry jumped to the railing and grabbed handholds for safety. As the rat sped past them, they all pounded off, howling and hooting in pursuit.

A few moments later the bosun and Tender inched forward toward the gangway platform. At the opposite end of the narrow deck, Whitcomb, Cadiz, Harrison and Perry closed in for the kill. They were cautious, intent. The rat was cornered against a jog in the frame of the housing. They all stood at a safe distance, staring in horrible fascination at the enemy.

— Jesus! Looka them eyes! Perry said.

— And those teeth, Harrison whispered.

— They must be an inch and a half long, Tender said.

— Go on, captain, the bosun said, what you waiting for?

Whitcomb gazed at the rat, who was down on all fours, quivering, waiting. Whitcomb lowered the broom handle.

— Look at the scars around his head and neck. Long dirty-looking streaks, Whitcomb said slowly.

— Kinda white, in the fur, yeah, I see 'em, Tender said.

— He musta had plenty of fights, Perry said softly. I bet a rat as big as he is was boss of this whole pier for a goddam long time.

— Yeah, Tender said.

The bosun reached out for Whitcomb's broom handle.

— Well, he ain't going to have anymore fights—

Whitcomb wrenched the broom handle from the bosun's grasp. He watched the rat, transfixed.

— He must be old. Real old, to grow that size and show those scars, Whitcomb said.

— What the hell's the matter with you, Cap'n! the bosun demanded. He's a fuckin' germ carrier. Useless. Never did nothing good in his life—full of diseases—

— He's favoring his forepaw, Whitcomb murmured. The others were infected by Whitcomb's fascination; they looked from Whitcomb to the rat, sensing that something was involved here that went beyond the game of catch and kill.

— He won't last long anyways. As soon as the others find out how weak he is, they'll crowd in on him, Whitcomb said.

Cadiz looked hard at Whitcomb.

— Let him die the way he lived, Whitcomb said quietly.

Cadiz dropped his shackle to the deck. The sudden shock of noise made all of them jump. The rat saw his chance and escaped straight down the gangway and into the underworld of pier piling and stringers.

There was a moment of stunned silence.

— Son of a b-bitch, the bosun stammered, that's the goddammedest thing I ever saw! Letting that old rat escape! Letting him get away, scot free like that.

Whitcomb whirled on the bosun. For a moment Cadiz saw Whitcomb as he remembered him when they had first met, years before—hard, capable, decisive. He reached out with one huge hand and grabbed the bosun by the front of his shirt. He yanked the man up and forward, pulling him to his toes.

— You got a loose mouth, Mister, and one of these days I'm going to take you out on deck and I'm going to beat you to a pulp. Don't you ever speak to me again, you sonofabitch, except in the line of duty, and then you had fucking well better have the mate's permission to do it. You got that, you big-mouthed bastard?

The bosun goggled.

— Answer me! Have you *got* that, Mister?

— I . . . got it—

— *Sir!*

— I got it, *sir*.

— Your heart and soul may belong to God, *but your ass belongs to me*.

— Yes, *sir*, the bosun said.

Cadiz saw that Whitcomb's tensions were flowing out of him like waste water down the scuppers. He had handled the bosun, but it had taken all there was in him. Cadiz stepped in quickly.

— All right, break it up! What do you think this is, a goddam class reunion? Tender!

— Yes, sir! Tender hopped forward as the others disappeared discreetly into the hatchway and the housing.

— Get your ass down on the pier and collar a cab for Captain Whitcomb.

— Yes, sir!

— And I don't care if you have to beat some of those kraut passengers over the head, get a cab and hold it. Tell the driver there's a ten in it for him if he can get to Penn Station in time for a seven o'clock train!

Tender, at the bottom of the gangway by then, scooted off into the milling crowds.

— You okay, Elly?

— Yeah. Yeah.

— The kid'll get you a cab, Cadiz said, trying to sound relaxed and casual.

— Yeah.

— Here's your briefcase.

— I don't know what got into me. Whitcomb started down the gangway. He stopped and looked back at the ship, searching the dark rigging aloft and the peeling paint on the housing. He spoke in a vague, abstracted way. Well, take good care of my ship, Mister Mate. She's all I've got at the moment . . . I swear, I don't know what made me do a thing like that—

— Remember, Elly, Cadiz called softly, when in doubt, take two half hitches, and there's nothing like a long lead—

— No strain, Whitcomb said, and shambled on his way.

Strain was what Cadiz felt after Whitcomb left. He sat amid his as yet unopened gear drinking a bottle of the poker players' beer. He listened to music drifting over the pier shed roof, coming from a party on the *Thuringen.* After such a short time aboard the *Sea Lover,* not more than four hours, he marveled that he felt so firmly and permanently established. He listened, responding to the strains and creaks of the *Lover* as she worked against her lines, ear attuned to the slightest variation in the rhythm of the silent ship.

The music paused on the *Thuringen,* and then it was started again. A lieder.

Now German ships depart
German ships and German men
Who will return?
She waits, she waits, in time
We will return.
Vaterland, Vaterland, Vaterland.

—Tender! Where the fuck is that Tender at! The bosun's voice split the stillness.

Cadiz could no longer resist; he had taken the ship and had, though he had been warned about Whitcomb, made a quick, hard decision, returning to the sea, resolved that he would see an end to it. He would, now that he knew about her, go out darkly upon a silent sea and fight his way out of a private hell, watch in and watch out, and do away with her.

Leaving home we sail out
Vaterland, Vaterland, Vaterland
She cries for me as I leave
She waits, she waits, in time
We will return from
Wasserland, Wasserland, Wasserland

He left his room and roamed the ship.

As he walked he deliberately thought about her—about them. He dove deeply into it. He let her presence fill him, and he began what he knew would be a battle for possession of himself.

He thought, too, of all that had happened since escaping from Jernegan, after seeing Hessian dead, after living like an animal in the sand cave. He traced it all from beginning to end. North from South Carolina in a slow, tortured night and day race to Baltimore and shipping out as a messman on a South America-bound tanker; jumping ship in Aruba, making his way to Panama, then to Panama City and a Peruvian guano shell; to Lima and a Britisher in the far east trade; then to Sydney and an American ship—A.B. on that one—then to London, then Sweden, then down from Stockholm to Malmo and A.B. on a Mo-Mac, and so back to the States. Four years with Mo-Mac.

Vaterland, Vaterland, Vaterland . . .

A year, then, on the bridge, after they discovered he held a ticket. And after running east for a year into the western oceans, he had come ashore with his money, still unable to forget her, and still compelled to know.

It had been difficult and expensive. He had hired an investigator. It had taken all the money he had saved and while the pursuit of Agnes was carried out, he slept in fifteen-cent bunks at the Institute. But he had learned, finally. After six months of hoping and waiting and spending his days in the New York Public Library, he had learned. She was married to a bread salesman and lived in Waycross and had two children.

Agnes, Agnes. . .

She cries for me as I leave
She waits, she waits, in time
We will return from
Wasserland, Wasserland, Wasserland

— What does it mean, Mister Mate? Tender asked.

— It means the sea, Cadiz replied.

— Oh. Tender studied the lights from the *Thuringen*. I snuck over there—

— You did what? Cadiz said sharply.

— I just wanted to see what was goin' on. They sitting around, a bunch of broads and sailors, drinking beer and singing.

— Stay away from the *Thuringen*, Tender, Cadiz said. That's an order.

— I just wanted to see what was going on, that's all, Tender said plaintively. I didn't do nothing, honest. They weren't very friendly.

— Oh?

— They got their piss hot and started jabbering at me. I tried to explain I was just being neighborly. I half expected they'd gimme a beer or something. Then they didn't wanta let me off the ship and tried to keep me from going down the gangway—

— What happened? Cadiz asked, feeling himself go cold.

— I got the idea they wanted me to wait for an officer. Sheet, I wasn't about to do that, so I left. Tender looked slantwise at Cadiz.

— But you said they didn't want to let you go?

— Well, I left anyway, Tender said.

— Did they try and stop you? Did you wait for the officer?

— Not exactly.

— You got into a fight with them, Cadiz said flatly.

— It wasn't no fight, Tender said stubbornly. No fight a-tall.

— But you hit somebody?

— Well—

— Jesus Christ!

— Only one time! Tender said. Jesus, Mister Mate, they acted like I stole something, or like that. So I cold-cocked him.

— Oh, you stupid punk, Cadiz moaned.

— I din' mean no harm, Tender said. It was just intended to be a little neighborly visit—

— Did you hurt him?

— He din' offer no resistance, Tender said.

— Meaning what?

— I busted his nose. And maybe—

— Maybe what?

— A few teeth. Nothin' serious, Mister Mate.

— You had better hope to Christ it's not serious, Cadiz said, and you had better stay aboard until they sail.

— Hell, I ain't scared of them.

— You'd better be, kid, Cadiz said. Across the pier the music and the singing stopped abruptly. There was not a word or a sound from the *Thuringen.*

— Would they go to the cops? Tender asked, and for the first time Cadiz heard a touch of uneasiness in his tone.

— I don't think so, Cadiz said. It's not their style. They'll handle this by themselves.

— Oh, Tender said. Then he flared. Jesus Christ! All I wanted to do was have a beer with 'em, talk to 'em, you know, like sailors. We're in the same racket, ain't we?

— Not exactly.

It was four o'clock Saturday afternoon and the poker players had been at it steadily since four o'clock the day before. The strain showed in their tired voices, their weary manner and their haggard faces. At one end of the table, dirty dishes had been piled up and shoved to one side. The messman sat in a corner and held his head, stupid with hangover. Tender was shaving Spanish with a straight razor. Spanish continued to play as he twisted his head, his face still half lathered. He sat in a slumped position, dealing with one hand, the deck flat on the table. As the play progressed, Tender had to stop from time to time as Spanish moved his head. Spanish dealt mechanically. Cadiz sipped coffee, watching.

— An ace, a queen, a niner and a trey.

The messman stood up painfully and began collecting the dirty dishes.

— The deal, the messman said, was for a hunnert dollars. Only I got so drunk, I slept and when I woke up she was gone. He sighed deeply. I didn't even get laid.

— Tough titty makes strong babies, Tender said, working around Spanish's lip with great care.

— Time for me to win one, the bosun said. This is my pot. I feel it. Ace bets twenty.

— I got an ace you can feel, Boats, Tender said.

The bosun glared at Tender and turned his attention back to his cards. They all saw the bet and Spanish dealt again. Tender was elaborate in his gestures as he shaved Spanish, getting the job done in short, quick strokes. He englished his body awkwardly to achieve just the right angle of attack.

— Into the old lady's crack, gents, Spanish intoned as he snapped the cards up from the tabled deck and placed them before the players. An ace with the ace and a pair, a nine with the queen and nothing, a king to the nine and no skin, and a fair spade four to the spade trey, and bet your aces, Boats.

— Aces bet twenty, the bosun said.

— I'm in, Perry said.

— See you, Harrison said.

— And the dealer kicks it twenty, gents, Spanish said.

—Tiredly, Perry and Harrison, without waiting for the bosun, threw in their money. Spanish had turned his head at that moment for Tender to stroke his chin, and on turning back, he tapped the deck one time and started to deal.

— Coming out, Spanish said.

— Hold it, Perry said. Bosun's shy.

— I'm thinkin', the bosun said testily.

— This ain't a waiting game, Boats, Spanish said, and then he winced. Ouch! Tender, goddammit, watch it!

— 'scuse-a me, boss, but-a de wife, she just had-a da bambino, and I am-a worried, and-a nervous—

Spanish grinned.

— Boats? Perry said. You *got* two fuckin aces, f'Christ sake!

— I said I was thinkin'!

— With what? Tender asked.

— Goddam you, I had about enough of your mouth. I oughta—

— Play cards, Boats, f'Christ sake and stop bellyachin', Spanish said.

— Okay for you to talk. This could be my last hand. I gotta squeeze it.

— You squeezed flat and don't know it, Boats, that's your trouble, Tender said.

The bosun ignored Tender and peeked at his hole card. Then he looked at the cards showing, then at his two aces, and finally made his bet.

Tender was having considerable difficulty shaving Spanish and stepped back in disgust. He watched as the cards were dealt.

— No help to the aces, a nine to the queen nine and a betting pair showing, eight to the king nine, no help, and the dealer shoots himself another fair spade with a tenner. Aces bet, or as the case may be, checks.

Tender screwed up his face and pulled Spanish's face around.

— Becky, make like this, Tender said, puckering his mouth.

— I gotta have this pot, the bosun said. Aces check.

— You brunser, Perry said. Well, screw you, nines check too.

— Check, Harrison said.

— Three little spades, Spanish said, bet fifty bananas.

— I knew it! I knew it! the bosun exploded. You bastard!

— A bastard with a spade, Spanish said. Four spades, to be exact.

The Bosun took a long time deciding.

— Okay, see your fifty, he said finally.

— And I kick it fifty, Perry said happily.

— Goddam you! The Bosun cried. A whipsaw! That's what you're trying to do!

— Only cost you fifty more, Boats, Harrison said, throwing in his money.

— You know something, Boats? Spanish said. You give me a pain in my ass. You always belly-gripin' about your cards, the money you lose, the lousy weather, everything. You a scared man, ain'tcha? Scared to death you going to miss something, and all the time you missing the big thing.

— Deal the goddam cards and don't hand me no mouth.

— No, really, Boats, you always crying the blues 'cause you ain't got it all your way. What the fuck do you want outa life, man?

— Everything I can git! the bosun said bitterly. And don't give me no snow job, Spanish. I know you trying to con me into losing my concentration.

— Boats, Spanish said heavily, you can't see the ass for the panties. You bitching and complaining about losing, and all the time you got more snatch around you than you can take care of in a lifetime.

— Deal the cards!

— You remind me of one of them eunuchs down off the Red Sea in one of them shakedoms. A guy with a big weapon hanging on him and all that nookey and him not able to do a thing about it. That's the way it is with you, Boats, a man with everything in the world and you can't rise to the occasion.

The bosun's face was blotched with anger. He half rose from his chair and leaned over the table.

— You gonna deal the goddam cards?

— You haven't met the bet, Spanish said gently. Put your money where your big mouth is.

— Don't get smart with me, Spanish, I *know* you.

— What do you know, Boats? Huh? What can you say about me? Go on, say what you think. Spanish, with a casual gesture, pushed Tender back out of the way. Cadiz came alert, watchful.

— Never you mind, I goddam well *know!*

— You, Spanish said, haven't got enough guts to say what you know, or what you think you know. There was a moment of silence. Make your bet, Boats, or roll over dead.

— The bet is fifty dollars, Perry said. And let's lay off the goddam he-man stuff. I wanta play cards.

— Fifty dollars is the bet, Spanish said, his voice still gentle, but deadly, and if you put your money in, Boats, you're going to lose.

— Well, I'll just see that bet, the Bosun said. He threw his money into the pot and settled back. We'll just see.

Spanish relaxed, tapped the deck once lightly, and eased back into a slumped position. Tender resumed shaving him.

— Last card, gents, here comes Destiny.

— Stiffen up, she's wide open, Perry said.

— We're all buck nekked, Harrison said.

— Mother can't help you now! the bosun said, rubbing his hands together.

— Heaven is on the way, Spanish said, and dealt the last card. There was a long, long moment of silence as the players studied their hands and the board. The bosun had caught a third ace. But Spanish had a fourth spade showing.

— Bet your aces, Boats, Spanish said.

— Aces check.

— The spade flush bets five hundred dollars, Spanish said, no nonsense in his voice. He dropped the money into the pot.

The bosun was stunned. He half rose again from his chair and glared at Spanish, at the spades and then at his own aces.

— Goddam you! Goddam you, and I say it again! You're bluffing! You ain't *got* no spade flush!

Perry and Harrison folded their cards and sat back.

— It will cost you five hundred dollars to find out if I'm bluffing or not, Boats, Spanish said.

— You're bluffing!

— You either put your money up, or I'm taking the pot.

— Goddam you! the bosun shouted.

— Five hundred to you, Boats, Spanish said, staring at him.

The bosun looked at the table. He stood upright, slowly, and then peeked at his hole card. He stared at the spade flush. He pushed back and stepped away from the table. He brushed past Tender.

— Get the hell outa the way! He walked back and forth behind the table several times, stopping twice to look at his hole card. He then looked at Spanish's cards. The room was silent.

Tender finished shaving Spanish and stepped back to admire his job. Then he slapped a palmful of shaving lotion hard on Spanish's face. He danced a little jig as he worked and sang, My Mama was a porcupine, *Annd!* My Papa was a woolly bear! *Annd!* I got quills where the pecker hair should grow! *Annd!* A whanger from here to there!

— Goddam you, *shut up!* There's over a thousand dollars in that pot!

— 'scuse me, bosun, Tender said cheerfully. He took a can of talcum powder and sprinkled it liberally all over Spanish's face.

— Five hundred is the bet, Boats, Spanish said.

— I ain't got five hundred.

Spanish started to reach out and pull the pot. The bosun stopped him.

— But I got exactly four hundred and twenty. So make the bet four twenty—

— I got you beat, Boats, Spanish said carefully. Save your money and let's go on playing.

— Never mind that crap! Make the bet four-twenty!

Spanish nodded. He withdrew eighty dollars from the pot and nodded again.

— All right, the bet is four-twenty, Boats.

The bosun threw in his money. Beat the aces, he said.

— I told you I had you beat, Boats, Spanish said. Spade flush. You lose.

The bosun was dazed. He looked at the cards, reaching over and checking them carefully.

— Goddammit! Goddammit! He wrenched away from the table and bumped into Tender again. I tol' you once, *git outa my way!* He lunged for the door. No one moved as Spanish collected, sorted and stacked his winnings. He picked up the cards and handed them to Perry, who was the next dealer.

— Shine, mister? Tender snapped the towel, bowing, posing. Manicure? Trim the hair around your balls? He lowered his voice confidentially. We also got nice girls, clean girls, out back. Little hair tonic to make you smell nice for the ladies?

The tension was broken; everyone laughed.

— We going to butt heads with three players? Perry asked. Now the bosun's broke?

— I don't like to play lessen four, Harrison said. And ain't nobody else got any money.

— How about it, Tender? Spanish asked. You want to sit in? One good hand could set you up for something.

— I only got seventy-three bucks I made serving you guys all night, Tender said. If you let me in with that, I'll play. But I'm warning you, until I get a pat hand, I'm just buying cards and holding'em.

— Sit down, gent, Spanish said expansively, and here's a lucky ten for the shave.

Tender winked at Cadiz and tossed the towel aside.

— This is what I been waiting for, Tender said. I snowed 'em, see? I been nibbling away at their money and now I'm gonna gulp it! He took the bosun's seat and dug the money out of his pocket. Here I come! Grab your cocks and lock up your money, the Man is here. Wheel and deal, the hotter the better.

— Tender, you kill me, Spanish said.

The bosun lumbered back into the room. He seemed shocked to see Tender in his chair. Tender continued his happy harangue.

— I'll kill ya! I'll spit in your eye, man! I'm going to get me enough for a suite in a big hotel and find me some big-league pussy. For once in my life, I'm gonna screw me a bee-yoo-ti-ful woman!

— Look at him now! the bosun said testily.

— Two grand oughta be enough, huh, Mister Mate? For one of them specials like you see onna front of them magazines? Huh? Man, a grand a week for two weeks in Capetown!

— That ought to do it, Cadiz said. Two grand should be just about enough.

— Every man has got to have himself a beautiful cunt at least once in his life, if for only one reason, Spanish said.

— What reason is that? Cadiz asked.

— Why, you know, Mister Mate, to prove to himself that there isn't any difference.

Perry dealt the cards. Tender's enthusiasm was contagious; they responded to the new energy injected into the game.

— A nice firm ass, not too big, Tender went on, and not skinny either. And a pair of big boobs that stay in one place. Ummmm-huh! And when I wake up in the morning, see, after giving her a good jazzing, I roll over, see, Mister Mate, I roll over and I see a *beautiful* woman—that's what I see, something *pretty* that I can *look* at.

— Ain't that just like a kid! the bosun sneered.

— Aces wired, Spanish, Tender said, ignoring the bosun. And here comes my first three jumps with that lucky broad, wherever she is. Aces wired and I bet twenty.

— Woman like that, the bosun said, the kind he's talking about, wants a man, not a kid, regardless how much money you got.

— I'll tell you, Boats, Tender said. I'm gonna win your money back, see. And *you're* gonna pay for my two weeks in Capetown. But I'll be nice about it. I'll come back to the *Lover* and tell you all about it.

— Do it and then talk, the bosun growled.

— You got the message, man, Tender said. I can do it. I don't have to spend a whole weekend aboard ship pissing my money away on a poker game 'cause I'm too old.

Perry delivered the next card and Tender caught another ace. He dropped his voice.

— It's only a little pair of aces, gents. Don't run away. Only going to cost you twenty more, just a touch.

Perry, Harrison and Spanish stayed, though they knew he would win. There was no doubt in Cadiz's mind as he watched and listened that they wanted him to win.

— I tell you, gents, now that you put in your money, I got three bullets. So don't throw your money away.

The next cards were dealt.

— Tender, you kill me, Spanish repeated.

— Just like a punk kid, the bosun said. A man would know what to do with a hand like that.

— Well, you must not be a man then, Boats, Tender said, 'cause you had one and you pissed it away.

— Who you calling not a man, you little bastard!

— If the shoe fits, Tender said. He looked around the table. Aces check, he said quietly.

— He's checking a cinch into you, Spanish, the bosun said.

Tender rose slowly and turned, facing the bosun.

— How about keeping your mouth outa the game, Boats? There's money on the table.

— Don't stand up to me, you fuckin' punk, unless you can back it up—

— I'll back it up right now!

— I'd cut your chicken heart out before you could take a breath, you little bastard—

With one flowing move, Tender leaped to the pantry shelf and snatched up a bread knife. The men fell back and left space for them to fight. The bosun dipped into his pocket, and there was a flash of a blade. Tender and the bosun squared off. Cadiz acted the moment the knives appeared. He stepped between the two fighters.

— Give me the knife, Tender, he said. Tender did not move. *Give me the knife.* His hand was extended, palm up; he exuded authority. His back was to the bosun, who did not move, or speak. Tender hesitated a moment longer and then he handed over the knife. As he did, he yelled past Cadiz to the bosun.

— You wanta fight with fists, you sonofabitch, I'll show you who's a man!

— There isn't going to be any fight, Cadiz said. He turned to the bosun.

The bosun made a move and Cadiz's reaction was quick; he stepped back and brought up the bread knife and faced the bosun over the blade.

— You take one step toward me, Boats, and you'll go to the Federal Pen for twenty years for attempted murder of your ship's officer—if I don't kill you first.

The bosun slowly lowered his arm.

— If I see you with a knife in your hand again, Cadiz said, tossing the bread knife to the pantry shelf, I'll drill you in the head.

— It's over, Mister Mate, Spanish said. There won't be anymore trouble.

— There sure as hell better not be, Cadiz said. Because if you want trouble, Boats, I'm the man to see.

It was very dark that night. Cadiz stood on the deck sipping beer. All evening officers and crew members from the *Thuringen* had passed back and forth through the pier shed, looking up at the *Lover* with flat hard faces. But no word of Tender's altercation reached the ship. Cadiz did not like it. He hoped the *Thuringen* would sail before anything happened. He doubted that it would.

He moved forward along the deck to the bow and settled himself on a coil of line and nursed his beer. He heard footsteps on the deck. It was Tender.

—You looked pretty good in there, Tender, Cadiz said thoughtfully. Real tough. Ready for trouble. A brine pecker.

—Don't con me, Tender said softly, a trace of bitterness in his voice. I was scared half to death. The sonofabitch.

—Oh? Is that a fact?

—I guess you got a right to tease, Tender said.

—Oh? Cadiz said again, looking at Tender more closely. The game over?

—Naw, they just shaking down. Takin' showers. We going to start up again in a little while.

—How are you making out?

—I'm up to six hundred, Tender said quietly.

—You don't sound very happy about it.

Tender didn't answer for a long while. He sighed, and when he spoke, his voice was harsh.

—He mighta got to me, but he'd sure as hell know his ass was in a fight!

—Maybe, Cadiz said. Where is he now?

—Gone ashore. Tender sighed again. Yeah, maybe you're right.

—Right about what?

—He coulda stuck me before I knew what happened.

—I'm surprised that you recognize that, Cadiz said.

—You looked pretty good in there yourself, Tender said. I know the bosun. He's mean. He coulda got to you.

—No, not him, Cadiz said, shaking his head. He knows better than to touch an officer.

—Well, just the same, Tender said, I owe you for breakin' it up when you did.

— You don't owe me, Tender.

— I might be all cut up and dying right now if it wasn't for you, so I'm owing to you.

— That's what a mate is for, Cadiz said, finishing his beer and tossing the can over the side. They listened to the small splash. This job is more than just handling a ship and navigating.

— You sound like you hadda lot of experience.

— Some, Cadiz said.

— What's it like, being a mate? Tender asked.

— You ambitious?

— If you mean do I wanta become a mate, Tender said, I been thinking about it.

Cadiz nodded looking at him. He lit a cigarette.

— You might make it with a license.

— Well, since I'm on your watch and all, sometimes would you give me a few pointers?

— Okay, and I'll give you some books to read, Cadiz said. But do you know why you want a license?

— I'm a coal miner's son, Tender said. That tell you anything?

— No.

— I'm twenny-two now, Tender said, and I been going to sea four years. Right outa the mines to Baltimore and a ship. If I'da stayed, I'da been married with two, three kids by now maybe. My wife woulda been a good, honest, hard-workin' woman, an' she'da looked like hell at the age of twenny-one. And the ony thing I woulda been able to do for a living, once I got married and had kids, would be a coal miner, 'cause I seen too many of them that lose their hearts and guts just scratchin' out a living. They *think* they'll go to night school and they *think* they'll save for a little business of their own, but when they come home at night, there ain't nothin' left. They want their glass of beer and something to eat and a piece of tail maybe, and then they git up and go back down the next day.

— You figured all that out? Cadiz asked.

— You think it's hard? It's easy, man, Tender laughed wryly. I said I was a coal miner's son. I grew up with it. Not only in my house, but everybody I knew had the same deal. So. There, look at it, I'm a coal miner with a few kids and a tired wife, paying fifty-sixty dollars a month for a car, for furniture, for this and that, and then suppose something happens to me? My wife goes on relief or moves in with her family.

His voice roughened as he continued to speak:

— I'd never been able to make any more, never git a chance to move outa the coal mountains. And if I did, what would I do? Work inna factory someplace and live inna dinky apartment? I didn't say good-by to nobody. The day I graduated outa high school, I went from the graduation exercises straight down to the bus station and went to Baltimore and to the Union and told them I had to have a ship. They laughed at me, but I learned you didn't have to be inna union, so I shipped out on unorganized ships. Ma's dead, and Pa's crippled up with arthritis. He's living with my brother. My brother hates my guts for dumping the old man on him. But I can't help that. I got out just in time. Just in time.

Tender stood and began to pace the deck.

— I got me something here. I got the whole goddam world waitin' for me and I ain't never going to let go.

— Good luck, Cadiz said.

— Yeah? Tender was skeptical. You sound like you putting me off.

— No, I didn't mean it like that, Cadiz said. I'll help you if you want to become a mate. I was thinking about your having the whole world waiting for you.

— Well, so? I got it all planned.

— How?

— Like the Old Man has, Tender said. I hear he's worth a hell of a lot of money with that farm of his down in Pennsylvania.

— You'd like to be like Captain Whitcomb?

— I don't see nothing that can stop me, Tender said. Look at you. I don't see nothing dragging your ass. I got enough education to learn navigation, and I know I'm a pretty good sailor.

Cadiz stood.

Tender sensed that he had stumbled onto delicate ground. I'm sorry, Mister Mate, I didn't mean nothing. I got a big mouth, that's all.

— Sorry for what?

Tender didn't answer.

— For what? Cadiz demanded.

— Well, I overheard you and Cap'n Whitcomb. You know, about you being hung up on a broad. I mean—I don't mean anything dirty, Mister Mate—

— You're a pretty sharp kid, Cadiz said.

— I don't know what I'd do if I loved somebody. I think it'd make a difference in everything.

— Everything?

— I mean, I just told you how I got it all planned, but I never seen a deal yet that meant anything to me.

— But you're the guy, Cadiz said, his voice hard, with the whole goddam world waiting for you.

— I know, I know. Tender leaned on the railing and looked down at the reflected lights of the cars on the upper highway. His voice was softly apologetic. Don't jazz me, Mister Mate. I don't know the answers. I don't know what's coming, any more than anybody else, but I gotta place here for myself and if it ain't much, it's mine. And there's hope that it'll be more. Like you, and Cap'n Whitcomb, maybe, if I'm lucky.

— Like me and Captain Whitcomb. You work on it, kid.

— I wouldn't want to make any more out of it than already exists, Mister Alberich, Cadiz said to the executive officer of *Thuringen,* but you know how these things can snowball.

Cadiz and Alberich sat in the spacious executive officer's cabin, facing each other over a glass of wine. Alberich was a man nearing fifty with pink skin and the curiously Germanic receding chin that was, in spite of this, broad and firm. He had a large nose; his face was strong and his eyes were bright and hard. He was bald clear back to the rear taper of the skull, and Alberich had let the ear-line fringe grow into very long hair which was swept directly over his baldness. Cadiz was sure that the jet black hair was dyed. It would follow, Cadiz thought.

— Was the sailor punished, Mister Cadiz? Alberich asked. He had a distinct British accent.

— Yes, Cadiz said.

— May I ask how, Mister Cadiz?

— He was restricted to the ship.

— I see, Alberich replied. He brought his hands together, making a ball of his spread fingers and tapping the tips together gently. May I say that restriction to the ship is a rather mild punishment for such a vicious attack?

— Not if you consider that this is our last weekend ashore, and he is a young sailor with a beautiful girl waiting for him.

— I appreciate that, Alberich said.

Cadiz nodded gravely.

— But my crewman has suffered a broken nose and several of his teeth are missing.

— The *Sea Lover* has a ship's fund which would take care of such details, Mister Alberich, Cadiz lied.

— Wouldn't you make the sailor pay? Out of his own money?

— Yes, Cadiz said, lying again, but only after he has signed off and been paid.

— Why not just enter it into the log? Alberich asked. It would seem to me the way to do it.

— If I do that, then it goes on his record, Cadiz said, still lying. And considering his motives for coming aboard the *Thuringen*—a neighborly visit confused into an issue by your crewman, and, of course, the language barrier—I wouldn't want to penalize him unduly. I've seen his girl, Cadiz said easily. Believe me, Mister Alberich, he is being severely punished.

— I see, Alberich said, and smiled. You are quite right of course. Quite right. But now, to compensation for damages.

— Whatever you think is reasonable and fair, Mister Alberich, Cadiz said instantly.

— Thank you, Alberich said, nodding. I would say—oh—twenty dollars.

— Done, Cadiz said. He pulled out his wallet and extracted two ten dollar bills and placed them on the coffee table. I'm glad you are so understanding, Mister Alberich—

— Please, I wish you would call me Bruno. The issue is closed.

— And I am Howard.

— Ah, Howard. Alberich stood and offered his hand. Cadiz rose and shook it firmly. Now, what do you say to something a little stronger than this wine. Brandy? I have an excellent one.

— A touch, Cadiz said.

They drifted into shop talk and were not surprised to learn they knew mutual captains and had been in the same ports at the same time and had visited the same infamous whore houses around the world. After several more brandies, Cadiz prepared to leave.

— Do you like poetry, Howard? Alberich asked as they walked the deck back to the gangway.

— I've read some.

— But you do not like it?

— Well, Byron, Keats, Emily Dickinson. Why?

— I rather—fancy myself a poet. I picked it up—Alberich laughed—Where else? At sea, of course! But I asked rather, because you see on Sunday mornings when we are in port, there are several of us aboard the *Thuringen,* unfortunately I am the only officer, a ship of this size—he shrugged—there are many others who get together and read pieces we have written since the last meeting.

— That's very interesting, Cadiz said vaguely. He started to shake his head, declining, when Alberich, almost as if he were reading Cadiz's thoughts, smiled and said, As you perhaps know, we have a crew of some seventy-odd women aboard. Have you ever seen a woman swooning with spiritual, ecstatic passion?

— Then it's not just poetry reading, Cadiz said.

— Essentially, no, Alberich said with a leer. Terribly uplifting, Howard. Will you join us?

— What time?

— At eleven. After services.

— I may see you, Bruno, Cadiz said.

— Good show! Alberich patted Cadiz on the shoulder. Cadiz was halfway down the gangway when Alberich called softly after him, I appreciate your coming, Howard. I hope to get to know you better. We of the Third Reich have a mission to become friends with all people.

— Well, Cadiz said, that has little to do with sailors like us, does it? Alberich nodded slowly, his face impassive.

— So, at eleven, Howard?
— If I can make it, Bruno.

— Tomorrow, Cadiz said to Perry, Harrison, Spanish and Tender, the shit may very well hit the fan for any member of the *Lover's* crew. And specifically for you, Tender, so keep your butt on the ship. They're out for blood. I just saw their mate. I got a snow job. I believe they've got it all set for about eleven.

— What about the squiffs coming back from ashore? Spanish asked. Half the crew will be falling down drunk.

— Can't we patrol the pier? Perry asked.

— They outnumber us, Harrison said.

— And besides, Spanish said, who wants to hang around the pier head? And face a bunch of goons?

— Would they really try to get even by—Tender stared at Cadiz. I mean, would they bust up just *any* member of the crew because of what happened with me?

— Kid, Spanish said, pulling in the cards and going through a shuffle, I've seen'em operate. They're crazy. The whole fuckin' country is crazy. I was in Bremen coupla years ago. They used to send their women aboard the ship while the men waited on the pier.

— Pimping? Tender asked.

— That's the story, Spanish said. We used to come back to the ship in a cab, cost a small fortune, but nobody was willing to walk down a long dark pier. I mean nobody.

— Jesus! Tender said.

— Don't worry about it, kid, Spanish said, They'll get theirs.

Tender stood up. I'll fight 'em! Why should somebody else get beat up for what I done!

— Sit down, kid, Spanish said quietly. And stay out of this. You don't know what you're messing in, ain't that right, Mister Cadiz?

— Cadizzzzz! Whitcomb roared, loud, stupid drunk. *Cadizzzzz!* CADIZZZZ! Goddammit! Where are you *at!*

Out of the darkness of the pier, Whitcomb staggered into the pool of light around the gangway, bobbing, weaving, hardly able to stand. His shirt was torn at the shoulder. Hatless, he had lost his jacket. He wobbled uncertainly at the bottom of the gangway, staring at his feet, then spun suddenly, as if someone had spoken to him, and cocked his head to listen.

Cadiz came out of the darkness on the boat deck and looked down at Whitcomb.

—Now that the children are here, I'm gonna change, Sara! Yes, siree! Change! You just wait and see. I'm gonna be a new man. This is gonna be my *last* trip! My very last trip. I promise—I *swear!*

Whitcomb turned suddenly and swung back and upward with his fist at an imaginary enemy.

—Listen! *Listen!* You smart little sonofabitch! You talkin' t'a man now! A *man!* A gut fighter! You think you gonna order me around? Why, boy, I'll break you in two like a worm-wooded fid! Yah! He lashed out with his fist. Yah!

Whitcomb settled, momentarily, and pulled himself upright. Cadiz listened to the old Elisha Whitcomb he had sailed with and known before he had become an old man, a drunken old man. Whitcomb tongue-lashing someone.

—You will not do this to me! *This can't be done!* Whitcomb roared. I'll fight you! Yes, by God, I'll—

He dissolved into the jelly of drunkenness again. He looked around, confused. He stumbled to the gangway and sat heavily.

—Cadizzz! For God's sake, Howard, oh, oh, f'God's sake—*Cadiz!*

He leaned to one side and began to cry. His rage was gone. With his cheek on the wood of the gangway, he began to plead.

—Sara, please, talk to me. I can't quit now. I just got my own ship. Don't you see what that means? *My own ship!* I'm the Man, now, honey! And the money, think of the money which is going to come in like it was pouring out of a hydrant. One year. Just gimme one year as master of my own vessel and I'll quit. I swear to you—

He jerked erect suddenly and tried to stand. He shook his head like a dog, trying to clear it. His head sunk low on his chest. From this position, he suddenly roared. I paid for this farm! Me! Elly Whitcomb! With my own money! Yah! Why, I held you in my arms when you were—

He broke off again, as if listening, cocking his head from side to side, trying to catch the words.

—You will not—kick—me—off—my—own—place! Sara! Sara! Please, talk to them. I don't wanta go back to sea. I wanta—I wanta stay here, with you—

Cadiz turned away from the boat-deck railing and went quickly into his cabin for his shoes and trousers. When he returned to the deck, Whitcomb was gone. Tender and Spanish were standing at the head of the gangway.

—He was here a minute ago, Tender said.

—Spread out, Cadiz said, hurrying down the ladder. Look for him.

—He coulda gone down on the pier, Spanish said. It's pretty dark.

—He couldn't have gotten very far, Cadiz said. Look fore and aft.

Above them, Whitcomb lunged out of the darkness and leaned on the boat-deck railing. The three men stared up at him, hypnotized.

—Watch it! Watch the wheel! She's broaching! Get the line secured. Hold it! Now surge it! Don't let it part—Goddam you sonofabitch! *Hold* that line! Hold it or I'll kill you! *Misterrr Englunnnnd!* We've lost three boats and we're taking water in the peak! I *know* you know, you stupid square-headed bastard. Now listen to me! If she goes down by the head—Whitcomb's voice became desperate and quiet—we'll never get her back into the wind again.

He swung suddenly, spinning around and pointing to the rigging.

—Get a purchase—get a purchase—Goddam you—take a turn on the cleat—surge it—Surge it!

Cadiz, Tender and Spanish stood immobile as Whitcomb roared and raged above them. Then it was over. Whitcomb seemed to notice something a few feet away from him. He took a few faltering steps toward it.

—Hello, babe. You just what I like. Small, thin, and eager. So, you're Portagee, eh? No speaka da English? Well, well, thas all right. Whitcomb turned and looked out over the pier shed. You gotta nice city here. He looked around the dark and silent pier with a smile on his face.

—He's off his nut, Tender said, awed.

—Shut up, Tender, Cadiz said. He ran up the ladder to the boat deck. As he gained the upper deck, Whitcomb turned and faced him. He spoke now with great dignity.

—I don't care if you are the Customs Officer, I'll lay off shore and let this cargo *rot* in the holds, but you are not going to—Whitcomb pulled himself up and pointed to the gangway. Mister Aldington! See that this man is put off the ship and that he stays off. And now, sir, I remind you that you are aboard an American flagship vessel. Your presence is odious, your manner insufferable, your mentality infantile, your spirit spongy and your politics criminal. Now git off my fuckin' ship!

Cadiz took a tentative step forward. Whitcomb peered at him. He wiped his face.

—What—what—Cadiz? Cadiz? Will you please tell me what the hell is going on? Are—you here, Cadiz? Howard?

—Right here, Elly, Cadiz said.

—Where the hell you been! Whitcomb demanded.

—Busy forward, Cadiz said. You know that work has to be done on the windlass.

—Oh, the windlass. I forgot for a minute. He leaned on the railing. Well, I been ashore. Had me a few. They got a nice city here. Everything all right? He looked around professionally. When we sailing?

—Soon, Cadiz said.

—Yes, sir, nice city, Barcelona. Always did like to come here in the spring, before it got too hot. Ever see anything like a moonlight ride along the Costa Brava? A picnic, man! With Spanish wine, leg o'beef, hot sauce and bread—and her—

—No, Cadiz said easily, relaxing a bit. Sounds nice, though. How about a drink, Elly?

—No! Whitcomb said. Not while we're working cargo. And we be sailing soon. A captain should always be sober when his ship is working cargo, or when his ship is going to move. Too many things can happen. That's a good lesson for you. Remember that. You going to be a good sailor, Howard. You already the best man with a sextant I ever saw. Work hard, Howard.

— Okay, Cadiz said. But one drink won't hurt. Come on, let's go inside.

Cadiz took his arm but Whitcomb wrenched it away.

— I gotta go back, he said. They can't do this to me!

Cadiz, with Tender and Spanish coming up fast, made a grab for Whitcomb.

— Lemme go! I gotta get back and fight for what's mine!

— Fight for what, Elly? Cadiz asked calmly.

— You made me do it! You! It's all your goddam fault!

— Elly! Cadiz struggled with him as Whitcomb tried to break free. Elly! Stop it!

— No! They can't throw me out! He twisted violently, trying to break Cadiz's grasp. With measured force Cadiz struck him across the face with the palm of his hand. The stinging slap rocked Whitcomb back into reality. He broke, leaning on Cadiz with both arms, embracing him, and began to cry.

— Oh, Howard, they did it. They did it, Howard. They said they didn't want a drunken bum for a father. They said they had done without a father all these years and—and they didn't want a—a bum to show up now and have to take care of him. I gotta go back and fight for what's mine.

— All right, Elly, all right. But let's have a drink first, okay? One for the road. Okay? Just one to get the Old Man's by-pass open?

Cadiz was not sure if Whitcomb was clear-headed enough to understand or not.

— Well, just one, Whitcomb said in a low voice.

— Just one, Cadiz said gently, his arm around Whitcomb. Come on, sailor, one for the road and then we go fight them.

Whitcomb nodded. They walked away. Spanish and Tender were left at the head of the ladder, where they had been standing throughout.

— Jesus Christ, Tender said. What the hell was that all about?

— Don't ask, kid, Spanish said. Don't ask. Come on, let's get back to the cards; it doesn't pay, messing in other people's business.

That morning the men came back, gray, faceless, weary sailors. Their eyes were red. Still dressed in their shore-going clothes, their suits were rumpled and dirty. Their expressions were blank. They were finished with the shore now. The holds were loaded and the men were spent; they hungered to get back to their oceans and be rid of the smells and demands of the land. They sat in the messroom, spiritless, all seemingly in the same mood, looking inwardly into private lies and deceits which were now like open sores. The poker game was still going on, but there was little of the intimacy between the four players that had existed over the weekend, when the empty, lonely ship had brought them together. With the return of the crew the need for companionship was lost. The ship was fleshing out. The spine of the *Lover* was being stiffened. The heart, spirit, muscle and grit that made the *Lover* a living organism was returned. Like prodigals, the crew had squandered a few wild, reckless days on the land and now they were penitent and anxious to be cleansed by the sea.

— See you and raise you fifty, Tender said, his voice hoarse.

Perry, Harrison and Spanish saw the raise and the next card was dealt. Behind them, a small, thick-shouldered man dressed in a cheap suit spoke to the roomful of men. His chin was tucked up under his shoulder protectively.

— And I told this guy to lay off me, but he wouldn't, so I grabbed him by the shirt and hit the sonofabitch so hard my elbow still hurts.

— Jacks check, Tender said.

— You checking *another* cinch, Tender? Perry asked amiably.

— Put your money where your mouth is, ya punk, Tender replied automatically.

— I'll never forget this broad, a second sailor said. He was thin almost to the point of emaciation, with deep worn lines around deep eye sockets; he spoke in a splutteringly angry way, making short chopping gestures with his bony hands. Jesus Christ! I hadda go and meet somebody.

The messman moved into the midst of the group, looked around, cigarette hanging out of the corner of his mouth, hands on his hips, and announced: Anybody want coffee better take it now, 'cause I ain't making no more until we git ready to sail. No one paid any attention to him. And then it's only for the work gang, he added emphatically.

No one bothered to reply. No one even looked at him. The messman moved to the coffee urn and began cleaning it out.

— Move over, the messman said to a third sailor who sat holding his head. The sailor moved instantly, with almost childlike obedience.

— It's crazy, the third sailor said. Like I was dead.

— What do you mean, dead? Spanish asked. I got you by the hocks, Tender. Raise you twenty.

— I don't know what happened, the third sailor replied, not looking up, still holding his head. One minute everything was all right—and then—nothing. Like I was dead.

— You got enough for a real first-class dingaling there, keed, Spanish said, reaching over and fingering Tender's money. And some left over to sober up on.

— Take your hand off my money, Spanish, Tender joked wearily. I'll climb all over you.

— This cop, the first sailor said, comes up, see? A big lanky stiff-necked Irish bastard and tries to lay me out with his billy. But I cold-cocked him with a full quart of whiskey. Then a car full of cops comes up and one of them draws a gun on me. I faded that with a bar stool. You shoulda seen his face when I hit him with that bar stool. The sailor leaped to his feet, his face taut, his eyes glassy. That sonofabitch will never call anybody else a name like that! The room was quiet. The sailor's shoulders sagged and he sat back down.

— It's meatheads like him, Tender said, jerking his head in the direction of the sailor, that give us decent sailors a bad name ashore, ain't that right, Spanish?

— Yeah, kid, Spanish said.

— She had green eyes, the second sailor said, greenest I ever saw, and her skin was the color of creamed coffee. She had just come up from Puerto Rico with her folks. They live in two rooms with rats in the halls. She was so skinny I could put my hands around her waist almost, like this. And her teeth were crooked, a little—

— Lover come back to me, Tender said.

— Shut up, Tender, Spanish said.

There was a shout, then a howl and then shrill drunken laughter from the gangway. Everyone looked up, startled.

— Here they come, Tender said, more of them knife-fightin', drunken, romantic Errol Flynns going down to the sea in ships.

— Sounds like Bernhart, Spanish groaned, and I'll have to hold his head, or stand his watch, or something.

— A sheer joy for you, Spanish, Tender said.

— A labor of love, Perry commented.

— I'm surprised at you, Spanish, Harrison said. Why, you know how we adventurous sea-faring men are, anything we can do for a watch partner is a *fucking honor*.

— Delighted that you could come, Howard, Bruno Alberich said, taking Cadiz by the arm and steering him through the cabin, which was crowded with pale, slim young men and women. There were around twenty people present, some sitting on the deck, some on chairs, some standing. A small group sat at the feet of a heavy-set, thick-featured woman. They glanced briefly at Alberich and Cadiz as they moved to the couch. A phonograph sounded in the background; the voice of a woman was pleading. Two homosexuals still in their stewards' uniforms slipped over and made room for Alberich and Cadiz on the couch, and almost immediately a short, thin, ruddy-faced young man in tight-fitting trousers and a flowing shirt appeared before them and offered Cadiz a glass of wine. He stood looking intently at Cadiz. The roomful of people watched and waited.

— Thank you, Hans, Alberich said, dismissing the young man. Hans turned abruptly and walked to the phonograph. But he went on looking at Cadiz.

— I'm particularly glad that you came at this time, Howard, Alberich said. Hertha was just about to read her latest work on the replacement of the old illusionary values with the unerring precisions of logic and order. But before we sit down and hear the work, allow me to introduce you to members of the crew of the *Thuringen.* Alberich turned and addressed the room in strident German, speaking rapidly. Ladies and gentlemen, our guest is the chief executive officer of the American ship across the pier, the *Sea Lover*. Chief Officer Howard Cadiz.

Cadiz nodded, acknowledging a warm general murmur of welcome. A few of the pale young men applauded delicately.

—Thank you, Cadiz said, and sat down.

Alberich smiled and nodded at a broad, solid-looking woman.

Hertha cleared her throat, pulled her skirt down over her fat knees and spoke in German with a deep masculine voice. At Cadiz's side, Alberich translated for Cadiz in a whispered monotone.

—This is a poem against the old illusionist idea that all men are created equal. She will speak out for the differences that separate. Her inspiration has come from the New Order. It has taken her many years to see that there is truth, a truth of ethnic guilt, first brought to light by der Führer. She dedicates this poem to der Führer.

Hertha rattled her paper and adjusted her glasses. She looked up once and then lowered her eyes to the page and began.

Freidich, ich, ich, ich, free deedich
free deedich free deedich freeich
Ich? Ich? Ich? free deedich?
Free deedich
Free deedich
Free deedich
Free deedich
Free deedich
deedich
deedich
dee
dee
Ich? Ich? Ich?
Ich! ICH! I C H ! Freidich, ich, ich, ich!
Free deedich
Free deedich
Free deedich
Free deedich
Free dee
Free dee
Free
Free
Ich? Ich? Ich?

Hertha stood, picked her way through the circle of young men and women at her feet and stood in the middle of the cabin. She waved her hands in a wide circular gesture. Her face was flushed. Her voice, huskier now, chanted rhythmically, the repetitious syllables becoming a blur of sound and cadence. The faces of her listeners were rapt. Her reading became more and more intense. She began to pause before each sound, turning to look at one and then another, jabbing the air with her thick, balled fist, forefinger extended, pointing, demanding, shouting.

—*Free deedich!*

Gradually the roomful began to chant with her, in response to her growing control over them as she varied her breathy, masculine voice, speeding up, then slowing down. Finally she pointed to Alberich, still standing in front of the couch. She was perspiring. Cadiz could see the small trickles of sweat running down her red, flushed face.

—*Freidich, ich, ich, ich, free deedich!*

—*Ich! Ich! Ich!* Alberich replied.

Cadiz became aware of a rhythmic clapping, soft and drum-like in the background, underscoring the gibberish. Hertha turned slowly away from Cadiz and Alberich and stepped back to the middle of the cabin. Her voice began to drop in volume and intensity. Slowly it returned to a normal tone and then on past it, lower and lower until it was a soothing, melodic whisper of unintelligible sound. Then it was over.

Alberich leaped to his feet and took Hertha in his arms and embraced her, kissing her sweaty face. The others crowded around, and Cadiz could see tears in the eyes of many of them. He was left alone as the circle around Hertha broke up and Alberich took the big-shouldered woman by the elbow and gently led her into his bedroom and closed the door. The phonograph was started again. The muse was still with them, however, and it was some time before two of the slim young men got up from the floor and started dancing together. A moment later, Hans came over and invited Cadiz to dance. Cadiz declined and the young man flounced off with a sullen pout. By the time Alberich reappeared there were a half dozen couples dancing. Alberich slipped through the dancers and came to Cadiz. His face was flushed and he was bright-eyed with excitement.

— Well, now, Howard, what do you think? Isn't Hertha one of the most overwhelming poets you have ever heard? The emotion—the cadences! Alberich cried. So rich, and so true! She is one of the great Dadaists. One of the greatest!

Cadiz put his glass down on the table and looked at Alberich. Did you get fucked? He nodded his head toward the bedroom.

— You are a gross pig, Alberich said coldly. She is a great poet.

— Or maybe you don't like women, Bruno, Cadiz said, standing. He looked significantly at the dancing male couples.

— It was a mistake inviting you here, Alberich said.

— Don't bother to apologize. Cadiz moved unhurriedly to the door and stepped out onto the open deck. The noon sun was strong. He took a deep breath, shook his head as if to clear it, and made his way below to the gangway, pushing through the small cluster of passengers just then beginning to arrive for the *Thuringen*'s midnight sailing. He knew, as he moved into and mingled briefly with the passengers and crew, that the German spoken around him was true German and not the gobbledegook Hertha had recited, and that the people were happy to be going on a trip. But he also knew that for the rest of his life, whenever he heard German spoken, he would be reminded of the big-bosomed, broad-shouldered Hertha and her red sweaty face as she boomed out the garbage of the New Order.

— Did you enjoy the poetry readings, Herr Cadiz? Martin Thale stood before him at the bottom of the *Thuringen's* gangway. His blue eyes were moist and bright. He smiled condescendingly.

— I thought of it, Cadiz smiled, as I think of most things that are what I think is called schizoid.

— Schizoid? Martin Thale was puzzled. Schizophrenia?

— Yes, Cadiz said. Something split.

— I'm not sure I understand.

— A thing that's impossible. There are two things, and they don't fit. Like a blivit.

— Vas is a blivit?

— Six pounds of sheepshit in a five-pound bag, Cadiz said, and without turning back, he strode across the pier and climbed his own gangway.

It happened in a way that Cadiz, thinking back on it later, could have predicted. At 1 P.M., after lunch, the barges came alongside and the *Sea Lover* began taking on bunker oil. Without thinking of the Nazi ship across the pier shed, or of Tender, whom Cadiz now considered a fixed member of the poker game, he sought out the third mate.

Chanofski, an amiable giant whom Cadiz had spotted soon after coming aboard the *Lover*, was the butt of good-natured jokes from the fo'c'sle. It was only the second trip on his license and Chanofski was still responding to the burly warmth and lustiness of the fo'c'sle. It always happened this way, Cadiz knew. It usually took several trips to instill the full feeling of authority a mate held in a new man on the bridge. For some it was difficult to leave behind the herd attitude of the men who lived and worked and ate together in the fo'c'sle. But Cadiz did not like jokes played at the expense of one of his officers, and he meant to speak to him about it. Cadiz wanted more of a margin between the bridge and the fo'c'sle than he thought Chanofski's amiability afforded.

—How long you been going to sea, Mister Chanofski? Cadiz asked.

—Nine years.

—Do you think you've got enough time in on that brand new ticket of yours to walk down on the pier, go aft, go forward and get me a true reading of the draft?

Chanofski colored. You got something to say to me, Mister Cadiz, come out and say it.

—'kay, I will, Mister Chanofski. The next time I hear one of the fo'c'sle hands giving you a hard time about riding on your brand new ticket, and you don't log him for disrespect, I'll log you for inefficiency.

—Oh! Chanofski's face broke into a grin. They don't mean nothing, Mister Cadiz. Just a little ragging, that's all.

—I mean it, Cadiz said. You're an officer now, Mister. That doesn't mean spit and polish and it doesn't mean being a stiff-necked bastard, but it does mean insisting on a proper respect for your position. You like the slobs in the fo'c'sle so much, I'll sign you on as A.B. That suit you?

— I get the message, Chanofski said grimly.

— Just one more point. We're para-military. You know what that means?

— Yes.

— Okay, that's the book. You're officer class now. You've got power, responsibility, and you're the captain's representative on the bridge and at all other times. Don't put down your captain. You try to be nice guys with the apes below, they'll eat you alive. You're on the other side of the line now. Act like it. You're drawing the pay. You back your captain and your captain will back you. The surest way to blow your ticket and get set down below is to give them an inch. Not one goddam inch, Mister Chanofski, understand?

— I got it.

— Okay, sit down and have a drink.

— I'll get the draft, Chanofski said, then I'll come back for the drink.

— One more thing.

Chanofski waited.

— Your name. Chanofski. Probably Polish.

— Polish. And Jewish. My folks came in on the Great Wave. I was born in the same bed I was conceived in. My old man even flew the wedding night sheet to prove to the neighborhood my mama was a virgin, though usually only the Catholics did that in my neighborhood. I'm the whole schmear. I'm strictly Greenpoint, Brooklyn.

— All Polacks are "Ski." But not you. Not anymore. You're Mister Chanofski. Get used to your new name. *Mister Chanofski.*

— You sound just like my old man, the third mate grinned. Can I ask you a personal question?

— Go ahead. But I might lie to you.

— Are you Jewish?

— No, Cadiz said, deadpan. But some of the best Jews are my friends.

They looked at each other a moment.

— I'm gonna learn a lot from you, Mister Cadiz, Chanofski said.

— You know most of it already, Cadiz said. You've made the biggest jump already. From the fo'c'sle to the bridge. The rest is easy.

— I'll get the draft, Chanofski said.

— To the quarter of an inch, Mister Chanofski, Cadiz yelled at the retreating figure, so huge it barely squeezed through the narrow companionways on the upper decks. I don't want to be cheated by some sharp-shooting barge captain putting the ace to me for an extra hundred barrels I didn't get!

— Down to a hair, Mister Cadiz, Chanofski yelled back.

Cadiz sat a moment, then grinned. It was going to be good to have someone like Chanofski around. He recognized the signs. Bright, alert, ambitious. Brine pecker. Good!

It was going to be a nice balance against Whitcomb. And then, reminded of Whitcomb, Cadiz walked to the captain's office and peered in. Whitcomb was sound asleep on the couch. Cadiz swore softly. An open bottle of champagne, with only an inch left in the bottom, was on the deck beside the couch. Well, at least he's asleep, Cadiz thought.

He stepped out into the open bridge, and then he saw it shape up.

Chanofski was walking down the pier stringer, staring at the bow, squinting to read the markings. He had just passed one of the open shed doors where the cargo had been loaded into number one hold when three men moved out of the door after him.

— Chanofski! Cadiz roared. Behind you!

Chanofski spun around on the balls of his feet and faced the three German sailors.

Cadiz took the ladder to the wheelhouse in two steps, grabbing the handle of the steam and depressing it. A deep-throated roar spread out over the quiet Sunday piers. He waited for perhaps three seconds until the steam rose in the lines and then began a rapid succession of blasts on the whistle. He heard the men below before he had cleared the boat deck.

The bosun, Perry, Spanish, Tender, Harrison, the messman and Cadiz all flowed down the gangway and intercepted a half dozen German sailors running across the pier shed toward Chanofski and the three Germans.

The men were separated by forty or fifty feet. The *Lover*'s sailors stopped and lined up. The German sailors stopped and lined up.

— Tender! Cadiz yelled. Get your ass over there and give the third mate a hand. We'll fade this bunch.

— Yessir!

No one else moved on either side as Tender detached himself, stooping a few feet away to pick up a length of two-by-four from one of the loading sleds. He ran forward alongside the *Sea Lover* to where Chanofski was pinned against the side of the pier shed, held there by two of the Germans. The third was punching him in the stomach.

Tender hit the third German with the two-by-four and dropped him, splintering the board. Chanofski was groggy and weak from a knee in the groin but he was still strong enough to grab one of the Germans around the neck in a hammerlock and hold him while the last of the trio faced Tender.

The German outweighed Tender by seventy-five pounds, and he moved in with confidence.

Tender still held the remainder of the two-by-four. He came in to meet him, holding the board high. They were five feet apart when Tender threw. The German ducked, but Tender had moved the instant the board left his hands. Before the German could recover, Tender was on him. He moved twice with the accuracy and the power of a West Virginia rattler, jamming his stiffened fingers into the German's eyes. The man screamed and staggered.

Tender circled behind the man and hit him in the kidney. The man buckled. Tender hit him again in the same spot. The sailor staggered. Tender moved again, lightly. Facing the man again who was still holding his eyes, he stepped in and pulled the man's undershirt over his head, enclosing his arms. Picking his shots, Tender stepped in and drove straight jolting punches to the man's face. Blood began to fill the inside of the undershirt as Tender worked on him. The man fell to his knees and Tender stepped in, ready to finish him off with a knee.

— Belay that! Chanofski roared suddenly. You wanta kill him?

— Yeah—yeah—I do, Tender said, and stepped in to finish off the German sailor.

Chanofski flung the German he had been holding to one side as lightly as he would a doll, his strength returning, and moved heavily and clumsily to intercept Tender. He picked the young sailor up in a bear hug and shook him. Tender fought and kicked to get free.

Chanofski slung Tender over his shoulder and started to walk toward the two lines of men.

Cadiz, the bosun, Spanish, Perry, the messman and Harrison had been joined by others of the *Sea Lover*'s crew by then, and from the Nazi gangway, Germans poured down until there were nearly a hundred of them. Martin Thale stood apart, observing, his clear blue eyes on Cadiz. No one moved on either side.

Alberich came down the gangway then, pushing through the German sailors and coming to the front, facing Cadiz.

Out of the corner of his eye Cadiz could see the rails of the Nazi ship lined with passengers and the crew of the stewards department. Hertha was standing at the head of the gangway, as if to descend.

Alberich and Cadiz gazed at each other a moment and then Alberich started to speak. Cadiz cut him off.

— Can't you control your men, Mister Alberich?

— Mister Cadiz—

— Start laughing at them, Cadiz ordered quietly. The bosun, Perry, and Harrison started it; soon the entire crew of the *Sea Lover* was laughing. It got louder and louder, peels of laughter aimed like stones at the thick knot of Germans opposite them.

Chanofski dropped Tender to the floor of the shed. Both of them roared with laughter. The Germans began to shift uneasily, with an ugly, angry menace.

Cadiz turned his back on Alberich, and, still laughing, walked toward the gangway of the *Sea Lover*, trailed by the rest of his crew.

The Germans remained on the pier for five minutes before Alberich gave Thale the order to have them return to the ship.

There was only one significant result of the unpleasantness with the crew of the *Thuringen;* the bosun had seen Tender beat the German sailor nearly to death without getting a scratch on him.

Whitcomb slept throughout the entire affair.

The fight and talk of the fight were over. The *Sea Lover* was making ready to sail. The rest of the Sunday afternoon had been spent securing for sea. There was none of the usual quick intensity that preceded a sailing. Cadiz did not insist on getting the men who were still drunk and sick out to work with the bosun. Late that afternoon the poker game was still going on, but the players were so tired they merely ran the cards out in showdown hands. The bosun was moving professionally and surely about the deck with his skeleton work gang. He too was finished with the land. And the poker game was behind him. He was a man working at his job, easily, with confidence.

— That boom cradle on the cross trees on the mizzen musta been sprung by them goddam stevedores, he said to one of his sailors.

— Well, we ain't got time to fix it now, the sailor said.

— I know it, I know it. Take a wire strap aloft and put a number two turnbuckle on it and lash it down. Pull it up tight now.

— Check, the sailor replied, and trotted off.

— Hey, Boats, said another sailor. They finished trimming number two. You wanta secure?

— The mate has to check it first. I'll go check it. You go find Mister Cadiz. After you see him and tell him, take one of the ordinaries and collect all the snatch blocks and stow 'em in the mast tables right by the winch. I don't wanta have to go looking for 'em when we get in the unloading position. Is Bernhart still puking?

— No, the sailor replied. He's got the dry heaves now.

— I need him to straighten out the wire falls on the Jumbo boom. He's got a way of taking out the pin—well, it'll just have to wait. Is there any coffee? Maybe we can sober him up a little.

— No, the sailor replied. The messman said he ain't going to make no more.

— When you find Mister Cadiz, the bosun said, ask him if he thinks I can secure this sonofabitchin' ship with a gang of drunks without coffee to keep 'em from vomiting their bile and liver!

— I'll ask him, the sailor said.

— And ask him when he's going to set sea watches!

— Hey, Boats!

— Yeah? the bosun turned, looked around, and spotted one of the firemen.

— You oughta see the party the Old Man is throwing in his cabin!

Him and Golden just come aboard with two of them strippers from across town. They puttin' on a private show right now topside—they gotta coupla cases of champagne an' everything.

— Strippers?

— Big-league stuff, and they dancin'! Golden just borrowed my Victrola and records!

— Jesus Christ, the bosun said.

Again Cadiz swore under his breath as he hurried to the doorway of Whitcomb's office. The Victrola was setting the pace with a dirty Dixieland horn. The office was jammed with crewmen. They were cheering, laughing, clapping their hands. Whitcomb stood before the desk waving a bottle of champagne in the air and urging the strippers on. He was more than a little drunk.

The women were not young. The bodies were flabby. They were naked except for their high heels and hair feathers. The sequins flashed dimly in the low-power light of the office. They did not actually dance; they gyrated, keeping the beat, bumping and grinding, shaking their shoulders and making their pendulous breasts bob.

The men roared their approval and when the record stopped they howled for more. The strippers held their fixed positions as the music stopped. Except for their heavy, labored breathing, they stood like statues.

Whitcomb swept one of them down in his arms and Spanish grabbed the other. There were loud demands for an encore as the two women drank champagne from the bottle. Someone put another record on. The beat was hot, driving. The women got back up on the top of the desk and started dancing again.

— Hold it! Whitcomb roared. *Hold it!* He spun around, waving the bottle of champagne. Stop that fuckin' record!

The music was silenced, and the strippers looked blankly at Whitcomb. He dipped into his pocket and pulled out a fistful of bills.

— A hunnert dollars—and a challenge dance! A hunnert dollars to the bes' one, and we all going to be the judge!

The men cheered and made room for the first stripper to dance. The music was started again. The blonde began, slowly, using her exposed breasts to advantage, stopping before one and then the other of the crew and throwing her shoulder at the sailor. The audience was quieter now, more critical, and when the stripper turned a good leg, they applauded and commented.

Cadiz stood at the door, looking from the stripper to Whitcomb. No one noticed him. The blonde was about halfway through the record when he slipped around the side of the men and shut off the machine. Whitcomb whirled around, angry.

— What the hell! Who turned that off?

Cadiz did not wait. All right! Knock it off! Every one of you bastards below! The party's over. Come on, move it, goddammit! If this ship is delayed one goddam minute because she's not secure for sea—

Whitcomb slouched toward him.

— Now, you just wait a damn minute!

Cadiz ignored him.

— I said *move!* He grabbed one of the men by the shoulder and shoved him. The man stiffened, resisted. Cadiz paused and looked the man in the eye. Are you really going to try something, Charlson?

The bosun grabbed the man and pulled him out of the cabin. The others filed out quickly. Cadiz picked up the women's dresses and tossed them.

— Good night, ladies, he said.

— Now just a goddam minute! Whitcomb bellowed. The party *ain't* over! Come back here—Helene, Stella—

— Tender! Cadiz called sharply, still ignoring Whitcomb. Tender appeared at the door. See they get off the ship. And I mean *now*. No side trips into the fo'c'sle for a little short timer, understand? Spanish! Lend a hand with these women.

— This way ladies, Tender said with a grin and mock bow. Too bad we ain't got more time, I could show you the world.

— Honey, the blonde said tiredly, I seen it awready.

As they departed, Whitcomb waved the bottle of champagne. He had subsided into a drunken amiability.

— See you next trip, Stella! Watch those grinds, Helene. That's a mighty sweet thing you got there!

The women yelled something back and Whitcomb, laughing, took a long swallow of champagne. He finished the bottle and, tossing it to one side, immediately picked up another and began working the wire away from the cork.

—Nice broads, Whitcomb said, his speech suddenly less thick than it was a moment before. He glanced sideways at Cadiz.

—Yeah, nice, Cadiz said.

—Too bad we didn't have more time, Whitcomb said.

—Yeah, too bad.

Whitcomb popped the champagne cork and drank.

—Ahhh! That Stella! He wiped his chin. What a bruiser she is, huh?

—Yeah, a bruiser, Cadiz said.

—What did you stop if for, Whitcomb asked. We sailing yet?

—You snuck ashore while I was sleeping this afternoon, didn't you?

—I went ashore, yes . . .

—How drunk are you, Elly?

—. . . but I wouldn't characterize it as snuck.

—You snuck, Cadiz said disgustedly, like a guilty little kid. I asked you a question. How drunk are you?

—Drunk, and I'm feeling fine. Why? Whitcomb took another swallow. We can't both be drunk. Somebody's got to be on the bridge when we sail.

—I want to know something, Elly.

—You want a drink? Good champagne. Some of that stuff I picked up in Port Said.

—No, I don't want a drink, Cadiz said.

—Say, what's the matter with you? You go ashore like old Elly told you and get laid? Naw! I can see you didn't. Well, you better screw on your head, Howard, 'cause I can see you still thinking about her and you going to get eat up alive.

—I told you, Elly, there's something I want to know.

—I don't want no conversation now, Cadiz, Whitcomb said, shrugging with irritation. Maybe you'd better take the bridge when we sail.

—I'll take the bridge.

—Fine, fine, I'll just hit the sack.

—Why didn't you stay with Sara?

— What?

— You heard me.

— I don't want to talk about it.

— Well, you're going to talk about it. Answer the question!

— Up yours, sailor. Now blow! I want to hit the sack. I'm tired.

— You're too old and too flabby to talk to me like that, Elly.

— I'll take you apart, Whitcomb said.

— You couldn't take a wet paper bag apart.

— What the hell's eating you! But I don't have to ask that question. I know what it is. It's a case of ass-ache-itus. Whitcomb smiled smugly and nodded. I seen it in sailors every time a ship leaves the pierside. Old self-pitying ass-ache-itus, poor little old me, having to leave her—

— Answer my question, Cadiz said.

— I ain't belittlin' it, Howard. I just want you to know I unnerstand how you feel. It ain't an easy feeling to carry around. No sir! I know.

— Why didn't you stay with Sara?

Whitcomb took a sip of champagne.

— I'd tell you if I thought it was any of your goddam business.

— Don't play four-stripe captain with me, Elly, Cadiz said.

— I ain't *playin'* nothing. I *am* the four striper! He drank again. Good stuff.

— Come on, Elly, Cadiz said. We've known each other too long.

— You know something? Whitcomb said suddenly. You remember what I said about you always being snotty and how you still snotty, and you changed and now you *mean?* Well, I wasn't so sure. But I am now.

— I want an answer.

— You *are* mean. You're turning sour. Right before my eyes.

— Why didn't you stay with Sara?

— *What* in hell's *eating* you *anyway!*

— What happened, Elly?

— Nothing happened.

— And then the boys came home and bounced you. What else happened?

— What the hell you askin' for, if you know already?

— Don't run, Elly, Cadiz said.

— Run from you? Jesus!

— I want to know.

— They *threw me out!* Okay! O-goddam-kay! They threw me out. Right out on my ass!

— That's what you said.

— That's what happened!

— That's only half the story, Cadiz said.

— Half?

— They threw you out. Okay. Now I want the other half.

Whitcomb sank to a chair. Go on, Howard, he said tiredly. I mean it, I'm hosed out and hung over and I wanta sleep.

— Come on, Elly, Cadiz said. The boys came home, found you there, and threw you out—

— That's what happened.

— *And what did you do?*

— Do! *Do!* What the hell *could* I do?

— Never mind what you *could* do, what *did* you do?

— Their mother was on their side, Whitcomb said vaguely.

— That's an excuse.

— She raised them, not me.

— Another excuse.

— I tol' you a thousand times how it was! We never shared anything, me and Sara—nothing. *Will you leave me alone?*

— Did Sara *tell* you to go? To *leave?*

— No—that is—she—Whitcomb was nearly on top of his anger again, and as Cadiz watched, it slid away from his face like rain water. He relaxed and sighed. Leave it alone, Howard, Whitcomb said wearily. Leave it alone.

— I won't go away, Elly, and it won't go away either.

— There is, Whitcomb said, raising his head, just so much of this that I will take! So just leave my personal life alone.

— Leave it alone, Cadiz repeated.

— Yes, sir, just leave sleeping dogs lie.

— Even if it's a flea-bitten old hound?

Cadiz knew at once that the remark had hurt.

— I'm sorry, Elly, he said quickly.

— That's okay.

— I didn't mean it, it was just a crack.

— I know you didn't, Howard, I know you didn't. Whitcomb looked helplessly around the room. Part of the problem—I mean—is, I never liked my sons. I never could talk to them. I couldn't get to them somehow. It was like talking to strangers most of the time. They didn't know anything about the sea. They weren't interested. They looked at me and thought I was different—not ever taking the time to find out *why* I was different. They looked at me and turned down the whole idea. I think that if I came home starched and clean and was master of a big passenger liner, like one of the Queens, they might have seen it different. Maybe I made a mistake there. I could have gone with one of the big companies and sailed with 'em until I got my seniority in and then got one of the big liners, instead of working for the one and two ship companies operating out of a phone booth at seventeen Battery Place. But I was a deck sailor. And there were so many things I didn't like about being on a liner. I guess it was a lot my fault. Them and me not getting on. On the other hand, Howard, they liked their stupid cows, but I never made fun of them for that. I—

Whitcomb slowly ran down and stopped. Cadiz watched him carefully. Did you ever try to explain that to them, Elly?

— Sure I tried. I tried hard. I wanted the oldest boy to come to sea with me. You know, it might sound silly, but right after the war, I had the crazy idea of owning my own ship.

Cadiz gave him a sharp look.

— No, I'm serious. There were hundreds of Hog Islanders tied up and I had pretty good connections. And with what I could have sold the farm for, make a bare boat charter out of one of those Hog Islanders and haul coal from Norfolk to Antwerp—

— That sounds reasonable enough, Cadiz said.

— Yeah, there was about twenty-four months there, right after the war, when a man coulda got himself a start.

— What happened?

— I talked to the oldest boy, Whitcomb said. I wanted him in with me, see. I never mentioned it to Sara.

— What did the boy say?

Whitcomb did not speak at once. And when he did, his tone was bitter.

— He asked me a question. After I had lined up the whole idea he asked me one question: when will I be able to come back to the farm, Dad? The only thing he was interested in was the farm and when I told him I would have to sell the farm to make the first charter, he cried. An eighteen-year-old boy, and he *cried*.

Cadiz got up and paced to the porthole, breathing fresh air, deeply, his rage barely under control. Behind him, Whitcomb continued.

— I guess I shoulda gone ahead and done it. I lost my feeling for it, though, after that. I mean, true, I was away at sea for months and years and only saw my boys a little at that time, but this was a chance to have them with me, see? My own sons, be with them, maybe make something lasting. Whitcomb and Sons Steamship Lines. My own ships, my own flag, my own colors. And you know something, Howard?

— What?

— When I left home, I went to Philly and signed on as master of a Hog Islander and sailed her for seventeen straight months in the coal trade from Norfolk to Antwerp, doing exactly what I wanted to do, and the owners made enough out of it to *buy* outright two Hog Islander's before the market dried up. They have nine ships in general cargo around the world today. Worth millions. Every time I see one of their flags I get sick to my stomach.

— And that's when you quit trying? Cadiz asked.

— Huh? What do you mean?

A slow realization spread across Whitcomb's face. His eyes hardened. Don't push it, Howard.

— Elly—

— We got a lotta water to cross. Whitcomb held both hands up, warding Cadiz off. Lotta water.

— Elly, goddammit, don't put me off, Cadiz said. I been a deck sailor since I was fourteen.

— Howard, please—

— My old man was weak and left my mother. I was raised by my mother and a maiden aunt. Both of them died in the flu epidemic after the war. I been on these goddam ships so long I feel like I got barnacles on my ass.

— Howard, don't eat yourself up, boy, it ain't worth it.

— It was all right when I was a kid. But I'm not a kid anymore, Elly. What does a sailor do when he's not a kid anymore?

— Howard, boy, I don't know what—

— Does he go on being a kid, Elly, until he's an old man and still a kid, Elly? Like you?

— I can't answer—

— Does he keep on with the broads and the booze and the good times?

— Why ask me?

— Because I want to know what you did when your sons bounced you!

— You ever think, Whitcomb said, busting in here, *just coming in,* that maybe I would just like to forget about it? Whitcomb stood and started for the bedroom door.

— Come back here, you sonofabitch, Cadiz said coldly.

— Now, Howard. It was almost a whine. Don't let yourself get all balled up over nothing. It's my business, ain't it? Well, *ain't it?*

— Tell me, Cadiz said.

— There ain't nothing to tell.

— Elly, I'd hate like hell to hit you, Cadiz said, taking a step toward Whitcomb.

— What! Are you out of your mind? *Hit* me!

— But I will, so help me God, I'll bust you right in the mouth.

— What kind of talk is that! By God! I wished I did know what you was talking about and wanted to know, so I could tell you and then, by God, maybe I could get some sleep and have a proper rest so I could sail my ship. When you get all cocky like this, Howard, I sometimes wonder if you didn't get hit with a cargo hook somewhere along the line and scrambled your brains or something.

— I'm talking, Cadiz said, about Elisha Whitcomb, who, if he wanted to, could go back down there to his farm in Pennsylvania and couldn't be stopped from staying there by his sons or anybody else.

— What?

— Yes, Elly.

— Please, Howard, I'm tired, I tell you. Goddammit! I gotta rest!

— I'm talking about Elly Whitcomb, who could still go down there to Lancaster and if his sons tried anything snotty, could take them apart. Even drunk and soft as you are, you're still twice the match for most men—

— Don't throw it off on me, Whitcomb shouted, avoiding Cadiz. They-threwn-me-out! Will you try'n understand that *once and for all!*

— I understand that you've been conning yourself all these years.

— Conning myself?

— Crying and whimpering and showing off about how guilty you feel, when actually all the time you've been setting it up for yourself. The truth, Elly, Cadiz said quickly.

— If you're so smart, then just tell me how I win the game now, if what you say is true, Whitcomb demanded.

— You tell me.

— Because they *did* throw me out, Whitcomb said. They came home and said they didn't want a drunken bum—

— The Whitcomb I knew would have torn their arms out of their sockets if they tried anything like that.

— I'm an old man, Howard.

— Yeah, Cadiz said harshly, an old fox.

— Leave me alone, now, huh? Lemme sleep.

— No.

— We gotta sail soon.

— No.

Whitcomb threw up his hands and flopped on the couch. He held his head.

— All right, all right, I see it coming. It's going to be one of those long, lonnngg talking jags of yours, but for Christ sake, can't you wait until we sail?

Cadiz reached past Whitcomb and picked up the bottle of champagne, tasted it and took a deep swallow. Maybe you see it and maybe you don't, he said wearily.

— See what? You tell me, you're doing all the talking. In fact, you the on'y one around here that knows what the hell is being talked about, 'cause I sure don't.

—You remember how you used to feel guilty about not going home? Cadiz asked. Well, now you've really got something worked out to cry over. A story that goes like this. I worked a lifetime building a farm and raising sons. And when it came time for me to retire, and after devoting my life to seeing they were cared for, they kicked me out because they didn't want a drunken bum to show up and claim them for sons. And how did you become a drunken bum? Why, while you were on the other side of the world, lonely, drinking to keep your sanity on those long, long late night watches in strange ports, drinking kept you from brooding too much. How's that, Elly? There oughta be a hundred whores like Stella and Helene that will cry over that one.

—It ain't bad, Whitcomb said. That's about the size of it. That's just about the truth.

—Truth my ass, Cadiz said. You wouldn't recognize the truth if it reached up and pinched your cock.

—What the hell are you trying to build, Howard?

—Why, nothing, Elly, nothing. But I just want to know *why?*

—Why what?

—Why did you do it all these years?

Whitcomb was suddenly cold sober. He stared clear-eyed at Cadiz.

—Leave it alone, Howard. Leave it alone and get out.

—No, Elly, not now.

—That's an order, sailor. Get on the bridge.

—No. You're tough. Let's see you face it, Cadiz demanded.

—*Face what?*

—The truth, Cadiz said.

—What truth? Something you concocted in that dippy fuckin' head of yours?

—The truth that you're a liar and a cheat and you cop a plea and you whine and beg and you con and sneak—

Whitcomb went white.

—I oughta beat your face in and throw you off the ship.

—Don't try it, old man.

—What are you trying to do, Cadiz? Crucify me? For what? Throw off on me? *For what?* What have you got tied to your tail that's eating you, anyhow?

—I want to know, Cadiz said slowly, letting it come out with control, if you knew what you were doing?

Whitcomb relaxed. His eyes were clear and sharp now. They sparkled a bit. He smiled. Then he wiped his nose with the back of his hand. He looked at Cadiz and grinned.

—Oh, you seen something, huh? You seen something ashore and it has to do with her, and you came running back to the sea as soon as you saw it, huh?

—Did you see it, Elly? Did you? Did you see it yourself?

—What the hell you think, Mister? I'm so stupid I didn't know what the hell was going on? Huh? Is that it? You think I don't know?

—Then you always knew you'd never go back to Sara?

—*Of course I knew!* Whitcomb said. I've known it for years now! *Years!* Now you ask me why I didn't do something about it? I seen this coming the minute you stepped aboard this ship! And all them years, the tolerant, smug way you took care of me. I seen you look at me when I was pukey drunk, knowing what you was thinking, that I was you, you in time to come, Mister Cocky Bucko Mate! Tough-minded, gristle-gutted—the honest man! Balls! They make'em like you and me a dime a dozen. A *dime a dozen* for tough cocks like you and me. Ever think about that! That you ain't so goddam unusual as you think you are!

Whitcomb turned and paced the deck several times.

—You think I don't know what's been going on in your mind? You think you the only one has any feelings? You think I don't get sick of those stupid dumb broads and their stinky sweaty bodies? Think I haven't stepped back and took a look at myself hunching over their ugly faces in a thousand ports? Think I don't get sick of being a slobbering, stinking, run-down drunken old man?

Red-faced, sweating, Whitcomb pounded the desk with his fist.

—I don't know when it happened. Years ago, I guess. On'y I remember saying to myself one day that I was over the line. I was committed. I'd never go back to her. And all of it was a dream. So. Don't sling mud on me! Don't ask me why I don't go home and snatch a half hitch in their kiesters and say, your old man's home, so watch your goddam step! Whitcomb looked Cadiz straight in the eye. How long would it last?

— You're drunk, Cadiz said.

— Sure I'm drunk. And I'm going to get drunker! and I might even go so far as to say I'll probably die drunk! But remember this, it ain't none of your business. So! You can get the hell out now. You got the story.

— What story?

You're tied up in a neat package like the rest of us, sucked in like the rest of us and just because you're beginning to see it, don't lay it off on me. I'm a drunk. With some of them it's women—French style—Turkish style—some go for punks and boys—some turn all the way queer and some take dope—but most of us, the majority of us, become drunks. I'm a drunk, but I came by it honestly. Yes, goddammit, don't you sneer at me. I'm an honest drunk!

— You don't know the meaning of the word, Cadiz said.

— I know! Whitcomb said furiously. But you oughta know what it means to me. I *don't* mean your simple "me good—you evil" crap. It means you look at the way things are. And you go along, and you tell yourself pretty lies, *after* you see you've gone too far to correct the mistakes. And then you lie and lie and lie until little lies are built into bigger lies, until one day those lies are the whole of your life and they look like the *truth!* And it is truth, because knowing that all of it is a big lie—*and then living with it*— is honesty!

Cadiz was now white-faced. He lit a cigarette and his hands trembled.

— You're a liar, he said. Nobody could look at it that way and make a deliberate choice.

— I ain't a liar, and the honest ones look, goddammit! And they do make their choice. And then they have to live with it. They live their life of lies and they cry and whine for sympathy because that's one of the ways you can live with it.

— You've got it down to a natural, haven't you, Cadiz said. But his voice was unsteady.

— A natural, Howard Tough Cock Cadiz. And the sooner you come to face it, the sooner you get to where life is easier to take. But

I oughta warn you that regardless of how well you've tied yourself up in your lies, there's always a little something slipping out. It's the crusher. It slams you in the gut. There ain't no way on earth to escape it. Whitcomb paused. He stared out of the porthole. We're lonely men on a ship, and nobody gives a damn. But you're committed. And then you find out that just living is the enemy. And you either lie down and let it take you, or you get up and like a man you do what you have to do.

They sat in silence for a long time before Whitcomb spoke again.

— What are you going to do?

— I don't know, Elly, Cadiz said.

— I can't decide for you, Whitcomb said.

— I didn't ask you to, I didn't expect you to do that.

— But I told you the truth, Whitcomb said.

— Yeah, I know you did, Elly. Cadiz got up and went slowly to the door. I know you told me the truth.

— I know what you're trying to decide, what it is that's building pressure inside your skull. You look around at us apes, down below *and* on the bridge and you ask yourself if there ain't a possibility that you going to be an ape too—maybe *already* an ape, and maybe you should go ashore and find her—

— It's too late for her, Cadiz said.

— or someone *like* her and forget all this. I can only say, make sure. Make sure. If this is your way, son, don't let it slip through your fingers.

— Get some sleep, Elly, you're going to sail soon.

— And when it comes time for you to fight it, to make your decision, remember me, Howard. And as hard as you fight, and as hard as you try to get rid of the pressure, remember this—

— Yes, Elly.

— I fought harder than you, longer than you, and I was *stronger* than you and I lost it.

Cadiz quivered inwardly and closed his eyes.

— Tell me, Elly, who ever wins this struggle?

— And *that* remark is the beginning! You know that, don't you? You listen to what you just said. Say it again in your mind and listen to it again. Hear it? It reeks with the first cry for understanding! For pity! God, I *pity* you, you poor sonofabitch. You're tough. Maybe, *maybe* even tough as me. And you're not going to give up easily. And you are going to take one hell of a beating. And you know what will happen, Howard?

— No, Elly.

— One of these days, one fine morning when you're heading back to the ship after a night of hosing and boozing, or maybe at sea, you'll wake up and it'll be a strange day for you, a hell of a strange day. It'll be twisted and turned around, and eating up its own tail, and that will be it. That will be the day you make your choice. You can't force it to come. It'll come in its own good time. It'll just come on you when you least expect it, long after you've thought about it, long after you've decided I was full of shit! It'll be there, like a fog bank, or a freak sea, seventy feet high rolling down on you at express-train speeds out of a dark and quiet ocean. And you won't have no time to prepare for it, and you'll either ride it out, like you do a freak sea, or you'll go down before it—like I did and like most of us do. Whitcomb picked up a fresh bottle of champagne. He worked the wire around the cork carefully. I can see it coming. You're tough and you're going to take a terrible beating.

Whitcomb took a long drink of champagne and did not bother wiping his chin as the wine spilled over.

— Elly—

— God, I'm glad it's over for me.

— Elly, listen—

— Don't bother to wake me for the sailing, Howard. I want to sleep in. Whitcomb closed his eyes and let his head fall back. Watch out for the ranges in the lower bay, Howard. There's a hopper dredge digging the channel. She digs red buoys coming up and black going down.

— I'll watch it, Elly.

— I've got a lot of serious drinking to do before I can get to sleep. You opened it up again, you sonofabitch, and now I'm going to have to pay for it.

— I'm sorry, Elly, Cadiz said.

— No, no you ain't. Just turn out the lights and leave me alone. And watch out for the dredge ranges. Don't let your pilot drift off the channel. They ony lose about one ship in five thousand here in New York, and I don't want it to be mine.

Cadiz looked down at the old worn-out sailor who had made a thousand crossings and a thousand sailings and who had been as far as a man can go on this earth. You've seen him, perhaps many times, and never looked at him twice, never knowing that he was the man who brought your chocolate from Holland; or took the first milling machine to Rio; or on one trip took three thousand tons of black powder to France for the Yanks Over There; or who had in his cargo on one crossing the first Model T's to go to Europe. You have seen him drunk, brawling, trying to screw that town whore you wouldn't spit on, and heard his filthy-mouthed language; and perhaps, too, you have seen him clean, brushed, returning from the sea with an aura of salt spray and mystery wreathed around his distant seeing eyes that you will never understand, and wonder what sights he had seen that you can only imagine; did you know this same Captain Whitcomb threaded the Gibraltar needle on a black and murderous night to carry Egyptian cotton bales to the New England mills that made your bedsheets? No, you did not know, or if you did, you did not consider it and you do not care. Most likely, you do not care because you do not hear . . .

Listen . . . The sea beckons with fluid arms, inviting you to escape. There, *out there*, are the illusions that make a man forget the muck of his life. It takes the ordinary man and teaches him to squander, and to be truly spendthrift with your life is not an easy thing. You find yourself reduced to the simple things, avoiding prejudices and pressures of any kind, because *out there* everything becomes so clear. It's all black and white. There are no gray shadings at sea. Life has no subtle, hidden meanings for the sailor at sea. It's different out there, a world that is not to be touched for its simple stark beauty. The sky and the water. And it looks different in every ocean. The sky and the water and the ships and the men . . . after a while it becomes impossible to argue with it, any more than a man can argue with his hand or his eye. But there comes an end. And you look at yourself and you discover that there is one more thing yet, one more thing, more simple and less complicated than being a sailor, and that is being an old man. The sea will do that. It will teach a man to be a spendthrift with his life and then he is old and feels cold and can never get warm again. He breaks his life down into the present hour by hour, and dismisses the past and the future. Thinking about the past only annoys and frustrates. And if he should dare think about the future, he stops and realizes that he is an old man and there isn't too much future left to him. He thinks only of the present. He breaks everything down to simple things, because the complicated things take too much time. And time is the one thing an old man, a very old, tired, worn-out sailor, does not have.

The next time Whitcomb comes your way, take a good look at him. You can see it all if you try, if you care.

Listen . . . Out there, far off on the distant horizon, just a whisper behind the voice of the attractive promise, it can be heard . . . When you become an old man, an old sailor, you will become lonely, not for people, but for the routine of your life. But who would bother his head about payment deferred when the whole world and your whole life is waiting for you? And though we know that all men are lonely when death comes for them, none is more lonely than a sailor when death comes for him.

Where will you bury him?

— Good night, Captain Whitcomb, Cadiz said.

Death slipped aboard the *Lover* four days outward bound southeast for Africa. Perry, Spanish, Harrison and the bosun came out of the housing, set up a hatchboard on a slight ramp at the railing, then left to come back with the canvas-wrapped body. The board-stiff body was placed on the hatchboard and then carefully draped with an American flag.

The crew, in their Sunday best, slipped out of the housing—awkward, silent, seeing yet unseeing. No one spoke. Bare-headed, faces bleak, they kept their eyes averted from the flag-draped body.

Cadiz moved to the wing of the bridge and looked down onto the deck. The bosun waved slightly and nodded.

— Stop the engines, Cadiz said to the second mate.

Slowly, evenly now, the beat of those engines that had pounded like the heartbeat in Whitcomb's body came to a slow and gentle stop.

Cadiz came down to the main deck and stood beside the body. He uncovered his head, opened the Bible he was carrying and began to read to himself. The crew shuffled their feet. Perry, Harrison, Spanish and the bosun waited stiffly.

— There go the ships, Cadiz said at last in a finely controlled voice, and this is one of the men who sailed them.

He stepped back and nodded to the attending bearers, who tipped the hatchboard upward. The body of Elisha Whitcomb was given to the sea. At that instant the whistle was blown for one minute as the *Sea Lover* rested silently on the face of Whitcomb's grave.

— These services are over, Cadiz said quietly. Bring her about. Full ahead, maintain standard course and speed . . .

December 1942

—Christ, it's cold! Captain Sparkle said. If I was a pious, God-fearing Bible-quoting old cockster like some of my salt-peter friends back in Tennessee, Mister Cadiz, I'd say it was time to pray. But since I ain't I won't. But I swear, I look at that rat-faced harbor pilot standing beside the wheel yonder and I can't help but raise a hard on for him and be a little jealous. He's got a master's license, I happen to know for a fact. How come he ain't taking war cargo to the battlefields of Europe like the rest of us crazy people?

— Somebody's got to read the river, Cadiz said. See that Canadian Canuck swinging on the hook, just off Red Hook Flats?

— What about him?

— If your rat-faced pilot wasn't in the wheelhouse, and on call for other ships, that Canuck might wind up on a sandbar.

— I don't want any of your reasonable answers today, if you please, Mister Cadiz. Just a little unlikely bullshit will do. I'm a little skit-terish with such a deep draft, and I just want to make noise with my mouth to take a turn on my fears, Captain Sparkle said.

Their ship moved down, at an angle, across New York Harbor and headed for Europe that cold December afternoon. They were just then taking the Statue of Liberty abeam.

— Like you ain't scared, Captain Sparkle said, seeing that Cadiz was grinning.

— I don't deny that I'm scared.

— Most of the time? Will you admit that?

— Only when I think about it, Cadiz said. Which isn't very often, thank God.

— Like you don't know where them crates, lashed to the deck yonder, is going? Like you don't have any suspicions where we're going?

— I know, Cadiz said lightly. But it doesn't help to worry about it.

— She's just about right in the head, wouldn't you say?

— She's riding well.

— We'll see when we get some weather.

— If everything stays down tight, we'll be all right. I just don't want anything loose on deck.

— No, or me either, Captain Sparkle said. He studied the water.

He shook his head, shot out his jaw, leaned back on the railing and kicked at the windbreak, studying the harbor movement around him. I counted a hundred and fifty-seven ships yesterday, Howard. A hundred and fifty-seven. It's a damn big war. No lights, no guarantees. Well, I say fuck 'em. When did a sailor ever get a guarantee of anything? I got me a good ship, and war or no war, I'm going to see she gets to her destination with her crew and cargo safe and sound. A good black night is what we want, then we pick up the convoy. Then, Howard, son, like that feller said, the one that gutted Macbeth at the end of the play, we will see if'n we really will be from this crummy world untimely plucked.

— Ripped, Cadiz said.

— Ripped or plucked or fucked, this is what I do and I ain't bowing to no sonofabitch for knowing my job. Now ain't it funny, Howard, that in the end of a good play-drama, the vilyan always learns the truth about himself and his misdeeds before he gets his comeuppance and his belly punctured? It ain't that way at all. I seen plenty of good men that went out, that got theirs, without a backward glance, or a chance to shout for forgiveness. It's a shame life can't be like a play-drama. Everything tied up in a neat half hitch. I tell you, son, it would be nice to know that just before you get yours, somebody's going to come along and tell you where you made your mistakes.

Both men turned their attention to an inbound tanker. It was a new ship with a clean lift to her bow, deeply loaded to within four feet of her tank tops. The tanker, being the burdened vessel, swung obediently out of their path and slipped past them, a dark and ghostly presence. Captain Sparkle waved and an officer on the bridge of the tanker waved back, and then it was gone astern of them. Once more Sparkle and Cadiz focused their attention forward.

They took the government piers on Staten Island on their starboard, easing past the maw of busy slips where blue-gray vessels, mostly Navy, balanced gigantic towers of super-structured steel on their racy hulls. One of the Queens, her gay colors washed over with a sickening wartime gray, was taking on troops. Cadiz got a glimpse of the soldiers being marched to the gangway from the train backed into the pier shed. At another pier a hospital ship was unloading the wounded. Further along, a vessel loaded tanks and tank carriers—which were the largest motor vehicles Cadiz had ever seen—and then they were passing O'Brian's dredging operation, and now they could see the Narrows clearly. They were entering the thieves' world where not yet, but soon, everything would be taken away from them except the tight, insecure world of a ship in wartime. Cadiz lit a cigarette.

— The war's picking up. You notice that, Howard, son? It's going to reach a peak pretty soon, then it'll start to coast downhill. That's the way it was in the first one. It hit a high, then we coasted downhill.

— Yes, Howard Cadiz said. I feel that we're not more than three or four years away from it.

— Look yonder, just off the starboard, just ahead. There's an old piling, or a log, or tree or something.

Howard Cadiz squinted. He had not seen it and looked admiringly at the old man beside him. Sparkle's eyes were still keen after forty years on the bridge.

— Yeah, me! She's just about right in the head. But not for a whole blow, Captain Sparkle said. For a whole blow I'd like to see her about four or five more feet out of the water in the head. Ever been in a whole blow before?

— Three times.

— Three times. That oughta make you an authority. Atlantic, Pacific or Injun?

— One in each.

Captain Sparkle laughed, leaned on the bridge railing and kicked again at the windbreak. They were both wearing heavy bridge coats. The sky held a threat of snow; the wind was freshening as they moved into the Narrows between Staten Island and Brooklyn.

— Lordy me! One in each. Howard, son, you're a good tight man. One in each. Why, I musta crossed that back Injun Ocean a hundred times, and the onliest blow I ever got was a light breeze that brought down the Calcutta stench. One in each, eh? Bad ones?

— Two were bad, one so-so. Cadiz stared out over the head of the ship. He was not sure, but he thought she was a little sluggish in coming right. It could be the set of the channel current. It wasn't important, but it was information about his ship, something to note.

— How low was the glass? Captain Sparkle asked.

— The one off Toyohashi was down to twenty-eight-ninety-eight.

— Bad?

— We lost everything above the deck except the bridge.

— Mast, booms, everything?

— We lost both hooks and the windbreak apron on the fo'c'sle head, Cadiz said.

The captain walked to the wing of the bridge, turned his back to the water and leaned way out, letting the railing catch him in the small of the back. He turned his head fore and aft, looking at the set of the vessel in the water, studying the waterline. So, Howard Cadiz thought, he too felt her sluggishness in coming right, and he's looking for a list. Captain Sparkle returned to Cadiz's side and started kicking at the windbreak apron again.

— You did a nice job of trim, Howard, son, Captain Sparkle said. She sets nice. That slow way she answers coming right must be the set here in the channel. Now, if we just don't get weather, we'll be all right.

— It's that time of year when there's always weather in these latitudes, Cadiz said.

— A little late for a hurricane, though. Them big southern storms never come when the weather is hard cold like this here now. But anything could happen.

Below them, led by the bosun, one group worked on the turnbuckles, taking the last turn on the deck cargo lashings; others were securing the booms and storing the lines. By the time they reached pilot station they were secure for sea. They stopped the engines and the little pilot skiff came alongside to take the pilot off.

— Good luck, Captain Sparkle, the pilot said. They shook hands.

— Thankee, Captain Sparkle said, smiling. Careful going down that ladder, now, you ain't so young anymore.

— Mister Cadiz, the pilot said. Good luck, sir.

Cadiz nodded. They watched as the always dangerous, always delicate job of handling the skiff and landing the pilot was accomplished, and then he was away.

The ship came to life again as the engines were rung up and sent full-ahead again.

— All right, Howard, son, Captain Sparkle said. That's the notch we picked for ourselves, so we'll give her a good fucking for the price. Now lemme see, we'd better have a boat drill right away before they eat, and you'd better check the windlass. Take that West Coast A.B. forward, the one that handles wire s'nice, to put extra lashings down as backups for the cat's-paws. And check the cement plug in the chain pipe. Don't let that stupid bosun mix the cement with salt water or it'll crumble.

— All right, Cadiz said.

— As a matter of fact, you'd better check those deck lashings yourself. I don't care if the bosun is the best deck sailor in the world, I want 'em checked.

— He's not the best, Cadiz said. I'm the best.

— That's what I like about you, Howard, son, you tote you own goddam brass around with you. As it so happens, *I'm* the best deck sailor in the world.

— I can lay eight wire into ten wire in a long splice with a spike, a hand vise and a pair of gloves. Can you?

— No, I can't, the captain said happily. I'm an old man and I don't care a shit if you can lay twelve into sixteen, I can't lay but one at a time and I'm in a hurry to get me a Russian cunt that's got patience. Say, now, listen, is that cock-loving second mate still asleep? He came aboard drunk, didn't he?

Howard Cadiz nodded.

— Whew! I saw that slut he was with, the captain said, wrinkling his nose. Think we can get him to let go his pecker long enough to come to boat drill? . . . Where are you going? I ain't finished talking to you.

— I want to get a bearing on Ambrose Lightship.

Sparkle watched as Cadiz spun the azimuth circle, flipped the vanes and glanced down at the gyro repeater on the wing of the bridge. He squinted, caught the awkwardly shaped, ugly little lightship as it was passed and took a reading. He nodded.

— Come left to steer one-three-five, sailor! Captain Sparkle yelled at the helmsman. They both watched as the bow came around slowly but evenly.

— She rides nice, Howard. I think we have a good ship.

— One-three-five, as she goes, the helmsman repeated.

— As she goes, Cadiz yelled. He looked around the ship. They say if she makes one crossing with her cargo in good shape, she's paid for herself.

— Ahh, they! *They!* They *who,* son? They give me a pain in the ass. Here they build a nice ship. Just look at her. Brand new. And they say a thing like that. It makes me sick at my stomach. You ever feel that way? About a ship, I mean. One trip and it's done its job and don't matter no more?

— No, Howard said. I don't feel that way at all.

— Did you know, Captain Sparkle said, that in all my years on the bridge, this is the first really brand new boat I ever had? The first one. Everything nice and new and stiff. Look down below, yonder, on deck. That running gear. The factory shine is still on the snatch blocks and the wire and—and looka them winches! Why I can still read the maker's name from here! And down below, why the sailor's fo'c'sles don't even stink yet. Ahh, *they!* Whoever the hell *they* are, they give me a pain in the ass. A ship like this, taken care of, will last for thirty, forty years. This ain't one of them hurry-up Liberty Ships. It took a hundred and seventeen days to get her skin wet. You been over her and so have I. She ain't all I could want for speed, going to war and all, but she's built for power, and—and—well, I say tuck 'em.

— Hold on, Jonas, Cadiz said. I'm on your side.

— I know it, Howard, son. I just get so mad. It seems such a waste somehow. Like the whole world has gone dippy, or like a rummy who's lost everything, respect for himself, wife and kids an' everything else. That's what this war has done. Here we are, standing up on the bridge of a brand new ship. Two smart, tough sailors with sixty-five years experience between us on all the oceans, and we playing some kind of stupid game with this war and all. It's all so useless to me, somehow. I don't see the reason for any of it. Captain Sparkle kicked at the windbreak. But I don't give a damn one way or the other, do you?

Cadiz scanned the horizon.

— Well, do you?

— You've read *Moby Dick?* Cadiz asked.

— I have, and Melville was a damned good sailor. It comes out plain in his writing. What about it?

— Oh, the gold! The precious, precious gold! The green miser'll horde ye soon! Hish! Hish! God goes 'mong the worlds blackberrying.

— That's a quote from it?

— It's an answer to your question about my giving a damn.

Jonas Sparkle leaned on the windbreak and stared out over the deepening gloom of the northeastern sky. His old eyes were thoughtful.

— You think, Howard, son, Melville wrote that book because he was rebelling against something? A faltering faith, maybe?

— Or had his faith fail him? Yes, I think so.

— They were pretty simon pure lily-whites back in his days. I never did like them Calvinists. All right, if his faith failed him, how did it?

— Maybe like everybody else, he expected his faith to do too much for him.

— That's true, we all do expect that, don't we?

— Or why did his faith fail him? Cadiz asked.

— Well, I don't go in for that black and white atheism of his either, Sparkle said.

— Maybe he did it to shock the narrow-minded of his time. Those lily-white Calvinists.

— Now you read *Typee*, didn't you?

— Yes.

— Well, that was shock enough, if that was the case. Shocked hell out of them. Some of them old dog-faced Pittsfield women musta peed in their woollen drawers when they read that book. Captain Sparkle laughed.

— But what about his black and white atheism—conscious man in hot, eternal battle with dumb nature? You think that's what he's saying?

— Well, Howard, son, he sure said a mouthful, if he meant to say it or not. But wasn't that a half-assed story now, that white whale? Lordy me!

— Let me ask you a question, Cadiz said.

— Go ahead, but make it snappy. We got to have a boat drill.

— Was Ahab more or less than the brute he pursued?

— You mean the whale?

— The white whale.

— Ahh, son, you can't snow an old brine pecker like me with that one. If I say Ahab and the whale were the same, then you say to me, nothing makes sense, and if I say they were different, then you say what was Ahab's reward in looking for vengeance on a whale. Lordy me! I will say this, though, Ahab was a mighty ambitious man. One whale, and him looking for it. Just one little whale in all that fucking ocean. Howard, son, that's a crock of shit. Look yonder, we're getting a little weather. It's going to blow cold as a beaver's ass tonight.

— Maybe that's the whole point, Cadiz said.

— What's the point?

— Ahab looking for a white whale in all the oceans. An example for all of us. Look at it this way. A creature of dumb nature searching for another creature of dumb nature. Was one any better than the other?

— Well, you might have something there. Remember, the whale took vengeance on them all. Was he so dumb? Captain Sparkle looked shrewdly at Cadiz. Well?

— Were we being warned off, then, from seeking into the ways of an angry, dumb God?

— Nature?

— Yes.

— Mebbe so.

— Warning us not to tamper?

— Could be. I know this much. You just can't throw yourself at nature, or it'll smack you down. Is that your angry God?

— I'm asking you.

— Mebbe so.

— Or, Cadiz said, are we precious, precious gold, not only to ourselves, but to a God of love?

— Who was he quarreling with? Sparkle asked after a time. Melville, I mean.

— Certainly not the God of love.

— No, Captain Sparkle said. Then the angry God?

— Dumb nature, Cadiz said.

— Who you quarreling with, Howard, son? Sparkle asked gently. I seen pain and disappointment in your face the first time I ever laid eyes on you. I read it plain.

— You can't read a damn thing, Cadiz said.

— How you feel about getting killed, Howard?

— Bad.

— That's a damn good answer, Captain Sparkle said. Cadiz, you're a good tight man. Look, weather's running in fast.

— I see it, Cadiz said.

— You and me, Howard, son, we could take on the world.

— Or a white whale?

— We're a team, all right. What do you do when the seas are running hard?

— Take two half hitches and a long lead, Cadiz replied.

— How's the great Cadiz brain feel about this war?

— You want it all?

— Snow me, Howard, son, give it to me.

— I would say we are misadventurers in the universe.

— I like that. Go on, fog me, boy, Captain Sparkle said, a grin on his face.

— And through some freak, I am—we are. Like Moby Dick, we are conscious man fighting dumb, menacing nature, beating at it, hacking away at it, trying to be secure in it, terrified of it.

— Sweet Jesus!

Cadiz tucked his chin into the bridge coat collar and studied the gathering weather ahead of them that was sure to bring snow, or at least a freezing rain.

— I would say, he went on, the only thing a man can do that answers nature is to have a woman to root on.

— By God! You're all man, Howard, son!

— To plunge into her.

— Lordy, son! Even old cocksters like me?

— Even old ones like you with dust in their balls.

— Be respectful, son, Sparkle said happily. But *do* go on.

— To give her, Cadiz said, all that is our greatest and sole reason for being at all, and by doing this, there, in her—

— Balls deep! Sparkle cried happily.

— Up to the hair, make our mightiest stand against the grand universe, by reproducing ourselves in all our ignorance and stupidity.

— Now, *ain't* we stupid, though, Howard, son. Here we are, going straight to war to get our ass shot off. Stupid.

— And if there is a reason for our being here in this world of chaos, it is to be found through her, the solemn device for progeny, the everlasting instrument, the warm moist passage to the womb and our immortality.

— I like that warm moist passage part, Sparkle said. I wish I had a warm moist passage right now.

Cadiz grinned.

— Then as a result of this union, through this vehicle, we come to be fathers to futility, and we grow old and become grandfathers to this same futility.

— How is it going to end, Howard?

— Like the beginning, Jonas. A dark nothing, without even your play villains' chance to learn about our mistakes. And finally we lose it all. Who we are, and what we are, and why we are here.

Jonas Sparkle laughed. But what about this war, Howard?

— I'm not denying it. *I'm* going to hang on until my fingernails bleed.

— Good boy! I thought for a minute there you was a pacifist.

— I'm a pacifist, Cadiz said. All my life I've avoided, as much as possible, a world and a life of violence that I've found everywhere. But it's pursued me and soiled me all my life. This war is just one more incident. And in a way, it is just another way to go down, as all of us must go down, before an imperfect world.

— Ahh! I like that.

— What?

— Go down before an imperfect world, Sparkle said. All our lives we've been taught it was up to us to make it perfect. My old daddy used to sit in his rocker back to home and read scriptures all day and half the night. He was a sailor. We're all sailors up my way, you see. I could never figure out why he read the Bible so much, but I know now.

— Oh?

— I'm getting ready to die, son. I'm trying to find out some fucking answers before I go down before your imperfect world.

— I'm scared of dying, Cadiz said, but not scared enough to prepare for it. Not the way you mean.

— Dying is dying, and as right as living. I don't put too much by it, but I've pissed away so much of my life and never bothered to ask any questions that I have to make up for lost time.

— Well, this war, it's stupid but it's man-made. It doesn't bother me nearly so much to go down in their war as to go down before the chaos of the universe that man has nothing to do with. Cadiz turned to watch the weather.

— I don't guess there *is* a hell of a lot of difference in whether a man prepares or not, or how you go down, or why. You know you gotta, sometime, sooner or later, and maybe sooner for me, and that's why I'm reading my Bible. It's the only guide I've got to that dumb nature you talk about. It ain't much and I don't draw much satisfaction from it, but I'm giving her a good mauling just the same. And I know what you mean.

— Do you?

— I think so, Howard, son. You're a stargazer. You looked out yonder at the stars and you, standing there on your puny legs and your big strong body and your hard head full of facts—and you couldn't help but throw down a challenge. Like a little feisty dog trying to take on a big dog. Lot of yelp and holler. And then because you're brighter than most I've met, you saw you didn't have much of a chance and you worked up your idea. But you're still young. You have time to hope for some other answer. Me, I can't take any chances. I'm reading hell out of that Bible.

— If you don't buy any of the ready-made answers, it—just ends, Cadiz said.

— So you go back to your woman, Sparkle said.

— Back to the woman.

— It ain't a bad thing, your idea about the woman. Of all the good things I ever had—a fine suit of clothes I once had made in London, a fine ship like this one, a fine house back yonder to home, good meals and good drunks—of all the really fine things I ever had, saying to you now, this was the best, or that was the best, there were lots of women. And if you lined up all the very best things I ever had, I would pick a woman every time. Two hours on a double bed with the best woman I ever had in a lifetime.

— But even then, Cadiz said quietly, it's the waste that bothers me most.

— Well, come on, Howard, son, see to it. The wind's freshened, and my head's blown clear of that New York stink and filth. There's that snow coming. We'll spin out yarns when the weather's past.

Cadiz smiled at the old man and then turned, quickly, whistling through his teeth, a sharp, clear blast that would carry through the highest wind and that had in it a note of urgency and demand. The most powerful quarterdeck voice found it difficult to carry windward. The bosun, just then returning aft, looked up and Cadiz signaled that he was coming down.

— It's going to be a hell of a crossing! Cadiz shouted at Sparkle, exhilarated by the bitter but fresh winds blowing from blackened skies in the northeast.

The ship had taken on a slow, gentle roll, and it was this that Cadiz had been waiting for in making his tour of the deck cargo.

— Let's go, Boats! Cadiz yelled against the high wind. Get the West Coast A.B. and send him forward to put wire backups on the windlass cat's-paws, and get your cement ready for the chain pipe plug.

— Going to get warm water for the mix right now, Mister Cadiz.

— And send two of your sailors with me!

The ship rolled easily, an even quartering motion that gave just the slightest pitch to the head. Avoiding the catwalk that had been constructed out of heavy timbers over the tops of the huge deck cargo to make passage fore and aft easier, Cadiz dropped onto the main deck and scrambled over and under the thick cables that had been lashed to cleats welded directly to the deck. As the ship rolled, shifting the massive crates, however slightly, Cadiz sprung the lashings, looking for slack. The bosun had done a good job; he did not find many that needed attention.

— Take a turn on this one, he ordered the two A.B.'s who waited dutifully with eighteen-inch marlin spikes. Inserting the spikes on either side of the turnbuckle they waited for the roll, caught the slack and tightened up on the tolerance. Then moving on, they followed Cadiz around the entire deck, checking and tightening. It was dark by the time they were finished, and the wind was driving straight ahead. The gentle roll had increased to a steady pitch and yaw in the head, and now they were taking green sea as far aft as the foremast table. The very last of the gray twilight was gone just as it began to snow.

Before returning to the bridge, Cadiz stopped off at his cabin and replaced his wet gloves with dry ones, wiped his face and had a drink. He had not turned on the light. He did not want to fight the burning afterglow on his retina that he would see for a good fifteen minutes when he returned to the bridge. He really did not need the light anyway. It was a small space, just large enough for a man to move around in without being cramped, just large enough to hold the possessions of one man; he knew where everything was and he could, in the dark, put his hand on the worn copy of *Moby Dick* (third from the right in the bookshelf, the first two being *Bowditch* and *War and Peace*). Next to this, taking up the space of several books, a photograph of his Aunt Meg and his mother. The picture had a stark black and white quality; his mother's face was not nearly so plump and Aunt Meg not nearly so gaunt as he remembered them. Next to this, the new books that he had not read yet and that would be taken up during the afternoons between watches.

The ship snap-rolled and he held out his hand and found the corner of the closet and braced himself. He then waited for the counter-roll, still braced. Another ship, a familiar ocean, the same stillness that was always there regardless of what the weather was doing, the reiteration of his past and the promise of the future. Howard Cadiz, chief officer of the ship. Though he held a master's license, he had refused to wait around for weeks until he could get a command of his own. Now once more he was settling into himself, alone on an ocean again.

He inhaled deeply, took a last pull on the bottle—he knew what was waiting for him on the bridge and that this might well be his last drink for a very long time—and then put it away firmly with the gesture of a man who has long ago come to a decision about whiskey, when to drink and when not to drink. Ramming his large hands into the good leather gloves, he pulled up his bridge coat and stepped out of the room into the dull red illumination of the companionway.

An ordinary, a bright-faced, pink-cheeked kid wrapped and girded in seaboots, sou'wester and slicker, his lips thin and indrawn from the bitter cold of his watch on the windward wing of the bridge, blocked Cadiz's way. Cadiz did not know the crew yet; there had been no familiar faces so far, but there was something about the ordinary (and Cadiz knew that the boy must be on his watch—the four-to-eight) that made him pause.

He got it then. The lad was underage.

— How old are you! Cadiz demanded.

The boy stopped short, shooting Cadiz a quick look that was entirely unafraid. He wiped his nose with his palm.

— Seventeen, sir.

— Name?

— Childers, sir.

— Childers, you're a damned liar. You're not more than fifteen.

The boy swiped at his nose again and returned Cadiz's gaze without blinking. He nodded, as if to himself.

— Mister Cadiz, sir, my papers say I'm seventeen.

— What the hell are you doing out here?

— I'm a sailor, sir.

— Sailor, my ass! You wouldn't make a gnat on a poor sailor's balls.

— That might be so, Mr. Cadiz, the boy said. But one way or the other, I'm on your watch.

— What do you do in a hard blow, Childers? Cadiz suddenly roared.

— Take two half hitches and a long lead, sir.

— And if the line parts, Childers?

— You tuck in your asshole and start spitting teeth.

— You're nothing but a sailor, Childers, Cadiz said. Did you know that? You're nothing but a dumb fuckhead sailor. Cadiz turned away.

— Yes, sir. Thank you, sir. But if you go out starboard when the port's the lee, you're going to get your face froze.

Cadiz stopped and turned back, looking down at the boy.

— Sir, can I ask you a question?

Cadiz nodded.

— How old were you when you went to sea?

Cadiz hesitated a moment. Fourteen.

— See what I mean, sir?

— Fresh coffee to the bridge, Childers, Cadiz said, and turned to the lee door.

They had been running for eighty hours, and Cadiz knew they had missed their rendezvous with the convoy.

Captain Sparkle had finally left the bridge and gone below for some rest, and then only when he had extracted a promise from Cadiz.

— Now, call me, Howard, son, though I don't expect anything to happen in this kind of weather, but don't fret about disturbing me. I know how you feel, but more'n seventy-two hours on the bridge still leaves me a margin, so call me. I'll only be resting my eyes.

— I'll call you, Jonas, Cadiz said. I promise.

Their weather, sighted on leaving Ambrose Lightship, had come down on them quickly, a gray-black cloud of icy rain that turned to snow, and for three and a half days they had been working northeast to make rendezvous with the convoy that had sailed from Boston. They should have picked it up on the second day out. Their weather had not given them a chance at a position. They rode dead reckoning through the day, which was only a little clearer than their nights, taking very special pains over their set, drift, wind and slip, but feeling even as they checked and rechecked that their figures were inaccurate. Not liking it out there alone, feeling sure they had missed the rendezvous, they were not, however, sure enough to make a decision and go back or, as the only alternative, make the crossing without escort and hope for eventual contact with the convoy.

Cadiz stood alone on the wing of the bridge, trying to shield his eyes from the driving snow, his head down inside his collar. He cast around the dark, washing, white-capped seas. He knew it would be almost impossible to see the pencil-thin wake of a periscope more than fifty feet from the ship, but he kept a constant watch, eyes half open, eyelashes holding a thin reed of ice, his temples frozen numb, surveying the familiar world of the North Atlantic during an average mid-winter storm.

The cold he felt was familiar; the fatigue of three and a half days with no more than an hour's sleep at a time was familiar too; and so was the brackish, rancid taste of too many cigarettes and too much coffee. Most familiar of all were the movements of the ship as it rolled, plunged, dove, taking black seas on deck. He could hear the crack of ice as blocks large as dining tables were slammed against the hatch combings and the skin of the ship. Then to yaw, the bow of the vessel sliding some forty feet as if skidding down the side of a steep cliff, then to slip violently as the stern rocketed over the crest of the same sea moving beneath the hull with the speed of an express train. Rising again, head and bow high, as if the whole ship were about to leave that terrible place, then poised there, like a prehistoric wingless bird on the back of the next sea, her screw thrashing the empty air, a shudder so violent passing through the vessel that though the ship was solidly loaded it was felt in every part of her. Settling easily, almost softly, as the screw caught good water and gave the momentary illusion of being on a calm sea—and at this moment she was rammed through the seas, making fifty feet.

Seconds later a new and more intricate pattern of motion began, at the end of which the vessel made another fifty feet.

Cadiz's responses to the movements, his understanding of what was happening to the ship and what was causing it, what would follow, how long it would last, were as much a part of him as his handwriting.

He stood on the wing of the bridge, a good twenty feet from the wheelhouse, and waited for the next roll. Timing it, feeling it in his legs and his body and not seeing it or bothering to look, he stepped off and walked on a flat and level deck the full distance to the wheelhouse door and was inside, braced, waiting when the roll came, snapping the laboring vessel as though it were a branch. He had done this in darkness, without thinking about it.

The air was fogged with cigarette smoke because he was one of the few mates that allowed the helmsman to smoke while at the wheel, remembering the agony of his own two-, three-, and sometimes four-hour wheel tricks without a cigarette, often having his torture made worse when the mate or captain would light up.

The steam-heated room, pitch black except for the dull orange glow of the gyrocompass repeater card, was filled with the odors of body sweat, wet cocoa matting and half-wet, steaming clothes dropped to the deck as the endless changes in the watch took place. Cadiz leaned low in one corner and snapped a match, lighting a cigarette, cupping the flame in his fist and smoking in deep, tasteless drags. The steam radiator clanked, kicked, knocked and went on in a monotonously irritating way. The gyro repeater clicked, clicked again, then took off, running free for fifteen or twenty degrees as the head was slewed about. The helmsman, a delicate, bony-faced, honey-colored Puerto Rican named San Juan, waited braced, watching the gyro card; he saw the head come back, running freely, too freely, and he put the wheel over opposite to check the wild swing and brought the ship on course with a sureness of touch that Cadiz admired. He never checked the course when San Juan was on the wheel.

He lifted the Silex from its snugly fitted place and poured a cup. The coffee was black, acidy and boiled down to a tasteless glue that was hard to swallow.

— Want to take a break, San Juan? Cadiz asked.

— Sí, yes, Mister Mate. You would like coffee?

Cadiz, without answering, moved to his side and handed him the Silex.

San Juan stepped back from the wheel. In a clear voice, he spoke the ritual.

— Steering fifty-one, sir. Five-one.

— Five-one, Cadiz repeated.

In a few moments the slender little man had bundled up and edged out into the bitter cold. Cadiz was alone.

He worked the wheel automatically. Checking her, bringing her back, braced on the wheel-spokes against the heaving vessel, he did not lift his eyes from the gyro light. But at two bells, as five o'clock passed, he glanced involuntarily toward the east, hopeful of gray dawn and clearing. He saw nothing but the orange hole of the gyro light.

Cadiz knew that Captain Sparkle would put great weight on what he had to say when the time came for a decision. He stood at the wheel, running the spokes around in his hands as unconsciously as he would chew gum, growing sleepy in the over-heated room and fighting it, thinking about what he would say when Sparkle put the question to him. Go on? Or turn back?

It would come, that moment of decision, within a very few hours. It would not be long before the steady darkness of the sea and sky, all one now, would separate with a murky, half-mile visibility, and Sparkle would turn to Cadiz for his opinion.

Cadiz was not afraid of the decision. He had learned about decision making and, more important, he had learned the true meaning of decisions. You made them, he thought, and you were either pleased with the results or you were not. But you made them.

A decision was the most meaningful thing a man had to learn to do. A good man or a sorry man could look back over his life at the decisions he had made or avoided and know much of what he was. Some men he had known never learned how to make decisions. By avoiding them, letting life situations meander past them, and surviving, they thought they had made decisions. They had not. And because life goes on, and they go on with it, they deceive themselves into thinking they have made important decisions, when they have made no decisions at all. Others place emphasis on how a man approaches a decision, and attach importance to how the man arrives at his decision. But this is foolish and only parodies the decision, and in the end, robs him of the sweetest, most valuable gift he has.

It is the choosing, and not a man's style, that matters. Style will muddy a clean, hard decision. The style of a man making a decision may even engage all of our attention, but in the end, it adds nothing to the conclusion. A less than stylish man, faced with a hard life-decision, will not be ashamed to go in splay-footed, shaking, fear stabbing, if he finds within himself the courage that no one else need see. The man of courage, and of true style, is the man who makes his decisions, he doesn't care how, and gets on with it.

— It would seem so, Cadiz said, half aloud.

He was finding it almost impossible to keep awake when San Juan returned with fresh coffee. Taking a cup, he left the steaming wheelhouse for his fixed position on the wing of the bridge. He loosened his collar and scarf and let the icy blast reach down and shake him up. The coffee was fresh and thickly rich, and he gulped it down quickly.

Refreshed, as alert as he felt he could be under the circumstances, he scrubbed his face with his knuckles and leaned on the rail and faced the bitter cold. But he could not think clearly. As hard as he tried, he could not get his thoughts to run in logical order; he was too tired, and he knew it. His fatigue stole away at his usual good discipline; the tight dimensions of his world as a sailor kept dissolving and reappearing, and he could not think. His aching tiredness ate at his very being. The cold reached him. His eyelids would not stay up. He grew hot and cold in turn. He fought back, refusing to give in, doggedly hanging on. He rubbed the snow and cold into his cheeks, cruelly, with anger. He would not stand there and dream and remember and reflect. He would not just stand there and search the seas. He would not be dumb with cold. He would not let Sparkle make the decision alone. He was support for the old man. His right hand. He was twenty-five years a sailor and this was not a small thing he had to decide. He hung over the railing, jaw to the wind, defenseless against his fatigue, furious with his body for failing him after ninety hours on his feet, with three one-hour intervals of sleep in between. He stirred. Somewhere in back of him he heard the bells go. Four times. Two and two. Six o'clock. It was still black.

The ship rolled and yawed, slipped and drove through the icy waters. He took a firm grip on the railing and braced, his legs spread, fought for each passing moment, gaining a half minute, then another half minute, then five minutes, then ten.

— Go on below, Howard, son, Sparkle's voice said.

— What? Oh, Jonas! What are you doing here? Go on below. Get some rest.

— You were sleeping, Howard, Sparkle said, nearly yelling in his ear.

— Who?

— You! Hanging over the railing like a dead man. San Juan got scared and sent for help. He was afraid you'd fall over the side or freeze.

— I was not asleep! Cadiz shouted.

— Son, I saw you. I been here three or four minutes. You were sleeping. With your month open. And ice on your lips. Now get below. You're lucky you ain't froze to death!

— What are you going to do? Cadiz asked.

— Whatever I do, you go below right now, Sparkle said.

— Are you turning back?

— I don't know yet.

— I'm not leaving the bridge until I know, Captain.

The ship made a violent snap-roll and they both caught at the railing. When they had waited out the lumbering movement and had straightened up, Cadiz saw that the sky was no longer black, but a queasy gray. It was not unfamiliar. He turned away from Sparkle, who stood clad in a huge bridge coat that swept to his ankles, woolen muffler and sou'wester. He clung to the railing, searching the graying world of their part of the ocean.

— There, Howard! Look! Sparkle yelled, pointing abeam.

— What is it? A hundred and fifty yards away, directly abeam, a submarine, enameled with snow and ice, rode well out of the water, an insolently designed craft whose sole purpose for existence was destruction, an assassin of the seas that hid in murky depths waiting to rise to the surface and fulfill its role as executioner of honest ships. Deception was its character, insidiousness its true nature, infamy its reputation. Cadiz loathed them.

— Hard left! Hard left! Cadiz yelled at San Juan.

On the deck of the submarine there was a flurry of movement as black-suited figures emerged from the side hatches and ran, skidding on the icy decks, to the deck gun. There was a flash of red, like the sudden opening and closing of a giant eyelid, revealing for a split second the evil eye of the killer.

The shell exploded on the lower deck, ripping a lifeboat from its davits, upending it and leaving it to trail over the side. The ship came about sluggishly, was caught abeam by the seas and rolled heavily until the decks were half under a greenish black sea.

Cadiz and Sparkle locked arms around the railing stanchion and hung on. When the ship snapped back on the counter-roll, at the same time being lifted high by a mighty swell, they had elevation for a clear view of the seas. The submarine was no longer there.

The force of the explosion had knocked Sparkle's sou'wester back off his head, and it dangled now down his back, caught at the throat by flannel earflaps and chin choker. His shingle of white hair blew wildly. They each moved at the same time, lunging to the after railing of the bridge, and stared below. Fire had broken through the gaping hole in the steel boat deck, and they could see the jabbing hands and arms of men who had been asleep in the fo'c'sle as they sought to catch hold of something and pull free of the wreckage. The lifeboat burned furiously as side tanks of gasoline in the number one boat, the only one of four that was motorized, leaked out and onto the wooden seats. Through a jagged hole in the bottom of the boat the liquid fire ran in a steady stream into the fo'c'sle and onto the men. A split second before he moved, Cadiz saw a man's whole face and head enveloped in flames.

Cadiz started to follow Sparkle to the boat deck and saw the old man making for a fire hose. He turned back to the wheelhouse, tore open the door and grabbed for the phone.

San Juan stood braced at the wheel. He looked wide-eyed at Cadiz. His legs trembled and his lower jaw jerked up and down in a spasm of uncontrolled terror.

Cadiz spun the telephone handle and yelled at San Juan as he waited for the engine room to answer.

— Keep that wheel over hard left. Keep it coming around until I tell you!

San Juan shook his head dazedly, then bolted for the door. Cadiz dropped the phone and lunged for him, catching his belt. They both fell to the deck as the ship careened back and down from the weight of an overwhelming sea that broke green water over the boat deck. Cadiz found his footing, pulled at San Juan, turning him over and saw the flash of a knife in the sailor's hand. Without thinking, Cadiz lashed out with the back of his hand, clipping the sailor's jaw. He seized the knife hand, twisted the thin arm, and the knife dropped and was immediately lost in the darkness of the heaving deck.

Cadiz righted himself and pulled San Juan to his feet. He slapped him hard across the face and shoved him back into the wheelhouse.

San Juan grabbed for the wheel as though his life depended on it, pulling at the spokes.

Cadiz grabbed for the dangling phone receiver, suddenly aware that there was an increasing noise in his ears, started to spin the handle and realized that the phone was ringing. He depressed the talk button.

— Hello! Hello! Goddammit, bridge! Answer, bridge! The chief engineer's voice rose to a shrill pitch in Cadiz's ear. Will somebody answer me! What's going on up there? Bridge! Bridge!

— Shut up, you goddam fucking idiot, Cadiz yelled into the phone.

— Cadiz! For God's sake, what is it—

— Shut up.

— Don't let us die down here.

— Shut up! Cadiz yelled again. Shut up and listen! We've been shelled by a sub.

— What? I can't hear you.

— We've been shelled by a submarine! But he's made his dive.

— Is it bad?

— Goddam bad! Listen, I want every turn you can get out of the engines.

— *What happened?*

Cadiz glanced at San Juan. The boy seemed to be pulling himself together. There was a burst of flame from the boat deck and someone started yelling. The chief was yammering in the phone again.

— Cadiz! For Christ sake tell me what's going on!

— I'll tell you just one thing, you stupid bastard. We've been shelled by a submarine. He's made his dive and he's going to try and find us and then give us one right up the ass, and I want every bit of steam you can get put to the shaft! You hear that?

— But—

— Goddammit, do you hear me? Open the bypass, I've got to get this ship moving. If we have to go over the side in this weather, we won't last five minutes. You understand that?

— Yes, I understand. What do you want me to do?

— Give me steam, all you've got. And stand by.

—Cadiz—

—What is it!

—Will you try to warn us, if you can?

—I'll do what I can, chief.

—Okay.

Cadiz hung up the phone and turned to San Juan. He took him by the jaw, pinching it, and spun his head around and looked into the man's eyes against the pale light of the flames that were slowly falling back on the boat deck. San Juan's eyes were clear. There was a draining cut on his cheek and a smear of blood over his brow.

—You all right now?

—Sí, I am all right, Mister Mate, San Juan replied in a small thin voice. Sí, okay. Hard left all the time. Hard over.

—Howard! Sparkle's voice ripped into the wheelhouse, and the old man staggered inside. His hair was plastered with water and the sou'wester still hung down his back.

—Are you all right? Cadiz asked. What's the damage?

—Howard!

—What is it? Are you all right?

—We lost the bosun over the side. He was there, hanging onto the railing, trying to clear away something so we could get the hose into the hole and on the fire, and he just fell backward and over the side.

Cadiz felt his throat close.

—I tried to do something, Sparkle said in a strangled voice. He was there, and then he wasn't. I saw him falling backward. He didn't even yell. I didn't hear him hit the water—the wind.

—Jonas, listen to me, Cadiz said decisively. We've only got one chance and that's to run from it.

—Yes, run.

—I'm bringing her about. We'll take everything astern and run before the sea.

—Yes, that's what we have to do, Sparkle said.

Cadiz started back for the compass and then the ship was lifted high with a sea and twisted like a cork and slammed back down again. The ship shuddered. He hung onto the doorframe and waited for her to break her back. Fore and aft the ship wrenched at the keel and the welded seams. Stresses were applied that nothing on the seas could withstand, flooding green water to the boat deck as the vessel and the sea fought each other. There was a sharp cracking sound like a pistol shot, and it was an instant before Cadiz realized that he had heard the parting of a welded seam.

— Amidships! Cadiz yelled, still hanging onto the doorframe. Check her! Check her!

— 'Midships! San Juan called in reply and pulled the wheel around, feeling the turn indicator with his hand, and feeling for the amidships spoke with the Turk's Head laced to the handle, then, finding it, checking the turn indicator that the wheel was centered, and two quick turns to the right. Half-right! San Juan yelled at Cadiz and Sparkle. Checking! Checking!

— Make your course sou'west! Two-two-two! Cadiz shouted, aware that now, with the wind and seas astern, they were in a pocket in the wheelhouse below the stack.

— Two-two-two! San Juan replied.

— Hold that until I change it! Cadiz ordered. He turned to Sparkle. You all right?

Sparkle nodded.

— Stay on the bridge, Cadiz said. I'll check below. She might be breaking up on us.

Sparkle seemed to come out of his stupor. He shook his head violently and went outside with Cadiz.

— There ain't a goddam thing I can do up here. I'm going with you.

— Let's go, Cadiz said, and they both plunged out of the wheelhouse to the boat deck ladder. The instant they were free of the windbreak on the bridge, the wind and sea spray drove in and tore at their faces. Blindly, Cadiz fought his way down the ladder, feeling with his feet and hands, and then reached the flat surface of the boat deck. He stepped on something soft and giving. He looked down and saw a man he did not recognize, who lay washing in the seas. There was something odd about the body, and then he realized that the man did not have a face, only a bloody pulp that gleamed whitely with bone now exposed to the eye of the world for the first time.

It was gray enough, light enough, for Sparkle and Cadiz to see their way below. The sun had risen, but far above the storm, not here below. Cadiz could see the ship and the sky above and the grayness of the ship's decks and housing made more gray by the dawn and the sea spray mists of the December North Atlantic. As he walked, with Captain Sparkle at his side and a little behind him, he realized with a sharp pang of despair that he had been living in this gray world all of his life.

The ship was driven forward. They ran before the seas and the wind, pushed by the surge of power from the engines that gave pressure to the canted propeller blades. They were fleeing the enemy in the underworld.

Below, in the midship housing, men were screaming, some in pain, some in hysteria. They milled in the narrow companionways, bumping into each other, clutching possessions, fighting over life jackets. The fiddley door was open, and the cries and shouts of the engineers and men below in the boiler room and engine room were like the squeaks of mice, dominated by the roar of the driving shaft, rods, pistons, the hissing of desperate steam and power.

Cadiz and Sparkle pushed through the mob to the gaping hole in the fo'c'sle. Green seas washed in, knocking Cadiz down. He was cold to the bone almost instantly. The foamy salt water receded out of the hole like surf on a beach.

Somewhere above him he heard Sparkle's voice, like a whip, getting the men under control. He regained his feet and wheeled, grabbing a man by the shoulders and shoving him into the hole and fo'c'sle.

— The wounded, Cadiz shouted. We've got to get the wounded!

— There *ain't* no wounded! the man yelled, and tried to break free.

Cadiz, his hands beginning to stiffen from the cold, could not hold the man, who succeeded in wrenching away and ran, stumbling, down the companionway.

Clinging to the doorframe, Cadiz waited until the ship rolled and the seas had spilled out, then stepped inside. The bulkhead between the two fo'c'sles had been ripped from the welded seams and lay flat to one side. He saw the naked body of a man, face down under the steel plate. He had no more time to look, for the ship rolled then and he turned, grasping a bunk railing that had not been completely torn free of its moorings, and turned his back to the seas and held on, taking a deep breath and closing his mouth and eyes as the force of the water hit him.

He was torn free of his handhold as easily as a matchstick is broken, but there was no need for holding onto anything. The incredible force of water slammed him face forward against a bulkhead and pinned him there. He was as secure in the grip of the sea, hanging him there on the side of the bulkhead, as if he were enclosed within a steel box. He no longer felt the cold. As he waited for the wall of water to let him down, he kept thinking that he had to get dry clothes on or he would freeze to death.

When the ship rolled and the water spilled out, he lunged, gripping the railing of the bunk. The ship was twisted so far over that he looked straight up into the overcast, dead gray world of the sky.

Someone clutched him by the arm and pulled him through the door and into the companionway. The man shouted something in his ear.

Cadiz shook his head, not understanding.

— She's cracking up! She's breaking her back! the man shouted.

Cadiz pushed the man to one side. It made no difference what the ship was doing, if he did not get dry, he would be dead in fifteen minutes, or so cold that he would be unable to move. His legs were like massive tree trunks that he somehow had to move. His arms felt as though they weighed a ton each. His mouth burned. His eyes were filled with salt and oil scum, and his vision was blurred. He felt his stomach muscles begin to cramp as his body fought off the cold.

He dragged himself upward, blindly, feeling along the side of the ship, holding onto the railing that ran around the engine room well, and began to pull himself forward. Men pushed and shoved him, but he kept going, a foot at a time, groping for handholds on the railing and forcing his fingers around the steel. He knew that he did not have much time. He pressed on faster: he kicked something but could not see what it was and did not care.

He gained the ladder and started climbing; there was only one deck above him, and then his cabin. He wanted to stop on the officers' deck. He wanted to stand, hold the railing and catch his breath.

— No! he shouted inwardly. No! You've only got five min

He staggered down the short companionway to his banged it open. The light was on. He stood, seeing it as l… it—calm, only a few things swinging in the roll of the ship. There was a book on the deck. It slid back and forth as the ship moved.

He could not use his fingers at all. He tried to pull at a button but it would not go through the hole. He pulled open a drawer and felt for his knife, and slowly, braced against the bulkhead, he cut himself out of his clothes. He was beginning to drowse by the time he was stripped. Suddenly he was thrown against the opposite bulkhead by a sudden roll of the ship.

He shook himself. He lunged to his locker and pulled the door back and found an unopened bottle of bourbon. He snapped the head off with a whip motion of his arm against the edge of the desk, held the bottle to his mouth and poured the liquid down his throat and over his face and body. He spilled much of it. Leaning against the locker, forcing his muscles with the last of his strength, he began to massage himself. He worked on his arms and shoulders and his legs and stomach. Slowly, methodically, not feeling anything in his hands, he rubbed himself with as much strength as he had.

He moved then, with a burning sensation in his stomach that he recognized as the bourbon, and began to dress. They might yet have to put the boats over, and he was going to be prepared. He pulled on two suits of underwear, two pairs of socks, wool serge suit trousers and seaboots. He added his warmest sweater, then a thick fleece bridge coat and, feeling the first signs of pain returning to his numbed fingers and toes he pulled a second bottle of bourbon from the locker, opened it carefully and took a long drink.

He concentrated on his dressing, putting his oilskin trousers with overall bib over his trousers and seaboots, then pulled on the jacket, snapping it closed. He put on a watchcap, pulling it down over his ears, then a sou'wester, and took out his best pair of gloves.

The pain in his hands and feet was beginning to reach him now, and he took another shot of bourbon. When he could manage it, he began to jump up and down while he rubbed his fingers, pouring bourbon from the bottle into his palm and washing his hands in it.

When his teeth stopped chattering and he could feel the intense ache in his jaw muscles where he had been involuntarily clenching his teeth against the cold, he knew he would be all right.

He opened the door. Captain Sparkle stood in the companionway, arguing with a sailor. He saw Cadiz step out of his room.

— Howard! My God, son! I thought you was drowned! Sparkle took several quick steps toward Cadiz, his face beet red from the cold. I thought you was washed over the side when you went into that fo'c'sle. I saw you washed over by that sea and then I didn't see you again. I thought you was gone!

The ship lurched, hard, and the deck seemed to drop away beneath them. Both Sparkle and the sailor, one of the A.B.'s, scrabbled for a handhold. Cadiz threw his foot up and braced himself against the opposite bulkhead.

— Are we still running before the weather? Cadiz asked.

— I don't know! Christ, how the fuck would I know? He turned back to the captain. Dammit captain, we we going to abandon ship or not?

— Now, Dorrence, just a minute. I thought the chief mate—Sparkle looked from Cadiz to the A.B. But now that he's—

— Screw the chief mate, the A.B. said. Are we going to abandon ship?

Cadiz stepped in quickly and struck Dorrence in the face with the palm of his hand. Before the man could recover, Cadiz took him by the front of his shirt and slammed him up against the bulkhead, pinning him there with the weight of his own body.

— Dorrence, I'll kill you, so help me, I'll kill you if I ever hear you speak to an officer aboard this ship like that again.

The A.B. tried to bring up his knee and Cadiz slapped him again, using the heel of his hand.

— I mean it, Dorrence, Cadiz gritted through his teeth. Now take an easy strain.

The ship heaved, down and over and up, buckling their knees as if they were on a powerful express elevator. Cadiz let the A.B. crumple to the deck.

— Get below, Dorrence, Cadiz said. The man struggled to his feet, fighting the action of the deck.

— But—

— *Now!*

Dorrence scrambled sideways, crab-like, to the ladder and disappeared. Cadiz turned to Sparkle.

— I don't know what's the matter, Howard. I couldn't seem to get going. I—Sparkle looked up, searching Cadiz's face.

— Don't worry about it.

— But I don't know—I don't know—

— Have you checked the damage? Cadiz asked.

— Yes, I did that. She's got a pretty big hole there—

— Where? Cadiz cut in. Both of them had to grasp the handrail as the ship plummeted again.

— Well, there in the fo'c'sle, of course.

— Is it into the engine room housing? Cadiz asked.

— The skin's cracked. Bad. Goddam bad, Sparkle said. Good God, son, when I thought you were washed over the side like the bosun up there on the boat deck—

— Is the crack on a seam, Cadiz cut in, or in the middle of the plate?

— No—no—not on a seam.

— You're sure? Cadiz demanded.

— I'm sure. They're getting a little spill into the engine room.

— Is it serious?

— No, the pumps will take care of it, but I don't know how long she'll take this pounding, Howard.

— All right, Jonas, Cadiz said. Go back to the bridge. Bring her about. Don't strain her. Get her back into the weather and hold her there. And send out our position.

— Send out our position, Sparkle said.

— Send it out, Cadiz repeated. Mayday—SOS—right flat out on the five hundred frequency and have that fucking Sparks send it out every two minutes until I tell him to stop.

— Is it that bad, Howard? Sparkle asked. That's like giving up, Howard. I wouldn't want to do that unless we had to.

— Jonas, we have to, Cadiz said.

Sparkle's shoulders sagged.

— All right, Howard, but—

— Have you got a gun? Cadiz asked.

— Gun? Why, no, what would I need a gun—

— Get one. And shoot the first man that comes up on the bridge. Don't fire a warning shot, just shoot him dead.

— Captain Sparkle! a voice shrilled below them. They both turned and saw the Navy gunnery officer climbing the ladder. He wore his life jacket, red signal light, whistle, knife, all jangling against his oilskins. He had forced his sou'wester down over his bridge hat, and the gold braid had been slung under his chin. He was red-faced and his eyes were too bright.

Cadiz turned on him. What do you want?

— We have to coordinate—

— Get your ass below, Cadiz said, before I throw you below.

— Now see here, you can't—

— I can, Cadiz said. Now get the fuck *below.*

The gunnery officer stood his ground. He glared at Sparkle, ignoring Cadiz. I will not order my men over the side without lowering the boats, and if your men won't do it, mine will. And we can't do it running before the weather—

Cadiz took him by the shoulder and shoved him backward to the head of the ladder. The gunnery officer tried to find a handhold and could not; Cadiz held him suspended above the chasm of the ladder hole.

— Listen you stupid fuckhead ribbon clerk, Cadiz yelled, you're not in the Navy now.

— Let go of me! I demand—

— You're aboard *my ship.* And you do as I say or I will throw your ass over the side.

— I'm an officer in the United States Naval Reserve and I demand—

— *You're aboard my fucking ship,* Cadiz roared. Do you understand that, you miserable sonofabitch?

— But—

— And you tell those Kansas shitkickers in your gun crew that if one—just *one* of them makes a move toward the boats I'll shoot his balls off.

The gunnery officer started to fumble for his sidearm. Cadiz waited until he got the pistol out of the holster and then wrenched it out of his hand, at the same time pushing the officer down the ladder backward and into the arms of the men crowded below.

—Get going, Jonas, Cadiz said. And remember what I said to you.

—About the gun?

Cadiz put a hand on the old man's arm. It's going to be all right, Jonas. I'll get you back to that rocker and your Bible—you'll see.

Sparkle looked at him expressionlessly.

—You can't beat that, can you, Jonas?

—No. Sparkle turned away. The ship dropped sickeningly and rolled sideways, throwing those at the foot of the ladder to one side and leaving the lower companionway momentarily free. Cadiz pushed his legs forward and out, gripping the handrails, and slid down the ladder on his palms. He faced the crew.

—Anybody want to argue with my authority? he asked. He held the gun straight down at his side.

No one moved. The gunnery officer stood in front of the men, half Navy and half merchant crew.

—There's a Nazi submarine out there, Cadiz said, watching their faces, alert for any movement that would signal a rush at him. He's got everything on his side. He's wounded us and he intends to finish us off.

The men muttered amongst themselves and there was a sudden general movement toward Cadiz. Cadiz brought the gun up and fired into one of the wooden doors leading to the messroom. The men ducked and froze.

With quarterdeck command in his voice, Cadiz said, You have a choice of facing me now, or the sub later. Any man who doesn't do exactly as I tell him will be shot.

He studied their faces again. They were listening to him.

—Haven't we got any chance at all, Mister Cadiz? one of the men asked.

—Sure, Cadiz said. If he suddenly blows himself up, or if he forgot to close the hatch of his conning tower.

—There must be something we can do, Mister Cadiz?

—There is, Cadiz said, nailing it down, looking at the gunnery officer, and I'm doing it.

— What is that, if I may ask? the gunnery officer said.

— I'm keeping shitheads like you from going over the side in an open boat where you'll freeze to death in fifteen minutes if you get wet.

— What the hell are the Navy guys here for if not to fight back? Dorrence complained. Let 'em get their ass up there on the guns instead of hanging around down here.

— Why should the sub come up for surface action, Cadiz replied, when all he has to do is sit on our tail and any time he wants put a torpedo up our hocks and go on about his business?

Cadiz noticed that the ship had begun to have a steady, predictable roll and pitch and knew that Sparkle had gotten her up into the weather. He looked at the faces before him. They waited, shorn of their mob courage, each man intent now on Cadiz.

— I've sent out our position, Cadiz said in a more deliberate voice, and with an offhand gesture stuck the gun into his coat pocket. The Navy will be along soon to give us help, escort us back inside, or pick up survivors.

— Do you think they could get here fast enough to get the sub, Mister Cadiz? Childers asked.

— I doubt it, Cadiz said. He straightened up. Okay! That's the story. We can get it any time now, because we're back into the weather. She can't take the pounding that running away would give her because of the hole in her skin. She might snap in two and we'd be up the same shit creek. You—Cadiz pointed to the gunnery officer—get your men to their gun positions and keep them there. Every man with a life jacket, ready to go over the side if we get hit. I want the merchant crew, including the black gang and everybody not on watch, except the steward and chief cook, to get their foul-weather gear and life jackets on and come with me. Steward!

— Right here, Mistuh Mate.

— Sandwiches and coffee. Make as much as you'll need for two, three days.

— Yes, suh. The steward, a tall, thick-necked Negro with sad eyes, touched his cap and nodded. Let's go, first cook.

— Now remember, Cadiz said, suddenly shouting at them with a ferocity that made several of them jump, *it's going to happen!* Now, today, tonight or tomorrow. He might not wait for the weather to ease. In this weather he could come alongside and shove the thing up our ass with his fingers, and we wouldn't be able to do a thing about it. The only chance we have is to stay on board as long as we can and make it a shorter time we have to spend in the boats. Now, you've got to stay *dry!* That's the key to the next piece of ass you've been dreaming about. Or the next bottle of booze, or getting back to your farm. *Stay dry!* Any man who gets wet reports to me for *permission* to change clothes.

They waited. There was no sign of the submarine. The Navy gunners stood their watches, bundled to the teeth in their foul-weather gear, their life jackets barely fitting around the bulk of their clothes. The merchant crew waited in companionways and in the crew mess and on the bridge. Every man nervously scanned the gray and furious seas. The clouds raced overhead, boiling and churning. The seas ran black, except for the white-crested caps. Wind scooped up the spume and sent it flying against the ship. Spray stung exposed skin like pellets of hail. The ship plunged, heaved, rolled, snapped and hurled itself forward.

There was nothing left for Cadiz to do. Every man was ready and the ship was ready and the boats were ready. They hung there on the skim of a raging ocean and waited for the death blow to fall. No one talked. They drank coffee and ate sandwiches and sucked on cigarettes and waited for their execution. They huddled, jamming the hatchways. Shrouded in their fear, they were lonely and tried to express this and could not. They tried to imagine themselves safe and sound ashore and could not. They tried to escape the present terror, seeking a world of their own making and could not. They wanted to be someplace else, or another person, or in another time, and they could not.

They were not soldiers. They listened to the wind and the seas and the hundred whines, stresses, strains and groans of the ship in that churning sea, and waited.

They knew all there was for a sailoring man to know about wind and water and weather, about how cargo should be loaded and how to fight the ocean, but they did not know anything about submarines or torpedo attacks or gunfire. What did this have to do with being a sailor? If they had wanted to be soldiers, they would have joined the Army. They raged helplessly. The only thing that prevented them from becoming a mob was their helplessness. No inner faith saved them from their terror. There was no direction or guidance except that of Howard Cadiz. So Cadiz became their faith. But one of them went mad. It took six men to subdue him. Cadiz had him bound tightly and placed near a hatch next to the lifeboats with two men standing over him. The man screamed and cursed for an hour; it was so unnerving that Cadiz had to give him a shot of morphine to quiet him.

Some of the younger ones cried. Others vomited. In the close quarters the stench became overpowering. Cadiz made them wash down, breaking out the fire hoses.

Four hours had passed since the boats were checked. The excruciating wait for the submarine to attack began to produce the first signs of a breakdown in discipline. Waiting for this, expecting it, Cadiz was on top of it at once. He put down three fights. Only one of them was a gut fight. A fireman was cut severely on one arm.

At noon that day, with still no attack from the submarine, their tense irritability quieted by the simple process of doing nothing. When the watches were changed, several of the men moved off to lie down in their bunks. A few still remained at the hatchways, but in general the stunning fear was dulled. For nearly seven hours they had waited. Their minds could no longer dwell on their own deaths. After hours of minute-by-minute tension, they had not yet been killed. They moved with the conviction that they had been spared. As much as Cadiz would allow, the ship quietly returned, under his steadying influence, to a semblance of normality.

At four that afternoon there was a slight break in the weather. The gray clouds dispersed and a path of unusually deep blue sky showed overhead; the sun streamed down on the dirty sea and picked up the droplets of spray, making them glisten. As quickly as it had come, the clearing was gone, and within a half hour they were returned to the ugly world of the North Atlantic midwinter. Cadiz climbed wearily to the bridge.

— Jonas? Do you know why we haven't been hit yet?

— I've been thinking about that since noon, Howard. He's been waiting for us to join up with a convoy. He's been hoping to get more than just us.

— He's not going to trail us anymore, Cadiz said. We could lose him in the night and he knows it. So—

— We oughta be getting it any time now, Sparkle said.

— I'll get them up, Cadiz said, and turned to the wheelhouse. He walked to the switch and rang the general alarm. Within seconds he heard the men cursing and running.

It was in the last moments of the clearing sky that the submarine, which had been lying well astern on the starboard quarter all day, pressed in for the attack. The first torpedo was wide of the mark; Cadiz spotted its wake. He and Sparkle watched as it broke clear of the waves. He did not see the torpedo that hit the ship. The explosion came just aft of the five hold. There were two explosions, and Cadiz heard them distinctly and knew that the magazine for the Navy gun on the stern had been hit. He saw four Navy gunners thrown high into the air and then into the sea; the gun itself was sent crashing below, into the steering-gear room. The Navy slept aft, above decks in a makeshift wartime stern housing. He knew there was no chance of anyone surviving.

— The screw and the steering gear are probably gone, Jonas, Cadiz shouted. We've had it.

— I'm too tired to care, Howard. Sparkle hung onto the railing, looking aft. Men poured out of the hatchways toward the boats.

— It's going to be cold in the boats tonight, Sparkle said. I hope that the SOS on the five hundred does some good. God, I'm tired Howard, son.

— Get into the boat, Jonas, Cadiz said, then made his way to the wheelhouse. San Juan, back on wheel-watch again, clung to the wheel and looked up at Cadiz. He was now quite calm.

— Get in the boats, Cadiz said. He picked up the phone and rang the engine room.

— All right, chief, get the hell out of there.

— That bad, huh, Howard?

— We're going down, Cadiz said simply.

He figured four hours in the boats. Not more. And if anyone got wet, maybe ninety minutes. Not more.

Something exploded somewhere below on the sinking ship and then he felt his back and left arm ripped and torn. San Juan was thrown clear and over the side. He never saw him again. The warm blood flowed down into his glove. The force of the blow on his left side threw him against the wheel, and he managed to grab one of the spokes and hold himself upright. There was a series of sharp reports, and for a moment he thought it was someone firing a machine gun, or perhaps Navy ammunition going off, but he heard a wrenching noise and knew then that it was the steel lashings on the deck cargo letting go. He was reluctant to go into the boats to die. If he remained where he was it would be over soon. He stood clinging to the wheel.

The wound began to pain him. The pain grew, but, like loneliness, it was something he had long ago learned to deal with.

— Don't, he said to himself, let everything go at once. If it comes while you're doing your job, then let it come. But don't, *don't,* let everything go at once.

He shoved away from the wheel and limped to the watch desk where he fumbled in the dark for the rough cardboard surface of the pencil log. He shoved it into the breast pocket of his coat. Then he took the code book and slipped it into his side pocket. He dragged himself to the door.

The cold stung him awake and he braced himself. He swung for the ladder and the boat deck below. Instinct, training, his pure professionalism responded when his eye caught the mistake they were making.

— Get that fucking painter outside those falls! he roared. Outside of everything. You'll never pull away. Get the painter outside of *everything—*

Good God, he thought as he sank to the deck, his consciousness oozing from him, was there to be no more?

The ship began to settle at the stern.

May 1943

Each time the train lurched, he would extend his left hand and lean with his palm flat against the wall and wait for the train to run smoothly again. At such moments he looked as if he might still be in pain, but the pain was all but gone now. He could remember it, though. His hands still trembled, but that and a little stiffness in the shoulder were all that reminded him of his experience.

They're getting better, he thought, regarding his hands. I would never have believed that I would find pleasure in shaving myself again. But I do. You're going to be all right.

He worked carefully around his lip, shaving slowly because he hated nicking himself. It occurred to him that shaving himself was the first thing he had cared about in a long time. His hospital pallor and the thinness of his arms made his hands seem bigger than they really were. Yes, he thought, they are definitely getting steadier.

The train lurched again. He held onto the sides of the basin with both hands, head down, an air of solemn gravity and patience in his attitude.

A welt of red, thick ridged and ugly, ran down from his left armpit and then was hidden by his undershirt. Hanging on the wall was a blue serge uniform jacket that looked new; four bright gold stripes gleamed on the sleeve. Over this was a white shirt and a black tie. A peaked bridge hat with a snow white cover, also fresh looking, hung on a hook nearby.

Cadiz dressed and staggered out to the companionway in jerky rhythm with the train.

— Savannah! This station is Savannah! the porter announced.

He was the first to get off. He started walking toward the station, down past the dirty, silvered coaches, glancing up now and then to see a face staring down at him; walking slowly toward a grillwork barrier that separated the loading platforms from the waiting rooms. People pressed in on him and once he had gotten to the station he stood still and waited for the crowd to thin. He wanted to sit down but he knew there was no place except inside the waiting room, and the crowd was between him and it. He did not have the strength to push his way through. He stood still, conserving his energy, and waited.

It was a full wartime scene, one that he had observed many times the past few years. People arriving and people departing, people laughing and people crying. Three fourths of the crowd, men and women, were in service uniforms. The accents jangled harshly on his ears. Naturally, he thought, they send the Georgia boys to Vermont, the Vermont boys to Kansas, and the Kansas boys to Savannah.

He gradually worked his way to the wide marble steps and sat down. It would be some time yet, he knew, before his luggage would come up from the train. He was in no hurry. He lit a cigarette and studied the ebb and flow around him. The station, he thought, is the same. Blackened and sooty from a thousand trains puffing in and out every year for—how many years? At least fifty. Two yellow cabs, their drivers in the two car wells that reminded him of a sally port in a European fortress. The same as ever. The two cabs were rapidly filled with soldiers and sailors and their luggage.

— Where yawl goin'? East side? Nex' cab, please suh. Ahm goin' to the south side. Yes, mam, they'll be another one along directly.

Cadiz watched and listened and remembered. It was all so much the same. Why should you have expected any change, he wondered. He leaned against the balustrade, conserving his energy. The change is in you.

He looked at his watch, and then up through the transom at the edge of the station roof to the sky. It was five-forty-five. If he were at sea, he thought, he would be standing on the wing of the bridge readying his sextant, searching the blue to graying heavens for his star. Not even six o'clock in the morning. It was much too early to call the office and find out where the ship was tied up. Nine o'clock would be the earliest. Three hours. He had his papers and knew the name, the *Thomas Moonlight,* and he could get a cab and search her down. Savannah was not New York or London or Baltimore where a ship could be in any one of three dozen places as much as thirty miles apart. He could find it, but he preferred to wait.

— Captain?

A porter was pointing at a truck full with luggage in the process of being unloaded.

— Which one's yours, suh?

Cadiz handed over the checks.

— The two black ones on the bottom.

— I see 'um, yes, suh.

The porter was careful not to scuff the bags as he fished them out.

— There you are, captain suh.

— Where could I get a drink this early in the morning, porter? he asked.

— Cap'n, six o'clock in the morning is bad enough, but six o'clock *Sunday* morning . . . Naw, suh. I'm 'fraid not.

— Is today Sunday?

— Yes, suh. It sho' is.

— Sunday, the captain said. I didn't know.

— Sunday, yes, suh. You might jest be able to get one of them bellhops to the hotels uptown to get you a little something. It cost you though, captain. Savannah is a hard town on Sunday.

There was almost no hope, he knew, of finding the office open. Not on Sunday in Savannah. Even a war would not change the habits of this city. They went to church on Sunday in Savannah. And they went all day. If not in fact, then in spirit. All of which meant that if he wanted to get to the ship that day he would have to track her down. The prospect of spending several hours looking for the *Moonlight* was not appealing, but he could rest and sleep once he got aboard. And he wanted to sleep. He was beginning to feel the effects of the sleepless night on the train now that he was alone and inside the tomblike station. He had to have some rest. He looked up. The porter was waiting, looking vaguely away, shifting his weight from foot to foot.

He reached for his wallet. The easiest thing would be to go to a hotel. But six o'clock Sunday morning, he thought, sorting out the facts, a weekend in a city filled with war workers and service people . . . Not a chance. Even the Saturday night one-timers wouldn't check out until noon.

He extracted a dollar from his wallet and handed it to the porter. The bill disappeared in the large palm and the porter dipped his head.

— Captain, suh, if you go to the Arrowsmith Hotel and ask for

Fats, he's the bell cap'n there, he might be able to fix you up with somethin' to drink.

— Do you think he could get me a room?

— He's a mighty slick man, that Fats, the porter said, smiling.

— I'll give you another dollar if you will call your friend Fats and find out if he can get me a room. If he can, and I do get a room, there's five more for you and ten for him.

— I call right now, Cap'n. If it can be done, he do it. Why don't you go on inside and have yourself a cup of coffee, suh, and I come and tell you.

The captain staggered and groped for the balustrade.

— You all right, suh?

— Yes, I'm all right, Cadiz said. I'll wait inside, as you suggested. He turned and started up the stairs to the waiting room. He turned back.

— I take care of your bags, suh, the porter said, anticipating Cadiz's instructions.

— All right, Cadiz said. Tell your friend, tell him—

— Tell him what, suh?

— Tell your friend that I'm an old Savannah boy. Tell him I would very much appreciate whatever he can do for me.

— You a Savannah boy, you say.

— Yes, Liberty Square.

— Cap'n, the porter said, you get yourself a cuppa coffee. I'm goin' get you that room, *an'* a bottle. What you drink, suh?

— Anything. Scotch.

— Scotch. Scotch. Go get your coffee, suh. I be along directly. And never you mind about your bags. I got 'em.

— What's your name?

— Goldsmith, suh.

— Ever know a colored man named Hessian?

— Hessian? The porter opened his eyes wide. Why, that's my friend Fats I tell you about, Cap'n suh. You know Hessian?

Cadiz closed his eyes. He's alive! *Alive!* He swayed and had to reach for the balustrade again.

— He is, he was, many years ago, one of my closest friends.

— An' your name, suh?

— Howard Cadiz.

— Goodgodamighty! the porter breathed softly. You Mister Caydeez, the bootleg man?

— You know about me?

— That Hessian! That Fats. He don' talk about nothin' but you. To everybody. The porter's voice was quietly excited and somewhat awed.

He threaded his way through the clutter of baggage, feet, legs and wandering children in the waiting room, arriving at the swing doors only a moment before he thought he would vomit. Outside, he gasped for air. He looked up and saw a woman approaching him. He was stunned for a second, at the same time realizing that it could not possibly be Agnes because she would be older now—and changed, as he was changed. A closer look as the woman, tall and almost as blond as Agnes, came toward him carrying a vanity in one hand and a spring coat over the other arm. She glanced at him, then brushed past him into the station.

Cadiz closed his eyes again. It clouded down on him. A ghost. But she would be older, he assured himself, older as he was older, and it is not likely that he would recognize her.

He opened his eyes and blinked into the six o'clock light of a quiet Savannah morning. West Broad Street was empty.

He lit a cigarette and studied the empty street and thought about being in Savannah again. It had all happened so quickly. A close friend in War Shipping Administration had called him at the hospital and asked if he wanted a ship, loaded and ready to sail. The ship was in Savannah, where her captain had been taken unexpectedly ill. This ship was his if he wanted it and was physically up to it. The Marine Hospital on Staten Island had really wanted to keep him another two weeks. They gave their certification reluctantly, and then only after he had shown up so well in the examination. The only thing that worried the doctors was his lack of strength. But he put pressure on them to let him go. The ship was a take it or leave it proposition, and he was weary of the hospital.

Well, he thought, Ulrica in Hyde Park and Agnes here in Savannah on a wild bootleg party. One was a domestic trap who wanted to play house and the other was a free wheeling playgirl, but they were both yours, and whatever they were, for whatever time, it was as close to love, as close to having *something* as he had ever had. Two times.

— You're a lucky man, Cadiz, he said to himself with a harshness that was less cynical than honest. Two times. Some only get one. And you got two.

— Cap'n Cay-deez, suh? You all right? The porter was back with a cab.

— Yes, yes, I'm all right.

— Fats say for you to come right down, suh, the porter said. And I got you this heah cab. An' yo' bags is inside. Just go right on down to the Arrowsmith Hotel and Fats meet you, suh. The porter grinned. He jump right down my throat when I said it was you. He is one excited man. He waitin' for you, suh.

— Goldsmith, isn't it?

— Yas, suh, the porter said.

— Thank you, Goldsmith.

— Captain Cay-deez, Fats say to tell you everything be *waitin'*.

They rode through the still sleeping city. Cadiz slowly became aware of the hostility of the cab driver who had watched stonily when Cadiz had shaken hands with the porter and thanked him for his help.

They passed down the street where he had once lived. He looked at the house as they went by. It had a worn-out look and he could not tell if there was anyone living there or not. At the next corner, as the cab slowed for a light and came to a stop, he peered intently at the corner. He and Shad had once stood there until one in the morning on a chilling January night talking about the American Revolution. Both of them had devoured their fourth-grade history books the first day of the new semester.

Before the cab reached the next corner, the names out of his past began to drop into his mind again, like drops of warm summer rain falling to a hot pavement.

He tried to blank them out as he had been trying to do all night. From the moment he had stepped aboard the train in New York and knew he was returning to Savannah, the names had been plaguing him.

— I've been ashore too long, he muttered aloud. Got to get back to sea.

— You said something? the driver asked.

Cadiz did not answer.

Inexorably, the names continued: Solly, Chocolate, Rufus, Sammy Kortner. Had he ever known anyone named Sammy Kortner? Lainy. Alfred S. DeCunningham, and Kolb, Danner, Bernice, Clyde West, Herod—Agnes—Agnes-Agnes . . .

— Of course, Cadiz said aloud, I'm still weak.

The driver turned and glanced at him. Sean Cadiz, Bowdry Calvert. Colbert, Dolly. Beau Cadiz. Aunt Meg . . . The names were all around him.

Elly Whitcomb, Captain White, Leon Tenderling, Sara Whitcomb, Boris. Sharkey. Jernegan. *Sparkle!* A blind and senseless rush of names, some accompanied with a scene, a snatch of conversation, a word, an expression around the eyes or a tightening around the mouth; names flooded through his mind.

The cab pulled to a stop and there in the window was the smiling face of Hessian.

They stood on the sidewalk in front of the hotel in the quiet morning, wordless, looking at each other, seeing the changes. Hessian was a hundred pounds heavier; Cadiz was weak and pale and thin.

— Mister Cadiz, it's been a long time.

— I never thought I'd see you again, Hessian, Cadiz said gently. I thought you were dead. If I hadn't thought so, I would never have left you.

— I thought I was dead, too, Mister Cadiz, Hessian said, smiling. When I woke up, I wondered if I wasn't dead. But the pain brought me back and I knew I wasn't.

— You were so still, lying there in the cornfield. I saw two holes in your chest and you weren't moving or breathing.

— I managed to crawl out of there and find a place, Hessian said. I crawled all night, clear across that cornfield and through the swamp. Then I found this place and a woman took care of me.

— I would never have left you, Hessian, if I had thought you were alive.

— It bothered me for a while, Mister Cadiz. But when I got to thinking about it—years later, I mean—I realized that's what you must have thought.

— I didn't know you were still alive until a half hour ago at the station, Cadiz said, still holding Hessian by the hand.

— I know, Mister Cadiz. Come on inside. I got everything set up for you. A two-room suite, hot coffee and two quarts of my best Scotch. I'm a kind of a bootlegger still. I cadge a few bottles here and there and then sell 'em to the guests. Hessian chuckled, lifting his hand to his mouth as Cadiz remembered him doing, snuffling at his nose. That Goldsmith, he said bourbon, but I remembered you as a Scotch man.

The cab driver stood to one side, having put the bags on the sidewalk.

— How much? Cadiz asked.

— Two dollars, the driver said. Then he turned his head and spat on the sidewalk.

Cadiz handed him the money. The driver took it and folded the bills over his forefinger and tucked them into his palm. He looked straight at Cadiz.

— You ain't no Navy captain, he said nastily.

Hessian glanced at him, then at Cadiz.

— What? Cadiz asked.

— You ain't no regular Navy captain, the driver said again. Once more he spat on the sidewalk.

— Mister Cadiz, Hessian said protectively.

— Just a minute, Hessian. Do you know anything about me? he asked the driver.

— All I need to know. You shook hands with a nigger porter at the station. Now you talking to this one like he was a long lost brother. The driver spat again. Yeah, I know about you.

— Let's go inside, Mister Cadiz, Hessian said.

Cadiz did not move. He would only have one shot and he had to make it good. His left arm would be useless, and he would be able to do nothing with just one arm. One shot, he thought to himself, assessing the driver.

— Mister Cadiz, sir, let's go inside.

— All right, Cadiz replied, turning slightly away from the driver. Hessian stooped to pick up the bags and Cadiz spun around and swung, pivoting, shifting his weight perfectly. He caught the driver squarely and the man went down, slamming his head against the cab door.

— Mister Cadiz! Hessian cried.

— Get inside, Hessian, Cadiz ordered.

— But, sir—!

— *Inside!*

The driver shook his head, trying to clear it. Hessian backed toward the hotel entrance with the bags, watching. Cadiz waited. He watched the man's eyes, and when he saw them clear and focus on him, he stepped forward and kicked the man in the head.

The driver dropped again. Cadiz stood over him. The man's nose was bleeding. There were no sounds in the morning streets. No one passed. Cadiz walked alongside the driver as he tried to crawl away and scramble to his feet. He turned and set himself to lunge at Cadiz from a squatting position. Cadiz kicked him again, not hard this time but hard enough to keep him on the ground and still conscious.

— You want any more?

— You sonofabitch, the driver gritted through bloody teeth. I'll kill you.

— No you won't, Cadiz said. You're going to get the hell out of here.

— I'll *kill* you.

— I'll call a cop. I'm a war hero. You tried to gyp me.

The man looked up and stared into the ghostly pale face.

— You're—you're crazy! the driver gasped.

— Get in your cab, Cadiz ordered. And don't think about coming back. You're not ready for that. You just wanted to push me a little. You're not ready to go all the way.

— You're crazy!

— Whatever I am, stay away from me, Cadiz said.

Hessian was at his side now, along with a white man in shirtsleeves.

— What's going on here! the man demanded. He looked at Cadiz and then at the driver. What's the trouble, captain?

— He tried to overcharge me for a cab ride from the station, Cadiz said, looking steadily at the driver. When I refused he got nasty. He shoved me, I pushed back, and he fell.

— That's a lie, you sonofabitch! the driver screamed.

— What's that? What's that? Watch your mouth! the man in shirtsleeves said. He pushed forward. I've got your number and I'm going to report this to Mister Davidson. He told me to do it the next time I caught any of you bastards overcharging servicemen. Now go on and get out of here!

— I'll get him! the driver shouted, but he stepped back. I swear I will.

— Now you listen to me, the white man said. You're in big trouble as it is. Your argument isn't with this officer anymore, it's with me. Now I'm telling you to get out of here and stop yelling and using filthy language or I'll call a policeman. You're not going to get anybody. You're just a lot of mouth. And if anything happens to this officer, I'm a witness that you threatened him.

The driver glared, slouched into his cab and sped away, gunning the engine.

— It's all over, captain. I'm sorry about this, but you know how it is in a city in wartime. Things aren't normal. I guess the cab companies are like the rest of us and take whatever help they can get, and it isn't very good sometimes.

Cadiz sagged and Hessian and the white man both grabbed at him.

— Mister Cadiz, are you all right? Hessian asked. Something wrong? Did he hurt you?

— No, it wasn't him. I'm just weak, that's all.

The fight with the cab driver had taken the last of his strength. He was nearly out on his feet and he knew it. His wound began to ache. He stood at the lobby desk and waited for the white man, Mr. Tuttle, to walk around to the back.

— Captain Cadiz, Hessian here, Tuttle said, told me you were an old Savannah boy and a close personal friend of his and that you've been recovering from a wound. I'm giving you the Governor Talmadge Suite at regular rates. You go on up, please, and you take care of him, Hessian. You can register later, captain. I hope that business with the cab doesn't bother you too much. You won't have any more trouble from him. This isn't the first time it's happened. The police Hack Division will hear about it. Just forget it, captain.

— Thank you, Mister Tuttle, Cadiz said.

Mr. Tuttle nodded and shook hands with Cadiz.

— And I might say, captain, that from the looks of that driver, from the push you gave him, with your being weak from the hospital and all like that there, I can't help but wonder what would have happened if you'd been in shape.

— I might have killed him, Cadiz said gravely.

With Hessian carrying his bags, they rode to the fourth floor in silence and then went down the long hall to a corner door. It was a large sitting room with a bedroom off to one side and a view overlooking a park. A room service table with two quarts of Scotch and a silver service of coffee stood just inside the door.

— Coffee or a drink, Mister Cadiz? Hessian asked, putting the bags down and moving to the table.

— Drink, Cadiz said. He sank to the Louis couch, tossed his hat to one side and settled back. He closed his eyes and felt the moisture in the palms of his hands. He had taken a chance with that one shot. It had been a stupid thing to do. If he had missed and the driver had gotten to him, the wound might have opened, and he would have been back in the hospital for a month. He would have missed his ship. His heart jumped.

— Sir?

He opened his eyes. Hessian stood over him with two glasses. Cadiz took one. Hessian smiled.

— I don't have to tell you, Mister Cadiz, what it means to me to see you here, and be able to do something for you. But that business with the cab driver, what you did and all, it makes it sweeter, Mister Cadiz, sweeter. You ain't changed much from the old days.

— Thank you, Hessian, Cadiz said. But you're wrong. I have changed. Changed a lot.

— Not to me, sir. Here's to seeing you again.

They both drank off their whiskey in one gulp, and Cadiz lay back again, letting the whiskey flow through him, warmly and slowly.

— I go off in two hours, Mister Cadiz. You just rest and sleep, and

I'll see you later. I got a hotel full of people I have to take care of. Want me to run a tub for you?

— No, I just want to rest here awhile.

— You rest. If you want anything, pick up the phone and ask for the bell captain. That's me.

— Thank you, Hessian.

— You just rest, Hessian said. How long you going to stay, Mister Cadiz?

— Not long. Probably be gone tomorrow. He spoke with his eyes closed. The whiskey was getting to work now and he felt that he might sleep.

— Leave Savannah, you mean?

— Yes.

— A ship?

— Yes, a ship.

— Was your wound bad?

— It's nearly healed now, Cadiz said.

— Nothing I can do for you before I go? Hessian asked from the door.

— You've done enough, Hessian.

— I never could do that, Mister Cadiz. You ever think about the old days, Mister Cadiz? Mister Al's store?

— I haven't thought about it in a long time. But I used to. I used to think about the old days a lot. Before the war. But the war has crowded out a lot of things that were important. You forget old times and old friends.

— Yes sir. You sleep now. I'm going.

The door closed. He was alone again.

The sun rose over the tops of the trees and buildings and shone straight into the sitting room of the Governor Talmadge Suite and into Howard Cadiz's eyes. He jerked awake.

Had he slept? It was five minutes to seven. He had been sleeping for twenty-five minutes. He got up and walked to the window and started to pull the drapes. He looked down. Bull Street. He felt the heat of the morning sun on his face. He thought of the many times he had walked that very street. Walking it once he had experienced for the first time the rhythm of the city and had been excited by it, had seemed to sense the secret of the city of Savannah, snugged into the side of the coast and protected from the onslaught of fall storms.

It had been a different city then, he thought, moving back through the dimness of the sitting room after pulling the drapes. The city had been alive then. It had had a coiling strength and snap to its step. The whole world had seemed that way. He had been young.

He poured himself another drink. Bull Street, the city of Savannah, the world at large could change, but his loneliness was immutable. He walked back to the window and pulled the drapes to one side. Sipping his drink, he looked out over the rooftops of the city to the river, a big, muddy red snake that wound its way through dun-colored buildings at the lazy riverside and worked its slow, sinuous way to the sea.

He watched a tugboat swing into the channel, churn powerfully, throwing a rolling wake, and then disappear into one of the nearby slips. Above the roofing of the pier he could see the rigging of a ship; from the height of the mainmast above the roofline he could tell that the ship was in deep draft, and the wisps of smoke curling from her stack probably meant she was about to sail.

How long ago had he sailed down that river as a boy? What were his thoughts that day? He could not remember. He studied the river, and for a moment it seemed closer to him than anything had ever been before; for a moment there was no red muddy river there at all, but a river of dreams, a promise of something more. Only he had not found the promise fulfilled, nor had he even discovered what the promise was. All he had really found, after touching in on every country with a coastline, were the very same things he had sought to leave behind when he had sailed down the river for the first time as a boy.

When war came, he had seen the men who sailed the ships learn to live with war and adjust to it. Their determination to survive became the focus of their lives. They found they could live like animals and accept the stench of their own fears, clinging to them like stale sweat, and still want to live. They went back upon their oceans carrying with them a grim refusal to die.

Was that the promise of life, he wondered, sipping at his drink, returning to the couch. To carry with you a grim refusal to die?

He got up at once and began pacing restlessly around the room, his mind casting back before the war, returning to old and used-up dreams that had the musty air of a closed-off room in a once fine house; returning to his loves, touching at their worn fabric. Ulrica. Agnes.

Was it in woman, then, the elusive offering of life? The promise? He could not honestly say. He had not given either of them a fair chance. And if he *had* given them time, which would have had the magic to give him and fulfill him?

He lay back down on the couch with a freshened drink and closed his eyes, the drink resting on his chest. In the distance, floating up to him through the Sunday silences of Savannah, mass bells, like the delicate forewatch singing of ship's bells, summoned the faithful.

I wonder, he said half aloud, what the new faiths will be? He stopped short. The bells had stopped. There was no new sound. It was still too early for street noises. Savannah was not yet ready to leave its Saturday night beds.

And then the lines of *Moby Dick* came to him, those lines that had always come to him at moments like this (especially when he had just left her room in Mexico, Bombay, San Francisco, New York, London, Paris, reeking with the febrile odor of her sex that he would not be able to get out of his nostrils for two or three showers and a cold salt wind, still smelling the acrid smell of her urgent body beneath his, a little high from his drinking, as he was now, but not drunk, nowhere near it). Then to hear those lines as he returned to his ship, an exhausted killer of the boredom of time. . . . *Oh, the gold! The precious, precious gold! The green miser'll horde ye soon! Hish! Hish! God goes 'mong the world blackberrying.*

— Why those lines, he wondered aloud, always returning at moments when he was facing some new, undefined threat.

— What is your terror now, Cadiz? What are you afraid of? Your loneliness?

He freshened his drink. It would be his last. He was almost groggy enough now to go to sleep. He downed it quickly and lay down on the couch.

Perhaps, he thought drowsily, your fear is that you will never find the promise of life, the promise of the river. You have been everywhere and seen most of it, and all of it is pretty familiar. Somewhere there may be an answer, perhaps somewhere in the past, when you moved right instead of going left or straight ahead; perhaps somewhere there was an awful error in judgment. But where? Where could it have been?

Cadiz woke with a start and stared at the alabaster ceiling of the Governor Talmadge Suite. He looked at his watch. The hands were divided into a perfect quadrant of ninety degrees. Nine A.M. He had slept more than two hours.

— Of course, he said aloud, remembering where he was. Savannah.

He touched the scar, running his fingers lightly over the thick ridge of fresh scar tissue, and remembered his return to Savannah.

Mass bells began again. They were not as insistent or as annoying as mass bells in Italy. These Savannah bells were remote, almost wistful, vaguely appealing. The bells of Italy, especially in Genoa, were demanding, unyielding. Savannah's bells held in them the vague hope of some reward. Gloria! Gloria!

He rubbed his face with his hands and walked to the window. He pulled back the drapes. Sunlight drowned the room and he opened the window and listened to the ringing bells and the murmuring noises of Savannah idly drifting toward mid-morning. And there to find, when it reached twelve o'clock high, nothing but a promise of more of the same to come. Gloria! Gloria! Gloria!

He stood motionless until the last note of the last Gloria! reverberated and vanished above the tree tops. Then he turned away. The coffee was cold. Cadiz reached for the phone.

— Bell captain, please.

— Mister Cadiz? It was Hessian.

— Yes, Cadiz said. Do you think I could get some hot coffee?

— Right away, Hessian said. How do you feel, Mister Cadiz? Did you sleep?

— Yes, I just woke up. The mass bells, I think.

— They sure are loud sometimes. I'll bring the coffee right away. Is there anything else you'd like? Eggs? Something to eat?

—No, not just yet, Hessian. Coffee would be fine. I'm going to take a shower now and I'll leave the door unlocked.

—I have a master key, Mister Cadiz. Keep your door locked and I'll just come in.

—All right, Hessian.

He undressed as carefully and slowly as an invalid, then started the shower. Oddly, he found himself thinking about his father.

As the water ran down over his body he remembered that he had vowed to beat his father to death for abandoning his mother. Promises made and promises broken. But they were a part of his mother's world, and so the argument was really between his mother and his father and should have no effect on him at all.

He wondered, as he toweled off, what he would do if he ever met Beau Cadiz? He did not know if he was alive or dead. He had absolutely no curiosity about him at all. It was a name, a place, a time, a moment in someone's life other than his own. His mother's. And his Aunt Meg's. Beau Cadiz belonged to them. Two sisters in love with the same man. He could not really share their tragedy.

He went to the bedroom and took the dragon silk robe that he had bought in China fifteen years before. Hessian was standing at the window. He had changed from a royal blue bellboy uniform to a pair of gray slacks and a thin white sports shirt tucked neatly into his trousers. A bright gold wristwatch was strapped to his arm and glittered in the sunlight. He did not look as heavy now as he had in the uniform.

—You sleep? Hessian asked.

—Yes, about two hours. I feel better. Much better.

—You look better, Hessian said. I was worried about you for a while. You didn't look none too good when you came in this morning. I slipped back in here about an hour ago to see if you were all right. You were sleeping, with your eyes open.

—Open?

—When I looked at you, they were open. It was like you'd woke up to the noise I made coming in. Then you closed your eyes again. But I didn't think you were awake.

—No, I didn't hear you, Cadiz said, and sat down on the Louis couch. He took a cup of coffee from Hessian and lit a cigarette. Hessian poured himself a Scotch and sat down facing Cadiz.

— How is your life, Hessian? Cadiz asked.

— It's fine, Mister Cadiz. I'm married. I have two fine boys.

— Two sons, Cadiz said softly.

— I'm paying off my own home.

Cadiz nodded. He sipped his coffee. He felt relaxed but was still tired. He was used to feeling tired. It was somthing he had learned to live with as a sailor. It was the tension that accompanied the tiredness that was what had to be fought down.

— And your mother? Cadiz asked.

— She died two years ago, Hessian said.

— I'm sorry.

— She was a very old lady. Very old and very tired.

— It's strange, Cadiz said, but I've thought often about your mother.

— You hardly knew her, Mister Cadiz.

— Yes, that's true, I only saw her just that one time. That night I came down to Yamacraw to get you, before the job.

— That was the only time, Hessian said, nodding. And you say you thought about her?

— Yes.

— That's strange.

— Well, maybe not so strange, when you think about it.

— She was just a colored woman, Hessian said. Yet you thought about her. To me, that's strange, Mister Cadiz.

— I thought about her when I thought about you. You were the only man working in the family, with your brothers and sisters depending on you. I thought you were dead, and I wondered what she thought and felt after her thread had been broken. Her hold on life.

Hessian watched Cadiz's face. He smiled. He sipped his drink, then put the glass down on the table. He chuckled. I don't often drink good whiskey like this. I can't afford it. I have to sell it. He refilled his glass but did not touch it. He leaned back in the straight chair and looked at his hands.

— Everybody thinks their own mama is the best, Hessian said

softly, but Mama was not an ordinary woman. She had a great way for getting things settled. Rent, food, clothes, education, keeping the family together, all these things she handled and got them settled.

— Did she know herself? Cadiz asked.

— I don't think so, not in the way you mean it. And that's what *I* mean about her. Hessian spoke slowly. She settled with herself a long time ago. I don't mean just being a Negro in the south, in Savannah. Or being a Negro at all. I mean, inside, she found out the best thing to do was to get things *done*.

— Make decisions, Cadiz said. Is that what you mean?

— Yes, Mama made decisions. Then it was law. For the house and us children and for herself. It was law.

— Was she educated?

— Not beyond the fifth grade in a country school. She could read and write, but only hardly, Hessian said. She wasn't educated, but Mama had it. It was instinct. A way. Her way. It was natural. It might have been different if Papa hadn't died—been killed.

— How was he killed?

— He walked into a drugstore over on the west side while the Doc was having an argument with a drunken nigra. The Doc called the police and when they came, they just grabbed everybody with a black skin. Papa tried to argue back. We never did find out just exactly when it happened—in the wagon on the way down to the jail, or later. I was just a kid at the time. Anyway, things might have been different if he had lived. But I don't think too much different. I think Mama would have been the same.

— Why do you think your mother went on, Hessian?

— I don't think Mama thought about it the whole time she was alive. Hessian paused and looked into his glass and then drained it off. I can tell you how. But I don't know why. Is it something you need to know?

— I'm sorry, Hessian, Cadiz said with a short laugh. I didn't mean to pry.

— You're not prying, Hessian said easily.

Cadiz walked over to the window and looked down at Savannah. The sun was catching flowers in the parks and private gardens and sandy plots where wildflowers grew to the sidewalk edge; the scene was calm and colorful. There was a little more activity in the streets now. The men wore panama hats and summer suits of pale, indefinite shades, and rimless glasses and air-vented, two-tone shoes. Starched, clean, dignified, solemn, dutiful people. On their way to church.

— Tell me what happened, Hessian.

— How much do you remember?

— Everything that happened until we were in the cornfield.

— Well, Hessian said, if you remember all that, there isn't too much else.

— Tell me, Cadiz said.

— I can't remember too well about what happened afterwards, Hessian said. I don't even remember getting hit.

— I remember you getting hit.

— I don't remember anything, Hessian said. There wasn't even any pain for me to remember. Not at first, when I was hit.

— Tell me what you remember.

— I woke up and that's when I felt the pain. Like two hot pokers rammed in my chest. I called for you. But I don't think I made a sound. I can't remember making any sound. I remember thinking I was going to die and I kept waiting for you to come back. I looked up at the sky—you remember there was no moon that night, how overcast and dark it was?

— I remember, Cadiz said.

— I didn't have anything to focus on, to see. There was just me and there was this pain and those two red-hot pokers in my chest. After a while, I knew you weren't coming back or that you were dead too. I think I slept, or I passed out, because when I woke up the sky was clean and I could see stars over me. That's when I started crawling.

— Why?

— Why? I don't know why. I just had to move. I don't know how many times I passed out. It kept happening again and again, and sometimes I could see it coming and I would say to myself, this time you're going to die and not wake up. And each time I woke up. It was almost a disappointment when I realized I wasn't dead. And I got to this place, and this woman took care of me. She called a doctor from another county and he took the slugs out. It was a miracle, or so I thought at the time. I went back up there years later and walked the whole way, the path I crawled. I couldn't believe it was so far, but it was an absolute fact. I got tired just walking it. It was two and a half miles, Mister Cadiz, that I crawled that night and most of the next day. When I got better and it was all over with, I came back here to Savannah and a friend helped me to get time in here at the Arrowsmith as an extra. Then I was put on. I haven't thought about that job in a long time.

— You crawled two and a half miles with two carbine slugs in your chest?

— Yes, sir. Like I said, I haven't thought about it in a long time. About dying, I mean. I died back there, if you know what I mean. I left it all back there, Mister Cadiz. I just been living since then.

Hessian stood, stretched and started to reach for the bottle of Scotch, then poured a cup of coffee instead.

— Mister Cadiz?

— Yes?

— What are you quarreling with, sir?

Cadiz had a sudden picture of Captain Sparkle, white hair falling like a shingle over his eyes, white beard wagging as he talked. And Elly Whitcomb, too, telling the shocking truth about his living lie.

— Mister Cadiz, sir? Do you feel all right?

— It's all right, Cadiz said. It's all right.

— What's all right, Mister Cadiz?

— I'm sorry, Hessian. What were you saying?

Hessian's face mirrored his concern.

— How is Savannah? Cadiz asked in a low voice. Has it changed much?

— Maybe I'd better go and let you rest, Hessian said, standing up. Here I see you so tired and all, yet I hang around talking my head off.

— No, I want you to stay, Hessian. Have another drink. Tell me about Savannah.

— Savannah hasn't changed much, Mister Cadiz. Lot of people in Savannah. People in the service, people working in defense, the shipyards, and like that. That's changed. But not underneath. Underneath, it's still the same. Kind of mushy on the inside. Hard on the outside, with all the war work and the money and the new people, but inside it's pulpy. The old faces you see around Savannah still have the Depression and the bad times in their eyes, almost like they can't forget it. I reckon they can't.

—I've seen that all over the country, Hessian. Most of the world, too, for that matter. People can't forget.

—I try to forget, but I can't, Hessian said. I got a bank account and my wife is working and we're making money hand over fist. I haven't got any worries, money worries, anymore. I got me a good job and I'm liked here, but I can't forget it. If Mama was alive, she would forget it.

—Would she? Now would she?

—Yes, Mama would forget. She had a whole lot worse than the Depression to forget about. She had *hard* times. Mama was pretty old when I was born. She had *hard* times. She was born a slave, Mister Cadiz. I can't forget it, though. I wake up in the middle of the night and go into the kitchen where I got a fine electric stove and a fine electric ice box and a whole pantry full of good food and I turn on the light and I just look at it, and I have to keep telling myself that the finance company ain't going to come and take it away from me. I work and I drive myself and save money. I get my shoes half soled and new heels put on instead of buying new ones. It's like a sickness. My wife, she's younger'n me. She had the Depression too, but she wasn't grown up during the time and she can forget it. So, you ask how Savannah is, and that's the way she is. The old faces around town that I've seen all my life but don't know their names, a face I've looked at a thousand times on a certain corner or the bus driver or the lady behind a counter in a store, they're all like me. They show what they went through. It's in their faces, Mister Cadiz, and they—they have a way about them that makes me know they're afraid on the inside, just like me.

Cadiz did not reply. Hessian thought he had a funny look in his eye. He studied the gray, thin face, observed the gauntness and the unlighted eyes and wondered what Cadiz was thinking.

Eight men died, Cadiz was thinking. Eight. With the last of his strength he had slipped Sparkle's dead frozen body over the side of the boat.

— Mister Cadiz? Hessian asked, are you sure you're all right?

— Yes, yes, Cadiz said, wrenching himself back to the present. Give me a drink.

— I wish I had your confidence, Hessian said. I've thought about it many times.

— What?

— The way you handle yourself.

— How do you mean?

— Seeing you downstairs with that cab driver. It was like you'd never been gone from Savannah all these years. Nothing seems to touch you.

— We all carry our fears with us. I'm not special. We all like to think we are, Hessian, but we're not.

— Back in the old days, around Mister Al's store, everyone looked up to you.

Cadiz looked hard at Hessian.

— Yes, sir, it was something special.

— I didn't know that.

— I don't know what it is you might be bothered with now. You got something in your craw. But—Hessian stopped and made a gesture of helplessness, then laughed.

— What's so funny? Cadiz asked, smiling.

— I just remembered how we all back at Mister Al's store was worried about when the next time'd be we were going to eat, or going to get another pair of shoes. Things like that didn't seem to bother you at all. I laugh because I can't imagine you ever wondering about where you going to get your next meal.

— I worried, Cadiz said.

— You can't say to me, Mister Cadiz, that you were worried about things like that. I won't believe you.

— Why was I different?

— You're asking why again, like you asked why about Mama. And I can't answer you why. But I can tell you how, Mister Cadiz.

— Tell me, Cadiz said.

— Most of us, all of us that I remember, were afraid of outside things.

— What sort of things?

— Jobs, money, food, clothes, all the things that are common to bad times, Mister Cadiz. You weren't afraid of those things.

— What was it then?

— You were, Hessian said slowly, like the way they used to talk about Mister Shad, the way he was before they put him on the chain gang, not like he was afterwards. You were afraid of yourself.

— You saw that?

— We all saw it. Mister Al, Mister Percey Kolb, Mister Danner, Policeman Herod—everybody. We used to talk about it and wonder what it was. And why . . . Well, I gotta go, Mister Cadiz. I been up since yesterday morning and I gotta work again tonight. If I don't sleep, I'll be dragging it by the time I get halfway through the shift.

Cadiz walked Hessian to the door. They shook hands.

— I told the day man about you. Anything you want, just call and ask. He'll get it. He's a good boy. His name is Joseph Joseph so they call him JoJo. He knows about you, so just ask him if you want anything.

— Thank you, Hessian. Perhaps I'll be able to sleep some today and we can talk again tonight. There's a lot I want to ask you.

— That would be nice, Mister Cadiz. And one more thing, I've got me a telephone now and it's in the book. Just call if there's anything I can do.

— You've done more than enough already, Hessian.

— Good-by sir. You rest now.

They shook hands once more, firmly and warmly, and Hessian left.

Cadiz poured a cup of coffee. As an afterthought he added a small amount of whiskey. Carrying the cup, he walked to the window. Golden sunlight poured down on the city, gilding the old and the decayed with radiance. This was his city. It had born and bred him. Of all the cities in the world, *this* one was his.

He was being challenged now, and he knew it. He did not know how, but he knew it was so: the names that had plagued him all night; the inexplicable, mysterious examination of things past; the search for answers to present problems.

Not too far away, the City Hall clock struck the half hour. Nine-thirty on a Sunday morning in Savannah.

He could barely remember leaving the hotel and walking (or had he ridden?) down here to the ferry landing.

He shrugged and marked it as part of this strange day that he had stumbled into, crossing and recrossing time from past to present. It would do no good to resist it.

Now he looked around him, at the river, at the familiar scene that was so very changed. The pier was rotting. The bright colors of the river traffic were gone, turned to a dead wartime gray. He walked over the pier and stood beside the bollard where he and Uriah had sat so often, and he squinted across the river as he had done so long ago, examining the ships taking cargo in the north-shore slips. His eyes sharpened as he studied the lines of a vessel and her name. *Moonlight*. It was his ship. *Thomas Moonlight*. They were naming all of the Liberty ships after second stringers, men who had contributed to the country but never changed it. Thomas Moonlight. Cadiz wondered who he had been and why his name and memory were attached to a ship, painted on the bow and stern, on the nameplates on the bridge, on all the lifeboat gear, the linen, bedding, formal and informal papers of all shapes and sizes, official documents, letters home, and how much more. Thomas Moonlight. A Judge? Governor? Senator? Diplomat?

Fathers and mothers with children, walking down to the river after Sunday dinner, eddied around him, and he could hear the parents' sometimes impatient answers to the children's questions about the river, the ships, the dock. He walked down to the floating dock. A few ferrymen waited in a group to one side, and as he came down, one of them detached himself and pointed to a large, flat-bottomed rowboat.

— Right heah, suh, cap'n, the ferryman said.

Cadiz stepped down into the boat, sat in the stern and shook out a cigarette. The ferryman picked up his oars, let go his mooring line and spun the boat into the river. The strollers watched him make his progress across the river.

— Which one, cap'n? the ferryman asked.

— *Moonlight,* Cadiz said.

— Yessuh, the boatman replied. She los' her cap'n. You gon' take her, suh?

— Yes.

— Good luck to you, suh.

The man was old, perhaps sixty or sixty-five. It would not be impossible that it was the same one who had taken him to the *Mandarin.*

— How long have you been on the river? Cadiz asked.

— Fohty years, suh. Yes, suh. That long.

Cadiz looked at him, watched the flawless touch the man had with the oars. He smiled, wondering what ten or twelve Savannah River boatmen would do in a racing shell against Oxford or Harvard. If he asked him straight out if he was the one, he would surely lie to get a big tip. Which Cadiz considered perfectly legitimate.

— You've taken a lot of people over, I guess, Cadiz said.

— I los' count, cap'n. I usta keep a record, but not no more. It was higher than I could figure, suh.

— I guess you've seen good times and hard times on the river, Cadiz said conversationally.

— Both kinds. Mostly hard, cap'n. Mostly hard.

— Get many little boys wanting to run away and go to sea?

— Not so much anymore, cap'n. Unions put a stop to all that. When they comes down to the ferry, they got they job already. But they used to be a few now and then. Back into the old days, when a man carries a discharge book. They come down and hang around. You kin almos' always spot 'em, suh. They hangs around and then works up they nerve to ax me if I think they kin git a job to a ship. I lets 'em down gentle like and tell 'em to go on home and make up with they family. They mostly do.

— But did you ever see one of them sail away on a ship? Back in the old days, I mean.

The ferryman was silent for a half dozen strokes, looking dead ahead, blinking away the sweat running into his eyes.

—Cap'n, suh, in all my time to the rivuh, ain't nobody eveh ax me close on that question.

—But there was one, Cadiz said.

—Yes, suh, I 'members one.

—You took him across in the early morning.

—Suh?

—Twenty-five years ago, Cadiz said.

The ferryman missed a beat of his oars and looked at Cadiz sharply. He shook his head. He licked his lips and shook his head again.

—The name of the ship was the *Mandarin,* Cadiz said.

—You? Cap'n, suh?

Cadiz smiled and watched the old man's face.

—Do you remember what the boy paid you for getting him the job?

—Five dollars.

—Do you remember what the captain did the first time the boy spoke to him?

—Knock him *flat* for not saying, *suh.*

—Knocked me flat, Cadiz said.

They were skimming into the landing then and Cadiz threw a line over the wooden post and brought the boat to a stop. The ferryman shipped his oars.

—Must *be* you, suh, 'cause I ain't told that story to nobody. Nobody.

—Didn't they come looking for me? Cadiz said.

—The police come for a week. I lied the fust time they come. When they keep coming back I couldn't say the other way then 'cause I scared they put me to the gang. I keep telling one lie after another, all the time. Then finely they stop coming.

—And nobody ever knew? Cadiz said.

—Not from me, suh. But you cause me many sleepy nights and long time after that I duck when I see a police come down to the river. The ferryman laughed. And now you a cap'n, and I take you to yo' ship. That's a strange thing, cap'n. I often think to myself about that little white boy I send out to sea, but I tell you, cap'n, suh, I thought to myself lotsa times that if you be any kind of man, that

Cap'n White on the *Mandarin* be all right for you. He was a fine cap'n, suh. He treat you all right?

— Yes, Cadiz said. Hard but fair.

— Well, suh, that's the sea's way, suh.

— It can't be too easy for you on the river at your age, Cadiz said.

— Hot weather is fine, cap'n, but the cold gits to me.

— How much do you make a day?

— Averages about twenty dollars, the ferryman said.

Cadiz reached into his pocket and took a twenty dollar bill and handed it over.

— I'm taking you for all day, Cadiz said. And as long as I'm in port, it's twenty dollars a day.

— But, suh, cap'n, it'n be *fifteen* if you takes me by the whole day, suh.

— Don't let it bother you, Cadiz said.

The ferryman took the money and looked at it.

— Suh?

— Yes?

— Suh, that's about the bes' thing ever done by me in my whole life.

Cadiz smiled.

— Yes, suh, the ferryman said, I be right here when you wanta go back acrost.

Cadiz walked up the dock, turned the corner of a warehouse and looked up at the stern of the *Thomas Moonlight*.

Climbing the gangway a little unsteadily—though the ship's deck was nearly level with the pier side, it was still an effort for him—he stepped onto the deck and glanced critically around. His eyes swept past the tangle of lines and gear trailing from the spot and yard booms, past the loose wire runners, snatch blocks, heaving lines, handy-billies, pots of fish oil and lamp black for the runners, and the hundreds of other necessities for the handling of cargo. He saw beyond this routine tangle of gear and tools to the heart of the ship, sensing that it was taut and clean. Everything he saw on deck belonged on deck. He walked aft and looked at number four and five holds, squinted aloft and grunted with satisfaction. Then, still tired and a little unsteady, he walked amidships and into the housing.

A steady, distant whine of the sanitation pump somewhere deep in the bowels of the ship greeted him. A toilet flushed, a door opened and a man staggered out, clutching his dirty clothes, and slapped in wooden shower clogs to his fo'c'sle, throwing Cadiz a cautionary glance as he closed the door after him. The galley was silent. It was clean and bright and did not have the usual smell of sour milk; he put this down to being a new ship. The messroom, pantry and utility were the usual clutter of dirty coffee cups and overflowing ashtrays. He walked forward, stopping at the saloon and inspecting the bright, clean, as yet unspoiled green, buff and red of its interior. He poured a cup of coffee from the Silex and tasted it, approved it and drank it off. When he looked up, he saw a man not much older than himself dressed in a pair of dirty chinos and an undershirt. He was barefoot and carried a magazine. He looked at Cadiz a moment and then scratched vaguely at his unshaved chin.

— Can I help you—er—ah, captain?

— Are you the mate? Cadiz asked.

— I'm the chief officer, the man said, his eyes narrow with wariness. Can I help you?

— Your name? Cadiz asked, almost lazily. He glanced idly at the slime of breakfast butter, spilled sugar, coffee stains, toast crumbs, empty beer bottles and cigarette butts on the serving table; it was more or less what he expected to find on a Sunday morning in port. But he knew it meant a slight edge for him, since technically the chief mate was charged with all responsibility for the vessel until the captain came aboard. He waited.

— O'Berry, the man replied. He stepped over the weatherboard and came closer to Cadiz. His toenails were yellow.

— Mister O'Berry, Cadiz said, staring straight into the other man's eyes, I'm your captain.

Cadiz watched as O'Berry's face turned a slow crimson, but he did not avert his gaze. He met Cadiz's stare. He did not twitch a muscle or move his feet or roll up the magazine or smile or drop his head; he used no tricks at all. He simply stood there and accepted the authority in Cadiz's voice without backing down.

— And your name? O'Berry inquired, hesitating a little longer than Cadiz thought he should before adding, sir?

— Cadiz.

— How do you do, Captain Cadiz.

— How do you do, Mister O'Berry, Cadiz said, and after an infinitesimal pause offered his hand. Cadiz looked him over as they held the grip, a big man in the belly with pale blotchy skin and hair the darkest red-orange Cadiz had ever seen. Freckles climbed his nose, fanned out and disappeared into the hair line. The eyes were blue, clear, though a little bloodshot at the moment, probably from working cargo day and night.

— Tell me about my ship, Mister O'Berry.

O'Berry backed away, tossed the magazine to one side and leaned against a table, one arm supporting him, while he dug at the thick mat of hair on his chest with his free hand.

— We topped off this morning and I had the gang on overtime all night. We're all set for the deck cargo, which I understand is going to be aircraft in crates. Welders are coming aboard sometime this afternoon to tack the deck cleats in place. We then shift ship to the Coast Line Docks, probably tomorrow morning, where we take 'em on. We're watered, bunkered, and stores are aboard except for the last-minute milk and vegetables. We've got a full crew, including a twenty-eight Navy gun crew and lieutenant. We've also got a purser. He's a fag, I think. But he's been riding steamboats a long time and seems to know his job. Hardly anybody aboard at the moment. The chief engineer lives in Brooklyn and is due back tonight. The first, second and third are across the river at some hotel. One of 'em is aboard all the time. They got some kind of shack job going but won't say much about it. O'Berry grinned. Cadiz acknowledged the information with a nod.

O'Berry rubbed his face and eyes and slid into a chair. Anything else, captain?

— What's the cargo?

— Five-hundred-pound bombs in number four, general cargo, mails and APO packages and such in five. Drugs, medicines, clap and syph pros, and Lord knows what else in three. Five-hundred-pound bombs in two, spread to the wings of the 'tween decks and to the top, and in one there's a lot of spare parts for the aircraft. That's it.

— Where does the Navy sack in? Cadiz asked.

— They have two fo'c'sles aft, built under the fantail gun. Twelve in each, wing and wing stacked like sardines. Kids mostly. The oldest is about twenty-three. The lieutenant, one of those Texas wha! wha! bullshit artists, Dade Strummer, is up on the chartroom deck. But he's a nice guy. Used to play football. Lotsa muscle.

— What kind of crew have you got, Mister O'Berry?

— Pretty good—on deck, that is. Only one ordinary is making his first trip. The others have made at least one trip, and the bosun is putting out for me and seems to know his job. The third mate just got out of New London and is a quiet sort of kid. The second mate is an old timer. He's been sailing on his license for nearly twenty years. He's a bottle-a-day man, but I don't expect any strain with him.

— Galley?

— Well, O'Berry said, so-so there. We have a pretty good baker, a kid just out of school and conscientious enough, and the chief cook, the fry and meat man, is a brine pecker been out here all his life. The steward is something else. I sailed with him once before. A Florida cracker who used to cook in a county jail and got his papers about eighteen months ago. He's liable to be a little prissy about being head of the department, but Rat—that's the chief cook—already made it plain enough to him to stay the hell out of the galley unless he was invited in.

— What's he prissy about? Cadiz asked.

— He thinks being the head of a department puts him up even with the captain and the chief engineer. Lean on him a time or two and he'll get the idea, O'Berry said with a smile. That's about it. Anything else you'd like to know?

— You, Cadiz said.

— You want to know the history, I guess.

— The history, Cadiz agreed.

— It's been eighteen years all together, and I been riding on my ticket four, four and a half years. I got two endorsements. City Island up to the Cape Cod Canal, open pilotage all the way around except for tows, and I got the Chesapeake Bay from Hampton Roads to

Sparrows Point. Had four years on tankers but never on the bridge. I been on the bridge about ten years now, and never spent too much time with any one company. You wanta know anything else, you gotta show me your F.B.I. badge. O'Berry stood. Right now I gotta take a piss, so 'scuse me.

Cadiz nodded, watching his chief mate move to the door and disappear. It was all there and he appreciated it. The professional brine pecker who knew his job and respected authority. He recognized himself, the many times he had been jacked up by a captain wanting to know the man to whom he would entrust his ship for long periods of time and who would make decisions in the name of the captain.

He climbed to the captain's deck, looked into the radio shack and the chartroom, and then opened the door to the captain's office.

Green, buff and red. A chair, sofa, desk, two pictures, two portholes, two wall sconces with electric lightbulbs, two steel filing cabinets and the ship's safe. The door beside the safe was open and he could see into the bedroom—neat, spare, sterile. He did not bother to look inside. He went to the nearest porthole, loosened the dogs and let the warm afternoon river smell flow into the room. He was on the open side of the slip, looking out over the river. Several Coast Guard craft, private pleasure boats converted for the war effort, spread out over the river and lazed along the piersides, sniffing for signs of the enemy. A tug washed upriver. The Sunday strollers on the opposite shore had increased in number. They lined the stringer on the dock and watched the Coast Guard craft. Slowly, easily, breathing like a man who has just taken a jackpot in a tight poker game, Cadiz relaxed and let an acute sense of melancholy spread through him like a fog. He watched the river scene for some time without moving. When he turned away, it was to a familiar voice.

— Hello, Howard.

It was an old man with gray hair and a thin, angular face. His eyes were bloodshot and his bad teeth were bared in a grin.

— Trigger?

— One and the same, the man said, stepping inside and offering his hand. Long time, huh?

— So you're the bottle-a-day man O'Berry told me about. Cadiz shook hands warmly, pleased.

— He's got a big mouth, Trigger said. Suppose you'd been some gospel preacher–captain, 'r something, an' heard you had a rummy for a second mate, it woulda been serious. How the hell you been, Howard?

— Okay, and you?

— Like as before, back on the old *Congo Palm*, running my life from bottle to bottle and broad to broad.

Cadiz saw that thin lines were beginning to cover the man's whole face; no amount of sun or wind or the deep, dark tan that Ike Trigger always had could erase them. He was much thinner and seemed less confident than Cadiz remembered him when they had sailed, Cadiz as third mate, Trigger as second mate, for the West African Line.

— You want a drink, Howard? Trigger glanced at his watch. I'm about due.

Cadiz nodded and followed the old man to the deck below and around to his cabin. Trigger broke open a fresh bottle of Wilson's and rinsed two glasses.

— Say when, Trigger said.

Cadiz took three fingers of whiskey and drank half of it in one gulp, then sat down on the side of the bed. Trigger took a much smaller drink, less than an inch in the bottom of the glass, but Cadiz knew that he would repeat the dosage every fifteen minutes.

— This your first wagon on your license? Trigger asked.

— My first.

— Long time coming. You're overdue.

— You know how it is. You want something to do. And a mate runs the ship. That's what I liked to do.

— Yeah, the mate runs the ship and the captain sits around.

— How long you been on the East Coast? Cadiz asked. When I left you in New Orleans, you said you were going to be nothing but a warm water sailor.

— Ahh, this goddam war, Trigger said. You can't call your shots anymore.

— Yeah, Cadiz said.

— How's it been with you? Trigger asked. The war, I mean. Been dumped yet?

— Twice, Cadiz said. We got one off Iceland (I was with Captain Sparkle. We were in the boats five days. Sparkle died.) And once down in Windward Passage.

— That's where I got it. Windward Passage. They just sat at both ends and caught us coming up from the Canal, or going down. Trigger shivered. Funny thing, I wasn't scared of anything except the sharks. I was in the water awhile and I almost went dippy worrying about the goddam sharks.

— I never thought much about it, Cadiz said. But of course we got our boats away.

— Well f' that matter, we din't, Trigger said. Three o'clock in the morning, and everybody stoned from Puerto Rican rum at ninety cents a quart.

You got no boats away?

— What boats? From number four and the housing forward there was one big fire, and with everybody half crocked, they all tore aft and jumped. The third assistant blew his stack. Came running up to the bridge balls ass yelling and screaming. The captain came up, takes one look, and starts yelling to jump. So he jumped.

— The third?

— Yeah, only he went over the wrong railing and landed on the deck. The twelve to four A.B. on my watch looks over the railing and curses him for a miserable sonofabitch. He owes me eighty-seven-fifty, the A.B. says to me.

Trigger poured himself another drink. Cadiz declined a refill.

— Yeah, this war has sure made a mess out of things.

— Things were a mess to begin with, Cadiz said.

— That's an unpleasant fact. But there's a lot to say for the old days.

Trigger was leaning against the basin, his arms folded across his stomach, staring at his shoe-tops.

— What good old days? Cadiz asked.

— Back in the twenties, the thirties. It was a great life. Very few places a ship couldn't touch that wasn't a paradise for the brine pecker.

—You mean the times in port or the time at sea?

—Even at sea, though I admit it was pretty rough. If you were on deck. But for a man on the bridge, it was great, Howard. Jesus!

—Like what? Give me an example.

—Well, working all day and all night and then going ashore and hosing and drinking all day and all night. You know.

—Maybe it was because you were young, Cadiz said. And all of it was new to you. New places, new faces, new women, and leaving it all behind you when you got tired of it.

—Well, that too, but—

—Crap, Cadiz said. As my Aunt Meg used to say. You're getting old, Trigger, that's all. Maybe you don't spring so good anymore, Trigger. Maybe your liver is more like a sponge than before. Maybe you're trying to cop a plea.

—What the hell's the matter with *you?* Trigger asked.

—Just don't hand me any of that shit about the good old days. We ran. Every one of us, we ran, from ship to ship, country to country, woman to woman, and for what?

—I don't see that a man has to put a reason to everything he does. Sometimes he just does it because it's there to do.

—Then why drag it up now? Are you crying because you don't have anything put aside?

—I got so fuckin' many war bonds I feel like I'm fighting Hitler all by myself, Trigger said. I got mine.

—I'm not talking about money and you know it.

—Well then I don't know what the fuck you're talking about. All I know is, it ain't like it used to be fifteen-twenty years ago. And I had some good times. That's all.

—And all you've got left now is your memories, right?

—All right, so I'm old and worn out, what goddam business is it of yours? You don't want to talk to me, get the hell outa my cabin, Trigger said. And if you don't want me on your ship why, just say the word. The way I see it, Ike Trigger is the best goddam navigator and dead reckoning man afloat, and I ride wagons that appeal to me, not the other way around.

—You want to pile off, Cadiz said, pile off.

—What's *eating* you, f'Christ sake!

Cadiz was silent.

— You lookin' thin and shaky, maybe you sick or something. And you ain't really worried about me, because you know that drunk or sober, you don't have to walk into the chartroom when I'm aboard. And you probably mean it when you said you'd rather be a mate than the man with the power. So what is it?

Ike Trigger pursed his lips and squinted at Cadiz, as if looking into the sun line and the horizon. A thought exploded in his mind and he rejected it out of hand. But it would not stay down.

— You scared, ain't you? he said. Since when? When you got dumped? You have a hard time? Lose a buddy? Sparkle! You got a hospital look about you. Sure, sure, I bet I look it up and I find you probably all busted up inside or something. Well, I'll be goddammed to hell and gone! Howard Cadiz, who I heard talk about long time before I met him or sailed with him as the raunchiest hard peter you could sail with—*scared!*

— Fuck you, Trigger.

— You scared of dying, Cadiz? Maybe you scared of living. I known plenty of guys like you. Run away from life and get themselves all twisted up. You thinking sailors with a hard-on for the whole world always did give me a pain in the ass. Now, lemme tell you a little something about being scared. It's human to be scared, Howard, see what I mean? You take me, for instance—

Cadiz watched the wagging jawbone in the tight-skinned face, like old, unused leather that was cracking at the folds, and listened to the gloating voice rising and falling like the cycling of a bilge pump on an old Hog Islander spurting sewage into an emerald sea. The ugly, ignorant blathering of the common herd pumped and spewed uninvolved, tidy philosophical leftovers; regurgitated, the insipid thoughts flowed out of the wagging jawbone and he was covered with them as sea slime covers the tide lip on a coastline beach of a southern ocean. He fought against the suffocation of the wagging jawbones' pronouncements on God, Humanity, Peace, Love, Security, Desire, Indulgence, Life and Death. He was powerless to stave it off. He felt the slime of shopworn ideas coating his mind in thicker and thicker layers and he yielded to the anesthesia, sinking into it and letting himself be drowned in ooze.

— You fell asleep on me, Howard, Ike Trigger said, an appreciative chuckle in his voice. He leaned forward and held a glass with whiskey in it under Cadiz's nose. I bet you ain't heard a word I said.

Cadiz looked up, focused, then closed his eyes again. He was aboard the *Moonlight*. Sunday in Savannah. He took the glass.

— You all right? You really look beat up, Howard, old buddy. You wanta lie down here and sleep awhile? Go ahead, I gotta few things I can do. Trigger started to go.

— No, don't go! Cadiz said sharply.

Trigger eyed him uneasily, unsure now what to say or do.

— You remember Muzzy Di Angelo? Cadiz asked.

— Little guy with lotsa hair? A third assistant outa Baltimore?

— He's dead, Cadiz said.

— Oh, I'm sorry to hear that.

— You remember Captain White on the old *Mandarin?*

— Yeah, Trigger said, his uneasiness growing.

— He's dead, too.

— Oh.

— You remember Dave and Aubrey?

— No.

— Both dead. Cadiz stood and glared at Trigger menacingly.

— Take an easy strain, Howard, Trigger said. Why don't you get some sleep?

— Can't sleep.

— I gotta pill.

— Fuck the pill.

— 'kay, Captain, Trigger said. He sloshed more whiskey into Cadiz's glass. He backed away, easing to the other side of the cabin, and leaned up against his bed.

Cadiz raised the glass. Here's to the eternal, infernal triangle: birth, life and death. We have nothing to say about our birth, and the way we live has no effect on our death.

He drank the whiskey off quickly, without taste or enjoyment.

— What comes next, Trigger? he asked.

— Are you drunk? Trigger asked. And then he paused. Naw, you ain't drunk.

— No, I'm not drunk. I've just been drunk all my life.

— I don't remember you being a boozer.

— Not drunk on booze, Trigger, but drunk on the easy way out. Seduced by the line of least resistance. I have for years been stoned, crocked, blotto, piss-ant drunk on *getting by*.

— So? The whole world seems to shape up about like that.

— Like you.

— Like me, Ike Trigger said, a little defensively. And like you, since you just admitted it.

— But you don't admit it?

— I do. But I don't have to discuss it. I'll let you hard-peter sailors with flim-flam souls eat away at your guts and make ulcers. I brushed it once, as it happens, with a broad I positively worshiped. Then I found her ass high and balls deep into a guy, and that ripped it. I been drunk, not on the easy way out like you said, but on good old eighty-ninety proof stuff. I took my lumps and backed off. So.

— Some kind of a nut, maybe, Cadiz said slowly.

— Rat-shit, sailor. I got a rule of thumb. If you can even think about yourself being screwy, you ain't. Maybe it don't always work, but generally speaking you can depend on it. You nutty like a fox. You nervous, is all.

— I feel I've missed something big and important along the way, Trigger. I'm up to my knees in sentiment, self-pity, self-doubt, all mixed in with fears I thought I'd clamped down a long time ago.

— So be practical. Get drunk, try to dodge the clap, run from the subs and live it up.

Trigger was smiling, friendly.

He believes it, Cadiz thought. But then, he added to himself, so did you.

— Anything else you wanta know, just ask me. Trigger was grinning broadly now. Another drink?

— You're a fountain of enlightenment, Cadiz said.

— So, I didn't ask to be raised. I did it all by myself and I'm pleased with the result. As a matter of fact, I can give you two very good reasons why I'm better off than you are.

Cadiz nodded.

— First, I got a cunt waiting for me at six o'clock. I had her three days ago for the first time. And I honestly believe I got her cherry. For the first time in my life, I think I got one. She's waiting. She loves me. She adores me. I even love her back a little bit. But I'm taking more than I give.

— It's an old story, Trigger.

— Yeah, but the second part ain't. I been through the motions of loving so many times in my life that I know *exactly* how to drop into it, take more than I give, and get out.

— Experience, Cadiz said. You're not unique.

— I know I ain't, and I know it's experience, but living those moments with her, those hours with her, *that's* unique and every one of them is different.

— And *between* times? Cadiz asked harshly. Tell me, Trigger, how long can you go without a fix? A broad? A love affair?

— You sonofabitch! Trigger said.

— And you nibble on your bottle, pickling your brain and your senses with booze, coming out of it only when you've hooked up with something.

— Not something, not *just* something! It's *all* there when *I'm* there! And who gives a damn what she feels like when I'm *not* there!

— And there, my rummy friend, is *your* way of getting by. You've got yourself *believing* that you're not just getting laid.

— You miserable sonofabitch! Trigger said. You ain't changed a bit. You got to take everything. You don't leave nothing, do you, you sonofabitch! I remember what you did to that big A.B. on the *Gold Coast*—

Cadiz jerked his head up.

— Yah! A nice guy who bragged a little about being a professional fighter. Nobody cared if he was full of bull or not. But you had to take him on. You had to show him up! You had to put him down and you damn near killed him. Who ast you to come sticking your nose in! Who the hell ast you, huh?

— He was drunk, Cadiz said angrily. He came looking for me.

— Sure he did, Trigger rasped. After you let it out that you doubted him, and in a way that he had to call you out. But you couldn't back down. No, not you. Not the Great Cadiz! You had to tear him to pieces.

Cadiz turned away.

— I saw him a coupla trips after that. He was on North Broadway down to Baltimore. A panhandler. So stripped down he didn't even *remember your name!*

— I didn't do it on purpose, Cadiz said.

— You're a fucking liar, Captain Cadiz.

Cadiz looked at Trigger with a face like thunder. Trigger stared back at him.

— You going to tear me to pieces too, Captain Cadiz? For calling you a liar? Go ahead, I been bounced before, I'll be bounced again. But you know a little of what it is to have a guy strip down for your pleasure, 'cause I just nailed you, Captain Cadiz, 'cause you know and I know, you took that A.B. apart *on purpose!* So get your ass outa my cabin and don't talk to me except in the line of work. Maybe I won't even sail on the same goddam ship with you.

— Trigger, I didn't mean—

— Go on, get out.

— You're right. Cadiz sighed deeply. I've been doing that for years.

— I don't want to hear about you or your problems. Just get the hell out and close the door.

— Come on, let's have another drink. Cadiz picked up the bottle and offered it to Trigger, who spun around, knocking the bottle out of his hands. It crashed on the steel and cement deck. Curiously, the shards were evenly divided and pointing straight up. The fumes of whiskey immediately pervaded the small cabin.

Cadiz stepped to the door, speaking over his shoulder without turning around. Pack your gear and get the hell off. Don't hang around. I'm telling O'Berry to have you off the ship in thirty minutes.

If the roses aren't red and you want them red and you have the power, then off with their heads. He climbed to the captain's deck and entered the office, slumping down on the sofa. He lit a cigarette and tried to force himself to calm down. He listened carefully to the sanitation pump and the rattle of pans in the galley. It was early for the galley to be alive, since it was Sunday and there would be a cold-cut supper, which was probably already prepared. It would be the baker, Cadiz thought. O'Berry had said he was conscientious.

He did not know how long he sat there before he looked up and saw Trigger in the doorway.

— I'm sorry, Howard. You really want me to pile off?

Cadiz shook his head.

— I'm going ashore, Trigger said awkwardly. You want to come along? My broad can get a cousin or somethin'.

— No, you go ahead, I've got to start looking over the papers and learning about my ship.

— 'kay, then, Trigger said.

— 'kay, Cadiz said.

— Everything all right, Howard? Between us, I mean?

— Yes, Trigger, Cadiz said. Everything's all right between us.

— Well, I'm going. Trigger shifted his weight uneasily.

— Take an even strain, Cadiz said automatically. He listened to Trigger's footsteps fade away on the lower decks, and then he was left alone again with the sanitation pump and the rattle of pans in the galley.

— Captain Cadiz? Sir?

— Yes?

— Good afternoon, captain.

— I—ah—I'm afraid it's been so long since I've been in Savannah — Cadiz stammered, not embarrassed but off balance a little.

— Tuttle. Of the hotel. The Arrowsmith.

— Ah, Mister Tuttle! Of course. I'm sorry. I'm afraid I was—ah—thinking.

— I beg your pardon, Captain Cadiz.

— It's all right, please. I'm glad you spoke to me. How are you?

— Yes, well, I'm fine, thank you. Captain Cadiz, were you thinking of going to church?

— I beg your pardon? Cadiz replied, startled.

— Church, Tuttle said, nodding up at the spire. This is a church. My church.

Cadiz turned.

— We're the Watch and Wait Pentecost Baptist Worldwide Missionary Alliance Church of God.

— I'm deli—that's—I mean, fine. Fine. Cadiz said. What is it you watch—and, ah—wait for?

— The Second Coming of Christ Jesus, our Saviour.

— I'm being rude, Mister Tuttle. Please excuse me. This is a strange day for me.

— Your wound? Tuttle asked reverently.

— Yes, Cadiz said, seizing on it. I'm still a bit weak. Now he wanted only to escape and try to hide his panic which he was sure was only too obvious to the other man.

They were standing on a wide, red-bricked sidewalk before a compact, white sandstone church. People passed through the huge double doors in a steady stream. Several of the men and women nodded to Tuttle and smiled at Cadiz.

— You would be most welcome, captain, Tuttle said.

— Church, Cadiz murmured. He could hear organ music.

— I must be getting inside, Tuttle said. You just slip in the back, if you like.

This was the quiet time. The city was still. Still and calm. If you only knew, John Wesley, and you, John Calvin, or you, Mary Baker Eddy, that generation after generation of youngsters would grow to hate you and everything about you for making them stay indoors on a beautiful late afternoon just because it happened to be Sunday.

Sunday, Cadiz thought, walking now along a narrow side street that was overhung with a row of fat-trunked, yellow-blotched sycamore trees. The rounded, brown-to-green nuts the size of golf balls covered the sidewalk. He kicked one, watched it skid into the street. A car passed and the nut was squashed.

Sunday.

He walked on, pausing to stop in a park and sit for a moment on a bench while the crowds of Sunday strollers paraded past. They were mostly soldiers, sailors and marines with pretty, giggly girls.

He left the park and continued on his unseeing way, lost in a private, burned world of his own. After some time he looked around him. He was on West Broad.

— My God, he thought to himself, *Here's* where Al died.

He stood trance-like. He stared.

He was weak. His wound ached. He had not eaten. He had drunk too much that day, and he wished he had another drink. He needed sleep and he needed to put an end to brooding and remembering.

The past was undeniable, he thought, walking away from the spot where Al had died. More than anything else, undeniable. It could be misrepresented. It could be made to look black or white, left or right. But it could not be changed. It was there. A testament of the man who had lived it and who would never escape it.

He swung into Broughton Street, stopping to look down West Broad, then turned his back on it and, facing east, moved away from the disaster of Alfred S. DeCunningham's store. He stopped in front of a drugstore and remembered there might be a few things he would need aboard the *Moonlight;* in time past he could depend on the slop chest for most of his needs, but not now, during the war. He had better go in and look around.

— I'll have two of these combs, please, Cadiz said. And two dozen of those handkerchiefs. And a half dozen packages of Beech-Nut Chewing Gum and . . . I'll just look around to see if there's anything else.

— Yes, sir, the girl said.

He walked along the notions counter, stopping, looking, aware of the girl—pretty face, dark brown hair, a neat slim figure in a knitted suit that clung to her breasts and thighs. Her cool, distant smile was an invitation.

He moved around the store and circled slowly back to his starting point. She was standing at his side, still smiling.

— Have you thought of anything else, captain?

— No, I'm still looking, thank you.

She would be about twenty-five or -six, he thought. He checked her left hand; there was a plain gold band on her ring finger. She made no effort to hide it, nor did she make it obvious. Or did she? She was still standing, waiting patiently. Cadiz nodded toward the ring.

— Serviceman?

— Yes, she said. A lieutenant in the infantry. She looked away a moment, and he followed her gaze to the soda fountain, where several harried women of indeterminate age were rushing to keep up with orders. There were very few civilians in the store. She looked at Cadiz again. He hates it, she said.

— I can understand that, Cadiz replied. I don't think anyone, except maybe a few generals and admirals safe and sound in their offices, really enjoys this war.

— He tried to get into his own line of work—he's a photographer—but they put him in an infantry company. He's in the South Pacific. Every letter I get he repeats how disgusting it is.

Cadiz nodded.

— It would be better if he did not question, or think at all.

— I tried to comfort him, the girl said. But letters . . .

Cadiz pretended to examine some cheap plastic sunglasses on the display counter.

— It's been eleven months now, the girl said. Cadiz raised his eyes level with hers. I have to go on too.

— I see, he said. A long time.

— Too long, she said. He keeps saying in his letters that it's a matter of individuality and self-respect. The war has stripped away all pretense of human dignity.

She leaned against the counter, surveying the store, her arms folded under her breasts, speaking without looking at him now.

— I remember one letter I received just a little while ago.

Cadiz fumbled for a cigarette. What did it say?

— His big argument, the girl said, was that the Army and all of his men and superiors took his self-confidence for granted. That was what he resented most. He's a naturally self-possessed man, even a little cocky, with a nervous pride in his ability as a photographer. But that was only with his *own* life.

— Has he seen much action? Cadiz asked.

— He's received the Distinguished Service Cross and two Purple Hearts, she said.

— Then it would seem, Cadiz said, that he's wrong and the Army is right.

— I wrote that to him, too, the girl said. Letters again, but he shot an answer right back.

— What did he say?

— It was all accident—all of it—pure chance. A split second either way and it could have been the Jap who received a medal, and not Mack. They put his picture in the paper back home.

— He's a hard man to argue with, Cadiz said.

She sighed and surveyed the store again; she shrugged and tossed her head, looking very directly at him again. Cadiz had been seduced before, but never in quite this way. There was something more here than simple female heat.

— Back home?

— St. Louis. We're both from St. Louis. He shipped out from Savannah and I decided to stay here for the winter.

— You don't sound midwestern, Cadiz said.

— I've been here long enough to go native, the girl said. It rubs off on you. I'm pretty alert to the casual things in life, captain.

— Such as picking up a southern accent?

— Yes, she said slowly. Among other things.

— You sound as self-confident as your husband.

— It's one of the things we have in common.

— He has—or had—his photography, Cadiz said, moving in, testing it. What do you have?

It jarred her. She flushed.

— I have everything a woman needs, she said.

She had, Cadiz decided, thought about what she was now doing for a long time. She had thought it out and she had made her decision. Once her spiritual contract with Mack, lieutenant, DSC, confident photographer, and now less than confident killer of Japs, had been broken (he wondered if it had not been just recently, the last letter, perhaps, some trigger in the letter setting her free), she was making her move.

— So, Cadiz said slowly, you've picked me.

— I guess I have, she said.

— May I ask why? Do I look like Mack?

— No. Not at all.

— Then why?

— You're handsome, she said, flushing again. And you're a sailor. I mean Merchant Seaman. I know the difference between that and the Navy. You didn't just join up because of the war, and you didn't get four stripes sitting at a desk in Washington.

— Very good, Cadiz said. Also, I am probably very romantic and vastly experienced.

— Yes, that and—

— And?

— You're a complete stranger to me.

— That would be true in almost any case, wouldn't it?

She made a dismissive gesture, contemptuous.

— Some of Mack's closest and dearest friends have had their hands all over me.

— A stranger then. And good-by the next day.

— Yes.

— Anything else?

— I can't think of anything, she said.

— Want to hear my side of it?

She gave him a startled look and he knew he had jarred her again. It had not, he saw in her face, occurred to her that she might be turned down. She nodded slightly.

— Why should I be your stud?

She shivered and caught her breath. She shook her head.

— I don't want that—not that, she said.

— Neither do I.

— Are you refusing me? she asked, trying to carry it off with a little laugh that, Cadiz decided, must have taken a great deal out of her.

— No, I didn't say that, Cadiz said. I'm just saying that in order to sleep with you, a complete stranger, there has to be something more than just the mechanics. Is that what you want?

— No, not that, either, she said. But what else do you expect? Love?

— No, not love, Cadiz said. Just something to keep it from being a mechanical piece of ass, which has no value for me at all.

She wheeled abruptly away from him and he was not at all sure she would come back. He watched her walk to the check-out counter and wait on a marine who bought cigarettes and paid his soda check. The marine talked to her a few minutes and tried to pick her up, but even though she joked back with the marine, Cadiz saw that his mission would not be accomplished. But he was still not sure she would come back.

The marine finally left and she sauntered unhurriedly back to him, resuming her position, her back to the counter, her arms folded under her breasts.

— You probably don't know it, but you've made yourself all the more attractive to me, she said. I've been thinking about the something else.

— Yes?

— I think, she said slowly, that it may already be there between us.

— That could be. But tell me how.

— One of the things that bothered me when I thought about this wasn't the problem of picking out a man, undressing before him, sleeping with him—though there was some problem there. The real difficulty was what would fill the vacuum afterwards, while I was still with him. How in Christ's name would it end? Now I think I know.

Cadiz felt the need and hunger now. No more talk.

— When? he asked.

— I'm off in a half an hour, she said. Do you have a hotel room?

— Yes, Cadiz said. He gave her the name and room number.

She nodded, hesitated, then moved off, taking his combs, handkerchiefs and chewing gum to the check-out. He followed her, paying for his purchases. She returned his change and, not saying a word, not really looking at each other, not touching, they parted. Cadiz pushed through the swing door to the street without looking back.

He mingled with the pedestrian traffic, most of it going eastward to the theater district, wondering about Mack, lieutenant, DSC, man about to be cuckolded, and his pronouncements on self-respect, individuality, human dignity, self-confidence.

— Here, let me, she said. She took the towel and Cadiz turned his back. Very gently she patted his wound dry.

— That's the ugliest—she paused. No, not the ugliest, the most obscene thing I've ever seen in my life. She tossed the towel to one side, leaving the bathroom, walking with a full stride into the sitting room, going directly to the bottle of Scotch and pouring herself a drink.

Cadiz watched her thoughtfully, slipping into his robe and then toweling his hair. He walked into the sitting room after her. He poured himself a drink, sat down on the couch and waited. She stood erect, shoulders back, looking out over the park at the darkening sky. She held a drink in one hand; a cigarette was held lightly in the other.

— Are you well enough, captain? she asked, not looking at him.

— I never went in much for acrobatics, he replied.

— A soft and gentle lover?

— I won't say I'm the soulful type, he said, but I've never regarded sex as a conquest. Or a contest.

She laughed, a free, uncluttered sound.

— I like that, she said. They both drank, and he lit a cigarette. She laughed again. You know, it's been eleven months—for me, she said. I told you that. Has it been a long time for you? I would think so, what with that wound.

— Yes, it's been a long time, Cadiz said, leaning back on the couch and shutting his eyes. Much longer than eleven months for something like this.

— Like this?

— Where there is at least the possibility of—

— Affection?

— Yes.

— How quickly it can be induced, she said.

— Desire?

— No, the possibility of affection.

— When you saw my wound? he asked.

— Yes, she said sharply, looking at him with a quick twist of her head; a direct, surprised stare. How perceptive you are. Yes. Lots of things hit me. Revulsion. Fear. A certain instinctive pity. Guilt over my husband, considering that he, too, has been wounded, though not as badly as you. And a good dose of the maternal impulse to take you in my arms and hold you and care for you.

— And all of these feelings separated from sex, Cadiz said, his eyes still closed.

— Completely, she said.

— What would you think of me if I took advantage of my wound? he asked. Would it be unfair?

— Whatever you did, you would not be taking advantage of me, captain. I'm wide open.

— It's a marvelous idea, affection. How much to receive, and how much to give?

— That's splitting hairs, captain, she said. Don't you have any of the vulgar, manly characteristics that can and will please me?

— I have a certain confidence, he said.

— And I am absolutely certain, she said, putting the drink to one side, stubbing out her cigarette, that I can please you.

He did not move his head from the back of the couch but merely opened his eyes. The room had grown darker. The glow of the street lights below fell softly on her.

He had seen a hundred woman undress before him. He knew the rhythms of every move—every bent knee, curved back, angled head, every slightly studied gesture.

Now, bit by bit, she unsnapped, unhooked, cast off her stockings, skirt, sweater, slip, shucking out of (very quickly now, almost with haste) the last remaining wisps of netlike silks. He stood, and seeing him stand, she moved quickly, forthrightly, into his arms, pressing her warmth against him, giving a quivering response, involuntary and complete, the last barrier down, feeling the honesty of his erection, moving her hips in a swaying, snakelike motion and rolling his hardness across her abdomen. They kissed. Their hands wandered, searching, testing, caressing; a flutter of fingers, hands, tongues, discovering in each other and in themselves the long-awaited, remembered scents and tastes and touches that now magnified, opening up layer after layer of their hunger which, once opened, drove them on and their lips were bruised and their legs trembled and their aching parts were flushing as he now, breaking off, moved her backwards onto the couch, pressing her back down, both hands on her shoulders, trailing his hands over her breasts. He moved and with one knee bent, foot dangling, to the side of the Louis couch, firmly taking hold of one and then the other of her knees, spreading her thighs; spreading them further, now moving in over her while she, dart-like, took hold of him; he probed. A suspended moment as she, in her abandon guiding him, sought the cleft. He tested. Good. He arched his back, waited, sensed the moment and swung his hips down and forward, carrying himself entirely within her. She screamed—caught her breath and bucked one time, meeting him. He stroked. She bucked again.

It did not last long. It could not. He responded to her pleas not to withdraw. Flushed but unheeding that he was finished, she continued to press for the moment long after it was gone; and as he held her, he knew that he had released all there was within her. Gradually her spasms ceased and there was left only the soft, bruised lip kisses and an exquisite silence.

The language of spent love, when lovers are still entwined, sighs, heavy breathing, gradually released pressures; small insulated sounds of withdrawal, the rustle of body against bedding, passion trickling away, eyes closed yet seeing all; quick touches and breathy whispers, this language carried them through to a repossession of themselves—who they were and where they were individually—and what they had done.

They lay side by side. With one hand he groped for the cigarettes, lighting one for each of them; she studied his chin, nose, brow in the glow of the flame, and in that instant he turned, seeing the spread of her breasts and he realized then who this girl so reminded him of.

— Agnes . . .

Cadiz opened his eyes and met hers. They were full of concern. She sat on the side of the couch pressing a cold towel to his forehead. He took it away.

— I'm sorry. I hope I didn't frighten you, he said.

She breathed deeply, relieved, and finally smiled.

— I'm glad to see you're all right. I don't know exactly when it was that you passed out.

— I did not pass out, Cadiz said.

— You were out cold.

— I may have fallen asleep, he said. From weakness. I have done that, or I have fainted, if you will, a number of times today.

— Do you want me to call a doctor?

— No, I'm perfectly all right, he said, holding her arm. It's just that—this has been such a strange . . . day for me.

— Very well, she said quietly. She sat upright, her hands in her lap, her back slightly arched as a balance against the imperfect seat she had on the edge of the down pillow. Her breasts were high and her hair, slightly disarrayed, hung down over her face and neck, a pasted effect where several thick strands adhered to her moist skin.

— This is a delicious moment, she said calmly. I'm not bothered at all by my nakedness. She turned to look at him. Or by yours. Thank you for that. It would have been so easy for me to feel shame and guilt. I feel none of that.

— I'm glad, he said. I must have given you a fright, going off the way I did.

— No, not really, she said, smiling down at him, her back still arched.

— It's just this—strange day. It's like re-experiencing energy used up and burnt out years ago.

— That is both foolish and beautiful, she said. Were you thinking of old loves, captain, as you made love to me?

— No, he said after a pause, not lying, remembering that he had not thought of Agnes until after they had made love.

— I don't mind, she said, if you were.

— All day I've been reliving my whole life, he said.

— That's not unusual for a man who has had trouble, she said. Not unusual at all. I think we often do just that.

— What?

— We go to the past looking for a way out of the present.

— I'm not in trouble.

— Perhaps not now, she said, tracing the wound on his side with a delicate fingertip. But there has been trouble.

— I wonder what has made me go back? That's not like me. I have never looked back.

— Perhaps you are just like the rest of us after all, captain, she said.

— I am not very extraordinary, he said.

— Oh, yes. Oh yes, you are. But not in the way I mean. Don't we all search for a mistake in direction? A pattern on which you can build and see, possibly, how it might end? We never bother to do that in good times. Just when trouble comes.

— Why would I go back, he said, reaching for a cigarette and lighting it, seeing her eyes gleam in the glow of the match. Why listen to old, old voices that may no longer be true? I've done that all day. I've been looking back. Only the past comes through diffused, like a bent ray of light. It's there, but not to be trusted. I've seen how easily the deceptions came about.

— Have you nothing to say for our search for love? I am at a disadvantage, captain. I don't know about your past. But even so, there are things about a man that a woman knows the moment she has submitted and he has possessed her. I am not being vulgar when I say how terrifying it is to—take a big prick after so long a time. She knows if he is gentle. Or if he is sad. Or if he is in pain. I think you are all three, captain . . . Tell me how, she said, brushing her lips against his hand. She leaned over him, half reclining on his chest, but careful of his wound, and brushed her lips over his eyes.

— How is a thing frightening? I suppose when we don't understand it.

— And there are things you don't understand in your past? she asked, kissing him softly, lightly.

— Yes.

— Are you trying to understand them?

— Yes.

— Why? she asked, kissing him again.

— I don't know, he said. I can only wait for it. I don't know if it is a beginning or an ending.

— Is that the part that's frightening?

— It would seem so.

— But you're not sure? She kissed him deeply. They parted.

— No, I'm not sure, he said, tightening his grip on her.

She moved her body over his, shifting her position, still careful of his wound. She knelt on the floor beside the couch and smoothed her face on his stomach. In the semi-darkness of the room, she stroked him.

There was a moment of loneliness for him as, stretched flat, he did nothing at all; he was unattached, yet she was attached to him and to his rising passion. With subtle, varied rhythms she expressed her tenderness and love with her lips and tongue, and practiced upon him the sublime expression of love, surrendering to him the very last of herself.

Unable to identify the woman for a moment, Cadiz did not know where he was; then he looked at her again.

— Oh, yes, he said to himself, remembering. He looked at the windows and saw an unbelievably spectacular dawn; gray mists foamed up out of the west over Yamacraw, partly ground fog and partly sulphur smoke from a thousand and one breakfast coke fires, shot through with brilliant sunlight.

— Are you back?

— Yes, he said. I'm back.

— It happened again?

— Yes, it happened again. I'm sorry. It's part of this damn strange day. He lay on his back. She sat, as before, on the side of the down pillow, facing him.

— Part of the energy burnt out and used up long ago? she asked.

— Yes, he said. He reached and touched her shoulder.

— Are you afraid of it?

— I don't think so. But it is frightening.

— Captain?

— Good morning, Cadiz said.

— Good morning, she answered, and sighed, brushing the hair out of her face.

— How are you? he asked.

— Rested. Played out. Relaxed. And you?

— Pleased, he said. And . . . involved.

— Involved? Where are you now?

— Why—here. With you.

— But you haven't been with me for some time. Where have you been?

— Well, Cadiz said, I'm sorry about that.

— Making love to you, she said, was a lesson in suspended animation. You were very much there with me, and yet you were not. Every move you made was right. Even your indifference was rewarding.

— It was not indifference, Cadiz said. It is simply that one cannot be in two places at the same time. These last twenty-four hours, I've been possessed. I've been fighting old wars. Examining old wounds. Resmelling the seared flesh where I was burned. Arguing with dead shipmates. And unlike Ahab and his damn white whale, *this* Captain Ahab has no white whale to seek vengeance against. There isn't any place for me to work out my vengeance and hatred.

— Do you want vengeance? Do you hate?

— Yes, Cadiz said. I want to curse and scream and give pain. But on what? To what purpose? Ahab was lucky. He had his goddam whale.

— I wonder, she said, what it was that got to you. Was it a woman?

— I have known two women, Cadiz said.

— You're a lucky man. Two puts you well ahead of the rest. Above average. But it isn't a woman, is it?

— No, not a woman, he said.

— Is it the war?

— Part of it.

— Your wound? Some people have such a high regard for their physical self that they go to pieces when something happens to it.

— That too, Cadiz acknowledged.

— A good man and his good right arm, she said.

— Yes, he said. How do you know that?

— I told you my husband was an arrogant man. He is very much like you. Oh, captain, she said. You tough, proud, confident, arrogant men. You people who are sometimes violent need to have your lives softened by the one thing you can't have.

— Love, Cadiz said.

— Yes. Love.

— The two women, Cadiz said. I loved them.

— Did you compromise for either of them?

—No.

—Sacrifice anything for either of them?

—No.

—The difference is in the doing.

—There were circumstances, Cadiz said, hearing in his voice an irritation, the echo of Whitcomb's excuse, and he completed his thought in a whisper as he listened to Whitcomb's resistance years before when Cadiz had asked why Whitcomb didn't go home to Sara and the boys . . . *Circumstances. . . . Circumstances!* Many years before in an Indian Ocean port when seventy-three letters came from Sara in one big batch and Whitcomb was too drunk to read them. Circumstances . . . yes. They alter cases.

He raised up on one elbow. No! he shouted. No, *no.*

—Don't be frightened, she said, putting her head on his shoulder, pulling him back down gently to the pillow. Don't—

—Perhaps, Cadiz said after a moment, perhaps that is the truth of the matter. And the reason for this strange day. Quite simply, I am frightened.

—Captain—

—It isn't so much the way things have been, or the way things are, but what they might have been.

—Don't be afraid, she said, and she poised her body over him. Let me tell you that you are not to be afraid, ever again. Hush, now. And let me—let me—don't cry, captain, don't cry.

She held his head against her breast and rocked him.

—Do you feel better? she said at length.

—It's been a long time since I've cried. The last time was here in Savannah. On a ship. Just before I made my first trip. A long time ago. I'd forgotten what it was like.

—What is it like? she asked.

—Comforting, Cadiz said. And secure.

The phone rang.

—Excuse me, Cadiz said, and lifted the receiver at the bedside table. Yes?

It was Ike Trigger.

—We're ready to sail, captain.

— I see, Cadiz said. Hold the line a minute. He put his hand over the mouthpiece and turned to the woman. She knows, he decided.

— It's my ship. I've got to leave.

She made a slight gesture with her head, then followed this with an effortful smile. It was a fleeting thing. A moment. And then it was gone, and she was not with him any more. A second before, they had been in perfect phase, but now his ship was sailing and though only a few seconds had passed, the intrusion of the *idea* had broken the pattern of what they had so carefully built up. It was a new shape now. To recapture what had been would require more, much, much more than had gone into it. A simple phone call, one sentence, and it was over. It made their time together illusory. It robbed them. It denied them.

— Just hold the line, Cadiz said, his voice cold.

— But I gotta get back to the ship, Howard. I'm down on the dock at a pay phone and—

— Do as I say. You wait there until hell freezes over, but hold the line.

He put his palm over the mouthpiece again, turning back to her. She had not moved physically, but she *had* moved from him, outward and away, back into her own skin.

She lifted the edge of the sheet and covered her bosom: Eve made aware of her nakedness.

— I don't even know your name, he said.

— Veronica, she said.

— My name is Howard, Cadiz said. Now the words framed slowly in his mind. All he had to do was say them: *Will you divorce him and marry me?*

There is no mistake about it now, is there, Cadiz, this *is* the day Whitcomb had prophesied. And what was it? Oh, yes . . . Whitcomb had said: *You gotta get the roots started and then forget about 'em!* Well, Cadiz, do you put roots down with this one and forget about the others? Her name is Veronica. She is good, standard sized, standard bred, a pretty woman with intelligence and passion. Why not her? Put down roots and forget about the others. Whitcomb had also said: *Most women satisfy*. Veronica had satisfied him, as Ulrica had satisfied him, as Agnes had satisfied him. So—most women satisfy. Do you see that? It could have been any one of them, at any time, anywhere . . .

— Captain?

— Yes?

— The phone, Veronica said. The phone. Cadiz looked up. She was dressed. She had her purse and she was ready to leave.

— Were their names Agnes and Ulrica? she asked.

He had to wait before he could answer; sobering, he realized that she knew.

— Have I been talking?

— Yes.

— Agnes and Ulrica, he said. And one more. Veronica.

— Don't you think you had better answer the phone?

— Yes, of course, Cadiz said. Ike? Are you there?

— Where the fuck you think I'd be?

— Hold the line a minute, Ike—

— Now, listen, goddammit, Howard—

— No, just a minute longer, Ike, Cadiz said, watching Veronica. I have to say good-by to someone. Call me back in five minutes.

— In five minutes! All right! Then I'm going back to the ship and you can do whatever you damn well want to!

Cadiz dropped the phone into its cradle and turned to her.

— I was going to ask you to divorce him and marry me, Cadiz said. But I can't.

Veronica said nothing. She stood, immobile.

— We sit out there and hold our breath and wait for daylight, Cadiz said. And then when it comes we sit out there and hold our breath and wait for night. And that's what we do, wind up holding our breath, waiting for it to come. Another ship. Another steak dinner. Another girl with juices hot enough to singe you. Another bottle. Another ship. Another crossing. Another everything. We sit and we hold our breath, trying to fend it off. We sit, afraid that what we have will be gone too soon. We're men carrying water in a sieve. And we're greedy. That's it. We're greedy. We want more. Always more. Holding our breath, knowing that the end has to come, but still wanting more, trying to push back the roll of time—because the *sea* is the enemy. I have something in common with the foretopman of the early centuries and the lookout man who sailed with Columbus. Each of us, in our own way, try to ignore it. We spend our lives trying to ignore the sea. We drink buckets of booze and get roaring drunk and we try to put roots down ashore and we do a million things to keep us from hearing the sea. But we always hear it.

The fact that there's a war on, well, that's a detail. The war won't last forever, and when it's over, those of us who have survived, well, we'll go on. I'm twenty-five years a sailor. It's too late for me. I love you as much as I have ever loved any woman in my life, and if I had met you at any other time except on this strange day, I would have moved heaven and earth to have you and hold you. But it's late for me. A friend once said that this day would come. And I see now that I am committed. It's not as bad as it sounds. I still have a lifetime ahead of me. Bigger and firmer tits, deeper and older whiskey, and then at last it comes to an end. I can't sell myself on the idea there will be anything else for me. I'm Captain Howard Cadiz and I am a sailor. Nothing more can be said about me. Except perhaps this: I am a lucky man because I have found my way. There comes a time when a man is sated with tits and booze and good times. And when that time comes, all a man has left is his own, private way. To try and change it now would be to force me into a hunger for something I could never be able to achieve. I can't have the comfort of a Christian conscience. I can't have the remedy of a Sunday afternoon with my wife and kids. Because for me, for us, every day is Sunday afternoon. It is my way—our way. And a man would be crazy to deny his way when it has been handed to him. There are those of us who never see that there's another way open. They are the lucky ones. They go on and on and they just vanish from the seas and no one ever knows what happened to them and no one cares. The unlucky ones—and there are a few of us—we are the ones that insult nature. And we always lose. I don't ask you to divorce him and marry me because I know that I can't win against the sea. And putting down roots, worrying about them, feeling guilty for not caring, indifferent to the needs of my children, who would be strangers to me when I returned, are the things that I avoid. Unless a sailor is completely selfish, he's a liar. Unless he stalls against every responsibility not part of the sea or his ship, he is a dishonest man. A lot of us make this mistake. Some of us die thinking we're sure to be up front when the roll is called up yonder because we didn't screw that lovely thing in Hong Kong or London or New York. Or we are teetotalers who rage against the sin of our shipmates, waving the Bible around as if it were a first-class ticket into Heaven. My argument is with the order of natural things which, by selecting me, has in its cold indifference sent me out a-voyaging. Where is the permanence for such as I? So I will not ask you to marry me, Veronica. I will try very hard, from this day forward, not to remember anything that has ever touched me. I will try to forget that you ever existed. The only thing that is important to me is that I exist. Not the reasons why.

The phone rang again. Cadiz picked up the receiver.

— Yes, Ike, you can talk now. What is it?

— I told you already. We're ready to sail.

— You said that.

— I know I did!

— Okay, I'll be right down. Have you got the calibrations for the degaussing?

— Yeah. And you've supposed to stop off at the Customs House, that's on Bull and—wait a minute, I've got it down here on a slip of paper—

— I know where the Customs House is.

— Well, see a Captain Gooch—Navy or Coast Guard. He's got the orders for you. That's the message. Now you can go fuck yourself, Captain Cadiz. Ike slammed the receiver down hard. Cadiz, on his end of the line, smiled wanly. When he turned, Veronica was gone.

For the last time he walked to the window and looked out over the city and beyond, to the river.

His life was there. The city, graced with a secret charm of a thousand oak trees and the wine-dark shadows thrown by ancient houses blocking a rising sun, was ultimately unimportant. The river of promise? Every place he had ever been and everything he had ever seen and all that he had ever done was there, tied up in a neat knot of innocence.

He stretched. He yawned. All of it was such a goddam bore. All that innocence and all that life and all that waste. Well, he thought, scratching, I've had it all now. You're Captain Howard Cadiz. On your own ship you can do as you fucking well please. Right?

— It would seem so, he said aloud.